HUNTING EVE

ALSO BY IRIS JOHANSEN

HUNTING EVE

IRIS JOHANSEN

**Doubleday Large Print
Home Library Edition**

ST. MARTIN'S PRESS ✄ NEW YORK

This Large Print Edition, prepared especially for Doubleday Large Print Home Library, contains the complete, unabridged text of the original Publisher's Edition.

This is a work of fiction. All of the characters, organizations, and events portrayed in this novel are either products of the author's imagination or are used fictitiously.

HUNTING EVE. Copyright © 2013 by Johansen Publishing LLLP. All rights reserved. Printed in the United States of America. For information, address St. Martin's Press, 175 Fifth Avenue, New York, N.Y. 10010.

ISBN 978-1-62490-565-0

**This Large Print Book carries the
Seal of Approval of N.A.V.H.**

ACKNOWLEDGMENTS

Many thanks to Roy Johansen, my son and cocreator of difficult and brilliant Kendra Michaels. He's always there to save me from drowning in her complicated and fascinating personality.

HUNTING EVE

CHAPTER

1

Rio Grande Forest
Colorado

It was Doane's mountain.

He was the hunter, she was the prey.

Was he still behind her?

Eve tore through the underbrush at the side of the trail, lost her balance, fell, then struggled to her feet again.

She mustn't give in to this weakness. She seemed to have been running through this wilderness forever. No, it couldn't have been as long as it appeared to her. It had been late afternoon when she had broken free of Doane and the house where he had been keeping her, and darkness was only now falling.

But why was Jim Doane still behind her, dammit? He was no young man, and she should have been able to lose him long before this. As a painful stitch stabbed her side, she paused and drew a deep breath, listening.

A crashing in the brush behind her!

She started running again.

"I hear you, bitch." Doane's breathing was harsh, labored. "Come back to me. If you do, I may not kill you . . . yet. But you're making me angry and I may lose control. I don't want to do that. It would spoil everything for Kevin."

Kevin, Doane's son, whose recon-structed skull Eve had hurled off this moun-tain, less than an hour ago, to distract Doane. Doane's obsession with his dead son was deepening with every passing moment. Did Doane actually think she'd trust him? Kevin had been a serial killer, a monster without a hint of conscience, and his father, Doane, had been his enabler, the one who had made it possible for him to kill all those helpless children who had crossed Kevin's path. While Eve had been Doane's prisoner after he had kidnapped her, she had begun to wonder whether it was father or son who had been the true monster.

Perhaps it was both. There had been moments when she'd had the eerie feeling while working on his forensic sculpture that Kevin was trying to break through the bonds of hell and death and merge with his father.

Crazy. Imagination.

Or truth.

It was hard to tell the difference in this nightmare into which she had been drawn.

"You shouldn't have thrown his skull off into that ravine. Did you think I'd go after it and let you escape?"

It was exactly what she had hoped. That damn skull was everything to Doane, and she'd gambled that he'd go down the side of the mountain to try to retrieve it.

She'd been wrong.

She felt the twinge in her side become actual pain. How long could she keep running?

Stop whining. She'd run as long as she had to run. She was far younger than Doane. She was strong, and she was frightened. Panic was a great spur.

And did she have Bonnie helping her?

For a little while she had thought that her daughter's spirit had been there beside her, putting speed and wings to every step. It had been a comforting thought . . .

But now there only seemed to be Doane and her in this deadly race. No loving presence that might warm and save her.

It's okay, Bonnie. I know you tried. There's nothing he can do to me that will matter in the end.

The stitch in her side was easing.

She was running faster.

She should have known Bonnie would not let her falter, she thought ruefully. Not if Eve showed even a faint hint that she would not do her best to keep herself alive.

I wasn't going to opt out, Bonnie. I wouldn't do that to Joe and Jane. I was just trying to be an understanding mother. I know you can't do everything. Well, I don't really know what a ghost can or can't do, but you seem to have some limits. I'll keep going.

As long as she could. Her heart was beating so hard that it hurt. She felt sick to her stomach.

She could hear Doane cursing behind her.

Farther behind than he had been before. Was he faltering?

Yes.

He was shouting at her, each word broken and harsh. "Don't think you're going—to get away. These are my mountains. Kevin and I spent months out here when he was a boy. He particularly liked to kill the deer. How do you think he qualified to be in the Special Forces? I taught him to be a hunter."

And had he taught him to hunt down those little girls and kill them?

"Do you hear me? I'm going back to the house and get my equipment and my gun. I'll hunt you down like Kevin and I did the deer. I just hope that hypothermia doesn't get you before I do. It gets cold in these mountains at night."

She knew it was true, but it was hard to believe when her entire body was hot and perspiring from exertion.

"I can hear every move you make in that brush. Do you know how easy you're going to be to stalk?"

She was pulling more away from him with every second. Close him out. She was **winning.**

"And then we'll go get Kevin and take

him to that butcher who murdered him. I'll let Zander see how it feels when I kill you in front of him. There's no greater agony than a father feels at the death of a child."

More madness. Lee Zander, the hired assassin Doane was sure had murdered his son, was not her father. How could he be? Eve's father had disappeared long before she was born, and her mother was never even sure of his identity. This particular insanity Doane had thrown at her when he'd been enraged after she had tossed Kevin's reconstruction off the cliff to distract him. He had thought it would hurt her in some way to know she was a killer's daughter and that she was to pay for Doane's son's death. It was just one more sign that Doane's cold-blooded, calculated pursuit and abduction of her was completely bizarre and totally without reason.

Forget that nonsense. She was not the child of a murderer who was probably more deadly and ruthless than Doane. It was all part of Doane's wild hallucinations. She just had to concentrate on getting out of these mountains or contacting someone to help her.

"Do you know how many people get lost

in these mountains?" Doane's shout sounded still farther away. "Some don't survive the bitter cold and the animals and the mudslides. You might be glad to come back to me after a night or two."

Not bloody likely.

"Do you think your Joe Quinn or Jane MacGuire will be able to locate you out here? You could be out here a week, and no one would catch sight of you. You'd have had a better chance staying at the house. I'm the only one who knows you're here and how to find you. And I will find you, Eve."

Keep running. He might be trying to fool her into thinking he'd temporarily stopped the hunt. Don't trust his words.

It was pitch-dark now. She couldn't see anything but the shrubs directly in front of her. This was too dangerous. She'd be lucky if she didn't tumble off the mountain.

She stopped and tried to hear something besides the pounding of her heart.

No sound.

Doane?

She stood there, listening. No rustle of brush. No harsh sound of his breathing in the stillness.

Safe?

Good God, no. There was no way she was safe, but maybe she'd have a brief respite from the fear that had been with her since she'd been taken from everything she knew that was safe and good.

Joe, Jane, the cottage on the lake where they'd lived so many years.

She could still hear nothing but the flap of an occasional bird's wings and the wilderness night sounds. But they weren't the same sounds as the ones she heard in the forest on the lake. This was wild country.

Keep moving. Put distance between herself and the place where she'd last seen Doane. Providing that she didn't move in circles. She knew a little about the basics of surviving in a forest, but she wasn't an ex-SEAL like Joe. He could survive anywhere with no problem. Her profession of forensic sculpting kept her indoors most of the time, and even as a child, she had been a city girl.

So there were a few obstacles against her. She wouldn't overcome them by self-pity or remembering how good Joe was at this kind of thing.

Or remembering Joe at all. The look of him, the way he'd tilt his head and stare quizzically at her with those tea-colored eyes, the **feel** of him. There were moments when you could afford to remember the ones you loved, but this was not one of them. The thought of Joe made her painfully conscious of the loneliness of being here without him. Perhaps that was what Doane had intended by mentioning him before he'd left. He'd meant to make her more aware of her isolation. Salt in the wound. Joe Quinn, her lover, and Jane, their adopted daughter, the two people she loved most in the world. Eve would never have wanted to have them here and in danger but it was the—

A sound in the bushes up ahead!

A large animal. A bear. A deer?

Or Doane? He might have circled around and gotten in front of her.

Damn, she had no weapon.

Freeze. Don't move. The threat might dissolve and go away.

Darkness all around her.

She tried to breathe lightly so that she wouldn't be heard.

Please, go away.

Doane wouldn't go away. She just had to hope it was another beast looking for prey.

She was not prey, she thought with sudden fierceness. She would get out of this. She would find a weapon.

To hell with Doane and this mountain he thought belonged to him.

It's not your mountain any longer, you bastard. I'm going to make it my own.

University of Southern California
Los Angeles

Idiots!

Kendra Michaels pushed open the heavy main door of Alexander Hall and stalked down the tree-lined pathway that would take her to the parking lot.

Idiots. Narrow-minded fools.

"Dr. Michaels." The voice came from behind her.

She didn't turn around.

"Dr. Michaels, please!"

She didn't have to look back to know it was Steve Whitty, one of the conference organizers. Kendra hated these things, and her experience here, at the American Psychological Association's Conference on

Autism Causes and Treatment, reminded her why.

She finally stopped. He wasn't going to be discouraged.

Whitty ran around to face her. "You were brilliant."

She pointed back toward the auditorium. "Try telling them that."

"You got a lot of people thinking in there."

". . . Thinking I'm some kind of fraud. Were you even listening to the Q&A?"

"Naturally they're going on the attack. You're on the bleeding edge in this field. Uncharted territory. Your work could make a good many of those people's life's work obsolete."

"That's not what I'm trying to do."

"Look at it from their point of view. You're telling them that music can actually help cure autism."

"It's not a cure. It's a treatment. And I never said it was the only treatment."

"But you told them that your study had results far more impressive than anything they've done. Of course you're going to ruffle some feathers. Which is exactly why I wanted you to be here." Whitty placed his hand on her forearm. "And when those researchers get over being scared and pissed off, they're going to examine your data and look at those hours of sessions you posted on the Web. They're going to see what I saw. They're going to see how this amazing young woman was able to draw patients out of their shells and help them join the human race."

Kendra took a deep breath, angry that she had let those fools get under her skin. She always tried to tell herself that the work was its own reward, finding the right instrument, the right chord progression, the right anything that would engage the interest of her patients and help coax them into a world beyond themselves. But she needed more, dammit. She needed to know that she was able to open those educators' eyes so that they would follow her.

She looked away from Whitty. "Look, part of me understands why they're skeptical. Believe me, I know that the music-therapy field is populated with all kinds of nuts and woo-woo, and they give my profession a bad name. But I treat it like the science that it is. I got input from ten researchers in that room when I was designing the study, and I was tougher on myself than any of them were in their initial feedback."

"They're surprised at your results. Just give them a chance to digest it."

"I've found a way to help those kids, Whitty. And that study is proof of it."

"Kendra, there's a significant variable that some people feel you haven't addressed."

She looked at him in disbelief. "Impossible. I considered every variable."

"Not quite." He smiled. "The variable I'm talking about . . . is you."

"Me?" Then she realized what he meant and cursed under her breath. He could be right. She had been nervous about the presentation and several times had caught herself trying to impress the other attendees. It was completely unlike her. "Oh, you mean the dog and pony show? I knew they thought I was a little weird. I just kind of slipped into it. I didn't mean—"

"Hell of a carnival act, but there's already been some speculation that's how you get your positive results. By being so perceptive and empathetic with your subjects, giving exactly what they need in terms of body language, tone, positive reinforcement, the whole package."

Kendra's eyes narrowed on him. "That's what they're saying? If they read the study, they'll see I wasn't the only therapist. My techniques got the same results from everyone."

He smiled. "I know that because I've read the study. And they'll know it soon enough. You just need to relax."

"If I'd wanted to relax, I would never have come to this conference. I thought for once that I could make a difference."

"Kendra, come back inside." He placed his hand on her arm again. He was trying to soothe her, dammit. He wasn't a bad guy, and the mistake had probably been her own, but it didn't matter.

She wanted to deck him.

Her BlackBerry vibrated in her pocket. Thankful for the opportunity to pull away from Whitty, she stepped back, pulled out the phone, and answered it. "Hello."

"Kendra? Joe Quinn. I need your help."

"Quinn?" She didn't like the tone in his voice. Grim. Ragged. She turned to Whitty and mouthed an apologetic "sorry." He nodded and headed back toward the auditorium. "What's wrong, Quinn?"

"You name it, everything. I need your help."

"Dammit, I'm not a detective. And I'm busy as hell. You can't pull me into—"

"You're always busy. You'll have to drop whatever it is." He paused. "It's Eve."

"Eve?" Kendra's hand tightened on the phone. "What's happened? Talk to me."

Forty minutes later, Kendra was at her condo throwing clothes into a suitcase on her bed.

"You didn't answer the door, so I used my key. What on earth are you doing?" Kendra Michaels's mother was standing in the doorway of Kendra's bedroom watching disapprovingly as Kendra threw clothes into the suitcase on the bed. "Besides packing with no regard to neatness or order. I taught you better than that, Kendra."

"That was when I was blind, and you thought I had to be superefficient so that no one would feel sorry for me because I was handicapped." She threw another pair of jeans and a sweater into the case. "After the stem-cell operation I discarded that guideline and embraced chaos."

"In more than packing," Deanna Michaels said dryly. "I was worried about you for a number of years after those doctors performed their miracle and made you see. I never thought that you'd sow quite so many wild oats."

"That's past history." Kendra grinned. "Now I'm just a boring music-therapy teacher. I leave all the wild oats to you." Her mother was a history professor at U.C. San Diego and was the most vibrant and young-minded woman Kendra had ever known. And the most caring. She had used that intelligence and forceful personality to raise a child blind from birth and make her as close to independent as was physically and mentally possible.

And every day Kendra blessed her for it. Though her mother could be difficult and definitely tried to manipulate Kendra and everyone around her to suit herself.

"That would be extremely clever of you. I like the idea of your leading a semiboring life." Her mother crossed the room and started repacking Kendra's suitcase. "But there are still lingering tendrils of that less-than-wise period you went through. Go get your things from your bathroom. Now that I've rearranged your clothes, I have a place for them in this corner of the suitcase."

"Mom . . ." She stared at her a moment and turned and went to the bathroom. She had learned to pick her battles, and this one wasn't worthwhile. A few minutes later, she brought her plastic bag to Deanna and handed it to her. "Keep it handy. I'll have to pull it for security at the airport."

"You're flying? Where?"

"Atlanta."

"Why?"

"I have something I have to do there."

"That's no answer. If you were still a teenager, I'd call it rude." She frowned. "Why didn't you answer the door?"

"I was in a hurry. I have to get out of here." She smiled. "I wasn't rejecting you. I gave you a key to the condo, didn't I? That means you're welcome anytime." She paused. "Why did you decide to come today? I don't think it's a coincidence."

"I dropped by your conference. I was going to take you to dinner."

Kendra grimaced. "And you saw me almost blow my cool."

"They were idiots. They should have known you were right. You were right, weren't you?"

"Yep. But not diplomatic."

"Thank God." She paused. "I followed you out to the parking lot, and I was going to save you from that earnest young man, but you got a telephone call." She shrugged. "You hung up right away and jumped in your car and left the conference." She met Kendra's gaze. "But I saw your expression. It's happening again, isn't it?"

"Wild oats?" Kendra shook her head. "I like my life, Mom. I'm not going to fly off and leave those kids I teach."

"You know what I mean. Who is it? FBI? The local police? Say no, Kendra."

Kendra hadn't thought she'd be able to deter her, but it had been worth a try. "I can't do that, Mom," she said quietly. "Not this time."

"Why not?" Deanna asked harshly. "Those law-enforcement people don't give a damn about you. How many times have you been hurt? And I've almost lost you before when they tapped you and ask—" She drew a deep breath. "You're too valuable to waste. You're good and giving, and you've worked too hard to become a complete person." Her lips twisted. "The only problem is that you became a bit more than complete."

"No, I won't accept that. Anyone can do what I do. All they have to do is concentrate." All during her childhood, she had trained all her senses to overcompensate for her blindness. At twenty, when she'd had the operation that had given her sight, she'd been amazed that the people around her weren't able to use those senses in the same way she did. In a way, they appeared more blind to her than she had been before her operation. It had been that ability that had brought her to the attention of the law-enforcement officers against whom her mother was so bitter. "And I assure you that most of those agents at the FBI don't consider me loving and giving. They consider me a bitch, useful but not comfortable to be around."

"I never taught you to suffer fools gladly." Deanna added, "There's a possibility I might have gone slightly overboard. But deep down, you have fine instincts. The rest doesn't matter."

"And since you taught me, it must be the

world and not me that's wrong." She leaned forward and gave Deanna a kiss on the cheek. "I'll sign on to that." She grabbed her computer case. "I have to go, Mom."

"Not until you tell me who you're going to see." She added grimly, "I need to know who to go to for the body if they get you killed."

Deanna wasn't going to be deterred. Kendra had hoped she would be able to avoid explanations. She didn't have time for them. "Joe Quinn. He's a detective with Atlanta PD. You may remember my mentioning him. I worked with him when he was out here chasing down a serial killer; and then later he involved me in a missing-person case."

"I remember you weren't happy to leave one of your students at a crucial time."

"It was okay. It worked out."

Deanna was frowning. "And you were working with an Eve Duncan. You had problems with her."

"We were a little too much alike. That worked out, too," she said. "I liked her, Mom. She was kind of special."

"So you're going to be working with her

again? That's why you have to become involved?"

"Yes, she's the reason." She shook her head. "But I won't be working with her. Joe Quinn called me and told me that Eve has been kidnapped by some nutcase. The man's name is Jim Doane. Quinn asked me to help find her. I have to do it."

Deanna sighed. "Dammit, then I don't have a chance of talking you out of going, do I?"

"It won't be that dangerous. I'm not going to be actively working the case. I just have to try to pull up any clues as to where this Doane took her. I'll go in and do my job and get out." She added softly, "I won't tell you not to worry because that's been your modus operandi from the moment I was born twenty-eight years ago. I celebrate that you think I'm still worth it. But this time, I honestly believe that there's not going to be any reason to do it. Okay?"

"No." She stared at her a moment. "If you don't get yourself hurt physically, you'll end up an emotional wreck. I've seen it before. And this time the odds are leaning in that direction. You told me yourself, you

like this Eve Duncan. You'll get hurt again."
She turned and slammed the suitcase
shut. "And I'll be here to pick up the pieces.
Maybe someday you'll develop a sense of
self-preservation."

"I already have. Things just seem to get
in the way. You'd like Eve, too, Mom."

"Would I?" Deanna asked as she turned
toward the door. "I'm driving you to the airport. You can tell me about her on the way."
She held up her hand as Kendra opened
her lips to speak. "I'm driving you," she repeated firmly. "I'm not letting you fly off into
the night without having a solid hold on the
situation. Grab your suitcase."

Kendra shook her head ruefully as she
hurried after her out of the condo to her
mother's Mercedes in the parking space
in front of her condo. "We might have to
go to a therapy session or two when I get
back. You're being domineering again."

"Am I?" She got into the driver's seat.
"Oh, well, you can take it. Talk to me. Tell
me about Eve Duncan."

"She's a forensic sculptor, one of the
best in the world. She does a great deal of
work re-creating the faces of skulls of victims found by police departments across

the country. She tries to devote most of her time to doing reconstructions of children. Perhaps you've heard of her? She's very famous."

"The name's familiar, but I tend to avoid looking at skulls unless it has to do with something of historical significance. It reminds me of my own mortality. But a person is more than a profession. You haven't told me about Duncan, just what she does for a living."

"She's illegitimate and grew up in the slums of Atlanta. Her mother was on drugs most of her childhood and didn't list any name for the father on Eve's birth certificate. Her mother wasn't sure who he was. Eve had an illegitimate child herself when she was seventeen. It was a little girl she called Bonnie. She adored her. The little girl was kidnapped and killed when she was seven years old."

"Dear God," Deanna whispered. "How could she survive a blow like that? I don't know if I could."

"Eve survived. She went back to school and became a forensic sculptor. She spent years trying to find the body of her daughter and only succeeded a short time ago. She

adopted a ten-year-old street kid, Jane Mac-
Guire, years after her daughter disappeared,
and she and her lover, Joe Quinn, raised
her. Jane's now an artist and temporarily living in Europe. Recently, Eve discovered she
had a half sister, Beth, and they're trying
to build a relationship, but Beth lives here
in California. They don't see much of each
other." She looked at Deanna. "Is that
enough personal background for you?"

Her mother nodded. "She's no light-
weight." She made a face. "Maybe I
shouldn't have asked you to tell me about
her. I don't have much ammunition to convince you not to go off and try to find her."

"No, you don't. She's strong, and she's
real. Like you, Mom."

Deanna didn't speak as she changed
lanes to get on the freeway. "If they know
the name of this man who abducted her,
why can't they find them without you?"

"I don't know. Joe said that Doane had
been planning this for years. His son, Kevin,
had been murdered and partially cremated,
and Doane only managed to salvage his
blackened skull."

"Ah, and he wanted Eve Duncan to do
the reconstruction on the skull?"

"Presumably. Doane let her call Quinn and check on the condition of Jane Mac-Guire, and she told him she'd made a deal with him to do it."

"Condition?"

She hesitated. Her mother was not going to like this. "Jane MacGuire was shot by one of Doane's accomplices, a man named Blick."

"Shit. And this isn't going to be dangerous?"

"I go in, then get out. Jane wasn't killed, only wounded."

"What a relief," Deanna said grimly. "Wonderful."

"It is wonderful." She wouldn't tell her about the CIA man who had been found with his throat cut on the lake property. "I'm not saying that Doane isn't dangerous. He's not stable, but I'm not going to have to deal with him. That's Joe Quinn's job. And he's fully capable of handling it. Before he became a detective, he was with the FBI, and before that, he was a SEAL. He only asked me to look around and see if I come up with something."

"And he wouldn't try to pull you into the case if he thought it necessary? You said he was Eve Duncan's lover. That doesn't bode well for cool professionalism."

Trust her mother to cut through everything to get to the truth. "No, Joe isn't at all professional about Eve." Kendra wouldn't lie. "He's crazy about her. They've been together for years, and it's still a love story. Nice . . ." She added quickly, "But no one pulls me into anything if I don't want to go. I'm not reckless. You know me well enough to realize that, Mom."

"But you don't have to be reckless if you get emotional. What about that case a few years ago, where there were kidnapped children involved? That nearly made you into a basket case."

Kendra didn't answer.

"Okay." Deanna sighed. "I'll shut up right now if you promise to call and give me reports how things are going."

"So that you can get on your white horse and come to my rescue?" she asked gently. "Mom, you have to let me go sometime. You were the best, the most extraordinary mother a child could have. You fought a thousand battles for me and taught me to fight them, too. Now you have to trust me to make good choices. And, if I don't make them, you have to trust me to make the situation work." She added softly, "Just as you did all those years. It shouldn't be so hard. After all, I am your daughter."

Deanna didn't speak for a moment. "Was that supposed to appeal to my ego? It is hard. You'll realize that when you have a child of your own." She pulled over in front of the terminal building. "And I will come to rescue you if you don't behave sensibly. I'll give you space, but I won't give you up."

"And that makes me a very lucky woman." Kendra opened the passenger door. "How could I ask for anything else?"

"You couldn't," Deanna said brusquely. "Now, have you told me everything you know about the situation? If I have to mount that white horse, I want to know how to program this GPS."

"How convoluted can you get?" Kendra got out of the car and retrieved her suitcase from the backseat. "I think you have the bare bones. I don't have much more than that. Quinn was rattling off names and details so fast that I still have to get everything straight in my mind. I'll probably be landing in Atlanta before it becomes clear to me." She leaned back into the car and gave Deanna a quick kiss on the tip of her nose. "Now you know as much as I do. Satisfied?"

"No." Her eyes were glittering as her palm cupped Kendra's cheek. "And if you don't want me to interfere, you'll call and keep me informed. That's not too much to ask."

"Blackmail." Kendra was laughing as she straightened. "What am I going to do with you?"

"I have no idea. I taught you to make your own decisions."

"True." She slammed the car door. "And there's really only one thing I can do with you." She turned away. "I just have to love you. I'll call you when I get to Atlanta."

She could feel her mother's eyes on her as she headed for the glass doors. She lifted her hand and waved as she went through the doors into the terminal.

Her smile faded as she went toward the kiosk. She had tried to comfort her mother and she wished she had been able to be more reassuring. She knew so little, and she hated it. She wanted to reach out, to see, to hear, to touch. She was going into this hunt for Eve as blind as she had been during the first twenty years of her life.

And she had a terrible feeling that she wouldn't be able to help Eve. Eve was very sharp, and if she'd been taken by this criminal, then he must be a formidable adversary. It was hard for Kendra to understand how the wary, intelligent Eve she had come to know had become a victim.

But most criminals left traces, clues that shined a light on their path. Doane surely wouldn't be different. All she needed was to go to the crime scenes and everything would come clear.

God, she hoped he wasn't different.

I'll find him, Eve. Fight him. Give me a chance. I'll do everything I can. I'll search so hard for you. . . .

CHAPTER

2

Rio Grande Forest
Colorado

The rustling in the bushes up ahead had stopped.

Eve listened.

The faint rustling was now to the right going down the slope.

Not Doane. A bear?

She didn't care what kind of predator it was as long as it was moving away from her. She started moving forward again.

Dear God, she was cold.

The moments when she had stayed still, waiting for an attack, had robbed her of the warmth from running.

And she would get colder. She didn't

need Doane to taunt her with the possibility of hypothermia in these mountains. She couldn't run all night to keep warm. She couldn't light a fire. She needed shelter and warmer clothing than she had on now.

And where was she supposed to get them?

Think.

Shelter would have to be found in a cave or trees. Clothing? It wasn't as if she hadn't made plans. She'd known she had to prepare for this frigid wilderness. Hours before her escape she'd packed clothes and a blanket into the duffel into which she had thrown the skull of the Kevin reconstruction.

But after she'd tossed the skull off the cliff she'd run only a short distance before she'd thrown the duffel to the side of the trail to get it out of her way and conserve her strength.

Retrieve it? It was possible. She'd made a mental note of the immediate surroundings when she'd tossed it.

If she could recognize the place in the darkness.

And it was only a few short miles from the house where she'd been held. It was reasonable that Doane would still be there, at least for the night. It could be insane to double back and give up the distance she'd already traveled.

And she'd be even closer to the cliff edge where she'd stood to toss Kevin's skull into the ravine. What if Doane had decided to camp out there to be close to his son? Considering his obsession, it was entirely possible.

And that possibility was very dangerous for Eve.

What if Doane had seen her discard the duffel and was waiting for her to come back for it?

So was she going to stay here all night, getting colder by the minute, trying to decide?

No, she had to assume that she was in this for the long haul. She mustn't count on someone coming to rescue her. She had no doubt that Joe would do everything he could, but she had to assume that what could go wrong, would go wrong. Stop questioning and weighing every step. Take a chance on getting what she needed to survive until she could find her way out of these mountains.

She turned and started back through the brush toward the trail that led down the mountain to the log house that Doane had told her had been formerly used as a factory.

She had a sudden mental picture of Doane sitting and waiting like a giant spider with a smile on that kindly face that hid the soul of a demon.

She firmly dismissed the vision from her mind. He would like the idea of intimidating her, making her hesitate, controlling her moves.

And he would probably attribute it to the force of his son, Kevin, reaching from beyond the grave. He had told her that he believed that Kevin was trying to break through the barriers between life and death, and there had been moments when she had believed it was true. She always felt a connection when she was working on a reconstruction, but with Kevin it had been frightening. It had filled her with terror . . . and nausea. She had been filled with profound relief when she had tossed that skull off the mountain.

Because she believed that the dead could reach from beyond the grave. Her little girl, her Bonnie, had begun coming to Eve a year after she had died. Eve had been spiraling downward and would probably have died herself if she had not begun to see and dream of Bonnie. Yes, the dead could cross that threshold.

But Kevin was not a loving, gentle spirit like Bonnie. In life he had been a serial killer of little girls, and there was nothing but evil in the force that Eve sensed while working on his reconstruction.

She was starting to shiver with cold. Don't think of Kevin. Don't think of the father who had given him life and helped him lure those little girls to their deaths. There was hope and good in the world. She was walking toward darkness, and she needed hope right now.

Think of Bonnie.

Vancouver, Canada

"It's Venable." Howard Stang handed Lee Zander his phone, which he'd left on the library desk. "Shall I leave the room?"

"Of course not. After all, he's CIA, not

the usual less-than-upstanding client whom you avoid like the plague. In fact, I'll turn on the speakerphone and let you listen. Haven't we reached a new plateau of understanding lately?" Zander smiled mockingly as he took the phone. "You're not only a trusted employee, you're actually becoming a confidant."

"Heaven help me," Stang murmured. He had no desire to be anything but the accountant and personal assistant he'd been hired to be. All these years he'd worked for Zander, the man had kept him firmly in the background of his existence. He was intensely private, and though Stang had been vaguely aware of occasional women who acted as brief sexual partners in Zander's life, that was the only aspect of the man he'd been allowed even a glimpse of. His contacts, clients, background, all were kept firmly under wraps. Stang had found it strange that Zander had lately chosen to reveal to him layers of his life and character that he'd never done before. But then, no one was more strange or intimidating than Zander.

"You might have to help yourself." Zander

spoke into the phone. "You again, Venable? I'm beginning to feel a bit of pressure. I can't say I like it. Why are you calling?"

"I'm sorry that I'm disturbing you in your safe harbor away from commonplace cares," Venable said roughly. "Too bad. Come out into the real world, Zander."

"I detect a hint of belligerence." He repeated, "Why are you calling?"

"I just got word that General Tarther was shot and killed at his home in Virginia."

Zander was silent a moment. "And so it begins." Tarther, the man who had hired him to kill Jim Doane's son, was dead.

"And Doane will be going after you next."

"Yes, he'll find me a more elusive target than the general."

"Is that all you've got to say? The general was a fine man and a patriot who served his country well."

"You'd appreciate that more than me. I never dealt with that side of him. He was only a client, but I respected him. He hired me for a job and paid me well and promptly."

"For assassinating the killer of his little daughter, Dany. After the court declared a mistrial, the general didn't see any other way to bring Kevin Relling to justice. Didn't

you ever feel even a little sympathy for
Tarther?"

"Would that have made me more efficient? No, it would probably have inter-
fered, and I wouldn't have been able to
give Tarther what he'd paid for."

"That's no answer."

"It's all you'll get from me. Stop trying to
read something in me that's not there. Your
wonderful general was just as much a murderer as me. Perhaps more because he
didn't go after Doane's son himself but preferred to lay the sin on my soul. Well, I took
that sin from him and made it my own." He
shrugged. "In the end, we all have the killer
instinct and just choose what circumstance
will set it free. The difference is that I let
others choose the circumstance and pay
me to execute it."

"God, you're cold."

"Is our conversation finished?"

"I promised the general that I'd try to get
that disk back from Doane. To do that, I
have to find him."

"My deal with the general didn't include
the return of the disk. That's your department, Venable."

"If you hadn't killed Doane's son, he

wouldn't have used the disk Kevin gave him as blackmail to hold over the head of those embedded agents in Pakistan. Now that Doane's broken loose, those men could be killed. It's all chain reaction."

"You're reaching. You must be desperate."

"I lost Dukes, a good agent, here on the lake property. The general was just killed." He paused. "And Eve Duncan is still being held by Doane, and I don't know how long it will be before he kills her. Yes, I'm desperate."

"Then it's not only the disk." He added mockingly, "I believe your sentimentality is showing, Venable. You really must watch that."

"Doane will be coming after you. He knows you're the hit man the general hired to kill his son."

"And I'll be waiting for him."

"A trap? Don't wait for him. If you're going to kill him, why not go after him now?"

"It will be more efficient to invite him into my web."

"Damn your efficiency. If you go after him, Eve has a better chance of coming out of this alive. She's not the most passive prisoner. She'll be trying to escape. Even if it isn't according to his plans, Doane could explode and kill her."

"I gathered that when Doane called me and made me talk to her." He chuckled. "She wasn't afraid of either him or me. I can see how she would annoy him." His smile faded. "But the sole purpose of Doane's call was to get me to come after him so that he would have the advantage. I won't give him that advantage. Let him come to me."

"You were planning to hunt him down when I first told you that Doane had left the safe house."

"I changed my mind. It wasn't worth disturbing myself when I could make him come to me."

"You can find him, can't you? You didn't seem to have any doubts."

"I make my living by finding people . . . and disposing of them. Yes, I can find him."

"Then do it," Venable said harshly. "And get Eve away from him."

"Eve Duncan wouldn't enter into the equation. If she did, then I'd lose any advantage. I'd go after Doane and not let any other concern enter into it. I'd think you'd realize that, Venable."

"Oh, I realize it. I just occasionally hope for a spark of humanity in you." He paused. "She's worth saving, Zander."

"Then you and Joe Quinn go do it."

"I'm tempted to tell Joe Quinn where you are and let him come after you," he said grimly. "I did tell him that Doane wanted you dead. That may be enough to turn Joe loose to stake you out. You may be in more of a trap than you'd like."

"You shouldn't have discussed me with him. It was bad enough that you didn't keep Doane's cohort from pulling the information out of that funeral director's family about my paying for Kevin's cremation. Now you're talking about it to Quinn? Our relationship is confidential, Venable."

"Bullshit." He drew a deep breath. "Okay, you won't help Eve. But I'll take you just going to get rid of Doane. Will you think about it?"

"Maybe."

"Answer me. Will you think about it? I'm not asking much. She's not asking much."

"She's not asking anything. Or expecting anything. I admit that's what impressed me about her. I'm hanging up now, Venable." He pressed the disconnect and turned toward Stang. "An interesting reaction from Venable, I knew he liked the general, but I didn't think it would trigger that degree of emotion."

"General?"

"That's right, you don't have the entire picture, do you? I must fill you in."

"No, you don't."

"Then I choose to do it." He moved toward the desk and flipped open the file on the desk. He gazed down at the photo of Eve Duncan in her dossier. "Venable is almost as emotionally involved with her as you are. You must be kindred spirits."

"Ridiculous. I'm not emotionally involved. How could I be? I've never met her." His gaze lifted to Zander's face. "All I know about her is in those dossiers and the snatches you've been giving me of what happened to her when she was taken by Doane. I just told you that I thought Eve Duncan appeared to be a worthwhile woman, and anyone would be sorry if she was killed by a mad dog."

"Anyone but me?"

"I don't judge you."

"You don't voice it if you do."

"I don't want to know anything about

your business." He tapped the photo. "Not this kind of business. I'm your accountant, and I handle your money. I don't know why you suddenly decided I should be anything different."

"Neither do I. A whim?" He smiled. "There's always that possibility, isn't there?"

Stang moistened his lips but didn't answer.

Zander waved his hand. "It doesn't matter. Where was I? Oh, yes, the general and how he's connected to Eve Duncan. General John Tarther was a client of mine several years ago."

"I gathered that."

"He hired me to kill Kevin Relling. Kevin Relling was previously with the Special Forces but when he was in the Middle East, he decided that the al-Qaeda was the way to power and insinuated himself into the group. The Army had no knowledge of that or that his killings didn't stop at the enemy targets. He was a serial killer who particularly liked little girls. He was very clever, and he left a trail of victims in half the countries in Europe. One of the victims was Dany Cavrol, five years old, and the illegitimate daughter of the general. The general was devastated and set out to catch her killer. He threw money and detectives and personal influence into the hunt. They brought Kevin Relling to justice." He shrugged. "But a jury member was tampered with, and the case was declared a mistrial. He escaped on the way back to jail."

"And that's when the general contacted you."

"Yes, you always have a wonderful grasp on the continuity of numbers or events, Stang. It's that fine orderly mind of yours. It didn't take me long to track him down. He was in Athens, and I knew it well. I shot him, then arranged for his body to be cremated by Nalori Crematorium. Unfortunately, his father was close by and rushed to the crematorium and retrieved Kevin's head from the furnace. He was a little upset and threw the man I'd bribed to do the cremation into the furnace."

"His father? Doane?"

"He was Jim Relling then. He took the name of Doane when Venable took him into protective custody. He'd contacted General Tarther and told him that his son had given him a disk with names of embedded CIA agents and Pakistanis who were searching for Bin Laden. He was afraid that al-Qaeda would find out and target him. He said if he didn't get protection, he'd have to turn the disk over to the newspapers." He shrugged. "He appeared a broken man just trying to understand what had happened to his Kevin. There was no evidence that he had any connection with his son's crimes, and I'm told he was very convincing. My instinct was to dispose of him immediately. I could see him trying to find out who killed his son and causing us trouble down the road. But the general was afraid that would be dangerous for those agents in Pakistan. I conceded graciously and let him live."

Stang's brows rose. "Graciously?" The gentle, old-fashioned word did not fit Zander in either profession or appearance. His close-cut white hair, the features that were more bold than handsome. He was probably somewhere in his fifties or sixties but he appeared ageless. His tall, muscular body, which he'd honed to perfection with daily workouts in the gym, was sleek and powerful. And so was that mind, which Stang had found to be sharper than that of anyone he had ever met.

"I'm always gracious," Zander said. "And I told Venable I'd let Doane live as long as he kept him under surveillance. That was truly gracious."

"And why did Doane target Eve Duncan?"

"He had a skull. She's a forensic sculptor."

Stang's eyes were narrowed on his face. "Is that all?"

"You're probing. You told me that you didn't want to know anything that—"

"I don't." He looked down at the photo. "Or maybe I do. I feel as if I've gotten to know her in the past few days. I feel . . . close to her."

"Really?" He studied the photo. "Are you attracted to her? She's not beautiful. She's just interesting. Nothing to make you—"

"Are you going to go after him?"

"I told Venable I'd think about it."

"Do it."

"I beg your pardon?" Zander turned to look at him.

"I know it's not my business. I've tried to stay out of it. I know it would be safer for me."

"Yes, it would." He tilted his head. "But it

intrigues me you're willing to take the risk of involving yourself. If you stayed on the outskirts of my iniquitous life, I'm much more vulnerable to ambush."

"You didn't give me a choice. It was either resign and leave you or take the next step." He forced himself to stare him in the eye. "And you don't know that I want to ambush you."

"No, but I'm a tolerable judge of character, and I've been suspecting it since the day you came to work for me. The prospect was interesting. Besides the fact that you're a genius at making my money grow there was another factor. I live a fairly boring life, and watching you and wondering what you're up to gave it a little spice. But now life is becoming more entertaining, and I may not need that additional stimulation."

Stang felt the tension grip him. "And that means?"

"I think I'll let you dwell on that and decide for yourself." He flipped the file closed. "I believe I'll go work out at the gym." He headed for the French doors that led to the detached building that housed the gym. "I'm a bit restless tonight."

Stang had been aware of that restlessness, and it had caused his uneasiness to heighten. Zander was usually in full control, and volatility was rare. "What if Venable calls again?"

"He won't. I won't need you for the rest of the evening. Set the alarm and go to bed, Stang."

"You told Venable you'd think about going after Doane."

"My, you're persistent." He paused. "And I will. There are reasons why it's not a bad idea."

"Eve Duncan?"

"No, the general. His death might tarnish my reputation. I mustn't have potential clients thinking that their lives could be in danger because of the aftereffects of the termination. If I'd followed my gut instincts in the beginning, none of this would have happened. I might have to show that I actively sought to correct the problem. Duncan has nothing to do with it." He glanced back over his shoulder. "Unless I have to use her to get to Doane."

"You **are** going to do it."

"Stop pushing me, Stang. I'm going to think about it." He smiled coldly. "And whatever I decide, it probably won't make an iota of difference to whether Duncan lives or dies."

"If you throw a different number into an equation, the answer is bound to change," Stang said. "And sometimes the answer is better than you hope. If you decide to do it, will you team with Venable?"

"No, why would I do that? He has his own agenda, and he'd get in my way."

"Just wondering." He turned toward the door. "Good night, sir. There's a jacket on the patio chair if you need it. It's cold outside."

Rio Grande Forest
Colorado

Lord, it was cold, Eve thought.

The temperature had plummeted in the last hour, and the cotton tunic she was wearing was no protection against the cutting wind. Her teeth were chattering, and her muscles were knotting with the effort to withstand the chill.

She didn't have much farther to go until she got to the place where she'd discarded her duffel. She would have been there sooner, but she'd lost the trail twice in the darkness and become disoriented. But now she was close, she knew it. The moon was up, and she'd recognized a few distinctive boulders.

It should be just around this turn of the trail.

And so might Doane.

She stopped and stared at the trail ahead.

Had he seen her discard the duffel? There was no way of knowing.

If he had, he could be up ahead waiting for her. If he hadn't, then she might be safe.

She moved off the trail into the shrubs.

Move quietly.

Listen.

Is he there?

No sound.

The wind was sharper, taking her breath.

Are you tucked under a warm blanket on your couch down there in the house, you bastard?

Stay there. Sleep. While I try to even things out.

She stopped again and listened.

Still nothing but the wind through the trees.

The duffel should be right before her . . .

No duffel! Dammit, no duffel.

Don't panic. Look for it.

She hadn't realized that the trail had skirted this close to the cliff edge at this point. What if the duffel had rolled down and gone off the cliff?

And what if it hadn't?

Look for it.

She might get lucky.

She slid farther down the slope toward the cliff edge.

There it was! She grabbed the black duffel and turned back to go up the slope.

And then she stopped on the cliff edge.

From this vantage point, she could see the house and the mine. The lamp-light was pouring from the windows. That was a good sign that he wasn't out here looking for her.

But she wouldn't take that small sign to the bank. He could still be out here.

Get away. She couldn't even stop to pull warmer clothes from the duffel until she was miles down the road. She started to climb the slope.

"You can't get away. I won't let you. Kill you. Throw you into the fire."

She went rigid at the gravelly whisper.
Doane?

Oh God, she'd been wrong. He was here,
waiting.

She whirled toward the road and started
running.

**"Hate you. Throw you into the fire.
He'll find you."**

Where was the voice coming from? The
other side of the trail? Wherever he was,
he'd had time to get his gun from the house.

No bullet.

No sound of footsteps behind her.

Where the hell are you, Doane?

**"Burn you like they did me. Never
get away."**

Like they did me . . .

Her pace slowed.

She hadn't thought she could get colder,
but she was suddenly icy.

Not Doane.

She looked over her shoulder at the
house where the lights cast a cozy glow out
into the darkness.

Then she looked down at the abyss
yawning beyond the cliff.

Burn you like they did me.

Not Doane. Kevin.

It was Kevin whose remains had been tossed into that furnace after he was shot.

She smothered the panic.

It could be imagination, a hallucination brought on by nerves and exposure.

Malignance and power coming from that darkness where she'd thrown Kevin's skull.

Or it could be that the evil presence she'd sensed while she did Kevin's reconstruction was real and waiting to forge across the barriers.

And attack.

But she hadn't heard his voice since she'd realized that it was either her own imagination . . . or Kevin. If the attack had come, she had been able to repel it.

"You're weak, Kevin," she whispered fiercely. "You can't touch me. You think you can use your father to break through, but you have boundaries. It's not going to happen." She started running up the path. "Go back to hell, where you belong."

He was coming!

Eve climbed higher in the tree, making sure that she made no sound.

Doane made no effort to be quiet. Why would he? He had a rifle, and she was the prey.

She had thought he had settled for the night in the house, but she'd been rudely disappointed. In the middle of the night, he'd come after her, and she'd had to go on the run.

And it was the second time tonight that Doane had gotten so close. He hadn't been boasting when he said he was a great tracker. She had resorted to going through the streambeds to erase the tracks and lose him. But she must have left some sign, or he wouldn't be here now. It wouldn't surprise her. It wasn't as if she was woods-savvy like Joe. She just had to do the best she could.

"I can feel you, Eve," Doane called out. "I can feel your fear and the panic. It's terrible being hunted, isn't it? No matter where you go, I'll be right behind you."

She wasn't in a panic, but she was experiencing that primal fear of being hunted. And she **hated** this feeling of helplessness.

Damn, she wished she had some kind of weapon. She'd found a branch earlier that she'd tried to fashion into a club, but that would not hold up when confronting a rifle.

Not unless she could stage a surprise attack, and he had given her no opportunity to think of a way to do that.

"Are you having a rough night? The temperature is near freezing, and I was thinking of you when I was curled up in the house. That's why I decided to leave comfort behind and go after you. I expected to be able to bring you in with no problem. You must be tougher than I thought to survive so well."

It had been rough. Even wrapped in the blanket and covered with leaves, it had been cold. The wind hadn't stopped, and she had only dozed for minutes at a time. It was probably a good thing because she had heard Doane when he'd tried to surprise her.

"Were you afraid that I'd be tracking you tonight? You'll never know when I'm after you or when I go back for a little well-earned rest. So never sleep too hard, Eve."

He was right below the tree.

Don't move. Don't breathe.

"If you sleep, I'll catch you, Eve. You must

be very tired right now." He lifted his head. "Do you hear me? I must admit that I'm enjoying our little hunt. I like the idea of running you to ground. I noticed that you were traveling the stream. Your feet must be wet. By morning, they could be frost-bitten. It will be hard for you to run then, Eve."

He had moved a few yards away and was going toward a stand of trees to the north.

Don't move. No sound.

"And you can't try to light a fire to dry out. Because I'll see it or smell it. I may go back to the house for the rest of the night, or I might keep stalking you. You won't know, will you? You might as well give up and come back to the house. You'd have a better chance of surviving."

The hell she would. He wouldn't kill her immediately, but it was definitely on his agenda.

"Though I am enjoying our little game. It brings back old times with Kevin. I loved those weeks in the woods. I never felt closer to him. I feel that way now. Do you feel close to him, Eve? Do you feel him hovering over you? Waiting?"

She made sure she didn't think about
Kevin. She blocked out everything but
evading Doane. That was a full-time task.
She'd been trying to locate a branch of
the rock road he'd driven when he'd taken
her to make the phone call to Joe, but
she hadn't succeeded. She'd probably
have to go back to the house and start
from there. But that would be like stepping
into the lion's mouth. Not yet. Not until
she had a better plan on how to either
avoid Doane or find the opportunity to
take him out.

"The sun won't rise for a long time. You'll
have to contend with the wind and darkness for hours yet . . ." His voice was fading away and she could no longer see him
through the trees.

Too soon to get down. She'd stay here
for a while in case he came back. She sat
back on the branch and took off her wet
right shoe and sock. He was right. Her
feet were already cold, and she had to
keep the blood moving. She began to rub
her foot and ankle roughly. After five minutes she did the same with her left foot.
Good, the blood was tingling. Once she

was settled for the night, she'd massage them again.

Chance making a fire?

No, a fire was an emergency measure. She would just make do as she had done earlier tonight.

And keep busy trying to make that damn branch into a viable weapon.

She settled back against the trunk of the tree. Give him another forty minutes, then get down from the tree and make her way back to the tree where she'd hidden the small duffel that contained her store of treasures. Treasures, indeed, she thought ruefully. The blanket alone was worth its weight in gold.

More, it could save her life. She'd been right to go after the duffel.

Hate you. Burn you.

She instantly rejected the memory. Kevin might be close to Doane but not to her. She was having trouble keeping Doane and Kevin apart in her mind. Perhaps that was also Doane's problem. Maybe it had been Doane projecting those thoughts to her.

Hate you. Burn you.

She shivered; the words seemed to reach out and touch her.

Time to get down and start moving. She could not let the thought of Kevin haunt her or get in her way. She carefully climbed down from the tree. She paused for a moment to lean against the trunk as she looked around the forest.

She rubbed her neck. God, she was tired and hungry.

Berries. Try to find some berries or something. Joe had told her about some of the edible ones on some of their walks through the woods at the lake. She had to keep her strength up. It wasn't as if she could build a trap for a rabbit as he could do. It definitely wasn't her forte.

Well, she might be able to do it, but berries would be easier.

If she could even see the bushes in the dark. She might have to wait until dawn. Or until she was sure Doane had gone back to the house. But she couldn't be sure of anything, as tonight had proved.

Get moving.

Carefully. Warily.

Hate you. Burn you.

Oh, yes . . . warily.

The Abyss

"I'll get her, Kevin. Be patient."

Doane stood on the cliff edge and looked down into the abyss where Eve had tossed his son's reconstruction.

Vicious bitch. He couldn't control the sudden anger that tore through him. He wanted Kevin **back.**

All of his careful plans and they had been destroyed by Eve Duncan.

In spite of the words he had earlier hurled at Eve, he was no longer enjoying the hunt. The pleasure had lasted only a short time, until he realized that he was losing control of the situation. He had no doubt he would catch her eventually, but she was faster, smarter than he thought she'd be in the woods. She made mistakes, but she was still good enough to be annoying.

And the hunt could take much longer than he'd thought it would.

Which would mean that his plans for Zander might totter and be destroyed.

No!

Make up time. Move the plan forward.

He reached in his jacket and pulled out

his phone. He would call Terence Blick and stir him into action. He was not alone in this. Blick loved Kevin, too, and would do anything to make sure he was avenged.

Blick picked up the call a moment later. "Doane?"

"Things are not going as quickly as I thought, Blick. I may need you to step in and help."

"What's wrong? You said you had Duncan."

"I did have her. There was a problem."

"Did? You let her go?"

"Don't be ridiculous. It's only a temporary setback. I just may have to spend time retrieving her. I need you to go to the safe house and retrieve the box. By this time, all of Venable's searches must have been done, and it should be fairly safe. Maybe only a guard or two to get in your way."

"You shouldn't have let her go." Blick's tone was ugly. "You yell at me for not doing what Kevin would want, but I'm the one who's making all the moves. I shot Jane MacGuire, I killed the general, and now you want me to risk my neck going to the safe house to get that box. You said you were going to do it."

"And I would, but I don't have time." He controlled his anger. "We want everything to be perfect, don't we? Get the box, then kill Zander. Remember what they did to Kevin. You said he was your friend. Is that how you behave toward your friend? You told me you'd die for him. Now you complain when I ask for one small change in the plan."

Silence.

"I'll do it."

"I knew you would. Remember to take the photo. I miss it." He hung up.

He stood there, looking down at the abyss, trying to control his rage.

He had been wrong. He was alone.

"He's not worthy of you, Kevin," he whispered. "He was good enough to serve you when you were alive but he's proving . . . lacking. When this is over, I may have to send him to you. You'd be able to shape him to suit yourself."

Yes, that would be the answer. He could feel Kevin's approval for the solution he had crafted like a gentle touch. He and Kevin had usually thought alike when he was alive, but lately he had felt that their minds were linked.

"I hate to leave you," Doane said regretfully as he turned away from the cliff. "But I have to go down to the house and get some sleep." He started down the path. "Eve Duncan has more strength than I thought. I have to be ready for the hunt . . ."

CHAPTER

3

Lake Lanier, Georgia

Kendra cursed her GPS as it struggled to calculate her route from Cornelia Highway to Eve Duncan's lake cottage. Eve had been urging her to visit ever since they had met the year before, but Kendra had no idea she would be finally making the trip under these circumstances.

It was after midnight, but the infamous Georgia heat and humidity were still living up to their reputation. She had lowered her car window to look at a road sign a few minutes before, and the air conditioner was only starting to overcome it. She glanced at her GPS device. It had now given up en-

tirely, locked in an endless loop of RECALCU-
LATING.

No matter. Joe Quinn had been thorough with his directions, and she was sure
she could find it on her own.

But to what end?

She had dropped everything and rushed
across the country to join the search, as if
she was Eve's last best hope. She had managed to impress Quinn and most other investigators whom she had assisted through
the years, but what if there was simply nothing for her to observe here? She knew it
had rained, and that had a way of washing
away a hell of a lot of clues.

But a muddy rural area made it almost
impossible to erase others.

And since when did she give a damn
what anybody thought of her? She was
here for Eve and no one else.

Eve.

Kendra didn't make friends easily, but her
bond with Eve was strong and genuine.
She had been touched by Eve's strength
and her quiet struggle to move beyond her
daughter's murder, which had defined her
for so long. Now that Bonnie had finally
been laid to rest, she could see a sense of

freedom in Eve, not unlike the sudden freedom she herself had felt when she was finally given the gift of sight.

Kendra rounded the bend and passed a cluster of tall pines. There, near the lake, was what she was sure was Eve's cottage. Half a dozen cars parked out front in a haphazard fashion and every light was ablaze. She could almost feel the tension radiating from the premises.

Kendra parked the rental car and climbed out. A front-window curtain parted slightly, and a moment later the door opened and a familiar silhouette appeared on the porch. Slim, powerful, every muscle tense and alert. He was always a presence to be reckoned with but tonight she could almost feel the intensity. His tea-colored eyes were narrowed as he watched her come toward him.

"You could have waited until tomorrow," Joe Quinn said. "But I'm glad as hell you didn't."

"You expect me to get a call like yours and just sit around twiddling my thumbs?" She reached the top step of the porch and gave him a quick hug. "Any news?"

"Only that General Tarther, who was on Doane's hit list, was shot and killed. We suspect Terence Blick, Doane's accomplice, but he hasn't been apprehended. Seth Caleb, a friend of Jane's, was in the area trying to guard the general and we hoped to hear from him but nothing so far."

"I'd say that's a substantial piece of news all right. Anything else?"

"We've been trying to pull a car that belonged to Doane from the lake." He nodded at the far end of the lake that was lit by floodlights and teeming with people and machinery. "We think Doane stole the truck of a farmer who lives nearby, then drove his own car into the lake."

"Why would he do that?"

"I have no idea. That's why I'm curious to get a look at that car and see if it can tell us anything." He added grimly, "Besides the fact that it might serve as a coffin for that farmer Doane stole the truck from. He's disappeared."

"It would have to be something else." Kendra took a step closer to the porch rail and looked out at the crane that was dipping into the water. "That's a complicated way to dispose of a body when he could just bury it. Why haven't you been able to pull the car up yet?"

"The lake's very deep at that area. First, we had to verify that the car was really there. There was no sign of entry."

She turned to look at him. "Then why did you bother to start looking there?"

Joe hesitated. "We had an informant."

"Someone saw Doane drive the car into the lake?"

"Something like that."

"Who?"

"It's difficult to—forget it. Let's just say it was . . . anonymous."

"No, I won't forget it." She frowned. "I'm feeling too much in the dark. I'm not going to tolerate your keeping things from me. A witness could save us a great deal of time. What else did you find out?"

"Nothing. It was a one-shot deal. I'm not going to be able to squeeze anything else out of the informant."

"Let me talk to him."

"He's already been released." He added harshly, "Drop it. Do you think I would have let anyone get away from me if there were a chance he could help Eve? I'll tell you about him later."

"I'd still like to—" She broke off and shrugged. "You don't have to be so touchy."

"Yes, I do." He drew a ragged breath. "I didn't mean to bark at you. I'm on edge. For a while we were fooling ourselves, thinking that Eve might not be in real danger. Doane kept everything low-key, and he's always been plausible. But now we know Doane was willing to kill at least three people to get Eve."

"Eve's smart. It doesn't mean he'll kill her."

"Not until he's done with her." Joe looked back at the floodlights on the lake. "But after that she's a witness and a—"

"I told you, she's a smart woman. Either she'll escape, or she'll find a way to stay alive until we find her."

"I agree." The woman who had spoken was standing in the doorway. She stepped forward and extended her hand. "I'm Jane MacGuire. You're Kendra Michaels?"

Kendra clasped her hand in both of hers, more as a gesture of comfort than greeting. Jane MacGuire was exuding a combination of strength and fragility at this moment. Kendra was not an instinctive caregiver, but she felt a sudden desire to shelter and protect. "Yes. Joe told me you'd been wounded. How are you feeling?"

"Like I've been shot by a high-powered rifle." Jane half smiled. "Aside from that, just fine."

Kendra smiled back. Jane was truly beautiful. She had Eve's coloring, hazel eyes, red-brown hair, and fine features but while Eve was interesting-looking Jane had glamour. Although Jane was adopted, she also had some of Eve's mannerisms, her purposeful walk, and the ability to deflect others' concern while smiling through her pain. She might be a total person in her own right, but there was no doubt about it, Jane was every bit Eve's daughter.

Jane moved a step closer to her. "Eve told me about you. You impressed her. She'd be happy to know that you came here to help us."

"Nothing could have kept me away."

"We can use all the help we can get, but . . . you're a music therapist, right? That's your specialty?"

Kendra sighed. It was coming. She had hoped to avoid it, particularly with Eve's daughter. But Jane was so like Eve that she should have expected it. Explore. No trust. Perform. "Yes."

"I'm having difficulty understanding what

you can do to help. I realize you did some amateur investigating work with Joe, but is it enough to prove value in our case?"

Joe moved toward Jane. "I asked her to come here."

Jane's eyes met Kendra's with a hint of a challenge. She said softly, "Maybe there are too many cooks in the kitchen already."

"Jane, don't be—" Joe stopped and smiled slightly. "What the hell, go ahead."

Kendra nodded. "Oh, we intend to, Quinn. It's okay, I understand where she's going. Believe me, I've been involved in enough investigations and seen too many crime scenes spoiled by investigators stepping all over each other. You've already had more than your share. You've had what, nineteen different law-enforcement officers here in the last day and a half? Eleven FBI, six local police, two CIA, give or take. Fourteen men and five women in all."

Jane wrinkled her brow and glanced at Joe. "Is that correct?"

"Hell if I know, but it sounds about right."

Kendra jammed her hands into her pockets and walked slowly around Jane.

"I know you were born here in Georgia, or at least lived here before you can remember. You've spent a lot of time in Europe, especially Paris, and probably lived there for a while. But you've been living in London for at least the past several months."

Jane glanced at Joe. "Did you or Eve tell her that?"

"Possible. But I don't think so."

Kendra shook her head. "In London, you lived in an older building, in a second-floor walk-up apartment. Or maybe even higher."

"Third floor," Jane said. "And now you definitely have my attention."

"You used to have a very nice pair of Gucci sunglasses, but you misplaced them. You must have liked them. You're still hoping they'll turn up before you take the plunge and have to buy them again. But it's been what, three months?"

Jane thought for a moment. "Two."

"In the meantime you've been wearing an inexpensive pair that are a little uncomfortable for you. They look similar to the ones you lost, but they're not the same, are they?"

"No." Jane smiled. "So now are you going to tell me where I can find my Guccis?"

"Under the sofa in your sitting room, probably on the left side."

Jane's eyes widened. "Seriously?"

"Nah, just kidding about that one. Who do you think I am?"

Jane shook her head. "I'm still trying to figure that out."

"But I can tell you that your favorite bracelet was made in the twenties or thirties, possibly made of silver and Czech glass. Your second favorite is very colorful, maybe amber, blue-and-white stardust patterns all around, with intricate gold settings."

Jane instinctively gripped her own bare left wrist. "You're right. But I didn't bring either of them with me."

"I'm sure you had more important things on your mind. You use an iPhone, and you don't own a car. Not that you really need one in London. Eve already told me that you're an artist, but she didn't say that you've recently been doing microscopic detail work, possibly photorealism?"

Jane was gazing at her in amazement. "Yes, I've been experimenting just in the past few weeks. I haven't shown anyone my work yet."

"I've always admired artists who weren't afraid to branch out and try new forms."

Jane didn't speak for a moment, then slowly nodded. "The admiration is mutual, Dr. Michaels."

Kendra inclined her head. "Kendra."

Joe smiled. "Didn't I tell you, Jane?"

"Yes," Jane said. She turned back to Kendra. "But are you sure that someone didn't tell you all this? Joe wasn't entirely certain. Not Eve or Joe?"

"I was told, but not by them."

"Then who?"

"By you." Kendra leaned back against the porch rail. "All those years I was blind, I used everything I had to make my way in the world. Everything I heard, smelled, felt, and tasted was crucial. I was like a voracious sponge absorbing everything. You just don't unlearn that. And now that I can see, I want to pay attention to everything. Vision is such a wonderful gift that I don't take anything for granted."

"Clearly you don't," Jane said. "So how did I tell you all that?"

"Your clothes tell me quite a bit. You're wearing a three-year-old pair of Feiyue sneakers and a pair of slacks from Maje that are about the same age. You could have bought them in many cities or even online, but each of those items is most popular in France. Odds are that you were living there at the time of purchase."

Jane nodded. "I was. But you knew I moved later to England."

"You replaced your shoelaces within the last few months, and those are different from any that Feiyues come with. Those are polyester flat-woven, five-sixteenth-inch-wide laces. Clearly from the UK, not France. Your shoes are scuffed with tiny marks of gray paint on the fronts and backs, some fresher than others. You picked them up by several months of banging your toes and heels against painted staircase risers, probably unavoidable because the treads are so narrow. That wouldn't be the case in a newer building. And you now obviously go to a hair salon in England, not France."

Jane flipped back her shoulder-length red-brown hair. "Obviously? I didn't know I had a British hairstyle."

"You don't, but you use a British shampoo. Indian Mulberry by Molton Brown."

Jane's mouth fell open. "How in the hell—"

"A very distinctive scent." Kendra tapped her nose. "When you're blind, shampoos and soap odors are fairly reliable indicators as to who is standing nearby. And sometimes where people come from."

"Well, you're dead right. About my hair and my clothes. You're quite the fashionista."

"Me?" Kendra tugged at the collar of her shirt. "Old Navy. But I'm good at recognizing designs. And dialects. Even if I hadn't seen you, I would have known about the Georgia upbringing, the time spent in Paris, and your most recent time in London. I could pick it up in some of your pronunciations. I knew it from the moment you said that 'maybe there are too many cooks in the kitchen already.' The rest just confirmed it."

Jane wrinkled her nose. "I hope you're happy. You've just made me incredibly self-conscious about the way I speak. What about the sunglasses?"

Kendra stepped closer and used her forefinger to trace an outline around Jane's eyes. "You wore your Guccis for a long time before you lost them. Those years made a slight tan line on your skin. It's very, very faint but defined enough for me to see that you had a very nice pair of Gucci double-bridged aviators."

Jane gave a low whistle. "Wow."

"And I see a ruddier, more recent outline of another pair of aviators with almost the same shape. But your skin is red and irritated on your nose and also behind both ears. Injuries inflicted by your replacement sunglasses. I'm surprised you stuck with them this long."

"Me, too. I was busy and didn't want to go to the bother of finding another pair."

"And once you find something you like, you stay with it. Your clothes are good-quality, but I'll bet you wear them for years and years."

"Yes." Jane raised her arm and gazed at her wrist. "My skin . . . Is that how you knew about my bracelets?"

"Yes, you should really use sunscreen more often. It's just the faintest color . . . It looks like cut glass separated by alternating patterns . . . Maybe a flower design?"

"Butterfly."

"In any case, very Eastern European, very art deco."

"But you described the other one in such detail." She frowned. "There was no way my wrist could have told you that, dammit."

"Not entirely." Her lips turned up at the corners. "But I could just barely make out a pattern I remember seeing on one of Eve's bracelets. I complimented her on it and she told me you'd made it for her. Given what I was seeing there, it wasn't a leap to think you'd also made one for yourself. Since the shape of the beads and settings were the same, it was pretty safe to assume that the colors were also the same as hers."

"I made mine first."

"There's a slight wear mark on your slacks that tells me you usually keep your iPhone in the front-left pocket, which also tells me you don't often carry a purse. But I don't see a wear mark for a bigger keychain, which is usually more abrasive. It makes me think you don't own a car."

"Not in London, but I've started looking for one here." Jane leaned against the rail next to Kendra. "Okay, now how in the hell did you know I was experimenting with a new painting style?"

"You've recently started using a monocle of some kind over your right eye. You squint to hold it in place, which has left faint, callus lines above and below your eyelids. The lines are fairly fresh, meaning you haven't been doing it for long. That suggests you've been doing intricate detail work unlike that in most of your other paintings."

Jane nodded. "I can see why Eve was so impressed."

"Okay," Joe said. "What I want to know is how you knew about all of our law-enforcement visitors."

"That was the easiest of all," Kendra pointed down, where hundreds of muddy footprints crisscrossed the porch. "Each agency has its own favorite shoe. Police have their uniform shoes, FBI favors dress shoes with rubber soles, and, when they're not on a mission, CIA types usually go for leather soles. Each set of footprints tells a story. It's just a matter of learning to read."

Joe studied the footprints. "I guess I'm just illiterate."

Kendra turned to Jane and tilted her head. "Enough? I could probably pull up some other details if I concentrated. But it's such a waste of time."

"Enough," Jane said quietly. "I hope you're as good at pulling up information about Doane."

"So do I." Kendra turned to Joe. "Where can I be helpful? What do we know? Where do we start?"

"What do we know? Damn little. I'd like you to take a look at the safe house in Gold-fork, Colorado, where Doane lived, and see if you can come up with something. Venable's agents have come up with zero leads."

"Then Doane is definitely not holding Eve at that safe house?"

"No way. But we don't know where he is holding her. Eve managed to make a call to me, but it was broken off before it made the final connection. Venable is trying to trace the tower now." He added grimly, "Trying isn't an option. He has to do it."

"You mentioned a grave where one of Venable's agents was buried?"

"You can check it out, but forensics has already gone over it pretty thoroughly." He looked out at the lake. "But I really want you to get a look at that car when they bring it up. I want to know why Doane drove it into the lake."

"You said that there might be a corpse in it. Isn't that what your informant told you?"

"Informant?" Jane repeated. "Oh, Margaret."

"Who's Margaret?" Kendra asked. "And how did she know that—"

"She didn't," Joe said. "Not definitely. But a body is a hell of a lot easier to dispose of than a car. Why get rid of the car?"

"Who's Margaret?" Kendra asked again.

"A friend." Joe stiffened as his gaze narrowed on the crane at the bank. "They're getting ready to lift. Come on, Kendra. Let's go and watch them bring it up." He started down the stairs. "Jane, you stay here. You've been doing too much today. You don't need to be walking halfway around the lake."

"The hell I will," Jane said.

Kendra shook her head as she started down the steps after Joe. "You can't help. All you could do is watch. Save your strength for the big push. Eve told me you were smart. Now prove it."

Jane hesitated. "Dammit, I wish you were wrong." She wearily dropped down on the porch swing. "I'll wait here. You come back and tell me what's happening."

"I will." Kendra hurried down the steps after Joe. A moment later, they were yards from the cottage. She stopped as they reached the shadow of a huge pine. "Go back to her, Quinn."

"What?"

"She's not good. She wanted to come with us. There has to be a good reason why she stayed behind."

"She was shot a couple days ago. Naturally, she's not a hundred percent."

"I'd say she's way under fifty percent. She's in a lot of pain."

"She hasn't said anything to me."

"Would she?"

Joe cursed. "Probably not. She left the hospital before she was due to be released, and she won't rest. She must be pretty bad if you noticed—what am I saying? You'd know before anyone else."

"It's pretty obvious. She was trying not to show it, but I could hear it in her breathing and see it in her footsteps. When she was leaning against the porch rail, she needed that support." She paused. "And I could smell it."

"Smell it?"

"The infection. It has its own scent. Ask

any nurse. That wound is festering. I'd bet she's burning with fever. Go back to her. Take her to the hospital and get her some help."

"I'm going." He turned on his heel. "Stubborn. So damn stubborn. Why wouldn't she tell me?"

"It's probably your fault. You and Eve raised her. You'd probably behave in the same way."

"Are you coming with me?"

"No, I'm a stranger. Jane wouldn't like me to see her when she's weak. I'll go down and take a look at that car they're raising from the lake." She started down the path around the lake. "I'll call you if I find out anything."

"You'd better," he said grimly as he took the porch steps two at a time. "Venable's down there running the operation. Tell him I sent you."

"I'd rather not have a CIA man hovering over me."

"Too bad. We're all in this together." His voice was harsh with frustration. "I keep going down blind alleys. I've got to find a way to get to Eve."

Vancouver

Zander shrugged out of his jacket as he let himself back into the library after spending two hours working out at the gym. He should be feeling tired, but he was not. He was alert, revved, every sense alive.

He didn't turn on the lights as he crossed the room to the desk. There was moonlight, and that was usually enough for him. He had trained his eyes to crystal sharpness over the years, and he kept them that way through constant practice. The gadgets and infrared glasses were all very well, but there was always that time when you didn't have them. Then natural weapons always prevailed.

He dropped down in the executive chair and stared down at the Duncan dossier.

Are you still alive, Eve Duncan?

And why should I care? I gave up the luxury of emotion years ago. Or it could be that it gave me up.

Perhaps he didn't care. He had dealt with death since he was a young man and knew to become involved was to open himself to defeat. At times he believed that defeat would be welcome, but he still had a keen sense of self-preservation and enjoyed some aspects of the life he'd carved out for himself. If he died, it would be his choice and not that of Doane.

Maybe what he was feeling was distaste at the idea of Doane's entering his space, not rejection at the possibility of his killing Eve Duncan.

Whatever it was that was moving him, he didn't like it.

Then face it and get rid of it. The worse thing that could happen was to sit around and think about Doane. He wasn't worth it.

He reached for his phone and quickly dialed Donald Weiner, his telecommunications expert. "Do you have it?"

"Zander?" Then the sleepiness left Weiner's voice. "Yeah, I think so. I wasn't sure that you still wanted it when you didn't call me back."

"I wasn't sure either. I'm sure now. Have you traced Doane's call or not?"

"It wasn't that easy. He didn't stay on the line that long and he had it bouncing off satellites and—"

"He stayed on longer than he should have to be safe. I thought at the time that

he might have wanted to lure me to wherever he is. Besides, you're a genius. If I'd
wanted excuses and easy, I'd have hired
someone from a Geek desk at BestBuy to
bug my phone."

"I wish you had."

"Don't worry. You didn't hear anything
incriminating that would make me nervous
in that conversation." That call when Doane
had phoned, spitting venom and threats
and put Eve Duncan on the phone, had
been more incriminating to Doane than to
him, and Weiner was too afraid of him to be
a threat. When Venable had told Zander
that Doane was on the move, Zander had
known that Doane might call him and taken
precautions.

"I didn't really listen to it," Weiner said. "I
just started tracking the signal."

"Liar."

"Okay, maybe a little. But I'm not stupid,
I hear lots of stuff in my business, and I
destroy the records as soon as I finish with
them. You can trust me."

"I don't have to trust you. All I have to do
is pay you; and then you give me the information. Where is Doane?"

"Somewhere in southern Colorado. Wild

mountain area. I couldn't zero in on the exact location, but I've got the tower."

"Map it and send it to my cell phone. Now." He hung up and leaned back in the chair.

Colorado. Mountain area.

Even if he had a start, it wouldn't be an easy hunt.

He had done his own research on Doane and his son five years ago, when Venable had snatched Doane away and stuffed him in that safe house. Doane was a hunter and very good at it. Zander couldn't see him exposing Eve to wild conditions when she was doing the reconstruction on Kevin, but it was possible. First, he'd check out houses and businesses in the area, then start doing some tracking himself.

He flipped open the dossier and looked down at the photo of Eve. The moonlight only revealed a dark shimmer of an image, but he found he didn't need any more. He knew her face by now. He had looked at it, studied it, thought about it for the last few days. Maybe, for the last five years. Why? Who the hell knew? He had thought he knew himself very well, but he couldn't deny he'd been drawn, fascinated, by the idea of Eve Duncan.

"It's not for you," he whispered. "I have my own reasons for going after Doane. I wouldn't do it for you."

His phone pinged, and he accessed the map Weiner had sent him.

The tower encompassed a hell of a large area. Google it for any likely buildings? No, he could do that on the way. Time to start moving.

He got to his feet and called Stang. "I'm heading for Colorado. Call the airport and tell them to get the plane ready for takeoff."

Stang was silent. "You're going after her," he said softly. "You're going after Eve, aren't you?"

"Don't be ridiculous. I'm going after Doane." He headed for the door. "I'll call you if I need anything."

Lake Cottage

Kendra could see the car's headlights jerkily emerge from the lake surface as the crane lifted it. The bank was swarming

with people, and it was daylight bright from
the floods. A tall, older man appeared to
be giving the orders. That must be Venable, she thought; he breathed authority.

She stopped some distance away to
avoid getting in the way and watched the
crane do its work.

"Hi, you must be Kendra. Joe Quinn told
me you were coming."

Kendra turned to see a young girl step
out of the trees. Slim, medium height, light
brown hair, probably not over nineteen or
twenty. She was tan and glowing with the
sheen of sheer vitality. She wore jeans and
a shirt, and her bare feet were in thongs.
She was smiling, and Kendra instinctively
smiled back. "Yes, and you are?"

"Margaret Douglas."

"Oh, the friend of the family?"

"Is that what they called me?" Margaret's
smile broadened to delighted brilliance.
"That's nice. What else did they say?"

"Not much. Except that you were an informant." No one could appear less likely
in that role than this young, vibrant girl. "Is
that true?"

"Well, sort of . . . more of an interpreter."
She giggled. "Informants hang out in dark

parking garages like that Watergate story about Deep Throat, don't they?"

"I'm not sure. I guess there are informants and informants. Where do you hang out?" She looked down at Margaret's semibare feet. "The beach?"

"Sometimes. I just came from an island in the Caribbean, and I'm used to my flip-flops. Where's Joe? Why didn't he come with you?"

"He had something else to do." She took a step closer to the bank as the blue car was lifted high by the crane. "Jane MacGuire wasn't doing too well. I told him to take her to the hospital."

"Dammit. I thought she looked bad earlier tonight." Margaret was looking back at the cottage. "And it looks like Joe's going to do as you suggested. I see the headlights of his car." She was frowning. "I should be with her."

"No one can take better care of her than Quinn," Kendra said. "And they're family. It's his job."

"You're wrong. It's **my** job. She saved my life and took that bullet for me. When Doane's partner, Blick, was targeting Jane, she pushed me aside. I owe her."

"And that's why you're here?"

"I owe her," Margaret repeated. "You have to pay your debts."

"You must be doing your best to do that if you're involving yourself to the extent of delving and acting as an informant to—"

"Wait." Margaret held up her hand. "I can see why Joe was casting around for a way to explain my presence without going into awkward details. He didn't want to have to defend me. According to what he told me, you're all high-powered brain-power and logical deductions. You're going to have problems with me. But I can't go along with it. I've found it easier to be honest with people if I can. Then they can take me or leave me."

"I don't have to do either," Kendra said. "I can't see that we'll do much interacting. I work alone."

"Do you?" Margaret beamed. "So do I. It's easier, isn't it? We may be more alike than I thought." She tilted her head. "Nah, not likely." She glanced at the suspended car, which was being tilted forward as it was being brought closer to the bank. "They'll have it down soon and you can get to work. I hope your magic works."

"It's not magic, it's observation."

"Whatever." Margaret was looking absently over her shoulder at the receding taillights of Joe's car going down the drive. "I should be with her. I'm not doing any good here. I've told Joe and Venable all I know about this car. It's up to you now."

"You told him that there would be a body in that car, the farmer from whom Doane stole the truck."

"That's right."

"You were wrong." Kendra could see the entire interior of the car because of the tilting of the crane. "No body."

"It's in the trunk," Margaret said with certainty. "Doane wrapped the body in a tarp and stuffed it in the trunk."

"Who told you that? Did you see it?"

"No, I didn't see it." She frowned as she glanced back at Kendra. Joe's taillights had disappeared from view and with them a little of her patience. "Look, I have to round up one of the officers to give me a lift to go after Jane. Go tell Venable to be careful when he opens the trunk. If there is any evidence left after that dunking, it will probably be there."

"If you didn't see it happen, who told you the body was in the trunk?"

"It's a bullet wound to the head, so I doubt if Venable will be able to get any forensic material after his being under water all that time." Margaret was already walking away from the bank and back toward the cottage. "But maybe I'm wrong. I'm not like you. I don't know much about all that scientific stuff."

"You're not answering me. Who told you that there was a body in that trunk?"

"A feral." Margaret's pace increased. "But he's pretty reliable."

"Dammit, what's that supposed to mean?" Kendra called after her. "Feral? Is that a gang member? Maybe some kind of private-detective organization?"

"No." Margaret was almost out of sight in the darkness beneath the trees. "Just a cat. I'll see you later."

"A cat?" Kendra was standing, riveted, staring after her. "What in hell do you—" Kendra broke off in frustration as she realized Margaret was out of range and couldn't hear her. The exchange with Margaret had been thoroughly aggravating and bewildering. The girl had a sunny appeal that reached out and enfolded you, but that didn't keep you from feeling as if you'd been caught up in a gentle whirlwind that left you far from the solid ground where you needed to be. It had been a little like talking to Peter Pan.

Venable. He was no Peter Pan, and she could count on concrete logical answers from a CIA agent.

She turned away and moved toward the agent in a brown leather jacket who was now motioning the crane to lower the blue car on the bank. "Agent Venable?"

"I'm busy."

"That's clear. I won't bother you. I just wanted to introduce myself. I'm Dr. Kendra Michaels. Joe Quinn thought I might be of service."

"Yeah, he told me." The blue car was safely on the bank, and he motioned the crane crew to take off the chains. "Though I don't know what you're going to be able to tell from this baby."

"Neither do I. But at least it's not salt water. That could seriously damage any remaining evidence." Her gaze went to the interior of the car, which was still a quarter filled with water that was pouring out of the closed doors. "We'll just have to see. Quinn said to call him if you learned anything. He was going to take Jane to the hospital to have her checked out."

Venable frowned. "Shit. I was afraid that would happen. She's been running on sheer will alone for the last couple days. Quinn didn't need this. He must feel as if he's been drawn and quartered."

"He'll survive. It's Jane who is fighting the infection." She walked around the rear of the car. "I ran into Margaret Douglas when I first got here. Interesting."

"You could say that," Venable said dryly.

"She said to give you a message. You're supposed to be careful of damaging evidence when you open the trunk. She said that's where the farmer's body has been stuffed. He's wrapped in a tarp." She met his gaze. "Though she doubts that you'll be able to get very much trace evidence. There was no struggle, and he was shot in the head."

"Shot? My agent Dukes had his throat cut."

She shrugged. "She said shot." Her eyes were still narrowed on his face. "You're taking this very calmly. You actually believe her?"

"Hell, no. But Joe Quinn believes her. And I believe in Quinn. So I'll go along with him until she's proved wrong." His gaze shifted to the trunk. "She says there's a body in the trunk. Let's see if she's right." He motioned to a man who was standing a few feet away, with BABCOCK'S LOCKSMITH stamped on the front pocket of his shirt. "Unlock that trunk. Carefully."

Kendra took a step closer to Venable. "Did it occur to you that Margaret Douglas could be an accomplice? She said that Jane saved her life by taking a bullet for her. Now she has a reason for staying close to her."

"It occurred to me. But she was already on Summer Island when Jane MacGuire arrived there with her sick dog." His lips twisted. "A plant? Maybe. Or maybe everything she says is true. Even some of the things that are a bit of a stretch."

"Did she tell you who told her about this car in the lake?"

"No." He looked at her. "But judging from your expression, I'd bet that she told you the same story she told Quinn."

"She didn't tell me anything that made sense. Just some babble about a feral cat."

"That's what she told Quinn."

She stared at him incredulously. "What?"

"Jane MacGuire says she's some kind of dog whisperer or animal whisperer or nature girl or something like that. She swore Margaret saved her dog's life by finding out that he was poisoned."

"He told her?" Kendra asked sarcastically.

"You'd have to ask Jane about that. I didn't discuss the details with Quinn."

"And this feral cat told Margaret not only where the car was driven into the water but where the body was put into the trunk."

"And that the farmer was shot and not stabbed," Venable said. "I know where you're coming from, and I'm a hundred times more cynical than you are. If she's in Doane's pocket, why would she tell us any of that?"

"I don't know. It's just too bizarre."

"But Margaret is very plausible. She makes you want to believe her." He smiled. "Maybe she's just crazy and not criminal."

He was right, there was something about

Margaret that lifted the heart. Which was probably reason to be particularly wary of her and a sad commentary on life. "And maybe she's both." She was gazing at the locksmith carefully trying to jimmy the trunk with a long-needled picklock gun. The crew dragged over a pair of high-wattage work lights and trained them on the vehicle. "What's wrong? Shouldn't he be—" She stopped short. "It appears Margaret hit the nail on the head. There is a corpse in there."

Venable raised his eyebrows. "Really? And did a fish just tell you that?"

"That's Margaret's racket, not mine. Can't you smell it?"

"Smell something that has only been dead for a day or two and submerged in fifty-five-degree water? Even if you're right, there wouldn't be much to smell here."

"The corpse will be bloated." She took a moment to prepare herself for what was inside the trunk. Detach. Focus on the irritation she was feeling toward the skepticism that she sensed in Venable. She didn't need to deal with that right now. "Eyes bulging, cheeks swollen, the whole nine yards. It won't be a pretty sight."

Venable shrugged. "I doubt if it will be that bad already. I've seen water corpses before."

"So have I."

"It's open." The locksmith with the pick-lock stepped back as the trunk swung open.

A black tarp.

Kendra inhaled sharply.

The scent of death was immediately in her nostrils.

It wasn't really shock. It was the confirmation that an innocent man's life had been taken and his body thrown away like this. It never ceased to bring her sadness as well as anger.

"Move the tarp," Venable said to the forensic tech next to him. "Carefully."

Kendra watched as the tech gripped the edge of the tarp and peeled it back. Half a dozen flashlight beams darted toward the open compartment.

"Holy shit." Venable instinctively stepped back.

Kendra's first instinct was to close her eyes, but she made herself look at the puffy and grotesque face inside. The eyes bulged from their sockets like something from an old cartoon. His lips and cheeks had puffed to five or six times that of any normal human dimensions.

A few minutes later, the sodden gray hair of the dead man was exposed.

"Okay, it appears Margaret Douglas was right on the money," Venable murmured. "The body was in the trunk. Though it could have been a guess."

She didn't like the idea of Margaret's being right, but she didn't know whether it was because the ridiculous concept of animal communication offended her or that she didn't want Margaret to be criminally involved with Doane. The girl was so appealing that Kendra liked her in spite of her suspicions. Get a grip. Think logically. "And the location of where the car went into the water?" Kendra asked. "How did the man die, Venable?"

"Let's see . . ." He took a step closer to the body. "It can only be a preliminary guess." He grimaced as he looked closer. "Maybe not so much of a guess. He has a bullet hole in his temple."

Margaret's prediction, again.

"You need to talk to her," Kendra said. "It's too . . . you need to talk to her, Venable."

She took a step back away from the car. "And I need to stop thinking about Margaret Douglas and start doing what Quinn brought me here to do." She watched as Venable motioned for the forensic team to come forward. The car was instantly surrounded by a swarm of techs.

Venable turned toward her. "And you were right, too . . . How in the hell did you know the corpse would look this way?"

"The odor. It wasn't just normal decomposition. It's called tissue gas. An anaerobic organism enters the body and runs amok because the immune system is no longer functioning. It results in a specific smell, accelerates decomposition, and causes the body to swell and discolor." She pointed back to the corpse. "The marbling on his face and neck is pretty common."

Venable nodded. "So now you're a forensics expert, too?"

"No, I've seen—and smelled—this on a case once before, and I asked the medical examiner to explain it to me. Force of habit. I grew up asking people to explain what I was smelling, feeling, and hearing. I guess I never stopped." Kendra backed away from the car. "I'll stay out of everyone's way, but I want to monitor what they're finding and doing. Then after they finish, I want time to do my own investigation before you take the car, okay?"

"Okay. Do you know what you're looking for?"

"No, how could I? I'll just use observation, logic, hope for luck, and try to put everything I find together." She added grimly, "But I guarantee that my findings will be a lot more solid than some feral cat's."

CHAPTER

4

Gwinnett Hospital

"How is she, Joe?"

Joe turned to see Margaret hurrying down the corridor toward him, her thongs slapping against the pristine tiles. "I don't know. She's still in the emergency room. I believe she'll be okay. She's not dying, but she's not good. She had a 104 fever when she got here."

"Shit."

"Exactly," he said grimly. "This must have been coming on all day, and she hid it from me. I should have noticed the signs, dammit."

"She hid it well. She was probably afraid

that this would happen. She didn't want anything to get in the way of her finding Eve." She added, "And she didn't want to get in your way and take your focus away from her."

"That didn't happen. I wouldn't have paid enough attention to Jane to get her to the hospital if Kendra hadn't pulled me up and told me to do it."

"That's right. You blew it. You can't see anything right now but what could happen to Eve Duncan."

"No argument?" His lips twisted. "No soothing words?"

"Why?" She shrugged. "It wouldn't help anything if I lied to you. What you did was natural according to your priorities. I have to accept you as you are. Besides, I should have been the one to keep an eye on Jane. She was wounded because of me. I guess I was too busy finding out the lay of the land."

"Jane would say that no one is responsible for her," Joe said. "And we're family, and that means that I'm the one who—"

"Kendra . . ." Margaret was no longer listening to him. "I can see that she'd notice anything wrong in her world. You were right about her, Quinn. She's like a mountain lion on the hunt, aware of everything, tracks, spoor, sounds . . . Interesting."

"I don't believe Kendra would appreciate your comparing her to a mountain lion. She's very civilized."

"On the surface. But underneath she has a few rebel qualities."

"Don't we all?"

"Yes, but Kendra is different." She smiled. "I think. What do I know? I was only with her for a few minutes before she told me about Jane. I'll have to make a judgment later. I do know that she and I are very different, and I can see a little friction erupting."

"That's not surprising," Joe said dryly. "She'd have a hard time accepting anything but what her senses tell her. You're a little hard to swallow, Margaret."

"I know. I'll try to stay away from her. It shouldn't be difficult. I've got to—Here comes the doctor." Margaret took a step back away from him as the ER doctor came out of the emergency room. "I'll let you deal with him. Please get permission for me to see Jane. I have a call to make."

"Right," Joe said absently as he walked toward the doctor.

Quinn was clearly focused on Jane for the moment, but how long would that last? Jane was still ill, and she would need someone to protect and care for her until she was better.

Margaret couldn't count on that being Joe Quinn no matter how much he cared for Jane. Eve was the center, and everyone else revolved around her. And if Margaret was going to do what she'd promised Jane to find Eve, then she couldn't be at hand to care for her either. She'd have to call in someone else whom she could trust.

Trust?

Trust might not come into the picture with the man she was going to call. He was one of the wild ones.

What the hell, he would at least be sure to keep Jane alive.

It was the best she could do.

Lake Cottage

"It's all yours." Venable turned toward Kendra and motioned back to the blue car. He handed her a pair of latex evidence gloves. "Go to it."

"So soon? I thought it would take the forensics team hours to finish going over it."

"More like days. They just needed to give it a quick once-over before we transport it to the FBI garage in Atlanta."

Kendra pulled on the gloves. "FBI? I'm surprised you're letting them take possession of such a key piece of evidence."

"They have the facilities to handle it here. The CIA doesn't." Venable shrugged. "We're not above a little interagency cooperation."

Kendra moved toward the car, watching as the body bag holding the corpse of Hallet was carried up the embankment to the waiting van. "I hoped I'd be looking at this in daylight, but these work lights should do."

Venable handed her his brighter-than-bright tactical flashlight. "This should help, too."

Kendra turned it on and stood over the trunk again. She glanced over the entire compartment, trying to catch anything that had escaped her attention when the farmer's body was inside.

"Two days underwater doesn't make it easy," Venable said.

"Definitely not. But it did wash enough

grime to see that the driver of this recently transported something."

"Something other than a dead body, you mean?"

"Yes." Kendra pointed to several indentations in the metal bottom and side panels of the trunk. "These are fresh. Probably made in the past couple weeks. See how shiny and reflective the marks are." She gestured up to the trunk lid's interior. "It was big enough that the owner had to drive with the trunk open."

Venable pointed to a frayed piece of nylon rope attached to the truck latch. "And tied down."

"Exactly. And you see fresh marks on the inside trunk lid that matched the ones on the bottom. Two symmetrical rails, maybe chair arms or some other furniture piece. Hard to say." She pulled out her phone and clicked off several photos of the trunk.

She glanced at the last shot on her photo screen. A shallow indentation of the trunk was filled with sediment and lake water, but something else was throwing back a reflection from her phone's camera flash.

She leaned inside, trying to ignore the still-pungent odor stinging her nasal passages. She slowly waved her flashlight back and forth over the bottom of the trunk.

There!

A metallic glint punched through the sediment.

Venable leaned over her shoulder. "What is it?"

"I don't know. It looks like . . ." She used the end of her sleeve to scrape up a tiny bit of the sediment, then turned her wrist against the large work light.

"Gold?" Venable said.

Kendra nodded. "Maybe. It's a little more granular than gold dust and a bit dull, almost unprocessed. Do you have an evidence bag?"

"Actually, no. Not my department." Venable stepped over to one of the FBI forensic techs and came back with a small envelope. He scraped the sediment from Kendra's sleeve into it. "I'll also make sure they take a close look at this stuff left in the truck."

"Good." Kendra moved around to the driver's side door and pulled it open. She'd noticed when she'd watched the forensic

team at work that the interior was empty of
ATM or cash-register receipts that would
help point the way home. Damn, that
would have been too lucky. Oh well, the
water might have destroyed them anyway.

She shined her flashlight beam onto the
dashboard. The vehicle ID number had
been crudely removed, as if pried off by a
screwdriver.

"The VIN has also been removed from
the inner wheel arch and the radiator support bracket," Venable said. "They knew
right where to go. It'll slow us down, but
if the car has ever been serviced in a garage, there's still a good chance we'll be
able to track it down."

"There isn't much of anything here."
Kendra pointed to the backseat. "Except
that those rear seatbacks were folded forward to transport whatever it was in the
trunk. The fabric was split by something
heavy, something that also crossed the
rear passenger compartment and pressed
against the back of these front seats." She
bit her lip. "I wish I knew what the hell it
was. Not a bicycle. Not bookshelves. Not
shipping cartons. I just can't tell."

Venable smiled.

Kendra glared at him. "Am I amusing you?"

"I'm amused that you could get so angry at yourself for being unable to immediately ascertain any great meaning from a few stray scuffs. It's obviously a feeling you're not accustomed to."

"I'm very accustomed to it. I see things every day I don't totally understand. When it happens, I immediately get on the Web or talk to someone until I **do** understand. But now I'm frustrated because there's nothing I can do to immediately figure out what those marks mean. And it's even more frustrating to think that they could somehow help me to find Eve."

"Odds are that they wouldn't," Venable said. "You said yourself they could have been left a couple weeks ago."

"But if they're irrelevant, I'd like to know."

"I just remembered something that one of the FBI guys who was familiar with your work told me. Is it true you cracked a case based on the amount of starch you noticed on a man's shirt collar?"

She nodded. "Santa Monica last year. But a malfunctioning treadmill actually had a larger role in cracking the case."

"A malfunctioning treadmill? Okay, now I may have to requisition that case file."

"Enjoy." Kendra shined her flashlight across the car's instrument panel. "Can someone get me power to this console?"

"I'm sure they'll be doing that back in the garage. I can give you the address if you want to go over there later today and—"

"I don't want to wait that long. Surely someone here has a jump starter."

Venable motioned up the embankment where two police cars' flashers were playing against the rapidly encroaching fog. "I'm sure one of those cops can help you out."

"Thanks. I'll keep looking here while you go ask them."

His brows rose. "I wasn't volunteering."

"I'll keep looking here," she repeated pointedly.

"That FBI agent also told me you had a reputation for being a pain in the ass." He smiled and started up the embankment. "It so happens I'm known to have the same reputation."

"It just shows you have initiative."

"If you say so."

Less than thirty minutes later, Kendra watched the car's illuminated instrument panel flicker to life. The hood was open, and despite initial doubts that the car's recently submerged electrical system would respond, the operation was a success.

Venable walked around from the engine compartment, where one of the forensics experts was high-fiving the police officer who had supplied the five-hundred-amp jump starter. "Now what?" Venable asked Kendra. "There's no GPS unit, so there's no history to draw from. Was it worth all this just to get an odometer reading?"

Kendra didn't answer, her eyes narrowed on the car stereo's display, and pushed a button. Then another. And another. And another. And another after that.

She pulled out her phone and tapped furiously on the keypad. After a few seconds, she looked up at Venable. "This car was in southwest Colorado."

"Are you sure?"

"Pretty sure."

"Doane lived in Goldfork, but that's in the northern part of the state. You're off by a few hundred miles."

"Do you know where Mineral County is?"

Venable shook his head. "Can't say that I do."

"Neither did I until about twenty seconds ago." She held up her phone, which had a map on the display screen.

Venable studied it. "How did you get this?"

"I looked at the radio-station presets and did a Google search of all of them together. This is the only area that has six major stations with these same frequencies."

He nodded. "I don't think Doane has any known associates down there, but we'll look into it."

"Good." Kendra stepped away from the car and thought for a moment. "So will I."

Gwinnett Hospital

"Hi, what do you mean worrying me? This is the third time tonight I came in to see you, and you wouldn't wake up." Margaret plopped down in the chair beside Jane's bed. "I was all happy to see you out of that hospital in San Juan and mending, and you decide to have a relapse. Are you trying to give me a guilt trip?"

"Stop right there." Jane scowled at her. "I just got that line from Joe, and I've had enough. I didn't want to come here, and now they're threatening to keep me here for **three** days. I'm not going to put up with it. It's just a minor infection."

"Which you wouldn't have contracted if you'd rested and let yourself heal."

"That's what Joe said. And those doctors. To hell with all of them. I couldn't have done anything else."

"I know you couldn't," Margaret said quietly. "But it's a little different now. That's a nasty infection, and if you don't get over it quickly then you're going to distract everyone around you who is searching for Eve. You don't want to do that."

"I'll get over it," Jane said. "It's just some freaky bug that—"

"Do you want to cut down the chances of Eve's being found because it's not you who finds her?"

"Don't be ridiculous. Are you crazy?"

"It's been suggested a few times." Margaret grinned. "But no one can prove it." Her smile faded. "I'm just saying you're being selfish. I'd probably be the same way, but that doesn't make it smarter or less self-serving. You're in everyone's way right now."

"Damn you." Jane's hands closed into fists. "Get out of here, Margaret."

"That's the fever talking."

"That's me, wanting to punch you." She glared at Margaret. The girl was sitting there, her face glowing and her eyes shining with that gentle, shrewd, almost loving, under-standing. But Jane didn't want to be understood; she wanted out of there. And she had a dreadful feeling that she was wrong and Margaret was right. "I can't stay here."

"You've already made the decision." Margaret leaned back in the chair. "You're too intelligent to do anything stupid that might hurt Eve just because you want your way. I'll call Joe and tell him that you've thought about it, and you'll stay here until they release you."

"I'll make my own calls," Jane said. "And I'm not the only one who likes to have her own way."

"True." Margaret chuckled. "But I don't have an infection or fever or any of those annoying things. But I'll stay out of your way for a while so that I won't irritate you.

This must be my night for avoiding con-
frontations. I promised Joe I wouldn't stick
around and risk arguing with Kendra Michaels."

"I can see that happening," Jane said
dryly. "She's a sharp scalpel, and you're
one of those water wands that sense be-
lowground springs. Did she find out anything from the submerged car?"

"I have no idea. I didn't wait to find out
after I found out you were on the way to
the hospital." Her head tilted. "See, you
were already interfering then. It's good you
decided that you weren't going to do it any
longer."

"Stop rubbing it in. Lying here, not able
to—I'm out of here as soon as I get the
okay." Her teeth sunk into her lower lip. "It's
going to kill me."

"I know," Margaret said softly. "Will it help
you to know that I'm not just going to be
around holding your hand? You can't go on
the hunt, but I'll do it for you. I'm leaving
your beautiful lake to see what I can find on
my own."

"No, it doesn't make me feel better. I
don't want you wandering off and getting
yourself hurt or killed."

"It was going to happen anyway. You said that you'd let me help you."

"Help. I was going to be there to—"

"Take care of me?" Margaret's eyes were sparkling with humor. "Jane, I've been taking care of myself since I was a toddler." She got to her feet. "And deep in your heart, you're glad to have a surrogate while these good people are keeping you prisoner." She headed for the door. "I'll call you every now and then and let you know what's happening with me. If you want to keep yourself busy, you should find some way to research or find—"

"Stop telling me what to do," Jane said. "Look, can I talk you out of this? Is there any way?"

"Not a chance."

She meant it, Jane realized. She had seen how determined Margaret could be. "Then I'll stop trying to do it. But you'd better call me, dammit."

"Or you'll worry yourself into another fever spike. I was only trying to keep you from being too on edge. I've already arranged for a safety wall and distraction, but you need to keep your mind working so that you'll feel useful and—"

Jane frowned. "Safety wall?"

"To keep you from changing your mind and trying to come rescue me as well as Eve." She stopped at the door. "Good-bye, Jane. Heal quickly."

"You bet I will." She paused. "And you're right, I must not be a very good person because I do want someone, anyone, to move ahead with searching for Eve while I'm stuck here." She moistened her lips. "But you have to be careful. Don't you dare do anything that would get you hurt."

"I won't. I promise." She turned to leave.

"Margaret."

"Yes."

"I'll be with you as soon as I can." She was silent a moment. "I'm sorry I yelled at you. You're a very special person."

"That goes without saying. But it's nice to be appreciated in a way other than the obvious." Margaret laughed and left the room.

Jane lay there gazing at the door. She was still clenching her fists, and she forced herself to relax them. As Margaret had said, she had made her decision, and she had to do what she could to get well as soon as possible. Keeping her temperature sky-high because she was upset didn't fall in that perimeter.

Control frustration.

Block the thought of Eve.

Neither of those things would be easy.

One of them would prove impossible.

Damn. Damn. Damn.

Okay, call Joe and tell him that she was calmer now and would try to obey the doctor's mandate. She had been rude and completely rebellious before he had left.

She was still rebellious. It wasn't fair that everyone around her was going to be able to go into action while she stayed in this hospital and pampered herself.

She took a deep breath. She could feel the heat and weakness attacking again.

Keep busy. See if she could find something worthwhile to do for Eve. As Joe, ask Venable, go over all the leads they had and see if she could find a way to do that.

She reached for her phone and dialed Joe.

What the hell was Seth Caleb doing here?

And he was there, Jane thought drowsily. It wasn't the fever. He was sitting across the room in a chair by the door. She could feel him in the darkness.

But it wasn't totally dark. She could see the light pouring through the door from the hall picking up the threads of silver in his dark hair.

And she could feel the vibrance, the tension that was only slightly masked by that lazy indolence he adopted on occasion. She was still half-asleep but that tension was reaching out and touching her, stirring her.

"You're awake," Seth Caleb said. "I tried not to wake you." He chuckled. "No, that's not true. I wasn't careful at all. I was getting bored, and I wanted you awake to entertain me."

"What are you doing here, Caleb?" She lifted her hand to brush the hair away from her forehead. Her head was no longer hot. The fever must be dissipating, thank God. "When I opened my eyes and saw you, I thought I was back in that hospital in San Juan . . ."

"Oh, that night you were shot and I stayed with you after you came out of surgery to guard you?" He turned on the lamp on the table beside his chair, and a soft light flooded the room. "That was memorable for me, too. I behaved with exemplary restraint. Don't you think so?"

"No. I don't remember any restraint." She watched him come toward her. Grace. Power. Darkness. Sexuality. She had always thought Seth Caleb was the sexiest man she had ever met. His face, his dark eyes that seemed to be almost hypnotic. But that power and sexual magnetism also brought with it a disturbing wariness. She had always been aware of that danger below the surface during the years she had known him. Eve had even warned her about him, though at one point that power and violence had saved Joe. But Jane had still called on him to help her take her critically ill dog, Toby, to an experimental research facility on an island in the Caribbean. He had given her support and strength during that hideous time as well as the period when she had been in the hospital with that bullet wound inflicted by Blick. That didn't mean she trusted him. He'd be the first one to admit that he was capable of manipulating any situation to suit himself and get what he wanted. And he had not been hesitant to tell her that what he wanted was a sexual liaison with her. "You tried to seduce me when I was barely out of the anesthetic."

"Not really. I only offered you a little mental stimulation that would have brought you extreme pleasure. I knew that you'd resent me later even if you enjoyed it, so I backed off. It wouldn't have been worth it." He was standing by the bed now, and she could see him more clearly . . . and feel that automatic tensing, melting, that was always a part of her response to him. "I decided a gradual assault would be better and let you become accustomed to the idea." He reached out and touched her cheek. "But if you persist in landing yourself in the hospital, I may have to get more aggressive. I'm very impatient."

"What are you doing here?" She moved her cheek to avoid his touch. "You were at General Tarther's house in Virginia."

"Which became an exercise in futility. I told you I'd go there to guard him." He grimaced. "Unfortunately, he was murdered before I even arrived. You heard about that, I assume?"

"Yes, Venable's agent he had guarding the general called him and reported that the general had been shot. We expected to hear from you."

"Why? I didn't think it would be necessary. I set about questioning neighbors and trying to get a description of the shooter."

"And did you?"

"Yes."

"Blick?"

He nodded. "One woman who lived down the street caught sight of a man of his description the day the general was shot. I was going to try to do some more scouting to get a description of his vehicle when I found out I had to come back here."

"Why? You're not needed here, Caleb."

"That's not what Margaret told me. I was ordered to show up here at the hospital tonight."

"Margaret? She called you? Why the hell would she—"

"I've already arranged for a safety wall and a distraction for you."

"I may murder her." She struggled to sit up in bed. "Go away, Caleb. I don't need either a safety wall or a distraction. I don't need you." She glared at him. "And stop laughing."

"Was that going to be my duty? Margaret

didn't mention anything but making sure that I stay with you until you were released." He tilted his head. "Safety wall doesn't fit my personality, but I suppose I can rise to the occasion, and distraction is one of my best talents."

"This is not amusing."

"It depends on where you're standing."

"I'm not standing; I'm lying in this bed, and I'm not going to have you forced on me until the doctors let me go. In spite of what a kid like Margaret decides is good for me. What right does she have to try to run my life?"

"Maybe it has something to do with that Chinese proverb about a person who saves your life belonging to you."

"Bullshit."

"Well, I tried." He moved back to his chair across the room. "Personally, I'm glad she chose me to watch over you in her place. She could have called Mark Trevor. After all, he was your lover for a few years. He's supposed to be arriving in Atlanta soon, isn't he?"

"Yes. And I don't need him either. All I want is to get out of this hospital and find Eve."

"And you will," Caleb said. "I'll help you. There are ways to do that I've never shown you. I've been thinking. I donated my blood after you were shot. That may offer a few options."

She gazed at him warily. "What's that supposed to mean?"

"Nothing that should alarm you." He smiled. "It's not as if you didn't know that I have a few bizarre talents and idiosyncrasies." His smile faded. "Though that may subconsciously be what's alarming you. Is it? Tell me, do you have nightmares about vampires?"

"Don't be absurd," she said curtly. "You're no vampire. You've just got this blood . . . thing. You're just . . . weird." More than weird, she thought as she looked at him. What would it feel like to be able to control the flow of blood in those around you? She hadn't believed it when she, Eve, and Joe had first become involved with him. He had been searching for the man who had killed his sister, and when he found him, he caused the man's blood to trigger death in the most painful way possible. And the medical examiner had never been able to declare it anything but a natural death. Caleb had told her later that the fatal gift had been passed down in his family for centuries. "And I don't dream about you at all." That wasn't quite true. She'd had a few very hot, carnal dreams for which she had been certain that Caleb had been deliberately responsible. She had an idea that power to move the blood might also have influence over mental and sexual responses.

"No?" He smiled knowingly. "I dream about you, Jane. And I plan on continuing to do so. Perhaps I can persuade you to join me . . . again."

"Screw you."

"That's my most earnest wish." He sat down and leaned back against the wall. "But until we're in complete agreement, I won't push. And I'll try not to overpower you with my presence. I'm staying tonight to make sure that your fever goes down entirely, and you're totally on your way to recovery. After that, I'll stick to normal visiting hours."

"Am I supposed to thank you? I don't need you, Caleb."

"But it's my duty to protect and distract

you. I have to obey Margaret. Close your eyes and go to sleep, Jane."

"I'd sleep better if you weren't here. You always—"

"Disturb you? I hope that I do. You've disturbed me from the moment that I met you. Have you ever thought that if we have sex, we might get it out of our systems and be able to walk away from it?"

"I can walk away from it now. You're the last person I want in my life, Caleb. I'm grateful for the help you've given me, but I don't want my life to be thrown into turmoil. You're too . . . volatile."

"That's without question. But have you ever considered how exciting it is to walk on the dark as well as the bright paths? Volatility can have its charms."

She didn't answer.

"Mark Trevor is all bright paths. But you tried him as your lover, and you sent him away." He paused. "I won't let him back into your life."

"I'll do as I wish. It's not your decision."

"That's true. We're all responsible for our own actions. But one action sometimes triggers another." He chuckled. "And I've noticed that what you do has a very potent effect on me. Actually, I welcome Trevor's arrival. It will make things even more interesting."

Jane was suddenly tired of fighting, tired of struggling against Caleb.

"This isn't a game, Caleb," she said wearily. "I can't care what you want or what Trevor wants. Not when I don't know what's happening to Eve. You're just not important."

"You're sad. And I don't like it." His smile vanished as he studied her. "You're such a wonderful, strong antagonist, I sometimes forget that you can be hurt. And then you show me your vulnerability, and somehow it robs me of any victory. It's not supposed to work like that." He shook his head. "If I were Trevor, I'd probably be over there holding your hand and making soothing but sincere noises. That's not me." He was silent. "But that doesn't mean I don't want to take the ache away. I'm finding it . . . surprisingly painful."

"I'm not vulnerable, I'm just . . . tired."

"Then go to sleep." He turned out the lamp next to him, plunging the room into darkness. "You won't even know I'm here."

"The hell I won't."

"And if you dream, it will be of your Eve. After all, she's the only one who is worth anything to you."

"Are you being sarcastic?"

"No, truthful. And since I find I can't bear the thought of your being sad, I believe I'm going to have to make sure that you're reunited without either of us going through that trauma." He paused. "I like Eve, too, Jane. I don't want anything to happen to her. But I'm just a man, and other more lascivious emotions get in the way occasionally." He chuckled. "Well, more than occasionally. I'll work on trying to exert more control."

"That will be a first. Margaret calls you one of the wild ones."

"I knew she was perceptive." His voice was soft, soothing. "Stop talking and go to sleep. Forget about me. Dream about Eve and the good times. You had so many with her, didn't you?"

"Yes." Her eyes closed. "Beautiful times, silver mornings . . ."

"What? Silver mornings?"

Sitting on the porch swing with Eve and feeling the love like a warm bond between them. Eve had more than saved her life and taken her into her home when she was a child. She had woven love and friendship into a bright yet mellow quilt of feeling. She could remember the smell of the pine trees, the breeze from the lake on her cheeks and Eve . . . always Eve.

"Silver mornings?" he repeated.

"Nothing." And everything.

Love. Warmth. Clear and bright as a silver morning that would never tarnish.

Eve . . .

Rio Grande Forest
Colorado

Walk faster, Eve thought. Keep the blood flowing; that would fight off the cold.

It wasn't doing a terrific job at the moment, she thought ruefully. She couldn't stop shaking. The wind was picking up again, and it cut like a knife. She wanted desperately to go back to the place where she'd left the duffel for safekeeping and cuddle down under the blanket.

Not now. She had a job to do. She'd been unable to find any trace of a road in the ground she'd been covering. That left only the rock road she'd traveled with Doane to make the call to Joe. A road led to civilization. A road led to people. Otherwise, she'd be stumbling around here just hoping to run across a way to save herself. But she had to make sure that she was not going down a blind alley when she tried to go down that road.

If she could manage to dodge Doane. She was getting more and more tired, and he had all the advantages.

She must be tired if she was permitting herself to get discouraged. Stop it. She'd get through this.

Find the road. The house was right over the next hill. She'd just get to the edge of the cliff and try to see where the road led after it left the house.

The cliff where she'd thrown Kevin's skull.

Kill you. Burn you.

Imagination. Only memory this time.

Don't look down into that abyss where she'd thrown the reconstruction.

She crested the hill and saw the house below. Was Doane down there? It was daylight, and she couldn't tell by lights. He could be there if he'd stalked her all night.

Maybe.

She couldn't be certain of anything. That would be a fatal mistake.

Look at the rock road. It curved from the front of the house around to the back and disappeared down a slope.

From this angle. If she got closer to the edge of the cliff, she might be able to see where that slope was leading. She started slipping and sliding off the trail.

Kill you. Burn you.

She felt the tension start to overcome her. Push it back. She was defeating herself.

She balanced on the edge of the cliff and stared down at the road as it disappeared down the slope. Still not the right angle. She moved a few steps forward.

Yes.

The road appeared to lead straight down the hill into the valley.

And it ended in a cluster of roofs!

A town?

Oh, God, please let it be a town.

Too dark, too far away, to be sure. She was looking from this strange angle and could only see these few roofs.

She tried to move farther along the edge.

No way. She'd topple over if she went
another few inches.

She'd just have to gamble and take the
road and try to reach that cluster of roofs.

Not now. She had to see where she was
going. Doane could not only track her but
could use the truck to go after her once
she started on the road. Go back and get
her belongings. Rest. Then, when the hunt
started again, she'd try to lead him in a different direction and double back.

Hope was zinging through her as she
turned and started climbing the slope back
to the path.

Kill you. Burn you.

She inhaled sharply, but she kept her
gaze away from the abyss.

I don't hear you, Kevin.

You hear me. Come to me. Bring me
back.

Don't think about him, she told herself
as she reached the path and started to
run. Think of something else. Anything.

Silver mornings . . .

Where had that come from?

Oh, she knew where those words had
been spoken.

Jane.

But it had been a long time ago, and she hadn't thought about them for years. Jane had been in college and come back from Scotland, where she had been hunting the answers to a mystery about Cira, an actress who had supposedly been killed in the eruption of the volcano at Herculaneum thousands of years ago. Dreams about Cira had been haunting Jane since she was a girl of seventeen. She had found her answers in Scotland in the form of a letter written by Cira.

In that letter, Cira had wished her sister, Pia, velvet nights and silver mornings, and those words had fascinated, puzzled, and touched Jane.

And she had shared that fascination with Eve one night when they had sat together on the porch at the lake cottage.

"You understand everything I've ever gone through," Jane said as she looked up at Eve from where she was sitting on the porch step. "That's why I can talk to you when I can't talk to anyone else."

Eve was silent a moment. "Not even Mark Trevor?"

Jane shook her head. "It's too new, just scratching the surface. He makes

me pretty dizzy, and that doesn't help for analyzing a relationship." She hesitated, thinking about it. "Cira wrote about velvet nights and silver mornings. She was talking about sex, of course, but the silver mornings meant something else to her. I've been trying to puzzle it out. A relationship that changed the way she saw everything?" She shook her head. "I don't know. I'm too hardheaded. It would probably take a long time before I let myself feel like that."

"A long, long time." Eve wasn't sure if she was talking about Jane or her own experiences.

"Maybe it won't ever happen to me. But Cira was pretty hardheaded herself, and she was the one who told Pia what to look for."

"Silver mornings . . ." Eve put her cup down on the railing and sat down on the step beside Jane. "Sounds nice, doesn't it?" She put her arm around Jane. "Fresh and clean and bright in a dark world. May you find them someday, Jane."

"I already have them." She smiled at Eve. "You give one to me every day.

When I'm down, you bring me up. When I'm confused, you make everything clear. When I think there's no love in the world, I remember the years you gave me."

Eve chuckled. "Somehow I don't believe that was what Cira was talking about."

"Maybe not. She never had an Eve Duncan, so she might not have realized that silver mornings aren't restricted to lovers. They can come from mothers, fathers, sisters, and brothers, good friends . . ." She contentedly put her head on Eve's shoulder. The breeze was chilly but brought with it the scent of pines and the memory of years past, when she had sat like this with Eve. "Yes, definitely good friends. They can change how you see your world, too."

"Yes, they can."

They sat in silence for a long time, gazing out at the lake. Finally, Eve sighed and said, "It's very late. I suppose we should go in."

Jane shook her head. "That makes too much sense. I'm tired of being reasonable. It seems all my life I've forced myself to be practical and sensible,

and I'm not sure I haven't missed a heck of a lot by not letting in a little whimsy. My roommate, Pat, always told me that if your feet are planted firmly on the ground then you'll never be able to dance." She smiled at Eve. "Hell, let's not go to bed. Let's wait for the dawn and see if it comes up silver."

And they had stayed up all night and talked and exchanged thoughts that had made the bond between them forge new strengths.

Silver mornings . . .

Jane had never really let that joy she had spoken about become part of her life, and Eve felt a sudden sadness. She had thought for a while Mark Trevor would be able to break through that wariness, but though they had become lovers, that had never happened.

A sudden gust of wind took her breath away. The temperature was dropping, and she had to get to the meager shelter she had made for herself. She increased her pace and didn't look back at the abyss. At least, that memory of Jane had banished the horror that had seemed to attack her.

It had made her think of Jane and love and family. It had reminded her that hope always emerged from despair if you opened the door.

It had reminded her of silver mornings . . .

Gwinnett Hospital

"Is your fever back? You're shaking like a leaf."

Caleb's voice.

Jane opened her eyes to see him standing over her. "Cold. So cold."

His hand was on her forehead. "You don't seem to have a fever." His gaze was narrowed on her face. "And you're not shaking any longer. Are you still cold?"

She shook her head as she struggled to sit up in bed. "I'm not cold. It was Eve . . . Eve was so cold. And trying to keep from being frightened of him."

"Who? Doane?"

"No, Kevin, but she seemed to think of them as one person." She drew a deep, shaky breath. "Crazy dream. So real . . ."

"Do you want to talk about it?" He sat down on the bed. "Sometimes it helps."

"It was just Eve looking down at a road. She was in the forest, and it was cold. She could see her breath as she ran. She was tired of being cold and knew she had to find a way out." Jane shuddered. And she, too, had been cold and wanting desperately to find a way to keep that cold away from Eve. "That's all. It was all jumbled. But it seemed very real."

"Do you often have stressful dreams?" He smiled. "I promise that any you have about me will be more pleasant."

"No, I rarely dream." She said jerkily as she reached for the bottle of water on the bedside table. "I used to have fairly frequent dreams but then she—they stopped coming."

"She?"

She should have known he'd pick up on that slip. What the hell. It didn't matter. "When I was about seventeen, I started to have dreams about a woman who lived in ancient Herculaneum. She was an actress, and her name was Cira. They were strange dreams and were almost like a serial unfolding about her life and her lover." She took a swallow of water. "They were so real, it was driving me crazy, and

I decided to go find out if she actually existed."

"And did she?"

"Yes. She was the one who wrote in a letter to her sister about silver mornings."

"Fascinating. And so unlike you to go investigate a dream image. You're the most stubborn realist I've ever met. Did it shock you to find that there was no sensible explanation?"

"There could have been a practical, scientific explanation." She took another drink of water. "There were statues of her, and they looked like me. Since I couldn't trace my own ancestors, someone suggested that it could have been a racial ancestral memory."

"That's a reach."

"So were the dreams."

"And you preferred to latch onto an explanation you could comfortably accept."

"Maybe." She finished the water and put the bottle back on the nightstand. "Turn out the light. I'm okay now."

"Not yet. I want to explore this a little further. I'm intrigued at seeing this side of you."

"You mean you're intrigued at the idea I

could be a little weird, like you?" She shook
her head. "I admit that those dreams when
I was younger were strange and disturbing, but I haven't had one like that in years."

"Not even tonight?"

Yes, that dream of Eve had been like the
dreams of Cira. The clarity, the realism,
the sense of being there with her. "Perhaps. Look, Eve believes in all that kind of
stuff. I respect her, but she's not me. It was
a dream, Caleb. Drop it."

"After I ask you a few questions. When
you were searching for answers to Cira's
story, did you find some of those answers
because of what you dreamed about Cira?"

She was silent. "Yes."

"You didn't want to admit that."

"As I told you, possible racial ancestral
memory."

"The dreams were very detailed?"

"Most of the time."

"Interesting. Could you remember the
details of your dream about Eve?"

"Probably. If I tried."

"Why don't you try?"

"What?"

"It couldn't hurt, could it?" He opened
the drawer of the nightstand and took out

a yellow pad and pen. "Describe the surroundings, what Eve was looking at, what she was thinking, anything you can remember."

"Why?"

"Details. It worked once, didn't it? You found the answers to Cira. You might be able to find where Eve is right now."

"It was a dream, dammit."

Caleb merely looked at her.

"And I wouldn't have any racial or ancestral memory with Eve. I'm adopted."

"But you have a connection with her whose power could supersede any vague ancestral memory like the one you're describing." He added softly, "Faith can move mountains. Love can move mountains. Maybe there's a reason you started to think about silver mornings."

"Good God, you sound almost sentimental. Not at all like you."

He smiled. "I have an agenda. It's not going to be simple to keep you in this hospital for a few days. If you have something of value to do that will push the hunt forward, it will be easier for me."

She gazed at him without expression. "And what's that supposed to mean?"

"How did you find Cira?"

"Scouring the Internet for info, tracking down esoteric books, calling academic experts when I had leads." She paused. "You're saying that I should do the same thing with investigating the area where I saw Eve in my dream."

"Or anything that she was thinking that might give you a clue."

She didn't speak for a long time. "You know it's crazy."

"What could it hurt?" he repeated.

What could hurt was the desperate hope she was beginning to feel, she thought. She was grasping at straws, and probably the disappointment was going to crush her.

But she had found Cira in the end. She hadn't given up until she had all the answers. So this was different, the odds even greater that she wouldn't be able to succeed. Take every chance, go down every road that might lead to Eve.

"They were new mountains, sharp, towering. Maybe the Rockies."

"Put it down on the notepad."

"Later." She sat up straighter in bed. "Get my sketchpad from the closet."

"Yes, ma'am." He went over to the closet.

"You're right, drawing it will make everything clearer for you." He drew out the pad and brought it back to her. "But maybe take a nap first?"

"Hell, no. I might forget something. I can do that while you go out and get me a load of travel books."

"Is that my first task?"

"Along with doing computer site work. I don't have time to do it all myself. And you might find something that I don't." She flipped open the pad. "Now be quiet and let me concentrate. Eve was moving all the time except for the time she was looking down into the valley. She was on the run. I'll have to make several sketches so I won't miss anything."

"Should I bring up the fact that I think you're supposed to rest while you're in here?"

"You should have thought of that when you turned me loose on this wild-goose chase. You can't stop me now."

"No, I don't believe I can. At least, medical staff will be on hand if you collapse from exhaustion." He leaned back in his chair. "And I'll enjoy watching you work. The intensity is like a comet streaking."

She made a rude sound.

He chuckled. "It's true. People never see themselves as others see them."

She didn't answer, frowning as her pencil flew over the page.

Minutes passed before he spoke again. "I've been thinking about your Cira. If you're right, and she was your ancestor—"

"I didn't say that. It's one explanation."

"And the other might be reincarnation, which is way too far out there for you to consider. At least openly. But haven't you wondered?"

"No."

"I would. But then my family is very ancient, very wicked, and the descendants of our founding fathers have been struggling for centuries to stamp out any trace of similarity. Reincarnation is a great excuse for failure."

"I don't want any excuse for my sins."

"But then your sins are almost nonexistent compared to mine." He tilted his head. "You mentioned Cira had a lover. What was his name?"

"Anthony."

"And did Anthony remind you of anyone you knew?"

She stiffened. "What does it matter? I don't want to talk about any of this, Caleb."

"He did remind you of someone. Let's see, Mark Trevor was very much in your life at that time, wasn't he?"

"Yes."

"Did Cira's lover remind you of Trevor?"

She didn't answer.

"Did he, Jane?" he asked softly.

She shrugged, her gaze still on the sketch. "Yes."

She wasn't looking at him but she heard him sigh.

"I was afraid of that. Oh, shit."

CHAPTER

5

Rio Grande Forest
Colorado

An ancient red truck.

Yes.

Venable had mentioned an old red truck that Doane had stolen in one of his reports, Zander thought.

This old log house was in the cell-tower area from which Doane had made the call to him. According to the Google map he'd pulled up, buildings of any kind were extremely sparse in this wilderness. There had been one possibility down in the valley that Zander had dismissed immediately after taking a quick look around. Then he'd driven up the mountain to the second habitation on his map, which had looked more promising. It was higher in the mountains, where there were seldom any hunters or tourists.

An ideal place to keep a prisoner.

Make sure.

He'd already reconnoitered the house and judged it unoccupied at the moment. He popped the lock on the truck and started looking for gas receipts or anything else that would ID Doane.

On the passenger seat was a folded black cloth. He lifted it to his nose. A faint fragrance. The cloth could have been used as a blindfold. The scent was definitely feminine.

He burgled the glove compartment and found the gas receipts for which he'd been looking. Not charged to a credit card. But one was from a station in Birmingham, the other a small town in Missouri. Both issued on the same day.

The path was clear.

He gazed speculatively at the log house. It was probably booby-trapped. Doane's son had been Special Forces as well as al-Qaeda-trained and had probably taught his father. It would take time to disarm even though it would be an ideal place to ambush Doane as he entered the place.

And where were Doane and Eve Duncan? The truck was here, and presumably this was where Eve was working on the reconstruction. Yet neither one of them appeared to be on-site. They would not be taking a casual stroll, and unless Blick was nearby, and they were using his car, there was no reason for them to be gone.

He quickly checked the area for other tire tracks.

No Blick.

It could be that Doane had become enraged with Eve and killed her.

However, that would be a last choice for Doane. He had the idea fixed in his head that he would hurt Zander more if he made him witness Eve's death.

Which left one other interesting possibility.

"Did you take it on the lam, Eve?" he murmured. "How unobliging of you to be so troublesome to Doane." He looked up at the path leading to wilderness country. "But it may make my task more of a challenge."

Hunting the hunter. Much more exciting than hunting prey.

The hunter seldom expected to be caught in the crosshairs when he was feeling the exhilaration of being the dominant one. He turned and headed down the rock road, where he'd left his Jeep a mile from the area of the house. He'd get his weapons and equipment and set out tracking.

He was already feeling the urgency, the excitement of the hunt.

She had said that she wouldn't count on anyone to protect her, but if she could hold out in that harsh country until he tracked down Doane, she might have a chance to save herself.

He found his pace unconsciously escalating at the thought. What was he doing? He deliberately slowed as he realized that his instinct had been to rush that kill just to get to Eve. He'd thought those instincts had died long ago.

He could almost name the date and hour.

He'd take his time, not rush the kill and risk making a mistake. If that time proved to be in time for Eve, then so be it.

If not, then she could take care of herself.

Lake Cottage

The sky had just begun to lighten to a dusty orange when Joe walked into the cottage.

Kendra stood up from the kitchen table. "How's Jane?"

"Extremely pissed. They're going to keep her there for a few days. They've pumped her full of antibiotics to combat the infection, and depending on how she responds to treatment, surgery may be necessary again."

"I could see that she has a lot of fight in her. Like Eve."

"You've got that right. It's going to be tough getting her to stay in that hospital. I halfway expected to come in this door and find her here ahead of me."

"Not yet anyway. Did you hear about the car?"

Joe grimly nodded. "I called Venable on the way back. They've just notified the farmer's family. Venable said you'd found a few other threads to go on. What were they?"

"Not much, I'm afraid. But maybe something to build on." Kendra told him about the scrapes in the trunk and passenger compartment as well as the information provided by the radio-station presets. She showed him the area map on her iPad screen.

Joe studied it. "Mineral County, Colorado. What's there?"

"Very little. It actually has the distinction of being one of the most remote areas in the Continental U.S. It's on the Continental Divide. Mountains, forests, and not a whole lot of anything else."

Joe studied it for a moment longer. "Does Venable know about this?"

She nodded. "But not about the additional stuff I found out about Mineral County. I've been looking it up while I sat here waiting for you. Venable is checking the area out against Doane's known associations."

"Good."

Kendra picked up a page of notebook paper from the kitchen table. "I was writing you a note. I'm leaving for Colorado in just a few minutes."

Joe stiffened. "You're kidding, right?"

"There's nothing left for me to do here, Quinn."

"For God's sake, you haven't even slept."

"And how much sleep have you had since you found out Eve had been taken?" When he didn't answer, she shrugged. "I didn't think so. You called me because you thought I could help. And I think maybe I can. But neither of us has the luxury of sitting around and seeing which move that we make is the right one. We're just throwing everything into the mix and hoping one of them sticks. It's all we can do when Eve is in danger every second she's held by that psychopath."

Joe's jaw clenched, and he looked away. "Do you think I don't know that?"

"Then stop trying to protect me. I'll sleep on the plane. I'll start at Doane's house in Goldfork. I assume you can arrange access for me."

"Of course."

"Then do it. There may be something at Doane's house that can help us," Kendra said. "Maybe point out a way to figure out where he's taken Eve."

"The CIA has searched that place several times over the years. And I guarantee you that they've been there almost nonstop since Doane left. They haven't come up with anything."

Kendra wrinkled her nose. "If I had a dollar every time a law-enforcement officer told me there was nothing more to see at a crime scene . . ."

"I know, I know. That's why I wanted you part of this, Kendra. You don't see, you experience. I just didn't want you to waste time crisscrossing the country."

"You all have things pretty well covered here. If it turns out to be a dead end, I'll catch the first flight back here. Or wherever else I can help." She smiled crookedly. "I know you won't be shy about sending me to hell and back if there's a chance of that."

Joe nodded. "Thanks, Kendra."

"But there's something you need to know." Kendra motioned toward a clear glass of water on the coffee table. Four tiny capsule-shaped objects rested on the bottom of the glass. Each object had a single thin wire lead protruding from the underside, almost like a long tail.

Joe stared at the glass, then gave a low curse. "Are those—"

"Listening devices. I put them in the water to neutralize them. I didn't want to destroy them on the off chance that you could trace them. Someone bugged the house."

Joe reached in and plucked one of the capsules from the glass. "Where?"

"Everywhere. One in the kitchen, one in the master bathroom, two in here. Doane may have used them to plan the timing of Eve's abduction. He knew when she would be alone."

Joe dropped down on the couch, still staring at the bug in his hand. "And if he was listening afterward, he knows exactly what we know. Every conversation we had here with the police, the FBI, the CIA . . ." He looked up at Kendra. "How did you find these?"

"I wouldn't have found them if they'd been put in by a pro. Evidently Doane wasn't as competent at this kind of thing as his son. I wasn't even looking."

"Then how?"

"Drywall dust. Not much, just a faint dusting. He drilled tiny cavities in the walls above three doorframes and the one wall mirror. He threaded the antenna wire and microphone into each hole. The holes are small and above almost everyone's sight lines."

"Including yours."

"But I could see small traces of drywall dust on the baseboards below some of the spots where the wall had been drilled. I wondered why. I'd bet a few of these bugs were planted more recently than others, or the dust wouldn't still be there. Maybe he decided he needed more bugs as the time approached for taking Eve."

Joe shook his head. "We've had a parade of law-enforcement officers through here, and none of them wondered why."

"Because they didn't see it. They weren't looking for it."

"Neither were you," Joe said. "But then again, you don't take anything you see for granted."

Kendra shrugged. "Two decades of blindness will do that to a girl. Anyway, I looked closer and found these. Venable might be able to track them through retail-sales channels."

"I'll let him know." Joe dropped the microphone back in the glass of water. "I can't believe it . . . I'm mentally replaying every conversation we've had in the past couple weeks. The thought of that sicko's listening to us is—"

"That's minor compared to the thought of his holding Eve someplace." She checked her watch. "I should really get going."

"Look, Kendra, about this trip to Colorado. I don't—"

"Knock it off, Quinn. I know what you're going to say. You'd never ask me to do it, but that doesn't change anything." She moistened her lips. "Look, I don't have a lot of close friends. Do you think I don't realize how abrasive I can be? But Eve is my friend. She puts up with me and slaps me down when she thinks I need it and makes me feel like I'm special to her as a person and not the way others look at me. Do you believe I'd give that up? You can't keep me from going to find her. I know she'd be out there doing the same thing for me."

"Are you finished?"

"Yes."

"Then may I say I have no intention of talking you out of going to Colorado. I'm much too selfish. I just don't like the idea of your going alone." He pulled his phone from his pocket. "Let me call someone to go with you."

"Like who?"

"Some of the guys I worked with in the

Atlanta PD and the FBI are now private security. I'll hire one of them."

"A bodyguard?" She laughed. "You want to hire me a bodyguard?"

"There's nothing funny about this."

"The hell there isn't. Put your phone away. I'll be okay." She shook her head. "Classic Joe Quinn. Always trying to take care of everybody."

"Not everybody. Just the people who matter to me and Eve."

"I'll be fine. The last thing I need is to be traveling with some muscle-bound ex-cop."

"There's nothing wrong with being either an ex-cop or having muscles. Both can come in handy."

"I'm joking. But seriously, put away your phone. I'll be okay."

"You'd better be. If you're not, it may be too late for me to tell you I told you so." Joe paused. "All right. But if you change your mind, just call. If I can't be there myself, I'll have someone on the next plane."

"I'll remember that." Kendra stepped toward Joe and awkwardly put her hand on his arm. "You know, that kind of makes me feel special, too. Thanks, Quinn. I know that it's naïve to tell you that everything is going to be okay, but I'll do my best to make it that way." She turned away quickly, instantly rejecting that moment of softness and headed for the door. "Keep me in the loop. Let me know everything you know. We're all splintering in different directions to find Eve, and that's not a bad thing. As long as we share information, the dominoes may start falling into place. We just have to cover every possibility. Good-bye, Quinn. I'll be in touch."

The front door closed behind her, and a few minutes later, Joe heard her car pull out of the driveway.

He sat down again and stared at the capsules in the glass.

All the time and painstaking effort Doane had made to take Eve was exemplified in those listening devices.

Son of a bitch.

The anger and helplessness were growing by the moment. The little pieces of information and leads that they were finding were not enough, dammit.

But at least Kendra had found out a few things that were promising.

Maybe.

His phone rang. Seth Caleb.

What the hell? "Quinn."

"I'm with Jane at the hospital. I was bored, so I thought that I'd come out here in the hall and call you. She told me she'd call you again later, but I decided I'd take it off her list. She's going to be busy."

"Is she sleeping now?"

"No, she dozed for a while but now she's wide-awake and in work mode."

"Work mode? You are not to convince her to leave that hospital, or I'll strangle you."

"I couldn't be less concerned about you, Quinn. I'm taking my orders from Margaret at the moment, and she's far more intimidating. As it happens, all our goals coincide."

"Not if Jane's not resting."

"She'll rest eventually, and the work she's doing will keep her at the hospital, where the doctors can keep an eye on her."

"What work?"

"Something she's evidently done before. She mentioned Cira."

"What?"

"She had a dream about Eve, and she was in some mountain location. Jane is going through computer files and books to see if she can find any matching terrain." He paused. "She doubts if anything is going to come of it, but she said it had results when she was searching for Cira. She's pretty desperate."

"She would have to be. Even when Jane's dreams of Cira seemed to have substance, she was still trying to find a practical reason why that was so and why she was having the dreams. She has problems with anything that's not reality-based." He added wearily, "But then we're all getting desperate and ready to embrace anything that gives us hope."

"What about you, Quinn? Did you believe there was anything in Jane's dreams of Cira that was . . . unusual?"

"Hell, yes. Do I believe that experience would translate to help for Eve? I have no idea. I haven't a clue why Jane's dreams of Cira seemed to have historical and geographic details of which she would have no possible knowledge. I used to be a total realist like Jane, but these days, I only know that there's nothing that's not possible. I keep bumping into impossible."

"I'm surprised you admit that to me."

"Why? I don't give a damn what you think about me. As a matter of fact, you're one of the impossibles, with that blood thing."

"Point taken." He paused. "I encouraged Jane to pursue this avenue. It seemed interesting and a way to keep her sedentary. I thought I'd let you know. I'm sure Jane will give you a call if it proves promising." He hung up.

Promising? Joe pressed the disconnect. He hoped to hell he'd hear something promising from someone. But at least Caleb had found a way to keep Jane safe until she was well.

Maybe.

If desperation was driving her as Joe thought, then she might become frustrated and give up the search for this dream location.

But that wasn't like Jane. She had bulldog tenacity when she was fighting for anything. It would be an obsessive determination if she was fighting to find Eve. He wished he could believe that dream of Jane's would give them a hint, a lead, a path. Maybe what he'd told Caleb wasn't entirely true and there were still strong elements of logic and realism that made him cynical of anything else.

"I saw Kendra driving down the road." Venable stood in the doorway. "Where was she going?"

"Airport." His lips twisted. "And then to Goldfork. Make sure your agents welcome her with open arms."

"I'll see to it." He came into the cottage. "She's sharp, very sharp. Extraordinary. I don't know if she'll be able to find anything that my guys missed, but I'm willing to let her take a shot at it." He went to the kitchen. "Mind if I grab a cup of coffee? It's been a long night."

Joe nodded at the glass sitting on the coffee table. "She's already found one thing. It appears that everything that's happened in the cottage has been monitored."

Venable glanced at the devices in the water. "Shit."

"Yes. How long before you're able to identify that metallic stuff from the trunk?"

"I put a rush on it, but it takes as long as it takes." He took his coffee cup from beneath the automatic coffeemaker and lifted it to his lips. "And I promised Kendra I'd call her as soon as it came in." He made a face. "Otherwise, I think she'd have been down at the lab harassing the techs."

"No doubt about it," Joe said. "Kendra's philosophy is that you throw everything you have at the wall and hope something sticks. She threw that metallic dust, and she's going to want to know if it stuck." He looked down at the glass with the capsules. "She also said she couldn't do anything more here. I don't think I can either, Venable."

"And?"

"Splinters. Kendra was talking about splinters. How we were all working at different points for the same goal, finding Eve. She's right. One of those splinters was here. The car and any evidence we could locate. Then Kendra branched off to Goldfork. Another splinter, we knew that Doane would try to kill General Tarther and Lee Zander because they were responsible for the death of his son, Kevin. You even tried to protect the general."

"Tried. The bastard got to him anyway."

"But as far as we know, Doane hasn't been able to kill Zander yet." Joe's lips twisted. "That's a very sharp splinter to explore."

"More than you dream." Venable's eyes narrowed on Joe's face. "It could be fatal."

"Why are you trying to ward me off Zander? You've been doing it since you told me about Zander and the general. He's an assassin."

"I don't want you dead." He added, "At first, it was just that five years ago I'd made Zander a promise that I'd keep his identity secret if he didn't go after Doane. I keep my word. Now, I'm having regrets about opening my mouth and not just trying to handle him myself."

"I want Zander's address," Joe said to Venable. "Now."

"Not smart, Quinn," Venable said. "Let me handle him."

"The hell I will," Joe said. "I have to get on the move. I can't sit here any longer. Kendra is on her way to Goldfork, Doane's safe house. You can't get me that damn tower location and the general was picked off as cleanly as if you didn't have anyone there protecting him. It's all been on Doane's side. I have to change it."

"Zander may not even be there."

"But someone will be there?"

"Stang, his accountant and personal assistant."

"Then I'll find out where Zander is and if he has any idea where Doane has Eve." He added grimly. "And if Doane is going to go after Zander, then I'll stay there and stake him out myself."

"What about Jane?"

"Stop trying to put obstacles in my path. Seth Caleb is there watching that she's not doing too much. He said he'd keep her occupied." He grimaced. "Which isn't very reassuring, considering the source. And I think Mark Trevor called Jane yesterday and told her he'd be coming here within a day or two. Jane will have more help than she's going to want. Give me Zander's address."

Venable hesitated.

"Venable."

Venable reached into his pocket for his phone and accessed Zander's information. "I'll send it to your phone."

"Good." Joe turned. "Then I'm on my way."

"Quinn."

"Don't try to stop me."

"I know better. Just be careful." He hesitated. "Oh, hell. I can't let you go without telling you. It could be a game changer somewhere along the way."

"What could be a game changer?"

"The reason Doane took Eve in the first place."

"The reconstruction."

"No." He grimaced. "The fact that Eve is Zander's daughter."

Joe froze. "What? That's not possible."

"Zander's daughter, and Doane knows it. It would just be too coincidental that he would pick Eve to do the reconstruction on his son."

Joe shook his head. "That's got to be bullshit. Eve didn't know who her father was. I don't think her mother did either."

"That would surprise me because Zander definitely knew about Eve. He told me about her five years ago. He always thought Doane would walk away from that safe house. He was looking at possible chinks in his armor that Doane might attempt to find. He thought Eve might be one. He told me if Doane ever split to look in Eve Duncan's direction."

Joe was trying to take it all in, but he was too stunned. "And you never mentioned it to Eve? You've known it all these years, and you never told us."

"I wouldn't mention it now if I didn't have to. Eve has made a decent life for herself. She didn't need to know that her father is probably the deadliest assassin I've ever run across. I didn't know what kind of effect that would have on her."

"No effect. Nothing could change what she is or how she thinks about herself."

"And you?"

"Are you crazy? Even if this crap is true, which I doubt, Eve stands alone." He took a harsh breath. "But if he thinks it's true, can I use it to get Zander to help me find Eve?"

Venable shook his head. "He doesn't care, Quinn. I've tried that card, and he doesn't give a damn. I've never seen a colder bastard."

"I can be colder," Joe said. "Watch me."

"That's what I've been afraid of. The situation between Zander and Eve may be . . . complicated. Don't jump until you know what's going on with him."

"I don't care what's going on with him as long as I can use him to get to Eve." He was going down the steps. "You just try to find out where that damn cell tower is." He opened his car door. "By the time my flight reaches Vancouver, I want answers, Venable."

Rio Grande Forest
Colorado

Threat. Danger.
  Doane!
  Eve's eyes flew open, jarred from sleep!
Yes, Doane!
  He was coming toward her, slowly, creeping through the forest to catch her off guard.
  And he **had** caught her off guard. She had allowed herself just a few hours to nap and regain strength.
  Too long. Too long.
  He couldn't be more than fifteen feet away from her.
  Run!
  She jumped to her feet and bolted.
  He was right behind her, his hand grabbing her shoulder. "Oh, no, Eve. I had you. You're not going to—"
  Her elbow lashed backward, plowing into his stomach.

He grunted, bending double with pain.
His grasp on her shoulder loosened.
She pulled free and ran.
So close.
She could hear him behind her.
Keep running.
He had not caught her though she had been helpless in those first few moments.
Instinct. Self-preservation. Bonnie.
Whatever had caused her to sense him and wake had saved her. She was making mistakes, but she was learning.
She was not helpless now. She had will and determination and the strength of her body and mind.
And she would not let him catch her.
"How long do you think you can hold out, Eve?" Doane's voice was mocking behind her. "I almost got you this morning, didn't I? But I managed to grab your duffel with all those treasures that are helping you to survive."
Eve ran harder.
She'd not had a chance to think about that loss. She had been forced to leave her duffel, blanket . . . and that spear she had made from the branch.
They **were** treasures. She had planned

on using that spear and maybe distracting Doane enough to get hold of his gun.

Or give him a karate chop that would kill the son of a bitch.

She had never thought she would plan to deliberately kill a human being. It had to be self-defense. It was always a last resort.

But this was beginning to feel like a last resort. The hours of being hunted and the sound of his voice telling her that he was going to kill her had taken their toll.

She would not let him kill her.

She would not be captured and forced to deal with that hideous skull that had sometimes seemed as if it filled her world.

Keep running. She had seen a vine-covered ravine up ahead where she could perhaps become lost in the heavy foliage.

He thought she was getting weaker, that he was wearing her down.

He was wrong. Perhaps that should have been the result of his stalking, but it had the opposite effect. She was feeling stronger, her body was becoming more agile, the muscles toned, her senses sharper. The berries and plants she'd found to eat had not been sufficient, but they'd warded off weakness. The worst enemy had been the cold and the early-morning frost, but she'd been able to withstand that, too. It would be harder now that she no longer had the blanket and extra clothing, but she'd get through it.

So that she could be hunted another day?

Sudden anger tore through her at the thought.

No way.

It was time she stopped being on the defensive and turned hunter herself.

She would find another branch, make another weapon, find another opportunity.

She would not let him beat her.

Even if she had to kill him.

CHAPTER

6

Goldfork, Colorado

The sun was going down when Kendra pulled up in front of the small house in a suburb that seemed to be composed of similar houses on every street. It had taken her almost as long to drive from the Denver Airport to Goldfork as it had to fly all the way from Atlanta. The town was located in a rural area just an hour from the Wyoming border, and it seemed an ordinary town and the people she saw on the streets also very ordinary. A typical American town in the beautiful state of Colorado.

It went right along with the story Joe had told her about Doane and his five-year stay in this safe house. He had taken on the coloration of the place and his neighbors like a chameleon and lulled everyone into thinking he was a good guy and good neighbor and not the psychopath he had hidden so well.

A young, uniformed police officer stood in front of Doane's house, leaning against his gold-and-white patrol car. He waved her toward a patch of gravel that had obviously been used as a parking lot for other vehicles in the previous few days. Kendra stopped her rental car and climbed out. She took a deep breath, taking in the aroma of dozens of plants in the subalpine woods surrounding the subdivision.

"May I help you?" The officer stepped toward her.

"I'm Kendra Michaels. I was told you'd be expecting me."

"Yes, ma'am. Can I see your badge or official ID?"

She showed him her California driver's license. "I'm afraid this is as official as it gets."

He checked her name against a list in a pocket notebook. "Thank you. They told me you'd be coming." His smile revealed a front tooth that was a shade browner than the others. "I'm Officer Tim Rollins, Gold-fork PD. I was told to extend every courtesy to you."

"Police? Isn't this an FBI investigation?"

"It is. We're just providing assistance and support to secure the scene."

"Have there been a lot of people through here?"

"Yes, ma'am. Pretty near every forensics specialty, K-9 units, bomb squad, you name it."

"Did they find anything?"

"I don't think so. I heard more than one agent say it was a waste of time to come here."

"Just what I need to hear after eight hours of traveling."

"Maybe you'll do better." He handed her a pair of evidence gloves and two disposable polypropylene surgical shoe covers. "Please put these on to avoid contaminating the scene."

"Sure." Kendra smiled as she pulled the booties over her shoes. "Boy or girl?"

"Ma'am?"

"Your baby. Boy or girl?"

He hesitated before replying. "Boy. Five months."

"Congratulations. How successful have you been keeping him on an organic diet?"

"That's my wife's thing, not mine." He wrinkled his brow. "Do you mind if I ask you how—"

"There's a bright orange spot on your belt buckle of a shade and texture of Gerber's baby food organic carrots. No artificial coloring or flavoring, or added starch or salt, which gives it a different appearance and odor than other foods. And your child spit up on your left shoulder when you were holding him this morning."

He pulled on the shoulder of his uniform shirt. "Aw, man. I thought I got it all off."

"You did. I can't see it."

"Then how did you—"

"I can smell it. Don't worry, I don't think most other people can. He spit up his formula, but it's a brand I'm not familiar with."

"Parent's Choice."

"Thanks. I'll remember that." That inability to place it had been bugging her since she had gotten close enough to the officer to detect the scent. It had been the only reason she had bothered to initiate the baby questions. She usually avoided the necessity for explanations if she could do it.

The officer half smiled. "Why would you remember something like that?"

"Because that's what I do."

She pulled on the gloves and walked over the stone pavers to the front door. The house was nestled in a thick clump of trees, almost as if the space had been hollowed out for the two-story structure. Kendra opened the front door and stepped inside.

Her first impression was that the house was very dark, despite the fact that every lamp and light fixture was turned on. The dense foliage outside blocked most of the sunlight, and the dark brown walls kept light reflections to a minimum. The dark Brazilian wood floors leached much of the remaining illumination.

She had read much of Doane's case file at the Atlanta Airport and knew that he lived alone. Indeed, there were none of the subtle clues that indicated there was more than one sensibility at work in the décor and arrangement of personal items.

The half-open drawers and slightly askew furniture were easy tip-offs of other recent searches of the house; but otherwise, things seemed to be in order.

Perhaps in too much order, she thought. As she glanced through the drawers, there was no mail, personal papers, or anything that left behind any real imprint of the man who had lived there. Did he really live this way, or had he deliberately swept away his footsteps behind him?

She climbed the narrow wooden stairs to the upper level, which contained only two bedrooms, a bathroom, and a loft area that overlooked the main floor. Doane had obviously used the loft as an office, with a desk, keyboard, printer, copier, and a stand for what probably held a laptop computer. Either Doane had taken it away himself, or the Feds' computer forensics teams were combing the hard drives in a lab.

Kendra walked into the master bedroom, which was furnished only by a bed, a chest of drawers, and a television cabinet. Kendra tugged on the front door of the TV cabinet and peered inside.

No TV. Something else.

She swung the door open wide and just stared for a long moment. Instead of a television set, the cabinet held a veritable shrine. Centered in the middle was a large portrait of a young, handsome man with the coldest eyes Kendra had ever seen. It had to be Kevin, Doane's son. The picture had obviously been taken during Kevin's military career. Surrounding it were news clippings, military badges, and award certificates, some dating all the way back to high school.

Kendra found herself recoiling at the sight of Kevin's flashing smile and those blue eyes that should have been attractive but were instead glittering with a kind of icy arrogance. It wasn't just because she'd been told what he had done, she realized. There was something intrinsically evil about that face, that expression.

Shake it off.

She had come face-to-face with bad people before, people capable of the most horrifying atrocities. Why should this simple photograph inspire anything other than revulsion?

Yet it did. And she was fiercely relieved that Kevin was no longer alive to inflict pain and suffering on so many children and their families.

But as long as his father was out there

with Eve as his captive, Kevin's horrible legacy would continue.

Detach. Scan. Analyze.

Her eyes flicked from one item to the next, trying to pick up anything that could help complete the father/son picture forming in her mind. Kevin had been left-handed, like his father. They had vacationed at least three times in Salt Lake City, twice in some ghost town, and Kevin never owned anything other than an American-made car. Doane dabbled as a carpenter, farmer, and auto mechanic, and his son was an amateur musician, a guitarist, probably self-taught and not very good, judging from the placement of his hands. Both were avid hunters and fishermen and comfortable with firearms. The son favored handguns, the dad liked rifles.

She studied the display a moment longer. There had to be something more here. Maybe in one of the photos, the newspaper stories or—

The cabinet itself. It was something Doane had probably made himself, she realized. It was similar in style and construction to pieces shown in photos of Kevin's home, including a coffee table Doane gave him on his birthday. Both featured a signature flourish of Doane's, a lathe-cut spiral design on the corners.

This cabinet appeared relatively new, Kendra thought. Where had he made it? She hadn't seen a workshop. Had he rented a place somewhere?

She closed the cabinet door, happy finally to be hiding Kevin's face from view. She stepped into the closet and immediately realized that a small suitcase had been taken, judging from the footprint left on the dusty floor. She scanned the hanging clothes, taking special notice of the few empty hangers. Doane had probably taken enough clothing to last him for at least a week.

She left the room and descended the stairs, this time stopping to look out the tall windows that lined the back of the house.

There, in the distance, was what appeared to be a small toolshed.

Which might be the answer as to where Doane carried out his woodworking projects. She reached the bottom of the stairs and quickly exited the back door. She crossed the large unfenced backyard and approached the toolshed, which was actually larger than it had appeared from the house. It was almost the size of a one-car garage though there was no easy automobile access on the uneven ground.

Kendra stopped. The toolshed's latch had been recently broken, and the door was ajar. The FBI's handiwork? Possibly, but not likely. The FBI was much more efficient. It would have been a simple matter to cut the lock, which was how they usually handled a padlocked door.

She pulled open the door. It groaned on its weather-beaten hinges.

She felt inside for a switch, flipped up, and . . .

Nothing. No power, or the bulbs were shot.

Fine. She was comfortable in the darkness. Sometimes she still preferred it. And she had her phone's illuminated screen to help her.

She turned on her phone, which gave her a view of only a few feet ahead of her. Her footsteps echoed enough to let her know that the structure was largely empty, with perhaps a few scattered pieces.

Up ahead. A shadow on the right. Table saw. Next to it, a short stack of lumber.

She squinted and made out a series of saw blades hanging on a peg board.

Something moved in the corner.

She stopped short.

A rodent? No, bigger.

Breathing. Low, rhythmic.

Not an animal.

Human.

Kendra switched off her phone and quickly moved several paces to the right.

More movement. Footsteps.

Heading toward her.

Kendra called out. "Who's there?"

The footsteps drew closer.

Kendra stooped and picked up a large, wooden dowel. "Stop, or I'll blow you away."

The footsteps stopped. But the quiet, shallow breathing was even clearer now.

Kendra's hand tightened on the dowel. "What are you doing here? Who in the hell are you?"

A woman's soft voice. "Kendra?"

Kendra went still. That voice . . . She'd heard it before.

"Kendra Michaels?"

Kendra lowered the dowel. She hesitated for a moment, then abruptly switched on her phone and thrust it forward.

The first thing she saw was that luminous smile.

"Oh, for God's sake, Margaret Douglas?"

Margaret nodded.

Kendra was trying to get her breath as she shook her head in disbelief as she pulled her phone back. "How on Earth . . . Why?"

"The same reason you're here. I promised Jane that I'd try to take her place while she was vegetating in that hospital." Margaret giggled. "Did you really think you were going to blow me away with that dowel?"

"I thought a bluff might send an intruder running."

"It could have worked, I guess." Her smile widened. "I wish you could see your face. I got the impression you didn't surprise easily. I guess I was wrong about that."

"No, actually you're right. Which should give you some idea about how shocked I am to see you."

"Which, I suppose, makes you more suspicious of me than ever." Margaret moved back toward the rear corner of the toolshed.

"Aim that phone this way, okay? There's a light switch back here."

Kendra held up the phone and lit the way for Margaret to reach a long workbench, where she flipped a switch and turned on a fluorescent hanging fixture.

Margaret spun around to face her. "Much better, don't you agree? I had this light on until I heard you coming. I thought you might be a policeman or an FBI agent."

"I'm still not sure how you knew where Doane's car was in that lake, but I've seen no evidence to indicate you've been lying about who you are and where you come from." She added dryly, "At least, in the short term. However, no one seems to know much about you before you showed up on Summer Island, where you ran into Jane. So the jury is still out. But Joe Quinn is no fool, and he appears to have a tentative trust in you."

"Good." Margaret nodded. "Tentative trust is better than no trust."

"You have Quinn's trust, Jane's trust, and you don't have even a smidgen of that commodity from me."

"That's okay, we'll work through it."

"I beg your pardon?"

"Well, we both have the same objective. I don't care if you trust me or not. I've been through all that before. I respect your fine logical intellect that tells you I'm full of bullshit. I can't expect the same respect from you until I earn it." She grinned. "And even then, you'll probably go crazy trying to figure out a way to keep yourself from feeling it."

"And so I should. This animal-communication business is completely ridiculous and probably bogus." She paused. "Why did you turn up here? Did your animal friends point the way again as they did to find Doane's car?"

"Don't be silly. Do you really think an animal could give me a street address?"

"You tell me."

"I could get a mental picture, but all creatures see things differently, and there are always memories, but they're tinted by a creature's experiences. It took me a long time to learn to be able to sort through either one. And an animal wouldn't pay any attention to a number on a house, so the address thing is out of the question."

Margaret was so straightforward and

down-to-earth that Kendra found herself half believing her. Sincerity, gentleness, and that innate radiance were hard to withstand. She shook her head to clear it.

Good heavens, what a con.

Or was it a con? Was Margaret just a little wacky?

Margaret's gaze was narrowed on her face. "Now you're in stage two. Not sure I'm a crook, but maybe a nutcase?"

"What's stage three?"

"Uncertainty, then toleration." She beamed at her. "Because you like me. And because together we'll make a good balance."

"We won't make anything together." She tilted her head as she had a sudden thought. "Wait, you're not Quinn's idea of a bodyguard, are you?"

"Bodyguard? Me?" Margaret laughed. "I've never been mistaken for that before."

"Quinn didn't send you?"

"Why would he?"

"He had some weird idea I shouldn't be alone."

"Well, he certainly didn't choose me to keep you company. Nobody knows I'm here. Except you."

"And why are you here?"

"I told you, I want to help Jane find Eve. I was with her on the island when all this began, and I could see how worried she was about Eve. It's a way I can pay her back for taking that bullet for me. There was nothing I could do for her in Georgia, so I decided to come here."

"Just like that."

Margaret nodded.

"It was an expensive trip to take on such short notice."

She was silent a moment. "Well, I really didn't think Jane would mind."

"Mind what?"

"You're not going to like this."

"Mind what?"

"I kind of borrowed her ID and a credit card from her bedside table when I visited her in the hospital. I knew she wouldn't need them in there."

"You stole from her?"

"I borrowed it. I'll give it back the next time I see her. I just didn't have time to finesse a way to get out here. If I'd asked Jane, then she'd have had a reason to not let me go." She added simply, "And I had to go for her. She was going to worry all the time she was in the hospital if nothing was getting done."

"How did you get on the plane? You don't look anything like Jane."

"Her ID wasn't that good, and my hair looks darker when it's pulled back. And I chatted to the security agent all the while she was looking at it. I'm good at distracting people."

"I imagine that's true. Did you steal money, too?"

"Of course not. I have a little money. I always manage to find a way to get money wherever I am. I just needed a way out here."

Kendra knew that she should have been appalled, but she couldn't help but be strangely charmed by Margaret. She moved through life with a dancer's agility and grace, with a fluidity that suggested a total ease in her skin and the world around her.

Not only charmed but also feeling a crazy protectiveness toward Margaret Douglas, Kendra realized. "And were you planning to rob a bank or two for funds?"

"No, of course not, I'm essentially very honest. It's just that sometimes you have to balance one thing against another.

Besides, there are all kinds of ways to earn money. I always manage. I'm very talented."

"I can hardly wait for you to tell me how you intend to find a way to do that in a strange town and—"

"I don't need money now. I'll worry about that later."

Kendra shook her head. Forget about worrying how the girl was going to survive. It wasn't her concern. "When did you leave Atlanta?"

"I was on the first flight out this morning. I've been here for a couple hours. I figured the police officer wouldn't let me in the house, so I've been spending time in the yard and in here."

"And has your time been productive?"

"I think so." She looked around the tool-shed. "There may be something here. I know that Doane lived here alone, and he was an angry and intense man. He hid it very well when he was with the neighbors, but the anger was always there. He was calmer after he worked out here on his furniture pieces. He never had guests except for the kid next door. But there was usually someone watching him and his house from the small road on the hill."

"Someone must have told you that." As soon as the words came out of Kendra's mouth, she realized it was exactly the same thing that people had always said to her when they didn't understand how she'd made a deduction.

But this was different, dammit.

Margaret smiled. "You might say some**thing.** I was able to pick it up from the birds in those trees out there on the hill. Birds are extremely sensitive to emotional states. And they're territorial. They can spend years in the same area. They recognize patterns of behavior."

Kendra nodded. Margaret's explanation was made in the same matter-of-fact, clear manner that Kendra herself used when explaining. It didn't make her believe in Margaret any more than she had before, but Kendra was surprised that she found herself wanting to believe her. "I . . . see." She asked mockingly, "And do these birds have any idea where we can find Doane now?"

"I'm afraid not." She chuckled. "There's a reason for the word 'birdbrain.' They were able to convey the idea of the person watching Doane, probably the agent Venable had assigned to him. But the rest I picked up from Carlie."

"Carlie?"

"Carlie's a German shepherd. She belongs to Ron, a teenager who lives next door. She's a very gentle, very friendly, dog. The kid came over frequently, and Doane helped fix his car. Lots of times, Carlie came with them and stayed with the boy." She shrugged. "Doane was friendly enough to the dog while the boy was with him. But when Carlie wandered into the yard by herself, Doane was different; he yelled and chased her away."

"So Doane was acting a part even with the dog?"

"People who love their animals would remember someone who was cold to them. Doane didn't want anyone suspicious until he was ready to make his move. He was smart in every aspect of his little masquerade. Onstage, he was perfection, model neighbor, model citizen, all-around good guy."

"But Carlie gave him a bad review."

"Only when no one else was around. Carlie was confused. He made her uneasy." She frowned. "That's why she watched him from the backyard next door. Doane spent a lot of time out here in the shed."

"Did he ever have a visitor?" What was she doing? Kendra thought with exasperation. She was playing Margaret's game and treating her as if she was being perfectly logical. "Never mind. Forget I asked."

"I know it's hard," Margaret said sympathetically. "It's a whole new way of looking at the creatures around you. And, you know, if you do start to believe me, you'll never look at them the same way again. That's even more scary for some people."

"I don't think I'm going to have to worry about that."

"Maybe. You can never tell. To answer your question, no one came to the shed, but there were times Doane left the shed and disappeared into the woods for hours at a time." She added thoughtfully, "I figure maybe Doane was picked up by someone out there who had a car waiting."

"Blick?"

"He was his accomplice and able to move freely. It would make sense. Or maybe Blick provided Doane with another car that he parked in the woods for him to use."

"So Doane might have come out to the

shed because it was easier for him to slip into the woods." She shrugged. "It's all guesswork, and I'm not about to take the word of your German shepherd."

"Why not? She's more honorable than most people. No axe to grind." She held up her hand. "You asked, I answered. Now we'll scoot away from things that might disturb you. You'll be more comfortable trying to put things together in a way that's more acceptable to you." She gestured sweepingly around her. "Go for it."

"I don't have to have your permission, Margaret," Kendra said dryly as she turned and glanced around the toolshed. Most of the structure was still cloaked in shadows, save for the slivers of illumination reflected by dozens of stainless-steel circular saw blades mounted on the wall. The area was centered by woodworking tools, including a table-saw router, lathe, and a few devices Kendra wasn't familiar with. She studied the contours of the machinery, but none seemed to fit the impressions she had seen in Doane's car.

"Doane's been working in here in the last week or so." Kendra pointed to the floor and waved her hands over large footprints in the sawdust.

"But I think other people must have searched this place in the past few days," Margaret said.

"They have. You can see their footprints, too. But these match the style and size of a pair of boots I just saw in Doane's closet. And this sawdust is freshly cut cherry-wood. It has a very strong scent. Can you smell it?"

Margaret nodded. "The whole shed smells like it."

"That means it can't have been cut much more than a week ago."

Kendra moved to a rack of hardware over a smaller lathe and fingered the intricate metal plates.

Margaret picked one up. "What are these?"

"They're used as patterns for the lathe, for cutting ornamental wood pieces. The one you're holding would make a clover."

Margaret's eyes squinted at it. "It doesn't look anything like a clover."

"No, but the pins act as a guide for pre-cisely moving the wood across the cutter to create the pattern." Kendra waved her hand across the other plates. "Each of these creates a different design. Before I could see, I used to love running my hands across intricate carvings, feeling the wonderful details and textures. I still think it's the best way to appreciate quality woodwork. You can admire some of its beauty by looking at it, but only by feeling it do you really appreciate how each cut contributes to the effect." She looked down at the lathe, which had a guide plate attached. "This has to be his most recent work."

Margaret leaned over it. "What's this pattern?"

Kendra studied it for a moment, then crouched to get a closer look. "Hard to say. Some geometric pattern. It looks like it could be a—" She stopped, frozen.

It was a pattern she had seen before.

Not the cabinet in Doane's bedroom. Something else . . .

Of course.

Kendra whirled and quickly moved toward the door.

"Where are you going?" Margaret asked, startled.

Kendra didn't answer.

"May I go with you?"

She didn't want company. The girl would probably get in her way.

But she didn't want to leave her out here alone either. That damn protectiveness again.

"Okay, come." She threw open the door. "Move. **Now.**"

CHAPTER

7

Gwinnett Hospital

"Did you pull up those **National Geo** articles on southern Utah?" Jane asked Caleb, as he came back into the hospital room. "I haven't found anything in Wyoming."

"Not yet. I've been busy persuading your doctor that you'd have a relapse if he didn't okay your making this room into your home office." He sat down and opened his computer again. "I'll get to it right away. Have you tried Colorado? That's where Doane lived in that safe house."

"I've scanned most of the areas around Goldfork, and I didn't find anything familiar." She looked down at the detailed sketches she'd made of what she remembered about her dream of Eve. "Though nothing is familiar, dammit. It could be any path, any scene in the mountains. I thought I'd try another state and hope I got lucky." She frowned. "That tree beside the path looks a little unusual. What kind is it?"

"I don't know." He took a picture with his cell phone. "I'll check on it."

"Hurry, will you? It might be important. It could—" She broke off. "And it might be nothing. I'm sorry, Caleb. You've been very good . . . and tolerant. I know you don't have to do this for me."

"You must be getting discouraged." Caleb smiled. "Or you wouldn't be this polite. I do have to do it, you know. Not only do I have an interest in helping Eve, but it's making you think of me as an ally instead of an enemy."

"I never thought of you as an enemy. I just never—"

"You don't have to put it into words. I know. I don't blame you." He looked down at the computer screen. "You see more than I'd like you to see. It's making it very hard for me. I should walk away from you. I could hurt you, and I'm beginning to think that would hurt me, too." He glanced up and smiled. "But I'm much too wicked to be that unselfish. I just thought I'd give you warning."

She tore her eyes away from him. "Utah. Give me the photos from Utah."

"Ten minutes." He looked back at the computer screen. "I've located the site and—"

"Why the hell didn't you tell me, Jane?" Mark Trevor asked.

Her gaze flew to the doorway. Trevor was frowning and definitely not pleased. "Hello, Trevor. Why should I? I had enough people interfering in what I needed to do."

"So I had to go to the lake cottage and find out that you were back in the hospital from Venable?" He moved toward the bed. "You should have stayed at that hospital in San Juan until you were better." He glanced at Caleb. "Hello, Caleb. And you should have gotten her to a hospital sooner so that she didn't end up like this."

"I won't even argue with you." Caleb got to his feet. "We both know that I was lucky to just be there for her when she needed me." He paused. "Which you weren't."

"I'm here now. I understand you stayed

here with her last night. Not necessary for you to repeat that tonight. I'll take care of her."

Sparks. Thunder. Antagonism.

Jane wasn't having any of it. "No one has to stay with me at night. And I didn't ask you to come, Trevor. It was your choice, and I'm not having you get in my way." She glanced at Caleb. "And you promised me those Utah photos."

Trevor opened his lips to speak, then shrugged. "Whatever. Getting in your way is the last thing I want to do. Providing I knew what the hell you're talking about." He looked at the open sketchbook on the bed. "What is this?"

"Dream stuff," Caleb said. "Jane had a dream about Eve last night, and she said it was eerily familiar to the dreams she had about Cira." His lips twisted. "It seems that you were with her during that period. I don't have to tell you anything more. You probably know more than I do."

"Yes, I do. Sting a little?"

"Yes. But I'm working through it."

He glanced back at the sketch. "It's very detailed. You're trying to find recognizable landmarks and sites as you did when you were exploring what happened to Cira. Any luck?"

"Not yet. It's somewhere in the Rockies. That's all I know." She made a face. "That's what I think I know. I don't really know anything. Half the time I was never certain that those dreams of Cira had any foundation in reality. And, if they did, who the hell can be sure those Cira dreams weren't one of a kind. I thought they were until I had that dream of Eve. Maybe it's wishful thinking."

"Hey, I can't tell you that it wasn't." Trevor took her hand. "But I can tell you that something special happened to you during the time you were investigating Cira. No one is more pragmatic than I am, and you blew me away." He was looking into her eyes. "Not that you hadn't done that before. But Cira was real, for you and for me." He smiled. "And there's nothing wrong with wishful thinking. I've been doing a lot of it lately."

She couldn't take her gaze from his face. It wasn't that he was stunningly handsome—she had grown used to that through the years. But there was something . . . different. He had been her lover during the most vulnerable time of her life, and she had thought that she knew his every expression. But there was an intentness that held no passion but something else, something deeper . . .

"Oh, yes," he said softly. "There's nothing more real to me than that time we had together. Except what I'm feeling right now." He lifted her hand to his lips and kissed the palm. "Do you feel it, Jane?"

She didn't know what she was feeling. She was suddenly short of breath and felt as if she were on the edge of a cliff looking down, no not down, gazing out at the horizon. She thought she had felt every emotion with Trevor, but she had never felt like this. It was strange . . . and frightening. She pulled her hand away. "It didn't work out for us. I didn't tell you to come back into my life, Trevor." She looked down at her computer. "And the only thing that's real for me right now is trying to make some sense of something that probably has no basis in reason at all."

He didn't speak for a moment. "Okay, I'll let it go." He glanced again at the sketch. "Tell me what you want me to do. I could go to the nearest library and check out anything they might have there that resembles this terrain. Or I could hit the computer and—"

"We don't need you, Trevor," Caleb said.

Jane inhaled sharply as she glanced at him. Darkness. Fire. Power.

"You may not need me, but Jane does," Trevor said silkily. "Ask her."

"Back off, Caleb," Jane said. "I need all the help I can get, and Trevor's helped me before."

"With Cira . . . and her Anthony," Caleb said. "That's right, you have a previous experience on two levels. It's hard to compete. But not impossible." He met Trevor's eyes. "By all means, stay and let's see how everything develops. It could be interesting."

"I'm glad I have your permission," Trevor said sarcastically. "Library or computer, Jane?"

Lightness. Darkness. Staring at the two men Jane remembered how she had thought that Caleb and Trevor were two opposite entities. That conflict was even more evident as she gazed at them now. They were both controlled and mature, but that didn't mean they weren't emitting disturbing vibes. She had no desire to have them in the same room if she could help it.

"Library. You might stumble over an old book that's not made it into an online database. I ran across a couple when I was tracing Cira."

"That's right, you did." He took a few pictures of the sketches and headed for the door. "I'll be back as soon as I find something to report. You're so hung up on reality, and I can't promise that I'll discover any evidence that Eve dream had any reality at all." He glanced back over his shoulder. "But **I'm** real, Jane. What I **feel** is real. You can count on it."

The door swung shut behind him.

"I feel vaguely like a Peeping Tom," Caleb drawled. "Except I'm sure Peeping Toms don't have this degree of irritation, only prurient lust." He tilted his head. "Though there is that present, too."

"You could have left the room."

"No, I couldn't. I wanted to have a deterring effect on Trevor. I couldn't have done that long-distance." He shrugged. "But it didn't have much effect anyway. When he wants something, he doesn't care who's in the way. He doesn't give a damn. I wouldn't either. In that we're alike."

"It must be the only way," she said dryly. "I was thinking that you're complete opposites."

"And you're right. He's tough, but there's a streak of something in him that I'll never have."

"What?"

"I don't know. Chivalry? Good Lord, what an outmoded idea. Softness? Whatever you'd expect from a Golden Boy."

"He's not soft, Caleb."

"Then you choose the word. I'm tired of talking about him. I'm glad you sent him away."

"He sent himself away."

"Because he's giving you space. I wouldn't do that, not if a man like me was this close to you." He smiled. "But then, I'm not a Golden Boy." He tilted his head. "However, I may give up my place with you tonight just to prove I can be civilized . . . sometimes." His smile faded. "But I found out one thing I didn't know before. He's more dangerous than I imagined. You felt it, too, didn't you?"

Standing on the edge of a cliff and not

knowing whether she was going to fall or be swept toward the horizon.

"You said you didn't want to talk about him. Have you finished Utah?"

"And you certainly don't, which is dangerous in itself." Caleb looked down at the computer screen. "I'll have the results on Utah in a moment. I'm checking out the forests in the ski areas . . ."

Rio Grande Forest
Colorado

Doane had **not** killed Eve.

Zander gazed down at the tracks for a moment, reading the story they told. The smaller, narrow prints, walking, then running, as the prey became aware the hunter was close. The larger boot prints, with a wider stride, not hurrying, confident that he'd overtake and destroy. He might not even be trying too hard, Zander thought. He could be toying with Eve before he caught and crushed her.

Or Eve might be more than he'd thought she'd be, lost in this wilderness. She could be wearing him down a bit.

Whichever it was, Eve was free and someone with whom Zander might have to contend. She could get in his way.

Or he could use her to get what he wanted.

Why not? A form of poetic justice?

Doane had been hoping to use Eve to bait his trap. That was why he'd called Zander and had her talk to him. Since he was obsessive about his own son, he could not imagine a father having no feeling for his offspring. Now Doane had lost his bait and was trying desperately to retrieve it.

Zander looked down once again at Eve's narrow footprints. If she had ever been trying to hide those prints, she had stopped. Maybe she had realized that Doane was too good a tracker and didn't want to waste her time. Or maybe she was fighting exhaustion and had given up that particular fight. Zander leaned toward the former, from what he knew of Eve, she would not give up even if she was completely exhausted. Though she should be exhausted. He had run across the history of her time on the run in the last few hours. It was clear she had no experience in the forest and was relying only on her senses and wits. Both of which must be phenomenal for her to avoid Doane this long. He just hoped she didn't make a slip on this particular stretch of the hunt.

It would spoil all of Zander's new plans if he had to do without bait for the trap.

Hold out, Eve. Keep him at bay. He lost you three times in the last five miles. He's a very good hunter. But not nearly as good as I am. I won't lose you.

He got to his feet and, ignoring Doane's prints, started following Eve's tracks.

Rio Grande Forest
Colorado

Cold.

Keep moving.

Darkness had fallen two hours ago, and temperatures were already plunging, but it would get even colder later, Eve knew.

She hadn't caught sight of Doane in the past two hours, and he might have gone back to that warm, cozy house for a while. That was his usual routine. Hunt, wear her down, then go back and rest.

The thought of that warmth and comfort made her even more angry.

Don't lose her cool.

Cool? Every thought seemed to be temperature-oriented, she thought dryly.

Keep moving.

Keep the blood stirring.

She'd make her way to the path that she knew Doane had to take to get to the forest from the factory. It was the best place to ambush him, and her decision was made. She had to get rid of Doane while she was still strong enough to do it. She had no weapons, but she had found another branch and that would do. She could spring out of the underbrush, stun him, then rely on the karate moves Joe had taught her to do the rest.

Could she bring herself to kill?

Don't think about it. Do what instinct told her to do.

Keep moving. She had to get close enough to that path to have to travel only a short distance before she made herself a shelter for the night.

Her feet felt heavy, leaden. She'd have to rub them when she stopped to make sure the circulation kept the frostbite away.

Run.

Twigs and branches were crackling beneath her feet, and she heard the call of an owl in the distance. She had become accustomed to the wild sounds, and they no longer intimidated her. It was the unknown that caused her heart to pound and the blood to chill.

Chill. Another temperature word. She'd better get to a place where she could stop and—

Someone was watching her.

Her pace faltered.

And so did her heartbeat.

Imagination?

Maybe.

Or maybe she'd been wrong about Doane's temporarily abandoning the hunt. Maybe he'd only tried to deceive her as he had before. He delighted in tormenting her.

Or perhaps it wasn't someone, but something. An animal in the brush or—

Whatever it was, human or animal, it was **there.** She could feel it.

She looked over her shoulder. She could see nothing in the darkness. Don't look for shape. Look for movement.

Nothing behind her.

Because it was ahead of her.

Darkness hurtling toward her!

Tackling, taking her down, taking her breath.

Taking her life . . .

Gwinnett Hospital

Jane screamed.

"What the hell?" Trevor ran into the room from the corridor. His hand brushed the switch, flooding the room with light. "Are you okay? What—" He sat down on the bed and gathered her in his arms. "Are you hurt?"

"Yes." She drew a shaky breath. Her heart was beating so hard she was in pain. "I'm hurting for her. He **hurt** her."

"A dream? Eve?"

"It didn't seem like a dream." She buried her face in his chest. "So real. She was so tired. So cold. And then he was there, and she thought he'd fooled her into thinking that he'd gone back to the house. He took her down and she didn't know if he was going to kill her and—"

"Shh." His hand was rubbing her back. "Think. Did he kill her, Jane?"

"I don't know," she whispered. She couldn't stop shaking. "If he didn't, then I think she was unconscious. It was all dark."

"Then you have to think positive."

"Don't give me that bullshit." She pushed him away. "I can't think, I have to know. And I don't know." She sat up in bed. "All I know is that it was too real to be a dream, Trevor, not an ordinary dream. It was **Eve**."

"Okay, it was Eve." He sat down on the bed. "One like you had when you were dreaming about Cira?"

"No. Yes. It was that real, but it was worse. It was terrible because it was Eve."

"And you think she might have died."

"That's what she thought might be happening." She closed her eyes. "No, I think I would have known if she were dead. I would have felt the emptiness." Her eyes opened. "And I've got to keep on thinking that. Because I've got to keep on trying to find her. Get me my sketchbook."

"Good God, your hands are still shaking." He handed her the sketchbook. "How do you think you're going to hold a pencil?"

"It will stop. I'll make it stop. I've got to get everything down while it's still fresh."

She met his eyes. "Before I only half believed that I had reached out to Eve before. You know me. I can't believe what I can't touch. But this dream was the same, the same place, the same thoughts. She was even thinking about the path that led to the house." She frowned. "No, she called it the factory this time."

"A factory in the middle of the wilderness?"

"Yes, I know it's crazy. But it was the same thing in her mind, that's how she was thinking about it. In the first dream, everything was jumbled because I was a little in shock because I wasn't expecting to—" She shook her head. "But I think that this dream was in sequence to the first one. Do you remember the Cira dreams were like that, unfolding like a story." She rubbed her temple. "Only the Cira story took place two thousand years before I was born. This story may be happening now. Am I going crazy, Trevor? Do I just want it to happen so badly that I'm grabbing?"

"If you are, I'll grab with you." He smiled. "And I'll hold on tight. I'd say you more than half believed in what you were doing. You were certain enough to get us all started on this wilderness-terrain hunt."

"Which hasn't yielded any results yet. I have to go farther than Eve's surroundings. I was afraid to attach any significance to anything else connected to her, but I have to go all the way." She drew a deep breath. "I think she definitely must have managed to escape from Doane. But he's after her, and she can't find anyone to help her. But the fact that she's free has to be good." She moistened her lips. "If he didn't catch her or kill her tonight."

"If he did catch her, it's no worse than we've expected all along." He took her hand. "And we've already ruled out the other. You said you would have known."

Dear God, she hoped she would have known. "That's right. I've ruled it out." She started drawing. "Be quiet, Trevor. I've got to remember everything she was thinking. She didn't even know who or what was after her. I'm trying to remember if she had any other impressions other than force and darkness when he took her down."

"Force and darkness," Trevor repeated speculatively as he got up from the bed. "It sounds like a demonic experience."

"That describes Doane." She steadied her hand as it flew over the pad. Don't give in to weakness. Eve had not given in to the cold or terrible aloneness.

"That scream was piercing. There's going to be a nurse in here any minute yelling at you for not trying to sleep."

"Then you'll take care of her. After all, you're irresistible. Ask anyone."

"Are you being sarcastic?"

"No, it's one of the assets you use whenever necessary. It's part of your character. When I first met you, I thought that was all there was to you, but you still made me dizzy."

"You were only seventeen, and I was fighting like hell not to prey on a teenager. It was hard to walk away from you."

"But you came back."

"You were older and I—"

"Never mind. I don't want to talk about our time together. It's over." She had found herself drawn toward those memories because they were also part of the search for Cira's story. No, be honest. Trevor had only to be near her, in the same room, and memories flooded back to her. "Just keep the nurse away from me. I want to call Kendra Michaels."

"Venable filled me in about her. She sounds intriguing."

"She's pretty sharp. Joe called me and told me she's at Goldfork. I need to talk to—"

"What are you doing awake, Ms. Mac-Guire?" A nurse in a red plaid jacket that displayed a J. RUDIN badge was standing in the doorway, frowning. "Do you need a sedative? Are you in pain?"

"No, I'm not in pain. I feel—"

"But she does have a problem." Trevor moved toward the nurse. "I'm glad you came by." He smiled. "I need you to answer a few questions for me, Nurse Rudin. Jane doesn't like drugs, but emotional and psychological problems can be hell, can't they? Will you step into the hall so that we can discuss it?"

"Who are you? She shouldn't—" Then she smiled back at him. They always smiled back at Trevor, Jane thought. "I'll be glad to help," the nurse said. "Let's get to the bottom of this."

"I knew I could count on you." He swept her from the room.

Irresistible, Jane thought. Never patronizing, just making you believe you were the most important person in his world. It was hard to fight that kind of magnetic star power. She had never been able to do it.

Until she realized that she was coming too close to surrendering herself totally to him. It had frightened her and sent her running away from him. She had never admitted even to herself that fear existed. Until now. Until she had faced the fear of losing Eve. As long as she didn't give herself, entrust herself, to anyone completely, she was safe.

But she'd had no choice with Eve. She'd made that commitment as a child, and the fear was growing with every passing minute. Her options were still open with Trevor, and she could send him away and save herself from that vulnerability.

Enough of soul-searching, the only searching she should be doing was for Eve.

Who was alive and well, she told herself fiercely. She would not believe anything else.

Kendra. She quickly dialed her cell number. She was half hoping it would go to voice mail. She didn't want the awkwardness of explaining why she wanted to—

"Jane?" Kendra had picked up the phone in two rings. "Are you all right? Where are you?"

"Still in the hospital. I'm fine, better all the time. I can't wait to get out of here. I've had enough of hospitals."

"I suppose you want a report. Sorry to disappoint you, but I don't have anything definite yet." Her tone was suddenly urgent. "And, look, I'm involved in something right now. I'll get back to you as soon as I can."

"It does disappoint me. And I'll only be a minute." She stopped, then went for it. "I'm going to send a few sketches I've drawn to your phone. I've been trying to locate the exact location. It appears to be in the mountains, somewhere in the wilderness. That's all I'm guessing."

"What the hell?"

"Just study them and see if you can identify them from anything you've seen."

"And why am I doing this?"

"Because I think that's where Eve might be. I believe she may have escaped Doane and she's—" Jane stopped. She could almost feel Kendra's skepticism, and who could blame her. "I don't know why you're doing this. Just do it, okay."

"Jane, do you still have a fever?"

"No, dammit, listen. And there's a house, only Eve thinks of it as a factory. I thought a factory in the middle of that wild country was peculiar enough to give you something to go on."

"Is that all?"

"Except that I don't think Eve has much time. Something happened to her." End the call. She had said all she had to say.

And hope that Kendra didn't think she'd completely lost her mind. "Don't shrug off what I've said. Please. Just keep it in mind and let it percolate. I'm hanging up now. You said you were busy. Good-bye, Kendra."

"Wait. I am busy, but you're not going to leave me like this. How? Where did it come from?"

Jane had been afraid that Kendra wouldn't let her escape without that question. She knew that in the same situation she would have jumped on her with both feet. "Nothing that you'll accept. Hell, nothing that I really accept. I just have to cling to it because I don't have anything else." She paused and then forced herself to say the words. "A dream, Kendra. Just a dream." She hung up.

She half expected a call back, but none came. Kendra probably was humoring her. Or calling Joe and telling him that Jane had lost it. Well, Joe knew the story, and she'd let him tell it. Maybe that would persuade Kendra to put aside logic and reason and at least accept tolerantly the information Jane had given her.

Yeah, sure. Not likely.

But she'd put a few seeds in Kendra's fine mind that might bear fruit.

And she'd make sure she threw a few other items at her to stumble over.

She took her phone and took photos of the sketches in her pad. Then she sent them to Kendra's phone.

She heard the familiar whistling sound. "Deal with it," she murmured. "I wish I was out of here and doing it instead."

"But you're not," Trevor said as he came back in the room. "And that kind nurse was tempted to come in here herself and stay with you until you went to sleep. After she gave you a shot."

"But you took care of it." She started to draw again. "She didn't have a chance."

"Sure she did. We all have a chance. We just make choices." He sat down in the chair. "Did Kendra choose to believe you?"

"Probably not. But I hung up before she could argue with me. I can only hope that I'm right about her and that she finds it impossible to discount any information even if it doesn't make sense to her. I believe she stores everything away and brings it out when she needs it."

"Efficient. I approve. Most of us store away only what is most important to us." He leaned back in the chair, watching her sketch. "You've stored away everything about Eve since the moment she came into your life when you were a kid. Have you stored away anything about me?"

Passion. Heat. Laughter. Golden hours with a golden man.

"Some things."

"But not the things I wanted you to store away and save." He smiled. "That's still to come. Sex is all very well. Sex is fantastic. It's also very powerful, and I'm having a few apprehensions about Seth Caleb. You're feeling a little too erotic where he's concerned. He taps that in you."

She didn't answer.

"But I'll handle that, Jane. I've just got to show you how much more there is to what we have together." He picked up his computer. "Now back to business. That library visit was no good at all yesterday. I'm going to send photos of your sketches to a few forestry friends I have in the park service and see if it will ring a bell."

"Forestry friends? Is there anyone you don't know, Trevor?"

"I've lived a full life. People are part of a full life. I like most of them. Those I don't like I find a way to ignore or get rid of." He looked up and smiled. "And then there are those I love and store away in a very special place." He didn't wait for her to answer but gazed down at his computer. "There's a brilliant guy, Joseph Hansen, who spends more of his time in the forest than he does in bed with his wife. Not popular with her, but very popular with the university where he teaches. Let's see if he's seen anything like these areas you've drawn . . ."

Rio Grande Forest
Colorado

Fire. Burning orange, blue.

The crackle of wood in the forest still-ness.

Forest . . .

Eve stiffened, her gaze flying from the center of the burning campfire to encircle the small clearing.

Tackled.

Pain. No breath. Death.

No, not death, darkness. She'd been knocked unconscious.

By Doane. Where was Doane?

She struggled to a sitting position.

Difficult. Her hands were tied.

Doane, again, dammit.

Where was . . .

"Hello, Eve."

He was behind her. No, she could see Doane coming toward the fire from the corner of her eye.

She went rigid and lost her breath.

Not Doane!

Powerful muscular frame and athletic stride. Dressed all in black, from jeans to wool jacket. White hair, closely barbered, dark eyes in a face that was lean and chiseled. Age . . . sixties? It was hard to determine. The way he moved spoke of a much younger man.

"You came around sooner than I expected." He crossed to the other side of the fire and dropped down on the ground. "I only wanted you out long enough to tie your wrists and make a fire, but it appears I just made it."

"Who are you?"

"Not whom you expected? But you knew I was there in the trees watching you, didn't you?"

"Yes."

"But I didn't make any sound. I've been at this a long time, and I don't make mistakes like that."

"You didn't make one this time either. I just knew you were there."

· "Instinct. It's a wonderful thing. It's probably what's kept you alive and free with

Doane after you. I saw by your tracks that you made some mistakes, but instinct can erase a lot of errors."

"Who are you? And how do you know about Doane?"

He smiled. "Think. Who do you think I am?"

"I don't like guessing games." She stared at him. Cool. Confident. His expression indicated only mockery and curiosity. "And I don't like to be tied like this." She reached up and touched her neck. "Karate. You pressed on my carotid artery to make me black out. I don't like that either."

"I understood you could be a formidable opponent. I chose to put you out and avoid permanent damage."

"Are you another of Doane's accomplices?"

"Another Blick? How insulting."

Her glance left his and went to the fire. "If you're not one of Doane's men, then you should put out the fire. The smoke could bring Doane running."

He smiled. "But I don't care, Eve."

And then she knew who he was.

CHAPTER

8

Eve's eyes widened as she went rigid with shock.

"Ah, you've put it all together." He picked up a stick and reached over and stirred the fire. "You should have done it sooner. After all, your situation doesn't have that many possible options."

"You weren't one that I expected. But now I recognize the voice." She moistened her lips, her gaze on his face. "You're Lee Zander."

"Yes."

"You told Doane that you weren't going to step into his trap."

"And I'm not. I'm going to let him step into mine. I decided that it would be boring waiting for him to close in and make his play. Better to have it over quickly."

"So you came after him."

Zander smiled. "And found an intriguing situation in play. How did you get free of him?"

"You're not really interested." She looked down at the ropes around her wrists. "And you weren't worried about any harm I could do you. You just staked me out like a goat for a tiger."

He chuckled. "You do yourself an injustice. You bear no resemblance to a goat, Eve. And Doane is no tiger. He's more reptilian in nature."

No, it was Zander who resembled the tiger, Eve thought, gazing at him. A rare white tiger, lean, powerful, and deadly. Though he appeared relaxed, almost indolent, she was acutely aware that laziness could change in a heartbeat. "Whatever. You're using me to trap Doane."

"He was using you to try to draw me into a trap. I thought that it was fitting that I steal the bait and set a trap of my own. It pleased my sense of whimsy."

"You'll forgive me if I don't see any whimsy in the situation," Eve said curtly. "I only see two vicious bastards fighting over a piece of meat. Why don't you set me loose and just go after each other?" She nodded at the blaze. "You've built that fire, and that will bring Doane running. Do you really need me as bait?"

"I'm not sure." He tilted his head. "It seemed a good idea at the time. I'll have to consider the possibilities. As I've been sitting here looking at you, I've been wondering if I could have had other motivations." He lifted his shoulder in a half shrug. "Though that's a hard admission for me to make. I have a habit of making up my mind and going straight for the target. I never second-guess myself."

"Well, good for you," she said sarcastically. "It must be wonderful to think you're always perfect."

"Perfect? I don't believe anyone could use that word referring to me." He paused, thinking about it. "Except I come very close in executing my profession."

"Murder," she said harshly. "Like Doane."

"We discussed this over the phone when

Doane tried to dangle you as bait. I'm nothing like Doane or his son. I do not kill children, and both Doane and his Kevin were amateurs compared to me."

"Murder," she repeated.

He nodded. "But I'm more like the assassins of the Renaissance, and they're like stockyard butchers."

"It's taking life. When you get down to the basics, that's all that's important." She paused. "Are you going to kill me?"

"You're not the target."

"But I'll be a witness unless you let me leave before Doane gets here." Her lips twisted. "A Renaissance assassin wouldn't leave a witness, would he? It wouldn't be clever or efficient."

"You're making fun of me?" His eyes narrowed on her face. "You're not afraid of me at all, are you?"

"Why should I be afraid? You'll either kill me, or you won't. If I can get away from you or take you out, then I'll do it. But there's no reason to let a two-bit killer intimidate me."

"Most people are afraid when faced by death," he said thoughtfully. "It's interesting that you aren't. I had that same impression when I spoke to you on the phone. Why aren't you?"

"I told you." She stared him in the eye. "Let me go. I'll disappear. I won't be a witness. I don't care if Doane dies. I was thinking about doing it myself."

"Were you?" His brows rose. "Yet your profession is based on compassion. Just thinking about it?"

She didn't answer. "Let me go."

"But then you might creep up behind me and attack," his voice was faintly mocking. "There's always that possibility. You appear to have such fierce instincts."

"You're enjoying yourself, aren't you? All I want to do is go home and live my life. I don't care anything about you. You're nothing to me." She held up her bound wrists. "I just want out of these ropes so that I have a chance when Doane gets here. I **won't** let him or Kevin kill me. If you won't let me go, just untie me so that I can fight him. I may save you the trouble of killing him."

"No trouble. I don't regard disposing of him as a chore. But I'm surprised you mentioned Kevin. We both know I killed him over five years ago."

"A slip of the tongue."

"Was it?" He studied her face. "I don't . . . think so."

"Think what you like."

"I always do," he said. "Are you hungry?"

"No."

"How long has it been since you ate?"

"I don't remember."

"And what was it?"

"Berries."

"Not very substantial." He took a leather case from his jacket. "Would you like some beef jerky?"

"Is that supposed to be my last meal?"

"No; just protein to keep you going if I find it necessary to take you on the run."

"But you have me so beautifully staked out here."

"True." He got to his feet and came around the fire. "But a little food is always diplomatically correct with prisoners. I always go by the Geneva Convention." He knelt in front of her. "Should I feed it to you? Or can you handle it yourself?"

"I can do it." She took the strip of jerky in one of her bound hands and lifted it to her lips.

"Such trust. What if it's poison?" He

snapped his fingers. "That's right, you're not to be intimidated."

"You could have killed me when I was unconscious. Why poison me?" She gnawed off a piece of the jerky. "You're right; berries only sustain. Anything that gives additional strength is good." She glanced up at him. "Even you, Zander. No, you're only tolerable."

He sat back on his heels, watching her chew the jerky. "You look like you've had a rough couple days. You're dirty and bruised." He reached out and touched her hair. "And your hair looks like a haystack."

She stiffened. "Don't touch me."

"Are you fearing for your virtue?" His gaze narrowed on her face. "No, that's not it. You know, don't you? He told you."

She didn't answer.

"I was wondering if he would," Zander murmured. "I rather thought he'd save it for the big surprise. When did he break it to you?"

"After I threw Kevin's skull off the cliff."

"What?" He started to laugh. "You did that? Priceless."

"He's crazy. It's all lies." She glanced away from him. "He had to find some way to punish you in a way that would hurt you the same way that you hurt him, and he made up that bullshit."

"Very logical of you."

"It's the only reasonable explanation for all this madness he's put everyone through."

"There is another explanation."

"No, there's not."

"I disagree. A much simpler one." He smiled. "That I am your father, Eve."

She inhaled sharply. "No," she said flatly. "I have no father."

"That's an impossibility, I'm afraid. Sandra was no Virgin Mary."

"Don't talk about my mother," she said fiercely. "You have no right. It's all lies."

"So defensive." He shrugged. "I'm just being honest. I'm not really attacking her. When I first knew Sandra, she was young and beautiful and hungry for everything that life held. That's not bad, that's human." He paused. "But from what I've heard about your childhood, she didn't deserve you defending her . . . You practically raised yourself when she got hooked on drugs. You had to take care of her from the time you were a kid."

"That's none of your business. She straightened herself out after I got pregnant with Bonnie. She was wonderful with my Bonnie." She threw the strip of jerky he'd given her on the ground. "I don't know what kind of game you and Doane are playing, but I'm not part of it. My mother wasn't even sure who my father was."

"She knew, Eve."

"Why should I believe you? You come into my life and say you're my father. Where's your proof?" She shook her head, her eyes glittering fiercely. "My mother might have not been the best mother in the world, but she was **there.** Even if I did believe you, my answer is still the same. I have no father."

"Fair enough. I have no intention of arguing with you. Though I might be able to furnish you with proof that would satisfy you." He smiled. "But then there are different degrees of satisfaction. If I proved I was your father, that doesn't mean you'd be happy about it. Quite the contrary. To call me a rotten apple on the family tree would be an understatement."

"You don't care if I'm happy. I'm bait, remember?"

"Certainly, how could I forget? But I'm beginning to think there's something else going on. I may have to explore it."

"The only thing going on is that you have me tied, and I want to be free." She looked at the trees. "He should be coming anytime."

"No, you'll notice I set the fire so that the flames are burning low, and there's little smoke. We may have a long time before Doane gets a visual or a whiff of the smoke."

"And why did you do that?"

"I'm not sure. Impulse?"

"But you want to get this business with Doane over with. That's why you're here instead of waiting until Doane came after you. Isn't that what you said?"

"Yes, and I'm sure that's my primary reason. I'm a professional."

"You're a killer."

"And that's my profession. It should be done well or not at all."

"Okay, that's the primary reason," she said impatiently. "What other reason could you have?"

"Curiosity? Boredom? I no longer have to rely on my profession to furnish me with either money or purpose. I haven't for a number of years. Loss of purpose can be a dangerous thing for a man like me, it makes one careless. But I've always had an inquiring mind, and that's still a force. I've noticed that I require a stimulant to keep me interested in life." His lips twisted. "Not surprising in a man who has dealt with death most of his adult life. I need something more."

"Then go join a monastery in Tibet."

"Actually, I spent some time at one during one point in my life. It was a total waste of time for me. There was mental challenge but little else."

Her eyes widened. She hadn't expected that answer to the suggestion she'd so scornfully tossed out. "So you went back to your true profession?"

"I never left it. I was sent to the monastery to kill Tenzin Dorje, a priest who was inciting political unrest in the country."

"And did you kill him?"

"No, I learned enough from the order that I figured that I was paid in full." He shrugged. "I don't like dealing with politicians anyway. They're never trustworthy."

"You didn't do your job?" Her lips twisted. "That's not professional."

"It would have been unprofessional if I'd taken their money and walked away. I did not. My reputation was still unblemished." He paused. "Though I might as well have made the kill. I knew that priest was a dead man."

"And was he?"

"Of course; six months later they sent someone else up the mountain to the monastery. He wasn't nearly as good or as clean as I was, but he did the job."

"And you had no regrets?"

"I didn't say that. Venable says I'm too cold to have any feelings, but occasionally I feel a stirring." He smiled. "They just aren't what other people usually identify as conventional emotions. That priest knew that he would probably die for what he believed. Part of me wanted to tell him what a fool he was, another part wanted to knock him on the head and take him away and let him convert Eskimos or something. But people do what they have to do. So I went down the mountain and let him do what he had to do."

"Die."

"Yes." He looked down at the fire. "Death comes to everyone. The bad, the good, the guilty, the innocent. You have a lot of experience in that particular truth, don't you? Your Bonnie was both good and innocent, wasn't she?"

"You have no idea. She's special. And beautiful, so beautiful." Eve's gaze went to his face. If by some wild chance what he had told her was true, Zander was Bonnie's grandfather. She found herself trying to find a resemblance. He had fine, strong features, but she could not see Bonnie in him.

His glance shifted from the fire and caught her appraisal. "You're relieved that Bonnie doesn't look like me."

And Eve was annoyed that he'd read her so easily. "There's no reason why she should. You're not my father. How do you know what Bonnie looks like?"

"Bonnie is a gigantic portion of your life and history. I told you, I'm curious. There are many photos of Bonnie from the time she was kidnapped. Naturally, I'd explore that aspect of your life."

"There's nothing natural about your being curious about me."

He chuckled. "It disturbs you more than I thought that you've found your humble, long-lost father. You don't like the idea that you have to claim me. Are you afraid I might have corrupted your genes?"

"The question is moot since I'm not claiming you."

"But would it bother you?"

"Hell, no. I am what I am. What I've made of myself. I don't believe that who started you on the journey has anything to say about what you do on the road. That comes from life experiences and who is on that road with you." She paused. "And we all have souls. Some souls are more beautiful than others. My Bonnie . . ." She paused. "She has a soul that could light up the universe. Do you think that I'd ever believe that a few degenerate threads of DNA from you or anyone else could change what she became the short time she was on Earth? What she gave to all of us?"

"No." His gaze was fixed intently on her face. "I don't think you'd ever believe that, Eve. If I were a more sentimental man, I'd feel a sense of comfort that you hold me free from blame." He grimaced. "But unfortunately, sentiment seems to have been left out of my makeup. Or perhaps it was scourged out of me at some point."

"Scourged? I can't see you being scourged by anyone."

"Of course not. Just an attempt to win your sympathy."

"Bullshit."

"Exactly."

"I don't want sentiment or lies. There's only one thing I want from you." She held out her wrists to him. "Let me go."

He didn't answer for a moment. "It's possible. But I'd be giving up bait for no reimbursement. After all, as we discussed that was my prime purpose. The idea appalls me." He paused. "Let me think."

"Don't tease me, dammit." She dropped her hands before her. For an instant she'd had a surge of hope, followed by disappointment and anger. "I won't beg you, Zander."

"No, I know you won't. I suspected that you had a sense of your own worth before I met you, and now I'm sure of it. It's a quality I respect."

"Because you definitely have a sense of your own worth."

He chuckled. "See how well we're getting to know each other?" He was silent. "You want me to let you go."

"I won't ask you again."

"You didn't ask me, it was more of a demand."

"Because you don't really need me to get what you want. Doane will come when he sees the smoke. Then you'll have him."

"That could be one way to handle it," Zander said. "But there's the question of reimbursement."

"You want me to pay you some kind of ransom? How much?"

"You couldn't afford me, Eve. Of course, I could go to your lover, Quinn. He's very rich, inherited money from his parents, I understand."

"Joe is out of this. It's between you and me, Zander."

"That's my take on it, too," he said softly. "You and me, Eve."

There was a note in his voice that caused her to stiffen. "And what's that supposed to mean?"

"Reimbursement. I didn't realize until I actually arrived in this godforsaken place that I might have another reason than Doane to be on the hunt."

"You wanted to save me from him?" she asked sarcastically.

"Oh, that would violate my prime directive as they say in the Sci-Fi genre. Yet as I was tracking you through the forest and learning the way you thought and used those valuable instincts, I realized that I had a need to know you." His brows rose. "It was very sobering. I've known you existed for most of your life and been able to ignore you. And for the past five years, I've had your dossier in front of me and your photo looking up at me, and I've been able to be very cool and calculating about you."

"So?"

"I didn't realize that it must have been exerting an insidious effect on me until I came here."

"But you're a man of no sentiment."

"So it must be intense curiosity. Why else?" He looked her in the eye. "Because, whether you believe it or not, I am your father, Eve. Since I appear to have trouble forgetting that at the moment, I need to explore who you are, what you are, so that I can dismiss you from my mind and walk away."

She could almost believe him. Zander would have no reason to lie to her when he was not trying to get anything from her, and she was clearly on the defensive. "I don't care whether you're my father or not. You can walk away right now."

"And I will." He smiled. "And so will you. All you have to do is sit there and answer my questions. Satisfy my curiosity. Then I'll cut those ropes and let you run into the forest while I wait for Doane."

She gazed at him warily. "What kind of questions?"

"Are you afraid I'll delve into your sex life with Quinn? Perish the thought. I'll skate lightly over your love life. It really doesn't interest me."

"What does interest you?"

"What you're doing running free in the forest. How you grew up. How you feel when you're working on those reconstructions. Jane MacGuire. Bonnie . . ."

"That's very personal stuff, Zander."

"But I don't believe you'll be hesitant about talking about it. You don't have many secrets do you, Eve?"

"No, but I know if I want you to—"

"Reimbursement, Eve. Not such a high price, is it?"

She looked down at her bound wrists.
"No."

He reached in his leather pouch and
gave her another strip of jerky. "Don't throw
this one away." He stretched out on the
ground and gazed at her over the flames.
"I'll wait until you finish before I start asking questions."

"I have a question for you." She took a
bite of jerky. "Why should I trust you to
keep your word and let me go?"

"You probably shouldn't. But I do keep
my word. It's the sign of a true professional."

"Just look at you." She slowly chewed
the jerky. "You're all relaxed and stretched
out there staring at me as if you were lying
on a living-room couch waiting to be en-
tertained by your favorite TV show."

"It would be a good simile if I watched
TV. I fully intend to stare at you while you
answer my questions. I'm looking forward
to it."

"Why? You've just told me what a mess
I am with all these bruises and the dirt."

"Sometimes both can be badges of
courage or interesting contrasts to what lies

beneath. After the first glance, I barely noticed them. All I could see was the defiance in your eyes and the tension in your body. You seemed to shine . . . Everything else went away." He added, "I want to see your expressions. It will be the best part of the show."

"And what if I refuse to perform?"

"That's your choice. But it would be a foolish one. It might be an easy out."

"This entire business is foolish."

"But I'm the CEO of the business at the moment. So humor me and get your chance to walk away."

"Just because you're curious about me." She stared at him for a long moment. "You **do** believe you're my father. It's not some scam." She shook her head in wonder. "Crazy. And so wrong."

"Perhaps. But I'm very seldom wrong. You don't want to hear why I believe it right now, and I understand. You reject me as a father and the fact that Sandra lied to you. But, since I do believe it, you should take advantage of the situation. Satisfy my curiosity. Then I'll be able to go my way and forget about you again. And you'll be free to take off again with the knowledge that

I'll be removing Doane from your path."
He added, "I'll even tell you where I left
the extra phone and weapon I always
stash for emergencies. A ticket to freedom,
Eve."

Her eyes widened. "Why would you do
that? I could have someone here in a matter of hours if I had a phone."

"I didn't plant them that close. I'll be able
to take out Doane and be away before you
can make your arrangements."

She stared thoughtfully at him. "Would
you have . . . difficulties if the authorities
knew you were here? Venable evidently
was working with you."

"My arrangement with Venable was unusual. There are a number of agencies
and governments who would like to talk to
me. Difficulties? You could describe it that
way." He smiled. "So, yes, I'll not be here
when the police or state patrol come roar-
ing to your rescue."

Her gaze searched his face. "I . . . think
you're telling me the truth. And that makes
you vulnerable."

"It's all manipulation. Though you're de-
nying it, I'm asking you to do something
that might make you feel a little vulnerable.

You're more likely to give me what I want if you believe we're on equal footing."

"Equal footing?" She glanced down at her tied wrists. "Not at the moment."

The smile never left his face as he gazed at her across the fire.

He was waiting.

She looked down into the flames.

He was wrong. Talking about her life would not make her vulnerable. She was far beyond anything in the past affecting what she was now. She had accepted the bad and the good and learned to work with them.

And lies or truth, the deal he had offered her was the only game in town. Or the only game in this wilderness, she amended ruefully. Take it and hope for truth. If it proved to be false, then worry about taking another step later.

She lifted her gaze to his face.

"Ask your questions."

He nodded. "I'll start off slowly and build. Though I'm tempted to go directly to Bonnie."

"Why?"

"Because every time you've spoken of her, it's been in the present tense." His brows rose. "For a man as curious as I am,

that was a red flag that was set waving."
He gestured. "But I'll restrain myself for a
while. Let's talk about where you grew up."

"Didn't your dossier on me tell you?"

"Yes, but I want to hear it from you. I
want to hear everything from you."

She shrugged. "I grew up in the slums
of Atlanta at Piedmont Housing Develop-
ment."

"Tell me about it."

"It wasn't any worse or any better than
any other slum. Children adjust and try to
find comfort and joy wherever they are.
Sometimes I could do that. Sometimes I
couldn't."

"When your mother was on dope?"

She tensed. "She was never abusive.
She had a problem. Which meant that both
of us had a problem."

"You loved her?"

"Yes, most of the time." She paused.
"I'm not talking about my mother anymore.
Ask another question."

"Tell me about your apartment. What did
it look like? Did you have friends?"

Eve relaxed a little more. She hadn't
been sure he would let her escape talking
about her mother. "It was small, on the

fourth floor, not terrible, just your usual de-
velopment flat. When I was older, I tried to
keep it clean, and I used a lot of bright lin-
ens. I hated drab colors."

"Friends?"

"Kids in the neighborhood. After I started
school, I didn't have much time for play.
Everyone told me that the only way to get
out of the slums was to either get very
smart in school or peddle dope or sex. I
wanted to get out so I chose the only way
I could tolerate. I knew about drugs, and
they scared me."

"Tell me about school."

"Why? It's just ordinary . . ." She stopped.
Give him what he wanted. School was a
subject that was boring, but it didn't reveal
any more of herself or her mother than
more intimate subjects. She relaxed a little
more. "Every wall in the school was tan,
and there was graffiti in all the bathrooms.
Most of the teachers were tired and scared
and wanted out of the projects. There were
a few teachers in the lower grades who still
liked being with the kids and tried to make
a difference. But once they had to deal
with some of the older kids who were already in gangs and on their way to be-

coming juvenile delinquents, everything changed. The teachers had to fight to survive, and if you wanted to get an education, you had to fight, too. I fought." She had a sudden memory. "But there was one teacher, Mrs. Garvy, when I was in the seventh grade who wasn't beaten down. She'd joke and try to make everything fun." She smiled. "I loved art but I was terrible at math and she'd come in early to sit down and work with me. It was . . . nice." She had another memory, they seemed to be tumbling back to her. Strange, she hadn't thought of the projects for years. But the past was always with you, waiting to be reborn. Now it was with her again, and she was scarcely aware of Zander. "And there was a Halloween party that she let us have that was fun, costumes and everything . . . Not that we could afford much. But a sheet makes a great ghost outfit . . ."

CHAPTER

9

Goldfork, Colorado

"What the hell?" Kendra murmured as she thrust her phone back in her pocket after talking to Jane. She slammed the door of the toolshed behind her and started for Doane's house. "Well, that was different."

"What was different?" Margaret said as she fell into step with her. "That was Jane, right? How is she?"

Kendra shook her head. "Damned if I know. I'd say, loopy from medication?"

"What?"

"No, maybe not. She sounded upset, not drugged. She wanted to tell me about a dream she'd had. She thought it might help find Eve. She said she was going to send me photos of a sketch she'd made, and I should be on the lookout for it." She grimaced. "Dreams. I'd never have thought Jane would be one to go around the bend like that. She must really be desperate."

"Maybe you should listen to her. Everyone dreams. So do animals. Some people think we're closer to everything around us when we relax our minds. How do you know that—"

"Margaret, I don't want to talk about dreams." She quickened her pace toward Doane's house. "I'll look at Jane's sketches because I respect her, but I—"

"What was the dream about?"

"She didn't go into it. She was vague. She was probably embarrassed. Jane impressed me as usually being very sensible."

"Then you should pay attention. It must have been important to her if she risked you thinking she was nuts."

"If you say so."

"I do. She should have called me. I'd have been more understanding." She increased her pace to keep up with Kendra. "Why are we going back to the house? What did you see in the shed that—"

"Margaret, this is no time for explanations. I'm in a hurry." Her gaze went to the house. "I'll explain as we go along. Maybe."

"I'd think you'd want to explain now so that I could be prepared to help," Margaret said quietly. "There's no reason to be impatient, Kendra."

There was every reason, Kendra thought. Between the weird phone call from Jane and now her own guilt feelings about being short with Margaret, she was feeling infinitely frustrated. "Don't lecture me. I'm trying to cope, but between your conversations with the dog next door and now Jane's dream, I'm feeling as if I'm in some bizarre nightmare myself. This is not how investigations should be conducted."

"Yes, Kendra," Margaret said solemnly.

Kendra shot her a suspicious glance. Dammit, it was clear the girl was trying not to smile. And why not, she thought suddenly. Kendra had sounded like one of the straight-and-narrow FBI agents who had driven her crazy with their insistence on their proper procedures and their blindness to what was so evident to her. She had always been considered different, too.

Different, but she couldn't embrace this degree of difference.

"It's okay, Kendra," Margaret said gently. "I understand. I've thrown you off-balance. You're probably angry at yourself, too. You're having trouble figuring me into your world as you know it." She smiled. "And you like me, which makes it harder."

Kendra did like her. But she didn't like her seeing that deeply into what she was feeling. "I don't need you to understand me. You're making me feel like that German shepherd you were chatting with. What's her name? Kelly?"

"Carlie." Margaret chuckled. "And I don't chat. I told you that it's only—" Her smile vanished. "Uh-oh." She was looking toward the house, where she had just caught sight of the young police officer. "Trouble?"

"No," Kendra said. "Don't say anything. Let me handle it."

"Whatever you say," she murmured. "But he looks very nice and . . . malleable. I could probably—"

"No," Kendra said firmly, as they stepped into the illumination of the outdoor lights.

She smiled at Officer Rollins. "Margaret Douglas." She gestured to Margaret. "She's with me. We're almost done here."

The officer nodded. "ID, ma'am?"

"Sure." Margaret reached into her pocket.

Don't let her pull out Jane's ID, Kendra prayed.

Margaret smiled as she handed the officer her passport. "That's all I have. I'm new here in the U.S. The FBI brought me over here as a consultant."

"How do you like it here?"

"Some parts are better than others. I love your Colorado." Her smile widened. "I bet you do, too."

He glanced down at her passport. "Greatest place in the world." He handed it back to her. "Welcome to Goldfork." He turned back to Kendra, his gaze going to the crowbar she had grabbed when she ran out of the shed. "Uh . . . anything I can help you with?"

"I'm not sure yet. If there is, I'll call down to you."

"You're not going to—You'll be careful not to disturb anything?"

"Forensics is through with the house, right?"

"Yes, ma'am. But a crowbar is . . . I guess you know what you're doing."

"I do know. Don't worry, I'll be careful not to do any permanent damage."

The officer nodded uncertainly and stood watching as Kendra and Margaret entered through the back door.

Margaret practically ran to keep up with Kendra's purposeful strides as they made their way across the living room. "He's wondering what you're going to do with that crowbar."

"He certainly was," Kendra said.

"So . . . what are you doing with the crowbar?"

"I suspect I'll be tearing apart a piece of this house."

"Oh, okay." Margaret looked around. "Any piece in particular?"

"Yes." Kendra led Margaret up the staircase and stopped at the landing. She pointed to four decorative wood panels that lined the wall's lower eighteen inches. "One of those."

"They're beautiful. Why?"

"Because Doane recently made at least one of those using that lathe we just saw. The Feds think he may have hidden something here, but they haven't been able to find it. It would be tough to find if he'd made a hidden panel into the wall, wouldn't it?"

Margaret crouched in front of the four panels. "They're all the same."

"You mean they look the same. The way things look is only part of the story." Kendra gently ran her fingers over the panels, then stopped when she reached the third one. She moved on to the fourth for a moment, then retreated back. "It's this one."

"Are you sure?"

"Yes. The fresh varnish gives it a different texture. The others have hardened for years, but this one is slightly tacky."

Margaret ran her fingers across the panels. "I can't feel any difference."

"Trust me, there is." Kendra pushed on the various contours of the panel's carved surface. "It seems a little medieval to think there may be a special catch that opens the secret panel, but Doane obviously had enough skill to pull it off."

Margaret pressed on the panel. "It could be a combination of things."

"You're right. But I don't want to spend all night here playing with this."

"Which explains the crowbar." Margaret smiled. "Would you mind if I took the first swing?"

Kendra studied her. Margaret seemed almost giddy with anticipation. "Uh, sure. Why?"

"Because you promised that nice police officer downstairs that you wouldn't do any lasting damage with that crowbar. I didn't promise anything."

"I could be careful and not destroy it."

"But that's not what I want." Margaret took the crowbar from Kendra's hand. "I've learned what a terrible person Jim Doane must be. He took Eve, and he's responsible for Jane's being shot. And then there are all those children . . . There has to be justice. I want him punished. I want him to suffer." She looked back at the panel. "And I know how hard he must have worked on this. It would be my pleasure to destroy it."

"Have you heard of 'It's the art, not the artist'?"

"Of course. But I don't believe it. Any art is an expression of the soul, and if the soul is ugly, I have no use for the art. No matter how beautiful it may appear."

Kendra gazed at her for a long moment. Before she had only been aware of Margaret as the soft, glowing girl who seemed to radiate sunlight and humor. That was not this woman.

Tough. Very tough.

Kendra stood and gestured toward the wood panel. "In that case, knock yourself out."

Margaret reared back with the crowbar and swung with all her might.

He'd rather die than live in this suburban nightmare, Blick thought.

He was parked down the street from Jim Doane's home, and there had been an endless parade of minivans and SUVs, each packed with kids bathed in the glow of backseat video monitors. What kind of job would he have if he were one of those SUV-driving dads? Gun salesman? Construction foreman? Cop? All decidedly less lucrative than being a hit man. Yet he might have ended up in a place like this if he hadn't met Kevin. Kevin had shown him how to live with power and independence. Kevin had taken him under his wing and given him the world to play with.

And they had killed him. Blick felt the tears sting his eyes as they always did when that sorrow and bitterness overcame him.

Forget it. He had a job to do. Though this job was not worthy of a man trained by Kevin. He felt like an overqualified errand boy at the moment. Doane could have called the kid next door to retrieve the package, for all the challenge this was going to present. There were no assault weapons, no attack dogs, no teams of federal agents swarming the place. Just one pathetic local cop passing the time on his mobile phone, probably catching up on Facebook or some moronic game.

Blick climbed out of the car and flipped the switch on the cigarette-pack-sized mobile jamming device tucked into his jacket pocket. He smiled at the cop as he approached the house. "Good evening, Officer."

The officer glanced up from his phone. "May I help you?"

"I'm Gary Deacon, ATF." He flashed a badge. "I was supposed to get here this morning, but I got held up. I'll go inside for a quick look, then—"

"Wait." The officer squinted at the badge.

"Bureau of Alcohol, Tobacco, and Firearms? You're not on my list."

"Like I said, I was supposed to be here this morning." He glanced at the cop's badge on his shirt. "Officer Rollins."

"Makes no difference." Rollins's jaw set stubbornly. "If you're not on the list, then I can't—"

"It might have come through yesterday or the day before. Is there another list someplace?"

The officer opened his book and scanned the pages. "No. You're actually the first ATF agent we've had."

Blick cursed. "Look, it's been a long day. How about I just go in, take a look around, and I'll get on my way."

"Hold on. I'll make a call." The cop opted out of his e-mail and punched a phone number. NO NETWORK CONNECTION appeared on the screen. "Weird. I've been getting four bars all day."

"Here. Use mine." Blick pulled out his phone and stared at the screen. "Damn. No signal for me either." He sighed. "Come on, buddy. I have to be on a plane to Washington in the early AM. You can even come in with me if you want. I just need to tell my boss that I looked the place over and that there's no evidence of a weapons stash."

"Weapons stash?"

"Yeah, that was in one of the earliest reports about this guy. None of the other agents have seen anything like that, but I just need to take a look for myself so that we can close our file. If you can't get your department on the phone, I'd appreciate it if you could just cut me a break. Ten minutes is all I need."

The officer was obviously torn. Rollins stared at his phone screen for another long moment before looking up. "I wish I could help. I'm sorry."

Blick nodded. "I know. Procedures." He put his phone into his inside jacket pocket. "It doesn't matter. It would only have bought you a few more minutes anyway." He pulled out his gun. Before the cop could react, Blick jammed the barrel into his chest.

He pulled the trigger twice.

Kendra looked up sharply. "Did you hear that?"

"Yeah." Margaret was on her knees, pulling out the splintered chunks of wood that had been the carved landing panel. "I heard . . . something. Kind of a . . ." She thought about it. "Pop."

"It came from out front." Kendra didn't want to tell her what she thought that sound might be. She had heard it before. She shined her phone light into the broken panel. "Quick. Is there anything in there?"

"A little to the left." Margaret was peering into the opening. "I think—yes!" She reached in and pulled a small, tattered, cardboard box secured by rubber bands. "It looks fragile. I'll hold it while you open it and see what—"

"No time. Let's get downstairs and go out the back—" She stopped as a flashlight beam suddenly jutted through the large landing window, illuminating Kendra and Margaret.

And the tattered box in their hands.

"Go!" Kendra whispered. "That was a gunshot. Silencer."

Margaret didn't ask questions.

They ran down the stairs, but before they reached the bottom, Kendra heard distinct thumps from the front porch.

Upstairs. It was the only way . . .

Kendra and Margaret half stumbled, half ran up the stairs as more gunshots echoed in the room behind them.

"Bitches!" The shooter yelled as he took cover in a downstairs hallway.

For all his firepower, the man was keeping his distance, Kendra realized. He probably thought they were cops or Feds. And armed.

If only.

"This way," she whispered to Margaret as she pulled her through a doorway at the top of the stairs.

They went perfectly still while Kendra tried to get a fix on the man's position.

Close your eyes. Concentrate.

She could hear his slow, measured breathing downstairs. Nothing nervous or intense about him; this man was comfortable firing a gun, accustomed to killing. Not someone to underestimate.

And he had probably killed Officer Rollins tonight. The young man would not be going home to his wife and baby.

Bastard.

He was staying in one place. For now.

Waiting for them to make a move.

Kendra turned to Margaret. She was holding up well. No tears, just intensity and steely resolve in her expression.

Good, Kendra thought. She was going to need it.

Kendra quietly removed the phone from her pocket and turned on the screen.

NO CARRIER.

Shit!

"No phone calls, ladies. That's against the rules. Why don't you come down, and we'll talk," the voice called from downstairs. He had obviously heard the barely audible beep from her phone.

So he must have incredibly sharp hearing. Maybe as good as hers, Kendra thought.

Good to know.

"Your phones won't work. And I've cut the home phone lines."

Margaret held up her phone toward Kendra and shook her head. The screen read NO SIGNAL.

He was jamming their phones. Clearly a pro.

"And I guarantee you'll die if you try to go out a window. You're too far up."

Margaret suddenly leaned forward and

shouted, "Come up those stairs, and I'll blow your fat head off."

Good God, Margaret sounded rough, like a world-weary street cop, Kendra thought, completely different from her usual tone. It would have been amusing if the situation had been different. The girl had moxie.

Still, it seemed to be working.

Silence down below.

But that bluff was only going to get them so far. Kendra pressed herself back against the wall. Concentrate. She replayed each room of the house in her mind. There had to be something she could use, some way out . . .

Footsteps downstairs. One, then two more. The guy was no idiot. It wasn't going to take him long to figure out that they didn't have weapons. And he certainly wouldn't want to chance hanging around until someone else arrived.

"Throw down the box," the man called out. "Throw it down, and I'll be on my way. We'll never see each other again."

Kendra looked down at the tattered box in Margaret's hand. Tempting, but no. There was a chance it was something that could help them find Eve.

"You don't even know what it is. Give it up."

"It's the disk. The list of Pakistani double agents."

"Wrong." He chuckled and took two more steps. "Why put your lives on the line? You don't even know what you have there."

Kendra couldn't argue with that.

"Who are you with? CIA? Do you think they'll care if you end up dead? All they want is that box. Give it up and live another day."

Kendra pulled off her shoes and motioned for Margaret to stay where she was. She quietly moved down the hallway toward the master bedroom.

"Good," the man said. "Explore. Trust me, there's nowhere to go."

That keen sense of hearing again.

Kendra entered the bedroom and approached the gas fireplace. She turned the key hard clockwise as far as it would go. Gas hissed from the fireplace. She grabbed a long fire starter from the mantel and moved quickly back down the hallway.

She heard another three steps downstairs.

Kendra tabulated the steps she had heard. One, three, five . . . Eight steps, which would put him about halfway to the staircase.

Need to stall, give the gas time to do its job . . .

"What's in the box?" she called.

"Why should I tell you? You'll be happier not knowing."

"I doubt that."

"Believe me. Toss it down, and you'll survive the night."

"You seem a little edgy. Calm down. We don't want to hurt you." She paused. "And we don't want to be hurt."

"That's better. You're being reasonable. Throw down the box."

"Give me a minute."

Kendra turned back toward Margaret and saw that she was pulling the rubber bands from the box and lifting the lid. Margaret peered inside, then turned it upside down over Kendra's outstretched hand. A worn, weather-beaten, moleskin notebook tumbled out.

Kendra quickly examined it. Not the data disk that she had been led to believe might be there. As she thumbed through the book, she saw that there were no lists of names, just pages and pages of erratic scribbling, like a journal.

Not like a journal, she realized; it **was** a journal. But whose?

"I'm waiting," he said.

Kendra slipped the notebook into her waistband and pulled her shirt over it. She quickly snapped the rubber bands over the cardboard box. "It's all yours."

"Smart woman. Throw it down."

Kendra glanced at the master bedroom at the end of the hall. If her timing was just a bit off, this lunatic would kill her and Margaret.

Make it count . . .

She stepped toward the staircase and hurled the box downward. It bounced off the landing wall and tumbled down the remaining stairs to the main floor.

"Good girl."

She heard him tearing into the box. Only another few seconds . . .

She reached toward a bookshelf and picked up three tiny ornamental wooden figurines.

Wait for it . . .

"Shit!" He started cursing viciously.

That was her cue. Hope you're still listening, asshole . . . She tossed one of the figurines through the open bedroom door, then tossed the other.

She crouched beside the bookshelf and pulled Margaret down beside her.

Would he fall for it?

Sure enough, he was charging up the stairs. He jumped the last few steps and sped past them down the hallway to the master bedroom.

Success!

Kendra pulled the trigger on the fire starter and adjusted the flame to its highest setting. She jammed the remaining figurine into the trigger guard to keep the flame ignited.

She stood and hurled the fire starter down the hallway behind him. She watched as it twirled end over end, almost as if in slow motion.

The shooter, now standing in the bedroom, whirled around, the gun extended before him.

And in the next moment, the flame hit the gas.

Boom!

Kendra instinctively shielded Margaret

from the explosion, using her body to block the raining splinters. She looked up.

Black smoke billowed down the hallway, pulsing with light from dozens of dancing, flickering flames.

No one was running out of the bedroom, but that didn't mean they were safe.

"Come on," Kendra said. "Out!"

Kendra and Margaret bolted for the stairs.

Blick pulled himself to his feet, still not sure if he was in one piece. His eyes stung from the smoke, which had choked off most of the breathable air.

How long had he been unconscious? Probably only a matter of seconds. Any longer, and the smoke would have killed him.

His ears were ringing, and the left side of his face throbbed. He cupped his palm over his cheek, and it felt cold and wet.

Blood.

His ears were blocked, ringing, but he thought he could make out the sound of footsteps on the stairs. It had to be them, those bitches.

But he couldn't hope to catch up. Not now.

Now he just needed to stay alive long enough to make it out himself. He pushed himself through the smoke and felt his way down the hallway until he reached the stairs.

The smoke was much lighter here.

One step, then the next. And over and over until he finally reached the ground floor. The front door was open.

Were the bitches waiting for him on the other side?

Doubtful, but possible. He had lost his gun in the blast, but he had a backup. He slowly, painfully, reached for the Beretta in his ankle holster. He held it in front of him and cautiously moved through the front doorway. No one was there.

Wait. He caught a glimpse of two women disappearing down the street. There was something familiar about the smaller woman . . .

His vision suddenly fogged, and he realized it was from blood dripping into his eyes. He used his sleeves to wipe it away.

Who had done this to him? Who had taken that journal?

The island. Jane MacGuire. The smaller woman was the one who was with

MacGuire when he had taken his shot. Her name would be easy enough to check.

But that hadn't been Jane MacGuire with her in the house tonight. Who was it?

He moved to the police car, where the officer's logbook still rested on the hood. Blick flipped through it, leaving bloody fingerprints on each page. Screw it. Get the information and get out. He could see neighbors pouring out of the houses into the street. There would be cops arriving any minute. At last he reached the final set of entries, where the most recent visitors were listed.

There, finally, the last name, the name he was looking for.

Dr. Kendra Michaels.

Kendra glanced in the rearview mirror as she sped down State Route 23 in her rental car. "Keep an eye out, Margaret."

"I've been watching." Margaret twisted back around in the passenger seat. "Though I don't know what I'm looking for. We don't have any idea what kind of car he was driving. You thinking he's following us?"

"I have no idea. I doubt it. But I don't want to be surprised."

"Do you think he might be . . ." Margaret's voice trailed off.

"Dead?"

Margaret nodded.

"Not likely. The blast wasn't that intense. I wouldn't mind if it took his arm or leg off, though."

It had been less than ten minutes since they had bolted from Doane's safe house, and Kendra's heart was still pounding hard. They had seen that poor officer's corpse on the front sidewalk, and narrow footprints on the ground of the lawn beside it indicating that his killer had coldly stepped over him on the way into the house. Then Margaret had grabbed her suitcase from behind the bushes bordering Doane's neighbor's house and they had jumped into Kendra's car.

Two fire engines, flashers on and sirens wailing, roared past them from an opposing traffic lane.

Margaret settled back in her seat. "He deserves whatever he gets for killing that officer. I didn't like his voice. It kind of scared me. I've never met anyone who sounded that . . . cold. Have you?"

"A few."

"I guess I should have expected it from the man who shot Jane."

Kendra's gaze flew to Margaret's face. "What?"

"It was Terence Blick. We only caught a fleeting glimpse as he ran toward the bedroom, but I recognized that red hair and freckles."

"Recognized from what?"

"Jane and Joe had a file on him from the security video on Summer Island. They shared it with me while I was at the lake cottage." She made a face. "Grudgingly. Joe's a little less protective than Jane but not much."

"You might have mentioned it to me."

"We were busy trying to get away from him. But now I've mentioned it." She smiled slyly. "But I would have thought you would have figured it out anyway. You're so logical and stuff. After all, Blick was Doane's accomplice. Who else would have shown up at that house?"

"Ask your friend, Carlie, the German shepherd," Kendra said sourly.

Margaret chuckled. "Next time." Her smile faded. "You know, I think he was going to kill us no matter what we did."

"It's a distinct possibility." Kendra pulled the worn-moleskin notebook from her belt-line and handed it to Margaret. "And we know he was willing to kill to get his hands on this."

Margaret thumbed through the pages. "Is that what those agents have been looking for?"

"I don't think so. All I've been hearing about is a disk." Kendra pulled off the road and parked in the illumination of a streetlight. "At first glance, it looks like a college kid's journal, packed with random scribbling, painfully obvious insights, and pretentious poetry."

"That's probably what you would think of my journals."

"It's also what I think of the ones I wrote when I was a teenager. None of us are immune."

"Yes, but I don't think anyone would ever try to kill anybody for ours. Maybe if we tried to force them to read them." Margaret studied a page for a moment. "Kevin. This belonged to Kevin. He was Doane's son, wasn't he?"

"Yes."

"Okay, it's not a disk. Do you think it

could have the names of those embedded agents in code?"

Kendra flipped through a few more pages. "Maybe. Not that we have any reason to trust anything Blick said, but he did say it wasn't the names at all." She nibbled thoughtfully at her lower lip. "Did you get the impression that he thought it was something more important?"

Margaret nodded. "Could be. His exact words were . . . that we didn't know what we have here." She shrugged. "I thought it was weird he'd be so open about it."

"Not so weird. Blick wasn't supposed to be the brains in the partnership with Doane." She lifted her gaze to Margaret's face. "And he didn't intend to let us live after he got his hands on this journal. He thought he'd be safe to say what he liked." Her glance fell to the journal again. "Well, I'd certainly like to find out why it's so important." She paused at one of the pages and stared in disgust at an entry. "This one's a letter to one of his victims, promising that her murder would ensure her of remaining forever pure and unspoiled."

"Sick."

"And here's one where he's boasting

and congratulating himself for besting the police." She looked up. "Okay, not the usual teen angst. But there has to be something else here."

"Should we turn it in to the FBI or maybe to Venable?"

Kendra hesitated. "Eventually."

"Why not now?"

"Because their interests and ours may not be entirely in sync."

Margaret gave her a questioning look.

"I don't like it that Venable told Quinn about some disk and not this journal."

"Perhaps he didn't know about it."

"Venable is very sharp, and he had five years to find out every detail of Kevin's past. Do you think he wouldn't have succeeded?"

"Go on."

"What I mean is . . . Our first priority is getting Eve back. I've worked with the FBI, CIA, and other agencies before, and they're standup organizations, but they often have their own agendas. Secrets and bureaucracies. It drives me nuts. It can muddy the waters."

"That's not all," Margaret said quietly. "What else?"

"I'm not saying Venable would . . ." She looked ahead. "But I've seen cases where some people in government would be willing to sacrifice—"

"Eve?" Margaret interrupted. "That's terrible."

"It is. But they would tell you that it's just collateral damage." Her lips thinned. "I'm doing this for Eve and Quinn. I don't give a damn about Venable and his spy games." She held up the journal. "I'm not going to give them this until after I've gotten what I need from it. Okay?"

"No."

"What?"

"There were a lot of I's and no we's in what you said. You need to rethink it." She paused. "And while you're doing that, what do you intend to do next?"

Kendra thought for a moment. "I think I've . . . we've done all we can here in Goldfork. I'm going to drive south."

"South? To where?"

"Mineral County. The radio presets in Doane's blue car corresponded to stations in that area, so he had probably spent some time there recently. It's only a few hours' drive. I'm going to leave right now."

"Oh." Margaret stared out the windshield for a long moment. "You're clearly not issuing an invitation, but I've decided to go with you."

Kendra laughed at her simple, direct tone. "Oh, you have?"

"Yes, I know you said you work alone, but you really could use my help."

"Just out of curiosity, how could you help me?"

"Even if you don't believe in my sensitivity toward animals, I'm also very good with people. Most people like me and want to help me. You believe that, don't you?"

Kendra nodded. "I didn't know you were so aware of it yourself."

"Of course I am, I've had to learn to employ every weapon I have for survival tactics. It can be a cruel world sometimes. Most of the time, it's pretty wonderful. But I don't take advantage. It could be useful for us, though."

Kendra studied her. It was possible that Margaret could help, but there was something about her that seemed especially fragile at this moment. Even though she had shown some very real flashes of toughness tonight.

Margaret smiled. "You think I need protecting. That's a mistake a lot of people
make. I'll be fine whether I go with you or
not, Kendra, but I won't quit. And, even if
we both were to go off on our own, you'll
probably just keep on bumping into me."

And Kendra would probably worry about
her when she was out of her sight, she realized with frustration. She might be as
tough as she claimed, but Kendra couldn't
help seeing her as vulnerable. Or maybe it
was just that when anyone saw someone
that bright and full of joyous life, they instinctively sought to find ways to make
sure that life went on. It might be Margaret's most powerful weapon. Whatever it
was, Kendra was caught. "In that case . . .
We might as well stick together for a while."

Margaret's smile brightened to brilliance. "Good decision."

Kendra started the car. "Really? I can't
tell you how relieved I am that you think so."

CHAPTER

10

Rio Grande Forest
Colorado

"Go on," Zander said. "Why did you stop?"

"Because I'm tired of talking," Eve said. "I've been answering your questions for over an hour. You can't want to know anything more. I'm not that interesting. I'm an ordinary woman with a few people I love and a career I tend to obsess over."

"On the contrary, I find you very interesting." He rested his head on his hand as he gazed at her over the fire. "Of course, it might be that I'm trying to find some fascination in you because we have a connection. There's a theory that people tend to develop passions for others because they subliminally remind them of themselves. In other words, they tend to love only themselves."

"That's bullshit, and cynical beyond belief."

He laughed. "I didn't think you'd go along with that philosophy."

"Do you?"

"Sometimes."

"And we have no connection."

"Oh, but we do. Even if you'll not admit to a paternal connection, this time together has definitely caused a bond to form. Don't you feel it?" He chuckled as he saw her expression. "I didn't say affection, I wouldn't presume. But I may know more about you now than your lover does. I'm sure you never discussed the details of your childhood or commonplace events that made up your life. Most people assume that those are too ordinary to be of interest to anyone else."

"Then why did you ask about them?"

"I've always found that if you want to learn about someone you have to take the tiniest details and put them together to form the big picture."

"And you believe you have the big picture?"

"No, but I'm on my way." He paused. "When you tell me about Bonnie."

She was silent. "I've told you about Bonnie."

"Very sketchy. If I were a man of senti-ment, I'd be considerate and either ignore or walk gingerly about your loss. But we've established the fact that I'm not a man of sentiment."

"Yes, that's carved in stone."

"You see? We do know each other," he said. "But I'll know you even better after you tell me why you speak of Bonnie in the present tense."

He had gone full circle, Eve thought. She had thought he might forget it in the multitude of information he had pulled out of her, but everything had led back to this point.

"You don't want to talk about her."

"Because I won't have you—" She shrugged. "What do you want to know?"

"I've already told you. Answer the ques-tion."

"Present tense? I can't think of her any

other way. She's always with me." She looked him in the eye. "She always will be."

"And yet I don't sense . . . sorrow."

"I've been through that and come out on the other side. She doesn't want me to be sad." She smiled faintly. "So I won't be."

"How do you know that she doesn't want you to be sad?"

Her smile faded. "You won't give up, will you?" She didn't speak for a moment. "Because she told me."

"Go on."

"You want all the details that constitute my particular form of insanity?" She lifted her shoulders. "Why not? The spirit of my daughter comes to me, and I'm grateful with every cell in my being. After Bonnie was killed, at one point I thought I was spiraling downward to death. Then she came, and I knew I could live." Her gaze shifted away from him to the fire. "There it is. Nothing mysterious. Just love. Just Bonnie. You can laugh now."

"No, I can't," Zander said. "And I do find it mysterious. Though I had a vague suspicion. And I can't call you insane because that would be insulting myself, wouldn't it?"

"Suspicion?"

"The way you spoke about your daughter, your expression. And I've studied After Life stories. I became interested when I was at that monastery in Tibet. There were some very bizarre experiences on that mountain. The stories varied, angels, demons, reincarnation. I take it your Bonnie is an angel."

"No, she's just Bonnie. And very special. I don't know anything about all that other stuff." She kept her eyes on the fire. "Do you think that demons—" She stopped. "I never thought much about demons before."

"Before what?"

She was silent. "Kevin. Sometimes I think that he's trying to break through and merge with his father. Crazy . . ."

He smiled. "You accept Bonnie but not Kevin? Good and evil. That's not crazy. The eternal battle."

"I'm afraid to accept Kevin."

"Why?"

"Because if he's a true entity, then I'm afraid he's with my Bonnie. And I can't reach her to protect her."

"Then she'll have to protect herself, won't

she? Don't you believe that good tri-
umphs?"

"Most of the time." When she didn't think
of the evil Kevin and Doane had done. "Do
you?"

"Not in my world."

"Then it's not a world I'd want to live in."
She grimaced. "Though my world probably doesn't seem all that inspiring to you
either."

"Inspiring? I'm far beyond being inspired
by anything. But your life is full of idealism
and hope. Incredible when one thinks
where you came from and all that's happened to you. Fascinating."

"I'm glad that I was able to entertain
you." She held out her wrists. "Now show
me that you're not a liar as well as a killer.
Let me go."

He gazed at her for a moment, then
slowly got to his feet and came around the
fire. "I'm many bad things, but I'm not a
liar, Eve." He knelt before her, took out his
knife and cut the ropes. "Unless I find it
necessary." He sat back on his heels. "And
you've paid your way. Now be still, I'm taking a souvenir."

"Souvenir?" She went rigid as the cold

blade of the knife pressed against her neck.

"Don't be so suspicious." He carefully cut the collar off her cotton shirt. "See, I'll trade you. And you'll get the best of the deal." He took off his black thermal vest. "I don't want you to freeze while you're on the run. It would be a waste. A lack of completion." He slipped her arms through the vest and fastened the top button. It felt warm from the heat of his body.

"You'll get cold yourself."

"Does that mean you want to give it back?"

"No, you can take care of yourself."

"Indeed, I can. Now stay still. I'm going to roll up the leg of your pants."

"Why?"

"Because I wish to do it." He was quickly rolling up the material. "Two pairs of pants. You were prepared when you took off from Doane."

"I tried to be. I knew what I was going to face out here. What are you—" He had pushed up his black denim pant leg and was unfastening a sheath and a huge bowie knife from his left leg. "Another knife? Isn't that overkill?"

"In my business, there's no such thing." He was fastening the holster to her bare leg. "Your legs are too skinny. It would be easier if you were wearing boots."

"It's not my style. I don't go around trying to choose my wardrobe to accommodate gigantic knives. I have a friend, Catherine Ling, I can see doing that."

"Catherine Ling?"

"She's a CIA agent. Very smart, very tough."

"Oh, one of Venable's team?"

"No, not really. She's more of a loner."

"Then I can see how you'd be drawn to her," he said absently as he drew the straps tighter on her calf. "You didn't tell me about her . . ."

"You didn't ask. You can't expect to know everything about my life in a few hours."

He sat back and pulled her trouser down. "Then maybe I should spend another hour or two."

"Absolutely not."

"I agree. I know enough. Do you know anything about handling a knife?"

"No."

"Just rely on surprise if you get cornered. Doane won't expect you to have a weapon."

"Why are you doing this?"

"You put up a good fight against Doane. I don't like the idea of his blundering across you on the trail and being able to kill you because you didn't have a weapon. For some reason, the thought offends me."

"Why?" He didn't answer, and she shrugged. "You're very weird. Where's the phone you stashed?"

He tilted his head and smiled. "Straight to the point."

"It's a way out. I won't let Doane beat me."

"The phone and the gun are in a building in a town down the mountain from the log house where Doane imprisoned you."

"A building?" Her eyes widened. "I thought I saw roofs down in that valley. People?"

"No, not for a hundred years or so. Probably since the mines played out in this area. Just cobwebs and rats. It's a ghost town."

Eve felt her hopes plummet. What had she expected? Nothing had been easy since she'd been brought to this place.

Make the adjustment. "Which building has the phone?"

"The saloon. No sign on the place, but it's the first building closest to the road leading up the mountain. Evidently the saloon was the town's main attraction, and it was the first and last place the miners wanted to visit."

"Where did you put the phone?"

"Behind the bar. I pushed it far back on the top shelf beneath it." His eyes narrowed on her face. "No mention of the gun. Tell me, would you use it? Would you use the knife I just gave you?"

"Would I kill Doane if I had to do it?" Her lips tightened. "I've been thinking about that while he's been hunting me. It would be difficult." She was silent. "Or maybe it wouldn't. I believe that monsters like him have to be destroyed. It wouldn't be the first time for me."

"Really? That's not in your dossier."

"Screw my dossier. During the years I was searching for Bonnie's body and her killer, I encountered a hell of a lot of monsters." She looked at him. "But it's different making a deliberate decision."

"No one knows that better than I."

"Did it get easier?"

"No, you just get harder and don't think about it."

"I wouldn't get harder. It would tear me apart." She got to her feet and headed toward the trees. "I'm out of here. I hope you kill Doane before he kills you."

"So that you won't have to do it?"

She looked back over her shoulder. "Maybe that's one reason. But I know Doane is a monster. Perhaps I should think that about you, too. I don't know why I'm not sure."

"I could furnish you with a collection of opinions to assure you that I am. One of them from Doane." He lifted his hand in a half salute. "That ghost town is quite a distance down in the valley. It will take you a long time to reach it on foot. Stay away from that road until you're sure Doane is away from the house, and you know I'm tracking him. He's probably familiar with the town. There were signs that someone might have been down there lately. I saw footsteps in the dust on the floor."

"Good-bye, Zander."

He nodded and smiled. "And you'll do exactly what you want."

"I'll do what I want."

"What can I say? It was my one and only attempt at fatherly advice. Since you won't believe I'm your father, it was bound to fall on deaf ears." He suddenly smiled recklessly. "I don't know why I made the attempt anyway. It was an impulse, and I'm not given to impulse."

"Any more than to sentiment?"

He nodded. "You have a strange effect on me, Eve. I don't believe it has anything to do with the fact that you're my daughter." He paused. "That caused you to stiffen, didn't it? You don't like me saying that. You're closing your eyes to the possibility. But someday, if we both stay alive, you're going to have to ask me a few questions, too. Because you're an honest woman and can't hide from the truth for very long."

"And would you tell me the truth?"

"If it suited me." He met her eyes. "I think . . . maybe I would. We'll have to see, won't we?" He turned away and started to smother the fire. "Get going. You're on borrowed time. Doane will be on the hunt soon."

"I'm going." But Eve lingered a moment longer, her gaze on Zander. The fire was casting a halo of light on his white hair, and he was moving with the athletic power and vitality of a young man. These hours they had spent together had been strange and bewildering and filled with emotions she had tried to smother. She couldn't believe him, and she had no desire to accept anything he said to her. But one thing she had to accept was that Zander had said he would let her go, and he had kept his word.

Zander glanced up at her. "Now don't get maudlin. I prefer you spitting cold little ice darts at me."

"Maudlin? Bullshit." She turned back to the woods. But she found she couldn't leave it like that. Not with Doane hovering and threatening both of them and so forming a united bond between them that might be unwelcome but was unquestionable.

"Take care," she muttered as she strode hurriedly into the woods.

Zander chuckled as he watched Eve disappear from view.

Those last two words had been difficult

for her. He could understand. They would have been impossible for him.

Or would they?

He thought about it. He was surprised he was even considering the question. Yet had he not done almost the same thing when warning her to stay away from the ghost town until he could distract Doane?

Good God, it had seemed entirely natural to offer her the protection of his experience if not his actual physical aid.

Forget it. He had taken what he wanted from her during those hours. He had satisfied his curiosity.

But had she also taken something from him during those hours?

Get to work.

When he had decided not to use Eve as bait, he had known that the game would be harder and more hazardous. He had put a plan in place, and now it must be executed. Doane was an expert in tracking, and he would know soon that there was someone else out here with whom to contend. He might know even now.

Zander could feel a tiny jolt of excitement at the thought. For years he had not felt more than the cool, logical, mathematical appreciation for a puzzle about to be solved. Was it because Eve was involved in this puzzle that it was different?

Take her out of the equation as he'd intended. Why go to the trouble of releasing her and sending her on her way if Doane was going to recapture her? It would be a failure for Zander if that happened. He detested failure.

He strode back to the trail where he'd taken Eve down and knocked her unconscious. He erased all signs of that encounter. Then he backtracked her trail, carefully obscuring her footprints by smoothing the ground and artfully dragging vegetation over them. Finally, he found two clear footprints of Eve's. These would do nicely.

Zander reached into his pack and pulled out the small container of instamold modeling compound. He broke the seal and immediately spread it into the footprints, knowing it would harden almost instantly once in contact with the air. It wasn't ideal; a silicone-based material would be a much better match for Eve's shoe prints when leaving a false trail, but that would have taken far too long to harden.

After a couple minutes, he pulled out

his casts. They would do. He could leave an occasional print in the frost-hardened mud. Just enough to keep Doane on the trail. It would not be foolproof but good enough to withstand scrutiny in the darkness.

Then he took the collar of Eve's shirt and ripped it into tiny shreds. Large enough pieces for Doane to occasionally catch sight of the material on a bush or tree.

He was back at the fire and erased all signs of himself but kept Eve's impressions clear. He put out the fire and faded into the forest.

It wouldn't take long to erase the direction of Eve's footprints as she'd left the campfire. Then he'd double back and start a new trail for her in the opposite direction that would go deep in the valley and totally away from the log cabin and the road leading to the ghost town.

It would have been easier for him to just go the same route as Eve and try to set a trap along the trail. He had carefully refused to ask himself why he hadn't done it instead of leading Doane completely away from Eve. Perhaps it was a question of the excitement that was gripping him at the thought of confronting Doane at last. It didn't matter what the reason. The decision was made.

He started moving, masking his own footprints, laying the Eve trail. He ticked all the boxes that a skilled tracker would be looking for: the occasional stone disturbed and turned muddy side up, vegetation broken and twisted in direction of movement, dew droplets brushed from leaves. He pulled scraps of Eve's clothing over the thorny branches, careful to leave only a few threads at a time. Mustn't overdo it.

Come on, Doane. Eve was good for an amateur, but you have no idea how much better I am. You'll get such an exciting surprise when you find me waiting for you instead of Eve.

Come and get me . . .

Gwinnett Hospital

"Shouldn't you be back in bed?" Caleb's brows rose as he strolled into Jane's hospital room and saw her in a chair with the bed table lowered so that she could draw up over her lap. "I know that Trevor has full control of the nursing staff around here, but your orders are for bed rest."

"I'm resting, that's good enough." She didn't look up from the computer. "And Trevor does not have full control around here. He's just persuasive."

"Whatever." He leaned against the bed. "Where is he, by the way? I left him to watch over you last night, and the sacrifice was for nothing?"

"He went to the Georgia-Pacific head forestry office in South Georgia to look at their maps and talk to a few of their forestry experts. He's hoping to nudge a few memories." She rubbed her eyes with the back of her hands. The glare of the computer screen had been bothering her for the past hour. She knew she should take a break, but the sense of urgency wouldn't permit it. "He said he knew a supervisor there."

"Male or female?" Caleb murmured.

"It doesn't matter. Stop it, Caleb."

"I just wanted to judge the possibilities of success." His gaze was narrowed on her face. "Are your eyes hurting?"

"Just tired."

"Do you want me to make it go away?"

She looked at him. "What?"

"We all have our own talents. I can't woo the birds from the trees like Trevor, but I bet I could make any ache in your body vanish . . . or begin." He smiled. "I'm particularly interested in your response now that I've donated blood to you, and you have my blood coursing through your veins. Don't you want to experiment? There are all kinds of stories in my family history about instances of cross—"

"Stories or myths?" Jane interrupted dryly.

"If we experimented, we'd know." He reached forward and gently put his hand over her eyes. "But this doesn't require any experimentation. This is easy."

Warmth.

A healing rush of blood.

Revitalization.

Soothing rivers of sensation . . .

"Easy?" She took his hand away from her face. "I've no desire to experiment, easy or not, Caleb."

"I know. You're very stubborn. Everything has to be completely normal and reasonable." He added lightly, "That's why I had to sneak that one in. But your eyes are better now, aren't they?"

She couldn't deny it. They felt totally normal, rested, and as if she'd had a full night of sleep.

"It could have nothing to do with you. I just had a moment of rest."

"True. And now they feel completely rested and you'll be able to use them free of strain or pain." He smiled. "It should last all day if you don't abuse them too badly." He took his computer out of his bag. "Now what other area do you want me to scan? I downloaded another site last night that has upper California and—"

He stopped as her phone rang. He glanced at the ID as he picked it up from the bedside table and handed it to her. "Venable."

She pressed the speaker, and her hand tightened on the phone. "What's happening, Venable? Have you heard—"

"Nothing about Eve." He cut her short. "Have you heard from Kendra or Margaret?"

"I haven't heard from Margaret since she left here. I called Kendra myself earlier. I didn't talk to her for long. She said she was in the middle of something, and she'd call me back."

"Oh, she was in the middle of something all right," he said grimly. "And did she call you back?"

"No." Jane had actually been glad that Kendra had not done so. She hadn't wanted to make explanations about asking her to look for that damn dreamscape. "Not yet. Have you talked to her?"

"I've been trying like hell to talk to her. She's not answering her phone."

"That's not like her. She's completely professional. Maybe something's happened." Dear God, she hoped that was wrong. She should have spoken longer to her, she should have— "Why are you trying to reach her?"

"To find out what she knows about a dead police officer at Doane's house in Goldfork."

"What?"

"You heard me. There was a young officer shot and some kind of explosion at the house itself."

"What does that have to do with Kendra? Joe called and told me she was heading in that direction, but she would never be involved in a crime."

"I'm not accusing her. I'm saying that

the first agent I sent who arrived at the house checked the entry book and her name was the last one on the page. It was close to the time of the officer's death. Chances are that she knows something."

"Or that she may have been hurt or killed or taken captive by the person who killed that officer. Why don't you send someone to look for her?"

"Do you think I haven't?" he asked roughly. "We have a dead cop and a house that looks like it's been bombed. The interior damage could also reflect a search and possible recovery. And all we have on the positive side is maybe Kendra Michaels who **might** have knowledge of what went on there. You're damn right I'm looking for her." He paused. "And possibly for Margaret Douglas. Someone of her description was reported to be in the neighborhood earlier in the afternoon. She's very memorable."

Yes, everyone remembered Margaret, Jane thought. "Have you tried to phone her?"

"Yes, no answer. That's when I tried you."

"I'll call them both and let you know if I get through. Have you called Joe?"

"He's next on the list." He was silent a moment. "If you get in touch with either one, tell them to call me and for God's sake keep a low profile. Goldfork is a small town, and everyone knows everyone else. They're not going to take kindly to the killing of one of their own. The West may have its own code toward women, but it might not be pretty if they don't give the right answers." He hung up.

"It appears that our Margaret is causing a stir," Caleb said, as Jane pressed the disconnect. "Explosions and dead bodies?"

"That's not Margaret. Most of Venable's suspicions were aimed at Kendra Michaels."

"I've never met the lady. I only know what you've told me. However, I do know Margaret, and I'd judge she's capable of more than you'd think. She'd definitely rise to the occasion."

"We don't even know if Kendra and Margaret are together. Kendra never mentioned—" But Jane had not given

Kendra the opportunity to tell her much of anything. She'd been too eager to get off the phone. But Jane had known that Kendra was going to Goldfork, and Margaret had told her the same thing before she'd left the hospital that morning. It was logical to assume that they'd run into each other and combined forces.

Maybe.

Her hands clenched at her sides. How the hell did Jane know what had happened stuck in this damn hospital room? "I can't be sure, can I? I wasn't there. I should have been there, but I wasn't."

"Jane."

"If you're going to be soothing, I'll probably deck you." Her hand was shaking as she dialed the number for Kendra Michaels that Joe had given her. "There's a dead man, and Kendra and Margaret are probably in trouble. Do you know what I told Margaret before she left? I said that I was probably a bad person, but that I was glad that someone was going to do what I couldn't while I was lying here in this hospital. Well, Margaret was in that town, doing what I should have been doing." The phone was ringing. No answer.

Then the voice mail.
"It's Jane, call me."
She hung up.
She dialed Margaret.
No answer.
Three rings. No answer.
Voice mail.
"Margaret, dammit, what's happening?"
She hung up, completely frustrated.
She was feeling helpless and she couldn't
bear it.
She drew a deep breath and called Joe.

Vancouver Airport

"Thank God, you answered. Did Venable
call you?" Jane asked.
"I just hung up from him," Joe said. "He
said you were upset about Kendra and
Margaret. Hell, I'm upset, too." He could tell
from Jane's tone when he'd picked up the
phone that Venable was right. Definitely
shaky and strained. "But Kendra's smart.
She'll be okay." He paused. "It sounds as if
she might have made a breakthrough at
Goldfork. And I'll bet she'll have info we
can use when she surfaces." He hoped to

God he'd win that bet. It seemed as if they were spinning their wheels, and it was driving him crazy. "Don't worry, Jane. After I finish here with Zander, I'll fly down there and find out what's going on if they've not checked in."

"Don't worry?" Jane's voice had a brittle edge. "Oh, that's right. Heaven forbid that I have to worry about Kendra or Margaret or you. After all, I'm the important one. Only that's not true. Eve is the important one." She drew a long, shaky breath. "I'm sorry, Joe. I'm just stressed, and I shouldn't take it out on you. Don't pay any attention to me."

"I always pay attention to you. That's what love's all about."

"Yeah, but in this case I should fade into the background. It's the least I can do. No, it appears it's the **only** thing I can do. Let me know about Zander. Stay safe, Joe." She hung up.

Joe slowly pressed the disconnect. He had probably said all the wrong things to Jane. He wasn't thinking too straight at the moment. She must feel chained and terribly ineffectual, and that would be pure torture for a woman of her character. She was like Eve in that.

Eve again. Everything came back to Eve. His every comparison, his every thought. Jane was right, nothing mattered next to the task of finding Eve and bringing her back home to them.

What was happening to her now?

A surge of pure agony.

Fight it off. He couldn't function if he let it overcome him.

He turned and headed for the airport exit.

Get to Zander.

Do your job.

"Okay?" Caleb was studying Jane's expression. "I gather from hearing your side of the conversation with Quinn that it wasn't particularly satisfactory."

"It was soothing and concerned and affectionate. Satisfactory? He told me not to worry. He'd take care of it when he had time."

"Uh-oh."

"I **am** worried. Something's wrong with Kendra and Margaret. Something's happened."

"On the threat of being decked, may I offer a possible explanation?"

"No. Kendra is professional. She believes in cooperation. Margaret is the furthest away possible from professional, but she has more empathy than anyone I've ever met. She'd know what I'm feeling. She wouldn't ignore me."

"Very clear reasoning. But what if neither of them wishes to explain what happened at that house at Goldfork? The simplest way to avoid it would be to not answer the phone." He smiled. "Of course, if you're bound and determined to think that they're both at death's door, there's nothing I can do about it. But exceptional people generally do survive, Jane."

"And is Eve going to survive, too?" she asked fiercely. "She's exceptional. No one is more exceptional than Eve. To keep her alive is the reason Kendra and Margaret went to Goldfork." She closed her eyes. "I was trying to fool myself that I was doing some good here, but it's all fairy tales. And you let me do it, didn't you, Caleb?"

"Yes. Does that make me the bad guy? Okay, I'm accustomed to the role. Sometimes, I even enjoy it."

"No, I won't blame you," she said wearily. "You just went along because you wanted to keep me occupied and docile in this damn hospital."

"Docile? You?" He chuckled. "That wasn't about to happen."

"Well, it worked, didn't it?" Her eyes opened, and she blinked to stop the stinging. "I wanted to be useful, and I thought it was happening."

"Maybe it was happening. We don't know yet."

"What we do know is that Kendra and Margaret were doing my job and ran into something they couldn't handle." She moistened her lips. "And I feel guilty as hell. I've got to get out of here, Caleb."

He shook his head. "There's no way that those doctors are going to let you go. They said three days, and they meant it. Look at you. You're shaking. You don't have a fever right now, but it will come back if you overdo it."

"I don't care. I **have** to do it."

"And have Joe rush back because you're on the verge of collapse before you can even get to the airport? You'd be more of a burden than a help."

That's what Margaret had said, Jane remembered. She'd been angry at the words, but she'd had to admit their truth. The last thing she wanted to do was to get in the way of finding Eve because she was too weak to get out of the way. And she was having to admit the truth that Caleb was speaking, she thought in desperation.

"I'll be okay. I won't get in anyone's way. We'll just have to make sure they don't tell Joe," she said. "Just help me get **out** of here, Caleb. I'm not thinking too well right now, but you know how to manipulate the system. Look how you managed to get papers for Margaret. There has to be a way."

Caleb didn't speak for a moment.

"Yes, there's always a way." He added softly, "But you don't usually like the ways I choose."

"I don't care. Get me out of here in a way that's safe for Joe."

He reached over and one index finger touched her damp lash. "I don't like to see you this way. It . . . disturbs me."

"It disturbs me that I have to ask for help. I'm doing it anyway. Help me." She met his eyes. "Or I'll help myself."

"And that would disturb me even more." His finger moved to her upper lip. "You'll have problems. You'll have to trust me. That's against your nature. You're sure?"

"Get me out of here."

He nodded slowly. "Get into bed."

"What?"

"You want out of here? The only way is to have a miraculous recovery and get the doctors to agree to dismiss you. That will appease Joe, and he won't rush back. Agreed?"

"Yes," she said warily.

"So get into bed." He pulled her to her feet. "And we'll get on with it."

"On with what?"

"Your miraculous recovery." He gently pushed her down on the bed. "What else?"

"We're going to fool those doctors into thinking I'm well?"

"You have very good doctors, Jane. Quinn made sure of that before he left you here. They wouldn't be fooled. They rely on medical science and experience."

"Then what are—" Her eyes widened as he began unbuttoning her pajama top. "Caleb?"

"I told you that you wouldn't like this." His dark eyes were glittering, and his smile was reckless. "But you can stop me at any time. Maybe."

"What are you doing?"

"Your miraculous recovery. I can give it to you. It may be temporary, but you'll be well enough to get a free pass from the medical staff here."

"What do you mean, you can give it to me?"

"Blood." He carefully removed the bandage covering the wound in her shoulder. "It's magic. We're going to see if my blood in your veins will answer me if I call on it." He unbuttoned his shirt. "I believe I can do it on my own, but the effect may be doubled. Wouldn't that be interesting?"

"I don't know what the hell you're talking about." But she couldn't take her eyes from the corded muscles of his chest, the dark thatch of hair, the sheer masculine virility. "And I'm not sure I want to know." He was coming toward her, and she instinctively tensed. "And I know the so-called magic blood stuff you seem to be able to pull off with your enemies. It's fatal."

"But that's only with enemies. You've only seen my bad side." He was standing next to the bed, and he reached out and touched the wound. "This is so ugly. It will be good to see it healed."

She inhaled sharply.

Burning.

Skin tautening.

Deep explosion of tension.

"You like that?" His fingers gently rubbed around the wound. "Yes, I can see that you do."

"Are you saying that you can cause that wound to heal?"

"No, I'm not a healer. But you can do it yourself." He smiled. "With my help . . ."

"How . . . can I do it?"

"Send the blood to the wound. Blood is healing. As a matter of fact, medical facilities all over the world are experimenting with laser treatments to cause the blood to rush to injured areas of the body. They work very well." He touched the wound. "But I'm much better at it."

She gasped.

Not pain.

Heat.

Exquisite, flowing, heat.

"You see, that's how it starts," he said softly. "I touch, we touch, the flow begins. But it becomes very intimate, and that's the part I can't control. Because even without a physical joining, the mind can become obsessive and doesn't want to release. All I can do is try." He tilted his head. "But you'll get what you want, Jane. If you're not afraid to reach out and take it. Yes, or no?"

She stared at him. She didn't underestimate anything he had told her. How could she when he had always been a mystery to her? When she had asked him for help, she hadn't dreamed he would go down this dark path. Perhaps she should have, he had always been a figure of darkness and fire to her. Once she had even wanted to paint him surrounded by flames . . . She should probably tell him that she had changed her mind and that she'd work the problem out for herself.

But she wasn't going to do it. He had said that he could give her what she needed, what Eve needed.

If Jane wasn't afraid to take it. He had thrown that challenge at her, and through all the frantic desperation, it had sparked fire.

"Yes or no?" he repeated.

She held out her hand to him. "Yes."

He smiled. "I thought so." He moved her to the side of the bed. He kicked off his shoes and lay down beside her. "Remember, I gave you the choice."

"What are you doing?" The warmth of his body next to her came as a shock. "Is this—It's a hospital. What if someone comes in?"

"I'll know if they're coming. As Margaret would say, it's part of the stalking instinct. Besides, it's unlikely anyone will interfere. You've practically set up your office in here."

"So . . . what do we do? What happens?"

"Relax, it's already happening. It will take a while. But in a few hours, you'll feel almost normal." He spread his shirt aside and took her in his arms. "Almost . . ."

Her softness pressing against his hardness.

No, her breasts were not soft, the tips were hard.

She couldn't breathe.

"It's not easy for me either," he murmured. He pulled her closer, enveloping her.

Flesh to flesh.

She was dizzy. Heat was surrounding

her. Every nerve in her body was alive, crackling.

And everything, every sensation, was coming from him, pulling her toward him.

"Is this . . . are you telling me the truth, Caleb?"

"Mostly. I lied about its not being easy. I have a few masochist tendencies that permit me to enjoy it."

"But about the rest?"

"You'll be well enough to leave here by late afternoon. As I said, it's not a permanent fix. If you don't abuse yourself too much, you'll be fine for a day or two." His lips brushed her temple. "If you start getting weak, all you'll have to do is come to me, and we'll do this again. I'm at your disposal."

"That's not going to happen."

"You can never tell . . ."

"And I won't forgive you if I find out that you're lying to me."

"I wouldn't dare."

"Or twist it to suit yourself."

"I would dare to do that. But how would you know whether it would work if I didn't do exactly what I'm doing? That's why it's important that I have your trust." He rubbed against her. "For instance, this is all part of the therapy. The tingling, sexual rush, and intense sensation is all beneficial."

"Caleb."

"Just a small lie. I don't know if it is or not, but I thought we both deserved it."

"I don't want this."

"Of course you do." He laid his head on her shoulder, his cheek on the wound. She could feel both the smoothness and the faintest roughness. It was wildly erotic. "You want it as much as I do. But I have to concentrate on something less entertaining. I made you a promise." His lips moved against the flesh of her shoulder. "Do you feel your blood surge against my mouth? I'm going to lie here and hold you, and the blood is going to flow and move and heat. Close your eyes and let it come to me."

Come to him.

Her entire body was tinglingly alive and coming, surging, to him.

"Shh, not that, not yet." His tongue touched the flesh of her shoulder. "Just give your body what it needs to heal. A few more minutes, and the heat will cause everything to blur, and the need will be gone for a while."

She didn't believe him. The need was too intense, too hot, the feel of him was too good. She instinctively moved closer.

"No. Later, anything you want. Not now." His cheek rubbed back and forth against her breasts. "Feel your heart beat? It's bringing the blood to every part of your upper body. But particularly where the wound is causing all that shock and trauma." She shuddered as he licked delicately at her nipple. "Burning? Stomach muscles clenching? It's all good, Jane."

She drew a deep breath. "The hell it is."

"It will have a good result." His cheek was once more on her shoulder. "But the blur is coming. You can relax now."

The blur.

The heat.

Dizziness and swirling intensity.

Relaxed . . .

The sexual need was still there, but it was like low-burning embers.

Everything was visible only through a red heat haze.

Blood haze?

It didn't matter . . .

All she wanted to do was lie there with Caleb and let the haze surround her. But should she—

"Shh, it's okay. Let go. I'll bring you back when you've had enough . . ."

CHAPTER

11

Jane's eyes flew open, startled.

"Don't be afraid," Caleb whispered. "It's just time for you to start stirring. They're starting to serve the meds. You don't want any nurses bustling in here."

"No." Not with Caleb half-dressed and in bed with her. "How long was—"

"Long enough for you." He sat up and carefully rebandaged her wound. "And not nearly long enough for me. Button your shirt. I'd do it, but I'm afraid you've been jarred out of intimacy." He swung his feet to the floor, and his fingers began buttoning his shirt. "But it was quite an intimacy, wasn't it?"

"Intimacy? I don't know what it was," Jane said as she hurriedly buttoned her shirt. "I've never felt anything like that before. I think you must have hypnotized me or something."

"You said yes, Jane."

"I know I did. I thought—I believed you when you said—" She looked at him. "Should I have believed you, Caleb?"

"Ask yourself that question. How do you feel, Jane?"

She thought about it. "Good, I think." Her eyes widened. "No, very good. Normal."

"High energy?"

"Yes."

"Any pain in your shoulder?"

She moved her shoulder in a half shrug. "No pain at all."

"Why don't you take a look at the wound."

She slowly pulled her shirt off her shoulder and shifted the bandage. "It's still there. No miracle recovery, Caleb."

"The doctors will think it's one. We accomplished three weeks' worth of healing in the last three hours." He headed for the door. "Now go wash your face while I go round up a doctor or two to give you the once-over."

"Do you think it really worked, Caleb?"

"It worked. Once you get on your feet and start moving, you'll know that it did." He glanced back over his shoulder. "And you may feel a little strange for a while, but you'll get used to it."

"What do you mean?"

"Your blood has become . . . accustomed to responding to me. It may continue to have a residual effect on your body responses. We were together for a long time. Action and reaction."

"You didn't say there would be any long-term effects."

"I didn't, did I? I wasn't really sure, but there was always that possibility. We'll have to work through it ourselves." He smiled slyly. "I wouldn't mention that to Trevor. It might make him feel a little . . . excluded."

She stared at him in astonishment, then understood. He hadn't liked it one bit when she had told him that Trevor had reminded her of Cira's lover, Anthony. It somehow made her closer to Trevor in his eyes. This was a little payback.

She said softly, "Why, you bastard."

She heard him laugh as he walked out the door.

Southern Colorado

"It's about time you answered your phone," Venable said sourly.

"How was I supposed to know it was you until you unblocked your caller ID." Kendra glanced over at Margaret, who was asleep in the passenger seat. They had passed construction sites and several wailing sirens on their trip down to southern Colorado, but she hadn't stirred. A simple phone conversation was unlikely to wake her. "I don't pick up for just anyone."

"I'm honored," he said sarcastically. "But I believe you might have suspected I'd be calling. And I know that Jane MacGuire must have been trying to reach you. She was very upset when she heard about what was happening at Goldfork."

"Then you shouldn't have told her, dammit."

"And I'll bet you haven't answered her calls, either."

He was right. Kendra had wanted to put off talking to anyone until she absolutely had to do it. She had to sift through the events of the past hours and decide what she could reveal. She hated lies, and deceit was just that in her eyes. "How was I to know that you'd bring Jane into this? Quinn wouldn't want her to be disturbed."

"Disturbed? We have a lot of questions about what went down in Goldfork. A lot of people are upset that you decided to flee the scene, especially since you left behind a dead cop in the driveway."

"A man tried to kill us up there in Goldfork. Excuse me for not wanting to stick around."

"Who?"

"Blick."

"Are you sure?"

"Margaret is sure."

"Margaret Douglas is with you? We had reports of a woman of her description in the neighborhood but no confirmation."

"She got to Goldfork even before I did. She recognized Blick from the photo in the dossier you gave to Quinn and Jane. I take it that he hasn't been apprehended?"

"No sign of him. When did you last see him?"

"At Doane's house."

"Could he be following you?"

"Yes, but I'm fairly sure he's not."

"Okay, putting aside that bit of news . . . What in the hell was Blick doing back in Goldfork? It looks like he tried to destroy the house with that gas explosion."

This was a bit awkward. "Actually, that was sort of my handiwork."

Venable muttered a curse. "I suppose I should have known."

"Why should you have known? It was purely in self-defense." She paused. "Is there anything left of the house?"

"Yeah. Most of it is fine. Just a couple rooms upstairs were damaged. Evidence teams are there now. They really want to talk to you."

"Later." Kendra drove in silence for a moment. It would probably have been better for her if the place had burned to the ground. She had an idea what his next question was going to be. She wasn't surprised when it came.

"So what did you find in that staircase, Kendra?"

"The staircase?"

"I received pictures. A panel on the landing was destroyed. More of your handiwork?"

"Yes."

"So what did you find?"

She braced herself. She hated this. "Nothing. We were still fishing around in there when Blick showed up. I was just going to suggest that your people give it a closer look. Doane went to a lot of trouble to make that secret compartment."

A long moment of silence. "We searched and came up with zilch. Are you positive you didn't find the disk?"

"No disk."

"Or anything else?"

Damn, she hated to lie. "I'm positive."

Another pause. He didn't believe her.

Tit for Tat. She wasn't sure she believed anything he'd told her about that disk either.

She looked down at the tattered notebook on the console beside her. Not yet, Venable.

"Okay," he finally said.

"Have the forensics guys pulled anything else from Doane's car?"

"Not a lot. That was gold dust in the trunk, but it wasn't especially pure."

"Unprocessed?"

"It was processed, but not in the way that it usually is these days. They found traces of cyanide in it."

"That doesn't sound good."

"It's actually not uncommon. Cyanide is one of the chemicals used to extract impurities from the gold. But the thing is that the gold dust we found in Doane's car wasn't processed like most gold is today."

"What do you mean?"

"Most gold undergoes a type of electrolysis to further separate it from other minerals. That wasn't done in this case. It's almost as if . . ."

"What?"

"That the gold dust we found may have been processed over a hundred years ago."

Kendra let that sink in for a moment. What in the hell was going on here? "Interesting."

"Yeah. I'm not sure what it means, but I thought you'd like to know."

"I do. Thanks."

"Always willing to cooperate. Cooperation is very important, Kendra." The words couldn't have been more laden with sarcasm.

Sorry, Venable.

"So what's your next move?" Venable asked. "Or am I allowed to ask?"

She hesitated while she decided whether or not to tell him. What the hell. "We're going down to the southern part of the state, in the coverage area of the radio stations on Doane's car stereo."

"We've been looking at that part of the state ourselves. It's a pretty big coverage area."

"I know."

"And did you say 'we'?"

"Margaret is still with me."

"Good God." Venable chuckled. "It sounds like you're a team. Shades of Thelma and Louise. How did that happen?"

"Long story. And we are **not** a team. Thelma and Louise? I find nothing laudatory in being compared to two idiotic women who drove off into the Grand Canyon. I'll be in touch, Venable."

Kendra cut the connection.

"Thelma and Louise?" Margaret asked drowsily. "Grand Canyon?"

Kendra glanced over and saw Margaret's eyes were open. "I thought you were sound asleep. How much did you hear?"

"From the beginning. Only from your side, but it was enough to put most of the conversation together. I was sound asleep, but I seem to have a built-in alarm for things I need to hear. Thelma and Louise?"

"It's an old movie. I'm not sure you were even born then, but it's kind of a classic."

"I like classics but more in the Frank Capra vein. That was a happier age. Anyone who drives a car into the Grand Canyon strikes of craziness or despair. Not my cup of tea."

"I can see that. Not mine either. Which is why Venable's comparison annoyed me."

"One reason," Margaret said quietly. "The main reason is that you're still having trouble with my coming with you. You'll get used to me, Kendra." She smiled. "You might even be glad I came. I know that you like to work by yourself and be totally independent, but that can also be lonely."

"I'm used to being lonely. I was blind until I was twenty." She paused. "That sounded as if I was sorry for the way I grew up. I didn't mean it like that. I had my mother, who was completely supportive and wonderful. I had a best friend, Olivia, and a few other friends who managed to tolerate my rather abrasive personality. The loneliness was my fault. There were times when I drew into myself and lived there." She chuckled. "Because I was damn good company."

"Really?" Margaret murmured demurely. "I haven't noticed."

"Ouch." Kendra glanced at her in surprise. "That was a sharp little jab. Not what I was expecting from Miss Sunshine and Light."

"Expect it. I'm only human. I believe in being cheerful and looking for the sun. But I also believe in being honest, and you left yourself wide open." She straightened on the seat. "You can be abrasive, but I like it. It's . . . stimulating."

"I'm so glad I meet with your approval," Kendra said dryly. "And I hope I've put your worries about my loneliness to rest." She tilted her head. "What about you? Did I detect a hint of empathy? You appear to be something of a loner yourself."

She shook her head. "No, I like people. I like to be with them and interact and feel their energy flow to me. The human race is a wonderful thing. Are you asking me if I need them?"

"Well, you seem to be leaning toward the animal kingdom."

"I like animals, too. And they can be very restful in comparison to people. They have simpler motivations. Food, shelter, procreation are central. But they also have emotional responses and often a sense of humor." She smiled. "It took me a while to be able to read those responses. After I ran away from home when I was eight, I lived off the land for three years. I was almost totally without human contact. That's when I learned the most about them."

"You ran away from home?"

"I didn't have a wonderful, supportive mother like you. She died when I was born. My father . . . was not kind. I decided it was time to go away and cheat him of the welfare check he was getting for me." She smiled cheerfully. "The only other attractive option was to persuade the Doberman down the street to tear his throat out."

"I . . . see."

"No, you don't. You're a little shocked that I'd say something like that much less think it. You're getting a glimpse of my dark side, which pops out now and then."

"I'm not shocked. I'm sorry that you were abused as a child. I hate it when children or animals are being hurt. That Doberman idea didn't sound all that bad to me."

"It was just a passing thought. I wouldn't really get a helpless dog into trouble like that. I just couldn't think of a way to do it myself."

"Three years living off the land is a long time."

"I enjoyed it. I was almost sorry when I decided I wanted to learn things that I couldn't in the woods. But then I found this wonderful couple, Bill and Laura Skanner, who lived on a farm in the next county, didn't believe that the law was always right, and thought that kids shouldn't be caught in the middle. They liked me, and I liked them, and I stayed with them for two years."

"And your father?"

"I don't know." She met Kendra's eyes. "I never looked back."

The words were clear and bold and yet held a hint of poignancy, Kendra thought. Or perhaps she was reading something that wasn't there into them. Maybe that was Margaret's philosophy of life.

"And what happened to the couple that you lived with during those years?"

"Bill and Laura had a few problems, but we straightened them out, and now they're living happily ever after."

"Do you see them?"

"Sometimes. But they're better off without me. I'm not cut out for happily ever after." She took out her cell phone and glanced at it. "I got another call from Jane while I was asleep." She didn't listen to the voice mail as she gazed at Kendra. "I'm not going to ignore another call just because it's hard for me to deal with. I only did it because I was hoping that maybe no one would tell her about Goldfork since she was in the hospital and couldn't do anything about it."

"Well, evidently Venable wasn't in a protective mood when he heard about the blowup there. He wanted answers, and he went to Jane to see if she could get them for him." Kendra frowned. "And he didn't believe me when I told him we hadn't found anything. So we'll probably have him on our trail right away."

"But you told him where we were going anyway."

"That was about Eve. I didn't have a right to keep anything about the search from him. The journal . . . I don't know. That may be another story and not one Venable was entirely honest about." She glanced down at the journal. "And I think we should get this out of our hands and into a safe place as soon as we reach Mineral County. It may not only be Blick who wants to get hold of it."

"Okay." Margaret took the journal. "But I want to read it cover to cover before we get there. It's pretty rambling, but there may be something that will strike a note. Maybe not immediately but when I look back on it."

"I should do that."

"Because you have such a fantastic memory and can put everything together and come out with dazzling answers?" Margaret asked. "And I'm just a kid who you don't trust to remember how to tie the laces on her own tennis shoes?"

"Yes."

"Then pull over and let me drive. We'll

take turns at the wheel while the other one
sleeps. Not that you'll sleep right now. You
can do the first read of the journal." She
smiled. "I don't mind your being the dazzling one. Though I should tell you that I
probably have a better memory than you
do. You were trained by your blindness. I
was trained by having to remember obscure trails and animals and having to put
all of the signs together during very distracting circumstances. Often when I was
on the run. Ever been chased by a bull
moose?"

"No." Kendra pulled over to the side of
the road. "I've never had that privilege. I'm
not looking forward to it in the future." She
smiled faintly. "And you almost had me
convinced how superior you might be until
I remembered what you said about my not
thinking you could remember to tie the
laces on your tennis shoes." She came
around the car and opened the passenger
door for Margaret to get out of the car.
"You're not even wearing tennis shoes
even though it's cold as hell here in Colorado right now. You're still wearing those
stupid leather thongs."

"Oops." Margaret gazed ruefully down at her feet. "I meant to change. I just didn't seem to have the time. Things were happening."

"I'm sure they were." Explosions and bullets flying and Margaret keeping calm and steady through it all. "But you have time now. Get those tennis shoes out of your suitcase and put them on before you start driving."

"Good idea." She reached into the backseat. "Thanks for reminding me."

No resentment. Someone else might have been a little annoyed to be told what to do, Kendra thought. Yet there was no lack of self-respect or independence in Margaret's attitude. She was beginning to realize that the girl was unique in a multitude of ways and possessed an inner strength that was fairly incredible.

Then why the hell did Kendra still feel the need to protect and guide her?

"There." Margaret double-tied the second New Balance shoe and jumped out of the car. "That feels better." She grinned knowingly at Kendra. "And it will make you feel better, won't it?"

Kendra didn't answer directly. "It's much more sensible. I can't see how you could stand traipsing around in this weather with feet that were practically bare."

"I just close it out." Margaret ran around the car and slipped into the driver's seat. "And keep moving. That's the trick. You just keep moving." She looked out the windshield at the snow-covered mountains in the distance. "But it would be harder up there. I hope Eve isn't . . ." She shook her head. "Wishful thinking doesn't do any good. Jane says Eve is strong. She'll do what she has to do." She started the car. "And so will we. Right, Kendra?"

Kendra's gaze followed hers to the mountains, then she glanced down at the journal on her lap. We. The inference of togetherness was both clear and deliberate. Margaret wanted a commitment. What the hell. Why not give it to her? It could be an uneasy partnership, but she was beginning to believe that Margaret would never fail her when the chips were down. "Right, Margaret. That's the only thing we can do."

She opened the journal and began to read.

Gwinnett Hospital

"Mineral County." Jane repeated with frustration, her hand tightening on the phone. "Where in Mineral County, Venable?"

"Kendra said she'd be in touch."

"Great. She didn't answer my calls. Neither did Margaret."

"They still consider you on the disabled list. They didn't want to worry you. Kendra didn't like it one bit that I called you and told you about Goldfork." He paused. "But I think that more happened there than she told me about. If you do get in touch with her, you might ask a few questions."

"Count on it. And I'll probably ask them in person. I should be discharged sometime before noon today. It would be sooner, but it's hard to get hold of doctors early in the day. Caleb has been trying to get them here to check me, but it's been like pulling teeth."

"Wait a minute. Quinn will kill me if I caused you to break out of there."

"I'm not breaking out. I'm getting a clean bill of health from my doctors. I've just got an okay from one of them. As soon as Caleb manages to get the other two specialists here, it will be all over. They'll all talk and argue, then decide to let me out of here."

"You seem very certain."

"I'm certain. I feel great, and they're not going to find any excuse to keep me here." She paused. "But you might wait until tomorrow before you tell Joe I've left the hospital."

"He'd come after me with a hatchet," Venable said flatly. "I'll call the hospital myself and get a report. If what you say checks out, I'll wait for a few hours. Besides, I need to know what's happening at Zander's place in Vancouver."

"Joe is in Vancouver? You didn't mention that little fact, Venable."

"Kendra and Margaret didn't think I was protecting you, but there were some things you didn't have to know."

She tried to smother the surge of impatience at his words. The entire world seemed to be in a conspiracy to keep her safe and ignorant when her neck should have been on the line like the rest of their necks were. "I don't like the idea that he's trying to deal with Zander by himself. Joe is in aggressive mode. Can't you call Zander and—"

"Zander's not answering. This seems to be my day for being ignored. Though that's not at all unusual for Zander." He added, "Look, Quinn wants cooperation from Zander. He won't be too violent."

"Maybe. I'll call him once I'm on the road and talk to him."

Silence. "You're not fooling yourself that you're well because you want to get into the action?"

"Yes, I want to get into the action. No, I'm not fooling myself. Call the hospital in a few hours and check for yourself." She added, "Blick. What are you doing about him?"

"What I've been trying to do all along. Get my hands on him."

"From what you told me, he might want to get his hands on Kendra and Margaret. Which means that we should get to them as soon as possible."

"I'm on it, Jane."

"So am I. Call me if you get a lead on Blick." She hung up.

Mineral County.

She'd start doing computer checks on the mountain territory as soon as possible. Why hadn't someone told her that Kendra had mentioned those radio stations?

She knew the answer. Why tell her when she had been so damn weak and ineffectual? Well, she wasn't weak now. She had never felt stronger and more full of energy.

Blood? Caleb's blood running through her veins? No, she wouldn't accept that. He had obviously managed to do something that had an amazing effect, but she was her own person, and she would not have it any other way.

"I couldn't believe it," Mark Trevor said grimly. He was standing in the doorway, studying her. "The nurse at the station said they may be ready to discharge you sometime today. When I left you, you looked so fragile that you might break if someone blew on you. Now you're . . . electrified. What happened?"

"What did they tell you happened?"

"A miraculous recovery the doctor said. But I think that he was quoting Seth Caleb. I saw Caleb going down the hall talking to him." His gaze was narrowed on her face. "What happened?"

"I decided I had to leave here. Kendra and Margaret were almost killed at Goldfork doing a job that I should have been doing." She went over to the closet and pulled out her suitcase and threw it on the bed. "We've been spinning our wheels trying to find an area that might not even exist. I have to go another route."

"What route?"

"Mineral County in Colorado. That's where Kendra and Margaret are headed. They must think there's something there that will give them a lead." She glanced at him. "Did you find out anything from the Georgia-Pacific office?"

"No, but that seems to be unimportant to you at the moment."

"Unless you made a breakthrough. I'll take any break I can get."

"That's clear. What I want to know is how you made this particular breakthrough. It's fairly mind-blowing." He came toward her. "Talk to me, Jane."

"The body is a wonderful machine. It takes its own time healing."

"I'm happy as hell to see you better. I'm not happy you didn't call me and tell me you were on your way to leaving the hospital." He added softly, "And I'm not happy that Caleb seems to be running things and looks like a cat who just devoured a quart of cream. Did he have anything to do with all this?"

She didn't answer.

"I told you that I'd heard some weird things about him after I had him investigated when I found out he was in your life. Most of it I didn't believe, but I'm leaning more toward doing so with every passing minute."

"What? Do you think he sucked my blood and gave me a high? He's not a vampire, for God's sake."

"I don't believe in ridiculous myths. I do believe Caleb is . . . unusual. How unusual, Jane?"

He wasn't going to give up, so she might as well tell him. "Unusual enough." She began putting her belongings into the suitcase. "He can control the blood flow in the body of anyone when he's close to them. It's a sort of gift passed down through his family. Eve said she once saw him kill a murderer by doing that."

"Handy. What else, Jane?"

"Bringing the blood up to a wound and keeping it circulating is very healing. He said that medical researchers are exploring the benefits by using laser treatments to accomplish manipulating the blood flow."

"But Caleb wouldn't need a laser, would he, Jane?"

She looked him directly in the eye. "No, he didn't need a laser. He asked me if I wanted him to help me get functioning and out of this hospital. He gave me the choice. I said yes."

He drew a deep, ragged breath. "I can see how you would. He was in the right place at the right time."

"With the ability to give me what I needed."

"And did you give him what he needed? What did he do to you, Jane?"

"It's none of your business, Trevor. I've told you more than I had to tell you."

"Did you screw him?"

"What do you think?"

"I don't know. I'm just jealous as hell and probably saying all the wrong things." He was silent a moment. "If you did, I'd understand. I might kill him, but I'd understand."

"You don't have the right to—" She stopped. Trevor was on the edge of an explosion, and the last thing she needed at that moment was a confrontation between him and Caleb. She couldn't count on Caleb not to exacerbate any conflict. "No, that didn't happen."

"What did happen?"

"He just . . . touched me."

"And that's all?"

"That's all." Swirling pulsing, heat, tingling arousal of every sense in her body. She turned away and closed the suitcase. "It seemed to work."

"Yes." She looked up to see his eyes narrowed on her. "But for how long? Is it permanent?"

"Maybe. If I start getting weak, Caleb said it might be necessary to do it again."

"Oh, I bet he did." He took her suitcase from the bed and put it by the door. "We'll just have to make sure that you get enough rest so that that won't happen."

"You're going to Colorado with us?"

"I wouldn't miss it. I'm sure that Caleb won't mind another passenger." He turned to Caleb, who had just walked in the door. "Will you?"

"Not at all. Why should I?" Caleb smiled. "This isn't about us; it's about finding Eve." He glanced at Jane. "I've been to the office and arranged to have the dismissal papers and paperwork made out in advance of the final approval you'll get when those other two doctors show up. All you have to do is go in now and sign the papers. That will save some time. I thought you'd want it handled like that."

"I do. I want out of here the minute I get the final okays." She grabbed her briefcase. "While I'm waiting, I want to check out the landscape of Mineral County." She added grimly. "And try to reach Kendra or Margaret again."

"Don't try to do too much. I mean what I said." Trevor took the briefcase from her. "Let me help."

"She looks just fine," Caleb said. "Look at the roses in her cheeks. How do you feel, Jane?"

She had an idea he knew exactly how she felt. His black eyes were glittering, and that smile . . .

Darkness and flame and something else.

"Good. Lots of energy."

He gazed at her searchingly. "And nothing else?"

Your blood has become . . . accustomed to responding to me. It may

continue to have a residual effect on your body responses.

She had thought that final idea he had implanted might have been merely to make her uneasy. Was it happening? Analyze, don't accept mere suggestion.

Heat, heaviness in her breasts, a faint tingling and breathlessness. Not like the searing sensuality when he had been lying next to her, with his hands on her body. But the sensation was there, and it was coming from Caleb.

And that knowledge was making her annoyed and faintly apprehensive. It was like being tethered to him. Block it out. Break it.

She turned away and started down the hall. "Nothing I can't handle. Come on, let's go, Trevor."

Rio Grande Forest
Colorado

It was going to rain.

That's all she needed, Eve thought, as she looked up at the sky as she hurried up the path from Zander's campfire toward the trail that led to the factory. There was still intermittent moonlight, but the cold wind already felt damp against her cheeks. When the rain started, it was going to be icy, and she couldn't afford to stop and shelter. That smoke would eventually draw Doane, and she had to get past the factory and start down the mountain toward the ghost town while Zander kept him occupied.

Occupied. What a bland word for what Zander intended for Doane.

The sheath of the bowie knife felt heavy and awkward on Eve's calf, and she stopped to pull up her pant leg to adjust it. The metal glittered in the moonlight, and it reminded her of how it had shone in the reflection of the campfire as Zander had put it on her.

Strange moment. Strange night. Strange man.

She pulled her pant leg down and continued quickly through the forest toward the trail that led to the coin factory. She had left Zander fifteen minutes ago, but she still felt as if he were with her. She could feel the lingering heat of his body in the vest he had fastened on her. The movement of that sheath on her leg was an even greater reminder. It was an odd combination. Protective warmth, cold aggressiveness. But no more odd than the hours that had preceded those actions.

Why had he done it? He had told her himself that he was not a sentimental man. He had also told her that he was her father. The first she had believed, the second she had found totally impossible. Even if she had believed it to be true, she could not have imagined that Zander would let it affect his hunt for Doane.

Yet he had let her go, made sure the elements would not harm her, and given her a weapon to guard herself from Doane. She must not read too much into those actions. She had no idea what forces drove a man like him. Curiosity, he had said. Perhaps he had only been telling the truth. What would it be like to be so drained of normal feeling that your prime emotion was something as remote as curiosity?

Remote? She had to admit that she, too, had been subject to curiosity during those hours, and she had not felt remote. She had experienced suspense, soaring hope, intense interest, and other less easily defined feelings. Zander was too powerful a personality to radiate anything but equally powerful emotions. In spite of her rejection, she had found herself considering the possibility that perhaps . . .

Stop thinking about it. Move. Get to that ghost town, get her hands on the phone that would be her salvation.

The phone that was a gift from Zander.

If he'd told her the truth, if he hadn't sent her on a wild-goose chase.

No, he wouldn't have lied to her.

She was startled at the instant mental denial. Why wouldn't he lie to her? He was a hired assassin, a man who cared only for himself and lived by a philosophy that was totally alien to her. He was familiar with most facets of her life now, but he was still a total mystery to her. He cared nothing for her.

But somehow she knew that he wouldn't lie to her and the phone and gun would be where he said they would be. It was his safety net, the extra weapon and cell phone that could save him as a last resort if he, too, was caught in a Doane trap.

And he had given it to her.

Not that he was vulnerable. Not that she should care.

She would **not** care. Even though Doane was the common enemy. She probably would not have been involved with Doane if Zander had not killed Kevin and started this macabre payback. She owed Zander nothing. Let them kill each other, dammit. She didn't—

A sound in the shrubbery up ahead.

She froze.

Doane?

She was close to the trail that led to the factory. She could still smell the smoke from the campfire wafting on the night air in this direction. Doane could have detected it and left the trail to investigate.

Or it could be an animal. It had happened before.

Don't move. Listen.

She held her breath. She could hear the movement.

Large, soft-footed.

Doane was astonishingly quiet for a big man. She had become accustomed to listening for him and to him in the last days. As he got a little closer, she would know . . .

Doane!

She slipped into the shrubbery to the

left of the path, every step silent. Just far enough to be out of sight. She couldn't risk any sound of crashing in the bushes that might alert him.

No trees nearby. Just low shrubs, then the cliff that plunged hundreds of feet to the winding river below.

Crouch. Hide. Watch.

Let him pass, then go for the trail that led past the coin factory. This could turn out to be a lucky diversion for her.

It didn't feel lucky. Her heart was beating so hard, she was afraid he could hear it.

He was closer.

Then he was directly opposite her.

Then he had passed her, and she heard the rustle of shrubs as they closed behind him.

She didn't move. Wait until he was a good distance away. He was going toward the campfire. He had a purpose. It would take him at least fifteen minutes to get there. By that time, she would have reached the trail and gotten a good start toward the factory area. Just stay here and wait until he was out of earshot.

She was suddenly aware of an abrasive roughness in her palm.

She looked down and saw that she had instinctively grasped the hilt of the knife in the sheath on her leg as Doane had come close to her.

The knife that Zander had strapped to her leg to fight their common enemy.

Common enemy. Why did she keep thinking of Doane in that way? He was **her** enemy.

And it was time that she started to escape from him and get back to her life.

She rose to her feet and moved out of the bushes and started up the rough path leading to the trail.

She could still smell the smoke that was leading Doane toward the campfire . . . and Zander. Unless Zander had left the fire and was laying a trap for Doane somewhere in the surrounding woods. It wasn't likely that Doane would go into the clearing even if he thought Eve was his only prey. He preferred to stalk, not confront, until he thought he could scoop her up. He'd have trouble scooping up Zander, she thought grimly. He was a powerhouse and probably more lethal than Doane.

Good luck to you, Zander. Bring down the enemy and crush him.

The common enemy.

Why the hell did that phrase keep repeating in her mind?

Common enemy.

She stopped in the trail, her fists clenching. What she was thinking was ridiculous, and it could be fatal. She owed Zander nothing.

Nothing but a knife that could save her life. Nothing but a chance at freedom if she reached that ghost town.

But she wasn't like Joe or her friend, Catherine Ling. She had no warrior instincts. However, she'd never been good in the woods either, but she'd managed to survive and learn.

And everyone was a warrior if the stakes were high enough. But, dammit, they weren't high at all where Zander was concerned. Unless you could call this frustrating sense of duty and obligation important.

It **was** important. It didn't matter who Zander claimed to be or whether or not Eve believed him. She had always gone by her own rules and code. She couldn't walk away from them now.

Stupid, she told herself, even as she whirled away from the trail and started back toward the campfire. Lord, what was she doing?

Maybe not too abysmally stupid. Doane would not expect her to be stalking him. She was the prey in his eyes. She would just monitor the situation for a while and make sure that Doane didn't surprise Zander and get the upper hand. Then she would take off back toward the trail and leave them both behind.

Surely that was not too much to do to help defeat a common enemy. . . .

CHAPTER

12

The campfire was just ahead.

What was left of it. Even from this distance, Eve could see that it was now only glowing embers. Which meant that Zander had left the clearing and was probably somewhere in the surrounding forest waiting for Doane to appear.

Doane was a good hundred yards ahead of her, and she could tell that he was slowing, his head lifted as his gaze circled the clearing.

Then she saw the beam of his flashlight pierce the darkness, spearing downward as he neared the clearing.

Tracks. He was looking for tracks.

She stiffened. And he would find her tracks because this was the way she had left the clearing. Then he would turn and follow those tracks . . . and find her.

But he wasn't finding her tracks, she realized in bewilderment. He was moving to the left, and the beam was focusing on the ground. Why hadn't he found her tracks? He was an expert, and he knew her prints well. Many times she had watched him from hiding and knew just how good he was. He had kept her on the run.

Just as she was watching him now. But he wouldn't find her prints in the direction he was going. He would find Zander's.

Unless Zander had erased all sign of his passing. That was possible, even probable.

"You're here, Eve," Doane called softly. "I can feel you. You must have been very cold to risk making that fire. But you were careful. I didn't see or smell it until I was nearly here." His flashlight's beam danced on the earth in front of him. "Maybe you kept the fire so low because you were afraid I'd do that. Are you afraid of me, Eve? I hope you are. It's been very frustrating knowing you don't fear me. If Kevin were still alive, you'd be afraid. He could make anyone afraid if that's what he wanted." He chuckled. "And he doesn't really have to be alive, does he? I think you're still afraid of him. I could see he had you by the throat whenever you were working on that reconstruction." He was going deeper in the circle encompassing the clearing. "If I don't kill you right away, you'll have to face him again. You will finish that reconstruction. That's something for us to look forward to."

Nausea. Smothering. A reaching-out to touch. To hurt Eve, to hurt Bonnie.

To hurt Bonnie.

God, yes, she was afraid of Kevin.

But if Doane died, then Kevin could no longer use him to try to fight his way back to the living. That merging she had been afraid would happen between father and son would not occur, and the evil that existed would be destroyed.

Was that why she had returned tonight? To make sure that Doane was killed? She had been struggling with the decision whether she could actually kill deliberately. She had told herself it was her duty to not opt out and run, but it could be that the other, more chilling, decision had already been made.

"Do you know that Kevin didn't really care anything about the sexual side of what he did to those little girls. He just found dominating them fascinating. He had to prove that the magical purity within them could be crushed and destroyed by him and him alone. He believes he can still do that. He's been trying to reach out for your Bonnie, but she's very strong. He's not used to little girls being stronger than he is. He thinks that you're helping her fight him."

Bastard. Son of a bitch. Every word was a red-hot brand that filled her with rage . . . and sickening fear. And Doane knew it and was pouring acid into that wound.

Yes, she would help Bonnie. Her soul would stay safe and full of joy in that special place. No monsters would be allowed to enter there.

"I can sense your anger. You didn't like that, did you? It's good to know we can reach you through her." He was on the far side of the clearing. "I'm sure that Kevin can find ways of hurting your Bonnie that don't involve the physical. He's such a smart boy and he can—" He stopped and the beam zeroed in on something on the ground. "What have we here?" he murmured. "Fresh tracks. Your tracks. How fresh, Eve?" He shined the light on the ground leading from the campfire. "Yes, you jumped to your feet and started running toward the forest. Did you hear me coming?"

What? She was totally confused. She had certainly not entered the forest from that direction. He must be looking at Zander's tracks.

"I can imagine you close, crouching, afraid to move because I'd hear you. Let's just see where you're hiding. These prints are leading toward the edge of the cliff. The earth is hard there, and you probably thought I wouldn't be able to track you." She saw the glint of moonlight on his rifle as he moved through the trees. "I'm getting impatient, Eve. I'm feeling a few raindrops, and I do not want to stalk you in a thunderstorm. I may have to blow one of your kneecaps to keep you from doing this again. That might work very well. You'd still be able to finish the reconstruction."

He was going deeper into the forest,

heading toward the bluff. His voice was fading as he put distance between them.

She heard a low rumble of thunder and the spatter of raindrops on the leaves.

Stay here or go after him? She knew what the decision should be.

But that wasn't why she had turned at the trail and followed him back to the campfire.

Common enemy.

And their common enemy was going after Zander.

She started to glide silently through the forest.

Zander left the path and pushed through the shrubbery. Not the easiest way to travel, but it was certainly the best means to hide his trail. Let Doane believe he was the hunter and not the prey. Let him think that he was alone in these woods with poor, defenseless Eve Duncan.

Zander smiled. Eve Duncan defenseless? Hardly. Defenseless like a grizzly bear, maybe. Even without the knife he'd given her. She was clever and clearly had a survival instinct that bordered on ruthless.

Where had that streak come from? She would not have admitted that he had anything to do with it, and he was inclined to agree. Eve's upbringing and the loss of her daughter had undoubtedly toughened her. It hadn't been an easy life that created the character of Eve Duncan.

He crouched low as he moved through an especially thick patch of brush. The ground was getting so uneven that he knew he might have to return to the trail. Even if it meant he—

The ground fell away beneath him.

Before he knew what was happening, he felt himself kicking and clawing at space as a sickening crack cut through the silence.

He tumbled over twenty feet into the void, trying to latch onto something, anything, that would slow his descent. He finally struck bottom with another sharp crack, this one even more sickening than the first.

It was the sound of his wrist breaking.

Pain stabbed him at every nerve ending, and a low, guttural groan escaped him.

Dammit.

He closed his eyes and gritted his teeth until the pain subsided.

There, finally.

He opened his eyes. Where in the hell was he?

His eyes adjusted to the darkness. He was at the bottom of a mine shaft, he realized. A gold mine dug and abandoned over 150 years before, like scores of others that probably dotted these mountains. He had stepped through the brush and rotted wood planks that covered the sealed mine, an entrance hidden and undisturbed by virtue of being off the trail.

Until he stumbled upon—and into—it.

Lucky guy.

Excruciating pain still radiated from his wrist. And his left ankle. Shit.

He pulled himself up and tried putting weight on his leg.

His ankle held.

No break, maybe a minor sprain. He could power through it. His wrist, however, was another matter. His left hand would be useless until he got medical attention.

Not the best condition in which to go mano a mano with a maniac like Doane.

A rustling sound up above.

He looked up. Not now, Doane. I need a little time.

He silently drew his gun from his holster.

If Zander was lucky it was only a wild animal . . .

"Are you all right?" a voice whispered.

Eve's voice.

She moved closer, and he saw her silhouetted against the starlit sky. "What the hell are you doing here?" He spoke louder than he meant to but the thunder muffled it.

"It looks like I'm saving your ass. I saw Doane go into the forest, and I was afraid that he might be tracking you. Then I heard a crashing sound, and I came to—"

"I'll save my own ass. Get the hell out of here."

"Do you think I want to be here? You're nothing to me. It just seemed . . . right."

"Oh, for God's sake. I should have known. You're a do-gooder who thinks she can change the world."

"I'm not a do-gooder."

"Close enough. A do-gooder and an amateur. God, I hate amateurs."

"And I hate men who take lives and walk away."

"Then get out of here," Zander said. "Move!"

"How badly are you hurt?"

He didn't answer.

"I'm not going anywhere. I'll pull you up." Eve backed away from the shaft entrance. "I need to find something I can use to—"

"Who asked you to do that? I'll get out on my own. Run, dammit."

"I can't leave you."

"Then stay here and let Doane catch you and pick me off like a duck in a shooting gallery. There's no **time**. Doane is on his way. He thinks he's trailing you, and I led him through a maze of shrubs, but he should be heading this way by now."

"What?"

"You heard me, I've been leading him here. Dammit, he should be on top of us anytime now."

"I have a knife."

"Are you willing to risk it? You can't win . . . Not like this."

"Can you get up here on your own?"

"Yes." He gazed appraisingly up at the craggy sides of the mine shaft, which appeared to present plenty of hand- and footholds. It wouldn't be easy, especially with this damn useless left hand, but he'd gotten out of tougher spots before. "I told you, I don't need you."

"He's coming." Eve's voice was suddenly tense. "I see the beam of Doane's flashlight near that bluff."

"Get out of here."

"No, I'll go toward him and let Doane see me, so I can lead him away from here."

"No! Don't you—"

"Stop telling me what to do," she said fiercely. "I won't have you shot. I won't have Doane and his Kevin survive if anything happens to me. Evil. So much evil. You're the only safety net I have to make sure that they're destroyed. You won't care about Venable or cops or politicians or anyone else. You'll run right over them. You'll go after Doane and keep on going after him." She whirled back toward the path. "Now shut up and start trying to get up that mine shaft."

Then, the next second, Eve was gone.

Eve started running, cutting back into the forest to where she'd seen the beam of Doane's flashlight.

The shrubs were wet, and she was soaked in seconds.

A light shining bright in the darkness.

The light was on her, targeting her.

She braced herself, standing there like a deer caught in the headlight. Then she turned and started running back through the forest.

Keep away from the mine shaft.

Had Doane caught sight of her? She'd thought that the beam had zeroed in on her long enough.

Just in case, make as much noise as she could to draw attention.

But the thunder that had been her friend was suddenly her enemy. How could you hear the sound of footsteps and crash of vegetation with that rumbling all around them?

But it didn't matter. Doane had seen her!

She could hear him cursing behind her. He must be close for her to hear him so clearly.

She glanced over her shoulder and her heart jumped in her breast.

Oh, yes, very close.

Should she pull out the knife? She jumped over a fallen tree stump and ran down the overgrown trail. If he caught up with her, she'd be ready for him.

"You won't win . . . Not like this."

Zander's words were still ringing in her

ears. He was right, of course, especially if Doane now had a laser-sighted rifle aimed at her back.

She glanced back. She couldn't see him, but she could hear the stomping of his rubber-soled boots and the jangling of keys on his belt. At least, she had drawn him away from Zander.

Now she just had to save her own neck.

"Give up, Eve," Doane called out behind her. "You'd never have lit that fire if you hadn't been exhausted. It's the end for you tonight."

She became aware of another sound. It was water, babbling and slapping over rocks. She turned toward a cluster of trees to her left.

A stream.

She bolted toward it.

She ran through dozens of outstretched branches, clawing at her face, her clothes, her hair. Just another few feet . . .

Doane's voice behind her, even closer this time. "You have to finish what you started. He's waiting for you."

She leaped into the stream and gasped as a million icy razors cut into her. The frigid water immediately took her breath away and slowed her movements. What was she thinking?

That he'd be crazy to follow her.

She dove to the shallow bottom and swam as far and fast as she could without breaking the surface. Doane was undoubtedly running on the bank alongside waiting for her to show herself.

She let the stream carry her along, moving faster than she ever could under her own power.

And, hopefully, faster than Doane, she thought desperately.

She swam until she felt that her lungs were about to burst. In one fluid motion, she broke the surface, hungrily gulped the air, then dove back under. Had he seen her?

It didn't matter. The current was picking up.

She could **do** this.

A bullet tore into the water only a foot from her head.

"The next bullet will be aimed much closer," Doane shouted from the bank. "Do you think you can swim faster than a bullet, Eve?"

No, and the stream was so narrow it

would make it easy for him to see her in the water.

Get out.

Take to the woods again.

She waited until she rounded the next curve, then left the stream and crossed to the other side. The trail was growing rougher and more overgrown here. She hoped she wasn't circling back toward Zander. She was so cold and tired, she was disoriented. Go deeper, toward the trail leading to the factory.

"Stop," he called. "Can't you see it's over?"

He might be right. He could be going to catch her, she realized in despair.

She might be able to fend him off once he brought her down. She had a weapon now.

But that weapon would let Doane know that someone had been here and tried to help her.

And so would this vest she was wearing.

Protect Zander.

Don't let Doane go back and shoot him while he was helpless in that mine shaft.

Fight the common enemy.

At a turn in the trail she instinctively shrugged out of the vest and threw it deep into the bushes.

Keep running. Don't let Doane bring her down until they were far away from the place where Zander had gone down.

Run.

Faster.

"Bitch!" Doane shouted. "I told you I'd blow your kneecaps out. I'll do it, Eve."

But he wouldn't do it unless he had to do it, in spite of his threat. She would be an encumbrance crippled.

Lead him away from Zander.

The bushes were scratching her arms and face as she tore into the forest.

But she'd lost time by making the turn, and Doane was even closer now.

Darkness.

Trees.

The sound of Doane's harsh breathing behind her.

Keep running.

Too late.

He was on her, taking her down!

She rolled over, kneeing him in the groin.

He grunted in pain.

While her leg was raised, she reached down and felt desperately for the hilt of the knife.

"Bitch." Her head rang as Doane slapped her.

She had the knife out.

"What the—" His hand brutally grasped her wrist and twisted it. The knife fell from her grasp.

He grabbed it and pressed the blade against her throat. "Move, and I'll slice you to pieces."

She froze.

"Now get up . . . slowly."

She got to her knees.

He stood up and towered over her. His gaze went to the knife in his hand.

"Where did you get the knife, you little viper?"

Think.

He slapped her again. "Where?"

"In an old, dilapidated hunter's blind about ten miles from here. There was a backpack and the knife and some spoiled food packs. I thought you and Kevin might have left them when you were up here hunting."

He shook his head.

"I was just glad to find the knife." She

glared at him. "I was going to skewer you, Doane."

"I'm sure you would. You're as blood-thirsty as your father."

"I have no father. That crazy story was a figment of your imagination."

"We shall see." He jerked her to her feet. "I can hardly wait to introduce you to him. I'm even more eager to watch his expression when I put a bullet in your head."

"He wouldn't care any more than I would to watch you kill Zander. Your plan is stupid, Doane. **You're** stupid."

"You're trying to make me angry. Do you want to die? Are you tired of the chase?" He pushed her ahead of him through the bushes. "Well, the chase is over. Now we get down to business. But first, we go get my Kevin. You wanted me to go down after him? No way. You'll go down the side of that abyss where you threw him and bring him home. That's what you call what you do to those skulls that you reconstruct, isn't it? Well, you're going to bring Kevin home." He pushed her forward again. "And then you're going to give him back to me just the way he was."

He wasn't going back in the direction

from which they'd come, she realized with relief. Keep him distracted. "If his skull is still in one piece. It's raining hard right now, and that will mean my work will take a big hit. You should have gone down that slope right after I threw it over. You might have had a chance of retrieving it. I've seen what the wolves do to carrion since I've been on the run."

"If he's been damaged, I'll stake you out, and those wolves can have you for dinner," he said viciously. "You'll bring him back to me, Eve." He pressed the barrel of the rifle into the center of her back. "You'll crawl down the side of that cliff and you'll go get him tonight."

Vancouver

Joe disabled the security alarm on the rear side of the palatial mansion and moved silently across the verandah to the French doors. It appeared Zander was very careful and extremely high-tech. It had taken Joe almost thirty minutes to disable the exterior alarm.

It took another fifteen to get into the house through the French doors.

He paused, waiting in the darkness for a motion detector to signal his presence. He had disabled two outside, but there could always be another.

No alarm.

He closed the door.

"Please, don't move. I have a gun, but I'm not overly familiar with them, and I'm afraid that I'll discharge it by mistake if I get nervous."

Joe froze, his gaze searching the darkness. "I'm not moving . . . yet." He could make out a tall, male silhouette framed against the drapes of the window. He hesitated, trying to decide if he should drop to the floor while drawing his own gun.

No, big mistake. He wasn't here to blow anyone away. He had wanted to make contact and get information. "I take it you're not Zander?"

"Good God, no."

"I didn't think so. Stang?"

"Venable told you about me, Detective Quinn? I didn't think I'd made that much of an impression on him." Stang reached over and turned on a lamp. "But, then, Venable appears to be a very clever man. Fearless, too. There aren't many men who aren't afraid of Zander." He smiled. "I think Zander appreciates that quality in him."

Joe's eyes narrowed on him. He couldn't detect any hint of menace in Stang's demeanor, but that could be deceptive. Stang was somewhere in his late thirties, a little over six feet, with brown hair and hazel eyes. He was dressed in a brown turtleneck and khakis and appeared to be fit without being particularly muscular.

He was also holding the Beretta revolver in his hand with an awkwardness that made his first statement about being unaccustomed to weapons ring true.

"You know who I am? You recognized me?"

"Yes, you're Joe Quinn." He made a face. "And I've been staring at your face in Zander's dossiers for some time. Of course, I recognized you."

"Dossier? Then you know I'm a police detective and not likely to attack you. It might be wise if you put down that gun."

He sighed. "It's not doing me much good anyway, is it?" He put the gun down on the table. "You're an ex-SEAL. You could probably take it away from me in a heartbeat. When I saw you on the verandah, I just thought that it might intimidate you for a time until I could see whether you were a danger to me."

"And not to Zander?"

"Zander? That's almost funny." He tilted his head. "Yes, Zander would laugh at the thought of my protecting him."

"You saw me on the verandah? I take it I set off an alarm?"

"Yes, you disabled most of them, but Zander always makes sure there's one more that you don't suspect. That's when I came into the library and looked to see who had come calling." He frowned. "Should I offer you a drink or something?"

"I just broke into your employer's home."

"But you didn't mean to burgle or hurt anyone. You probably only meant to talk to Zander and try to find Eve Duncan. Isn't that right?" He went to the bar and poured himself a scotch. "Well, if you don't want one, I believe I do. This isn't my forte."

"You appear to be very well informed."

He shrugged. "For some reason Zander wanted me to know about Eve Duncan. I found it very unusual." He lifted his glass to his lips. "I didn't want to know. I didn't like the idea she might be killed or hurt."

"But Zander wasn't upset at the prospect?"

"No. Maybe. I don't know. I've never been able to read Zander." He took a drink. "Well, perhaps a little, but it's mostly guesswork. I never wanted to delve past the surface. I always felt it could be . . . lethal."

"Then why did you work for him?"

"I had my reasons. The pay is good, and Zander can be fascinating."

"And where is Zander now?" Joe asked grimly. "I have a few questions I need to ask him."

"I don't know."

"Shall I repeat the question?" Joe asked softly. "I intend to talk to Zander, Stang."

"You see, that's why I got the gun out of the desk. Yes, you're police, but I think the way you feel about Eve Duncan probably overrides your respect for the law. From what I've learned about you, I should have kept the gun handy." He grimaced. "You can shoot me or beat me up or waterboard me or whatever. I still wouldn't be able to tell you where he is. He never talks to me about assignments."

"And was this an 'assignment'?"

He was silent. "Not exactly. But he still—" He met Joe's eyes. "He went after James Doane, Detective Quinn. He was tired of waiting for him to try to pounce and decided to go hunting."

"And where did he go hunting?"

"I have no idea."

"Then you'd better get one," Joe said softly. "Fast."

"I told you, he doesn't talk to me. Never about specifics. I like it that way."

"I find your relationship with Zander both bizarre and annoying. I can accept the bizarre. The annoying is going to be dangerous for you."

He shrugged. "I've lived on the edge for long enough to accept it as a fact of life. I've told you the truth. You should be happy that Zander is going after Doane. Eve Duncan has a better chance that way. Zander is exceptional at what he does."

"Why will Eve have a better chance? Is he going to try to get her away from Doane?"

Stang shook his head. "That's not what he said. He was only concerned about Doane."

Joe muttered a curse. "And what's to prevent Doane from killing his hostage if he thinks he's going to die anyway? That's what happens in situations like this."

"He said that Doane was his focus."

"And screw the fact that Eve is his daughter?"

Stang's eyes widened. "What?"

"You didn't know? Venable said that Zander knew."

"No, I didn't know." His brow wrinkled in a thoughtful frown. "But that might explain a few things. He's been behaving rather . . ." He looked at Joe. "But you can't count on that having any impact on him. Zander's not like other people."

"Do you think I don't know that?" Joe asked between set teeth. "I don't even know if Venable is right, and he is her father. I don't know, and I don't care. If I could use it to persuade him to tell me where I can find her, then I'd do it. Otherwise, he can fade back into the shadows where he's been all her life."

"He may not know where to find her,"

Stang said quietly. "I told you, he went hunting."

"But you think that he had an idea where to find Doane. She's with Doane, dammit."

Stang was silent.

"Answer me, Stang."

"I'm thinking about it. Zander would look upon it as a betrayal and he doesn't tolerate traitors. He always expects to be betrayed, but he'd still tend to set an example. I've lasted this long because he has a minimum degree of trust in me."

"Which must make your life hell."

"Sometimes."

"Then why do you stay? Venable says you could get a job anywhere, that you're some kind of financial genius."

"I have reasons."

"Your brother, Sean?"

Stang went rigid. "You know about Sean?"

"Venable has as big a report on you as he does Zander. On the plane here, I accessed every bit of information I could on both of you."

"Very clever. Just what I'd do. I'd bet there wasn't much on Zander."

"No, even Venable couldn't pull more

than a few lines on him." He paused. "But on you . . ."

"I'm very ordinary." He smiled. "Just your typical genius next door. All brain but with no larger-than-life characteristics. I'll leave that to you . . . and Zander."

"You can't compare me to Zander."

"Yes, I can. I see a few similarities. You will, too, once you make his acquaintance. But only a few, he's something of an enigma."

"And so are you. For instance, you were born Colin Daklow, in South Africa of American parents, missionaries who ran a medical facility there. You had an older brother, Sean, with whom you were very close. He was a doctor at the hospital. You spent most of your time in New York. First at Harvard and then at Merrill Lynch. You were the golden boy there, but you still made frequent trips back to South Africa. You and your family were very close." He paused. "But you weren't there when the village and hospital were attacked by rebel insurgents who killed your parents and fatally injured your brother Sean. He died two hours after you saw him the morning you flew back there from New York."

"I asked the doctors why they couldn't save him," Stang said. "Until I saw what they had done to him. Then I only hoped he'd die quickly." His lips tightened. "Butchers."

"Then you buried your dead and went back to the U.S.," Joe said. "But not to Merrill Lynch. You disappeared for a while. To grieve, Stang?"

"Yes, and to think."

"About the reports that the South African government was sending you about the suspicions that Lee Zander had somehow been involved in that massacre?"

Stang was silent.

"The nurses at the hospital filled out a report stating that Sean was coherent and talking before his death. What did your brother say to you before he died?"

For a moment Joe wasn't sure Stang was going to answer. Then Stang said slowly, "He made me promise that I would never leave Zander until the day he died."

"Yet there was no proof," Joe said. "But it must have been agonizing to know that Zander would probably never face punishment for those killings. It was about that time that you changed your name and purchased an entire new identity on the black market."

"Yes." He took a sip of his scotch. "It's remarkably easy if the money is available, and money has never been a problem for me."

"Then you hunted down Zander and applied for a job. I presume to look for your opportunity."

"It's always a mistake to presume anything, Detective. Since you are a law-enforcement officer, I'm sure you're aware of that." He put his glass down on the table. "And I'd like you to dispense with this raking over very painful coals. I still find the memories excruciating."

"I can see that you would," he added harshly. "Evidently your opportunity never came. Well, make it happen now. Walk away from Zander and help me. Help Eve."

He didn't speak for a moment. "I think I'd like Eve Duncan. I'd look at her photo and see . . . I don't know." He shrugged. "She reminded me of my mother and father, and Sean and all those other foolish souls who let themselves be butchered. Some people take, some people give. The ones who give shouldn't suffer, but they do."

"Then help me," Joe said urgently. "Zander is bound to find out about who you are eventually. Walk away from him now."

Stang smiled faintly. "I think Zander knew who I was before he even hired me. I know he knew a few months later. He doesn't take chances without knowing all the details about the people surrounding him."

"Then why the hell would he keep you near him?"

Stang shook his head. "Enigma. I believe he enjoys the risk. He works hard at protecting himself, but lately I've wondered if he doesn't really care whether he dies or not."

"Like Eve," Joe muttered. He hadn't meant that to come out. Eve never said anything, but he knew that she would not be sorry to go to her Bonnie. But not yet, dammit. He wouldn't let her go yet.

"Eve? Maybe that's what I saw when I was looking at her photo," Stang said quietly. "A reflection of Zander."

"That's not what you saw," Joe said. "Eve will fight. Eve will have a good life ahead of her if we give her a chance." He took a step nearer. "If **you** give her a chance. Where did Zander go hunting?"

"I don't know." He held up his hand as Joe opened his lips to speak. "But I may be able to point you in the right direction."

"Talk."

"Zander expected Doane to contact him, so he had his phone bugged and an expert on hand to monitor any transmissions and try to trace it."

"Did he call him?"

"Yes, and the night he left, I know that he made a call to verify that the trace had been effective." He paused. "I don't know if he got an actual trace. I wouldn't think so since he was in hunt mode. Maybe a tower, though."

"What tower?"

He shook his head. "Guesswork. You need to talk to the source."

"Who is the source?"

"Zander uses a man named Donald Weiner. He's very, very good. And he's completely discreet when it comes to Zander." He grimaced. "You won't find many of his associates alive who aren't discreet."

Joe typed the name into his phone. "Telephone number?"

"You're not listening. He wouldn't answer

any calls from numbers with which he's not familiar."

"I'll call on Zander's house phone."

Stang shook his head. "Zander calls from his cell."

"Roadblocks."

"That's the way Zander likes it."

"How do I get to—"

"If he knows you're looking for him, he'll take off and go underground. We'll have to go to see him personally."

"We?"

Stang shrugged. "He knows I work for Zander. It might help."

"Where does Weiner live?"

"About four hours' drive from here. On the other side of the city. We'll take my car." He went to the closet and took out his coat and a muffler. "We'd better get started."

"Why are you doing this, Stang? It's far from being discreet, and you said Zander didn't forgive indiscretions. Are you breaking with him?"

"And lose this fine job? No, I can't do that. I told you, I made a promise. But I believe this time Zander may be acting a little indiscreetly himself. Who knows? It might strike him as amusing. One can never tell with Zander." He shrugged into his coat and turned toward the door. "Besides, I like your Eve's face." He opened the door. "Better bundle up if it wouldn't offend your macho image. It's turned very cold in the past few hours."

CHAPTER

13

Rio Grande Forest
Colorado

Dear God, it was cold.

The rain was spiking hard against Eve's face and body, and her hair was clinging to her neck like coiled snakes. At first, the rain had felt almost warm in contrast to the icy waters of the stream. It did not feel warm now. The wind ripping out of the abyss was whip-sharp, taking her breath away.

"It's going to be slippery going down the side of the cliff." Doane was shining his flashlight on the straight stone of the cliff wall that merged thirty feet below into a rough slope. "I'll tie a rope around your waist and under your arms to make sure I don't lose you." He smiled grimly. "That would be a shame, wouldn't it? Don't worry, once you get your hands on Kevin, I'll pull you back up."

"I'm not worried. You'd be too afraid I'd drop him again if I took a header." Her breath was pluming in the cold air. Doane didn't seem to be feeling the cold, she noticed. His face was wet from the rain, but he was eager, charged with energy. It was because he was about to get his precious Kevin back, she thought. "Providing that I can find him down there in this muddy mess. He might have rolled halfway down to the valley by now." She added maliciously, "And then there are always the wolves . . ."

"You'd better hope that's not true." Doane was tying ropes about her body. "But I don't believe it is. I've been stopping here frequently every time I passed this way while I've been on your trail. I think that I saw Kevin about thirty feet down in that patch of jagged rocks jutting out of the slope." He shined the beam down into the darkness. "Do you see it?"

"I can't see anything in this rain." She didn't want to see it. She didn't want to know that Kevin was that close, waiting for her. "What am I supposed to carry the skull back up in once I've retrieved it?"

"Just drop it into the big compartment in the backpack." He took off his backpack and fastened it on her. "But make sure you don't damage the skull any more than it is already."

"Heaven forbid," she murmured.

"Don't mock me." His lips tightened. "I'm very angry with you, Eve." He pushed her toward the edge of the abyss. "And I'm tempted to cut these ropes and throw you off this cliff." He stepped back. "But I won't do it. This is much better. You're making yourself useful to Kevin." He wound one loop of the rope around a tree at the edge of the cliff. "Now get down there and bring him back. I'm afraid this rain may damage him."

"I'm not a climber, you know." She moved toward the cliff. "You may lose your Kevin if I slip or—"

"You won't lose him." He stood looking at her, the rain pouring down his face. "He won't let **you,** Eve."

She felt a chill that had nothing to do with the weather.

"Go on," he said softly. "Now."

She hesitated, then sat down on the edge of the cliff, grasped the rope, and began to crawl her way down the rough stone precipice.

The rope was abrasive, tearing her hands as she tried to place her feet against the stone to take pressure from her upper body.

Rain.

Cold.

Thunder.

Wind whipping up from the valley and swaying the rope and her body.

"Hurry," Doane shouted.

Hurry? There was no way to hurry. Did the bastard think that she was enjoying hanging here over this nothingness?

Keep calm. The one thing she could count on from Doane was that he wouldn't let her fall. He wanted Kevin.

Ten feet.

Another twenty until she reached the start of the slope.

That twenty feet seemed to be more like a hundred.

But she reached it, and her feet touched the dirt and stone that was the slope.

But the dirt was mostly mud now, and she was slipping and sliding.

Another ten or twelve feet before she would reach the cluster of rocks Doane had said had halted the slide of her reconstruction of the skull.

Steep, slippery feet.

She fell and felt the embedded stones in the dirt cut her knees.

She struggled up again.

Another four feet to go.

Those rocks were right ahead.

But she didn't see any sign of that damn reconstruction. Could it be Doane's imagination, and he had sent her on this wild-goose chase?

Two more feet.

She still couldn't see anything.

But she could feel it. She could feel him.

She stopped and inhaled sharply.

Kill you. Kill her.

Swirling darkness. Darker than the storm around her.

Nausea.

Fight it off.

Move. Get over it. She couldn't stay here paralyzed, huddled in the mud. That would be a victory for Kevin, a victory for Doane.

She felt a tugging on the rope around her body. Doane was becoming impatient.

Screw you, Doane.

She took another minute and moved forward.

Nausea. Struggle against it.

Then she saw the skull.

She stiffened, her hands clenching into fists so hard her nails bit into the palms.

Dear God, she had hoped all her work would be destroyed by the fall from the cliff.

It should have been destroyed.

Incredibly, the reconstruction was still miraculously intact. The nose was a little askew. The plane of the left cheek would have to be smoothed, and the eyes would have to be inserted.

But then Kevin would be complete, brought back to Doane the way he was before Zander had killed him and destroyed that face.

Kill you. Kill him.

Snarling evil. Clamminess. Smothering.

She braced herself at the assault. It might not have come from Kevin. It might have come from Doane on the cliff. She had come to the point when they were becoming one to her.

She could try to finish the job. She could take the skull and toss it the rest of the way down to the valley below.

Nausea. Panic. Smothering.

"You don't like the idea?" She crawled the rest of the way to the skull. "That must mean it's a fine plan."

Except that it would only mean that Doane would make her climb down to the valley and search for the skull. It would be a waste of time when she had to find a way to escape from him again.

Escape. She felt a sudden plummet of despair at the thought of having to go through that nightmare again. She had been free, and now she was back in Doane's cage.

Stop feeling sorry for yourself, she told herself in disgust. She had made choices tonight that might have been foolish, but she could not have done anything else. She would do it again.

So find a way out of Doane's cage. She had advantages that she hadn't had before she had escaped the last time. She knew where she could find a phone and a gun if she could just break away from Doane.

And if Zander managed to work his way up that mine shaft, he would be going after Doane.

Common enemy.

No, she couldn't count on Zander. She had told him she knew she was on her own.

But a gun and a phone were still valuable assets for a woman on her own.

"Stop wasting time," Doane yelled down from the cliff. "Bring up my son!"

Bring up the monster.

She stared down at the skull. The empty eye sockets seemed to glare up at her. "I'm going to give you back to him," she whispered. "You deserve each other. But I promise I'll find a way to destroy both of you."

She shrugged out of the backpack and opened the rear compartment.

She took a deep breath, then reached out with both hands and picked up the skull.

Nausea. Heaviness. Breathlessness.

She dropped it quickly into the backpack and closed the flap.

She let her breath out in an explosion of sound. Closing that flap didn't really contain the evil that was Kevin, but it closed him away from her for the moment.

She put the backpack on again. She jerked on the lead rope to signal to Doane she was ready and started crawling up the slope.

Lightning.

Thunder.

Rain.

And that horrible heaviness on her back that was an almost unbearable burden.

She had reached the steep stone of the sheer cliff, and she pulled herself to her feet. "Doane!"

He started pulling her up the cliff.

She braced herself against the stone and pulled herself hand over hand.

She could make it.

Don't think of Kevin.

Move. Climb.

Block the monsters from your thoughts.

Don't think of Doane waiting for her at the top.

Think of Joe. Think of Jane.

Think of Bonnie.

• • •

Shit!

Agonizing pain shot through Zander as he grabbed the exposed tree root and pulled himself another few feet up the mine shaft. He threw the strap of his backpack over the root and fastened it under his arms in case he lost consciousness again. His body was going into shock. He had been blacking out during the last hour of the climb. He had ripped the front of his shirt and formed a support bandage around his wrist. But there was no question that the wrist was broken.

He checked his phone. Still no signal, of course. The tower was too far away. Even after he climbed out, he would probably have to walk a good two miles to get any kind of reception at all. Inside the mine shaft, it was a totally lost cause. He winced as searing pain jolted through him as he put away the phone.

Ignore it. Use that technique the Buddhist priests had taught him to block it all out.

But the priests had not had to climb up a narrow, muddy mine shaft, with only the occasional rock or outgrowth of vegetation to support him. Nor use that broken wrist to catch himself when his other hand-hold was in danger of failing him. Like right now, when he was hanging from a slender tree root with his whole weight swinging from the grip on that fragile plant and his hip wedged in a small cavity that gave meager support. Or digging his fingers into stone cracks or into the slippery mud as his feet and knees pushed him up toward the top.

Yet the priests had probably gone through even more severe challenges for their faith. Zander had seen them do some fairly incredible things. Unfortunately, Zander had no blind faith to keep the demons of weakness and pain away. So close out the agony and concentrate on the job to be done.

In a minute. When the throbbing stopped. That last lunge had caused the bone to pierce the skin.

He closed his eyes. At this rate, it would take him several hours to reach the top.

Rest. There was no hurry. Eve had either escaped Doane or been captured.

Or she had been killed.

None of the three options required

instant response. If she had escaped, then she had proved she could take care of herself against threats. If she was captured, then Doane would try to keep her alive to accomplish his purpose.

If she had been killed, he could not bring her back to life.

Emptiness. Why was he feeling this emptiness?

"You can't rest. Go on. She needs you. I don't know how long she's going to be able to hold him off."

He opened his eyes and struggled to focus at the voice that had come from the top of the shaft.

A little red-haired girl wearing a Bugs Bunny T-shirt was sitting on the edge looking down at him.

Shit. Now he was having hallucinations. He knew who that little girl staring at him was supposed to be. He had read the newspaper reports, and Eve had told him about Bonnie. It was entirely natural that he was having visions of her in this shocked state. "Go away."

"I can't go away," she whispered. "I can't get to Mama. You have to do it for me. He's keeping me back. I'm fighting him, and it's getting a little better, but I don't know if I'll reach her in time."

"Who's keeping you back? Doane?" She shook her head. "Kevin."

Now he knew he was out of his head. "Demons and goblins, oh my."

"Stop it. I don't have time for this. I can feel my strength fading away. Kevin is too strong." She moistened her lips. "You have to get her away from Doane. I want to be with her, but it can't be like this."

"Sorry. You'll have to handle it yourself. Ghosts and demons are out of my realm of expertise."

"Don't you tell me that." Bonnie's eyes were suddenly blazing at him. "You have to help my mother. I won't have it any other way." Her voice dropped to a desperate whisper. "Don't you see? The darkness is closing in around her. And beyond the darkness is nothing but . . . silence."

"All I know is that you're a figment of my imagination and I refuse to—"

• • •

He was talking to air. There was no longer a little girl looking down at him.

There had never been a little girl with red hair and eyes that blazed with panic and anger and love.

Hallucination. Pain-induced craziness.

And again this feeling of emptiness was sweeping back to him at the thought that Eve might be dead.

Emptiness and rage. Rage at Eve for not doing what he'd told her to do. The same rage he'd felt toward the priest when he'd refused to let Zander take him off his mountain to safety. Didn't they know that all of their fine humanity and efforts to heal the world would only bring them to this? Death was always there, waiting for the good as well as the evil.

Who should know better than he?

Where was Eve now? Lying dead in the mud a mile away from here? He doubted if she would manage to escape. Doane had been too close, and she had deliberately run back across his trail.

To save him.

The rage was growing. Idiotic woman. Didn't she realize he could save himself.

That he didn't need her. God knows she should have realized that by now.

Okay, she was dead, or Doane had her again. He would know as soon as he managed to get out of here. If they were lucky, then she'd be alive and probably back at that coin factory by now.

They? It was Eve's life, Eve's fate. She had made that clear to him, and that was the way he wanted it. It was her decision, her destiny whether she lived or died on this mountain. He would not allow himself to care either away. She was not Zander's concern.

The darkness is closing in on her. And beyond the darkness is nothing but . . . silence.

Block that moment of pain and hallucination and think clearly.

Eve was not his concern.

But that knife he had given her was his concern, he thought suddenly.

When Doane discovered she had a knife, then he would be immediately suspicious. He would question her, and if he didn't believe the answer, then he would torture her.

And she would not tell Doane that Zander

had given her the knife. No matter what he did to Eve, she would not tell him that Zander was here in these mountains and vulnerable.

Because she was a fool, like the priest. She would take the punishment for some obscure reason that had no bearing on reality. She should tell Doane and let Zander take his chances. That would be the sensible thing to do.

And beyond the capability of the Eve Duncan he had grown to know tonight.

Which meant that there was an urgency after all whether he liked it or not, even if it took all night to climb out and battle back this damn pain.

He started to curse as he began to wriggle up the muddy shaft, grabbing the shrubs and rocks where he could to keep from slipping. And with every movement of his body, every flash of pain, the rage began to be transformed, alter, change, burn with white-hot intensity and shift away from Eve.

And focus like a laser on James Doane.

Eve took off the backpack and dropped it at Doane's feet. "There's Frankenstein junior. May you enjoy each other."

"Be careful." He opened the flap and shined the beam into the interior. "Why, he's not damaged very much at all." He lifted his gaze, and said maliciously, "What a disappointment for you."

"There is some damage."

"Not enough to cause any great delay. I knew he wouldn't let you win." He reached into the backpack and gently touched the forehead of the reconstruction. "He always was a survivor."

"Because he destroyed everyone around him. Even you, Doane."

"He didn't destroy me, he enriched me," Doane said. "And he completed me. We'll always be together." He took off the ropes around her. "And now I've got to get you to a place where you can finish what you started. You should be able to complete it within a few hours, maybe half a day." He nudged her with his rifle. "Come on, we have to stop at the factory and gather some of your equipment to take with us."

"Take with us? We're not going to stay there?"

"No, I'm not sure I believed your story about where you got that knife. We're going to change locations."

Which meant it would make it harder for Zander to trace them, she thought. It would be logical for Doane to take her directly to the factory. But logic seemed to have nothing to do with this roller coaster she was riding. "If I'd blundered into someone who would give me a knife, do you think I'd still be here?"

"No." He frowned. "But I still don't like it. We're moving."

She shrugged. "Whatever." She started moving toward the trail. "Where? I can't work outdoors in this rain."

"I have another place. I told you I'd planned this for years. Do you think I wouldn't make alternate arrangements in case something went wrong?" He smiled. "Alternate arrangements, alternate ending. Not as satisfactory as the one where I take you to Vancouver to Zander, but still a very interesting conclusion. But I'm still hoping to bring the other scenario into being."

She had reached the trail and looked down at the lights of the coin factory. "What a shame. After all your hard work, setting up those gas vents. It all went to waste, didn't it? I hope you were equally inventive in your second attempt at containing me."

"You'll have to judge for yourself. But you can be sure that you won't get away from me again." He looked down at the backpack. "We won't be taken in by your tricks again, will we, Kevin?"

She shivered. Doane's tone had been so loving, so matter-of-fact that it struck her as particularly eerie. She should be accustomed to it by now. Don't let him see it.

"I'm fresh out of tricks," she said as she started down the hill. "So I suppose I'll just have to find a way to send you to hell to join your son. May I ask where we're going?"

"Why not? There's an old ghost town close to here. No one has gone there in years . . . but me. It will be a perfect place for you to finish your work on Kevin."

Ghost town. She tried to keep any hint of eagerness or excitement from her expression. It had to be the ghost town Zander had mentioned, where he had stashed the phone and gun. Yet she couldn't be that lucky. "Then why didn't you bring me there first instead of that coin factory?"

"I told you, an alternate solution, an alternate location." He pulled out his phone. "Now be quiet. I've got to call Blick and tell him that we're moving in a different direction. He has his own part to play." He gestured with his rifle. "Keep moving. Don't think I'm not paying attention to you." He was dialing quickly. "This will only take a minute. I have to—Blick?" He spoke quickly into the phone. "I'm leaving the coin factory and going to the ghost town. You know what you have to do. I'll expect you up here right away. Wait, don't hang up. What about Goldfork? Did you get it?" An instant later, he was cursing. "Failure after failure, Blick. Find her and get that journal from Kendra Michaels." He drew a deep breath. "No, afterward, I told you where your priority lies. I have a feeling that everything might be closing in on me here. Things aren't quite what they should be." He hung up.

"Kendra Michaels?" Eve said. "What's Kendra got to do with Blick?"

"Your friend, Kendra, is interfering in my plans. She's searching for you, but she's getting in my way," Doane said grimly. "Another sign that your Quinn and Venable may be getting a little too close." He nudged her again with the rifle. "Come on, let's get out of here."

Lisbon, Colorado

"Hey." Kendra leaned in the passenger-side window and shook Margaret awake. "Ready to join the living?"

Margaret opened one eye, then the other. "It's light out."

"Excellent observation. And to think I was having doubts about bringing you with me." Kendra pushed a tall drink cup through the window.

"What's this?"

"I got you a green tea. No one who sleeps as soundly as you could possibly be a coffee drinker."

Margaret smiled and took the cup. "It doesn't make any difference. I lived next to a rock quarry for a while, and dynamite charges couldn't wake me." She glanced around at the old-growth trees and mountains in every direction. "Where are we?"

"Lisbon, Colorado. That's the Continental Divide you're looking at."

Margaret nodded and gazed at the scenery a moment longer before looking at her phone. "It's seven A.M.?"

"Yes. We got here a couple of hours ago. I thought this valley would be a good place to watch the sunrise, but I slept right through it." She nodded toward a small white shack situated next to the lot where they were parked. "The coffee place just opened."

"You're not mentioning the journal. When we changed seats a few hours ago, I was too tired to ask you any questions. Did you find anything interesting?"

"Only a sadist would find Kevin's journal interesting," Kendra said soberly. "He was terrible. But there were a few things in it that sort of puzzled me. I'll have to read it more closely."

"By all means." Margaret climbed out of the car and stretched. "Beautiful place, Kendra, but I have to ask—why here?"

"We found traces of gold in the trunk of Doane's car. It wasn't processed, at least not the way gold is now. This area was big during the gold-rush days, and some people still pan for gold around here."

"Really?"

Kendra nodded toward a man, a woman, and three children climbing from an SUV. "Mostly tourists. There's a gold-panning operation on the other side of that hill.

There might be someone over there we can talk to."

They followed the family up the path running alongside the parking lot, over a small hill, and found themselves looking down on a gentle stream babbling over rocks and a large tree that had fallen into the water. Two tents were set up next to the stream, staffed with young men and women renting out waders and pans. Two dozen or so people, mostly families, stood in the stream awkwardly moving their pans back and forth.

"Cool." Margaret smiled. "But nobody here really looks like they know what they're doing."

"He does." Kendra pointed to a bearded man, about seventy, who wore a bright orange vest adorned with the same company logo as on the equipment-rental tents. He was moving from party to party, demonstrating the proper technique for gold panning. "We'll talk to him."

They moved down a series of stepping-stones in the water and walked alongside the stream.

The bearded man looked at them and

pointed back to the tents. "You rent your waders and pans over there, ladies. You might just strike it rich!"

Kendra smiled. "Do you own this operation?"

"Yes, ma'am, Martin Salle, at your service. I have over forty years' experience working this area."

Margaret's eyes widened. "Forty years? In all that time, I'm surprised you didn't strike it rich."

There was nothing critical or catty in her tone, but her remark still caused Salle to look at them suspiciously. "Do you want to rent a pan or not?"

"We're more interested in information," Kendra said.

Salle raised his hand to shield the sun from his eyes. "What kind of information?"

Kendra pulled out her phone and showed him a photo of Doane on the screen. "Do you know this man?"

He studied it. "Afraid not. Should I?"

"Not necessarily. We think he may pan for gold in this area."

"Huh." Salle lowered his voice. "Did he run out on one of you?"

"No, nothing like that." Kendra paused. "Are you sure you don't know him?"

"Oh, I'm sure. It's just that . . ." He stepped closer to them. "Look, the only people panning around here are doing it for fun, for a hobby. Like fishing. No one really thinks they're going to score. It's like buying a lotto ticket. They do it because it relaxes them. I know most of them, and this guy isn't one of them."

"Are there others who do what you do?" Margaret asked. "For tourists, I mean."

"Sure. There are four or five companies that operate more or less regularly. And half a dozen other people who lead private gold-panning tours. But again, that guy isn't one of 'em." Salle looked downstream over his shoulder. "Sorry, but I gotta get back to my group. You might want to ask around at the visitors' center if you haven't already."

"Where is that?"

He pointed to another hill behind him. "Over there. There are bathrooms, a little museum, and a gift shop all in one building. I seriously doubt he pans around here, but if he does, maybe someone there knows him."

Salle turned his attention back to his group, leaving Kendra and Margaret to step across the stream's most shallow section and make their way up the hill.

"Do you think he was telling the truth?" Margaret asked.

"About not knowing Doane? I'm pretty sure. If he had, there probably would have been at least a flash of recognition when I showed him the photo. There wasn't one. I was looking for it."

Margaret smiled. "You have a lot in common with animals."

"Is that supposed to be a compliment?"

"No, just an observation. Animals are very perceptive about people. They don't understand our spoken language. So they depend on everything else to make judgments about us. Our tone of voice, body language, the way we smell . . . Kind of how you absorb everything to form a complete picture. It's interesting."

"If you say so."

"I do. That's why many animals are such good judges of character. People rely almost entirely on their words to deceive. If you're not focusing on just that, you have a much better idea about the kind of person you're dealing with. Of course, you take it to an entirely different level."

"You mean you're giving me more credit than you would a poodle?"

"Sure, dogs are terrible judges of character. They like almost everyone they meet. It's probably from being away from the wild for centuries."

"I don't have to talk to them to realize that."

"Of course you don't. Unlike people, animals don't try to hide their feelings. I think that's one reason I've always felt so comfortable with them."

Kendra studied Margaret as they proceeded up the path. She was obviously accustomed to the skepticism that greeted her, and she didn't seem at all concerned with convincing others of her abilities. It was yet another factor that made Margaret and her eccentricities easier to accept, Kendra realized. What you saw was what you got, and she didn't really care what you did with it. "And you don't trust what your fellow human beings are telling you?"

"Some of them. But I instinctively want to believe people are good, and that gets in the way of my judgment." She shrugged.

"But I couldn't live any other way, so I just have to try to be careful."

"You appear to know yourself very well."

"You think so? It's kind of hard when we all change with almost every experience." She slanted her a look. "You're an experience that will most likely change me, Kendra. It probably has already. I wonder what—" She broke off as they came over the hill. "Is that what they call a visiting center? Tiny, very tiny."

"Well, it appears to only serve this particular tourist area."

It took them another couple minutes to reach the visitors' center, which turned out to be a small one-room building staffed only by an elderly woman passing out maps and pamphlets. The "museum" consisted mainly of framed black-and-white photos taken during the gold-rush era, interspersed with a few scant displays of vintage mining tools and clothing.

Kendra pulled out her phone and once again accessed Doane's photo. "I have a feeling we're wasting our time here. As soon as the lady is through talking to those people, I'll see if she recognizes Doane. I guess then we can get on the road and try to find—" She froze, her gaze caught, held by something that she'd seen out of the corner of her eye. She whirled to face the wall.

Could it be?

"Kendra?" Margaret's glance shifted between Kendra and the sepia-toned photograph that had grabbed her attention. "What is it?"

"That picture over there." The photograph showed a clunky mechanical contraption, perhaps four feet tall, resting on four iron legs. A long handle jutted from the top, perpendicular to the rest of the device.

"It looks like some peculiar robotic animal," Margaret said. "What about it?"

"Trust you to see an animal in a machine," Kendra said absently as she stepped closer to the framed photograph. "This is incredible."

"What's incredible?"

"This . . . thing. Whatever it is."

"The little sign says it's a nineteenth-century coin press. What's so amazing about it?"

"Doane had one of these in his car recently."

"How do you know?"

"I saw fresh marks in his car after it was brought up from the lake."

Margaret shook her head. "I don't see how one of these things could even fit."

"It could fit. I **know** it." Kendra could understand why Margaret was doubtful. She should be questioning herself. She had to figure out why she was so certain that this was the answer. Yet the minute she had caught sight of that press, something had clicked. She had **visualized** that machine in the trunk. From the time she had seen those indentations in the trunk at the lake, it had been there in the back of her mind. She had been working at it, trying to puzzle it out. "Okay, I see what you mean. It does seem a little too large. Let me think about it."

Kendra concentrated, studying the contours of the press for a moment longer. Then she began replaying in her mind's eye each scratch, dent, and impression she had observed in Doane's car.

How had he done it . . .

Then it all came together. "It was disassembled and moved in three trips. The iron legs extended from the trunk all the way through the backseat. Trip one. The bottom half of the body went in the trunk for trip two. The top half of the body went into the trunk for trip three, and the handle might still have been attached to it and poked through to the backseat."

Margaret stared at her in amazement. "You're sure of the order?"

"I'm positive. Given the way the marks intersected with each other, it's the only way it could have happened." Kendra raised her phone. "I have photos of the trunk right here. Do you want me to show you?"

"No, thanks." Margaret smiled at Kendra's burst of intensity and excitement. "I'm not sure I'd see the same thing that you do."

"Of course you would. Once I explained it to you. It's very clear."

"If I marched to your drummer, maybe." She chuckled. "But I don't have to see what you see to believe you. I march to kind of a different drummer myself."

"I noticed that." And it was enough that Margaret believed that Kendra's deductions were valid. That faith was more than Kendra had offered Margaret.

Kendra turned to the elderly woman

who had just finished her conversation with the center's only other occupants. "Excuse me. May I ask you something?"

The woman walked over to her. "Yes, honey?"

Kendra pointed to the photograph. "This device was used to make coins?"

"Yes. Most gold-rush towns had their own coin factories. Sometimes more than one. Prospectors would bring their gold to be weighed and get gold coins in return."

"So it was kind of like a mint," Margaret said.

"That's exactly what it was. Back then, not all money was made by the government. Private companies could manufacture it themselves. Believe it or not, the Denver mint began as a private coin factory." She pointed to the photograph. "That's where this picture was taken. This press is still there."

"Are there others around?"

"Oh, sure. Museums have them, some belong to private collectors."

"Any in this area?"

The woman thought for a moment. "Hmm. I don't know of any offhand." She glanced at a family that had just entered the center. "You'll have to excuse me now."

Kendra gave one last look at the photo of the coin press, raised her phone and snapped a picture of it, then jerked her head toward the door. "Let's go, Margaret."

Margaret was frowning as they left the center. "Okay, I accept that Doane had a coin press in his trunk. Why? And where did he get it when he was under surveillance?"

"Pretty faulty surveillance, or he would never have been permitted to leave Gold-fork. As to why, that's what we've got to find out. He was either transporting it from one place to another or perhaps disposing of it. Either way it's a damn odd object to be moving when he was focused on going after Eve." Kendra was taking her phone out of her pocket. "I think we may need a little help." She was quickly dialing a number.

"Who are you calling?" Margaret asked.

"Hello, Venable." Kendra spoke into the phone. "Miss me? Didn't I tell you I'd keep in touch?"

"I don't miss you as much as that dead police officer's buddies. You might find yourself on the receiving end of a state-wide APB if you don't talk to them soon."

"Don't you think I'd do that if I could? I just don't have time."

"Somehow I thought that might be your answer," he said dryly. "So what's keeping you so busy?"

"I need information. Quinn says you're good at marshaling resources among all the government agencies and coming up with the right answer. Is that right?"

"Of course," he said sarcastically. "Why else does the CIA exist but to provide you with what you need?"

"I'm transmitting you a picture I just snapped of an antique coin press. It was used to make gold coins during gold-rush days. I'm positive Doane had one of these, or a similar model, in his car recently."

Now she had Venable's full attention. "'Positive' is a strong word."

"As positive as I can be without actually seeing the machine in the trunk. Pass this photo along to the forensic team going over Doane's car in Atlanta right now. They'll back me up if they compare it to the impressions and scratches on the trunk and backseat. This thing was disassembled into three major parts and moved. That's why there was gold dust on the scene. It had probably been caught in the press's inner workings for over a century."

"Okay, good. I'll see what we can find out about it. I'm not sure what it will do for us, though."

"I'm not sure either, but we're not exactly swimming in leads. I'm excited that we managed to find this one."

"I'm a little excited myself." He paused. "So are you coming in? We have a lot to talk about."

Kendra eyed the tattered journal protruding from the oversized pocket of Margaret's jacket. "Not quite yet."

"Why not?" His voice held a trace of urgency. Or was she just imagining it?

"The amount of gold dust we saw in Doane's car leads me to think maybe the press had never been moved before. It may have come from an old bank or mint around here. While your people are researching this, we'll do some looking around ourselves."

"Kendra, I'm really not sure that's the best—"

"Will you call Jane and tell her what Margaret and I found out? How is she doing?"

"Very well. The doctors gave her a pass out of the hospital, and I imagine you might see her before I do."

"That's great. But a surprise. She was pretty sick."

"They wouldn't have released her if she wasn't much better."

"Yeah, I guess so. I'm transmitting the photo now. Thanks, Venable."

She cut the connection and turned to Margaret. "Jane's out of the hospital. Venable says she's doing well and that we can probably expect her to show up."

"I'll be glad to see her," Margaret said. "She needs to be here helping to find Eve. It was hurting her to feel that helpless."

"If she's back on her feet, then she'll probably be trying to forge ahead like a bulldozer."

Margaret smiled faintly. "Like you, Kendra?"

"Maybe. But we'd go at problems from different directions."

"Will Venable cooperate?" Margaret asked. "He sounded a little surly."

"He'll cooperate." She thought about it. She was becoming slightly uneasy about

Venable. "He wants to find Eve. He just likes his own way."

"Don't we all." She wrinkled her nose. "And my way is to get to a motel where I can take a shower. I desperately need it after what we've gone through since we landed in Colorado."

"I'll second the motion," Kendra said. "We've had enough sleep in the car, but I feel filthy, too." She headed for the car. "Then we'll get on the move and see what we can find out about antique coin presses."

CHAPTER

14

Kendra's phone rang as she was getting dressed after her shower.

Jane.

She picked up. "I heard that you were released from the hospital. How are you feeling?"

"Fine," Jane said curtly. "I'd feel better if you and Margaret hadn't decided to go incommunicado on me. You could have called me back."

"You were ill. We didn't want to upset you. If there had been anything definite that you should know, we'd have called you."

"I'd say almost getting blown up in Doane's house would qualify as something I should know." She sighed wearily. "I'm sorry. I'm just so damn frustrated. Everyone was just trying to protect me, but I had no right to be protected when everyone else was in danger."

"No one is in danger now. We haven't seen Blick since Goldfork. And I did tell Venable to call you and tell you everything we'd found out. He said you were probably on your way out here by now. Where are you?"

"We're at the Atlanta airport. We'll get to Denver around midnight. So after we rent a car and drive down, it'll probably be sunrise by the time we get to you."

"We?"

"I'm with Seth Caleb and Mark Trevor. What about this coin press? You think Doane got it from somewhere around there?"

"I think it's a decent possibility. It's gold-rush country. They had coin presses. His radio was set on this listening area."

"Why would he want a gold press?"

"The more I consider it, I'm leaning toward wondering why he might want to get rid of a coin press." She paused. "And where he got rid of it from."

Silence. "Eve," Jane whispered. "He wanted to prepare a place for her. Maybe it was in his way."

"That's my guess. Margaret and I are going to be driving around the area and talking to locals and trying to find out about any known coin presses. I asked Venable to try to find out anything he could about them and let me know. Maybe you could help cover a couple of the mining tourist spots when you get here."

"Fine. We're going to stop before we leave Denver and talk to a friend of Trevor's who works in the forestry department of the university. He says he's more familiar with the forests in this area than anyone else in the world. What else can I do?"

"I have no idea. The same thing we're doing? Playing it by ear. You're on your own, Jane."

"Did you access photos of that sketch of mountain country I sent you?"

"Yes, none of it looks familiar. I'll keep it in mind if I run across anything like it."

"I know it sounded bizarre, but don't discard it because of that. We can't afford to discard anything that might help."

"Look, I'm traveling around with your

friend, Margaret, who evidently communicates with sundry creatures from field and stream, and I hardly question it anymore. What's more bizarre than that?"

"Where can we reach you?"

"We'll be traveling, as I said, but we'll answer the phone. I promise." She added, "I have a feeling we're close, Jane."

"I hope you're right. You've **got** to be right. And you're damn right you'll answer the phone. We've got to work together from now on. No one protects anyone but Eve. I'll call you if I learn anything." She hung up.

Kendra pressed the disconnect. Jane had sounded worried but strong, very strong, she thought. Clearly the medical staff at the hospital had been right in dismissing her.

And there would be no way anyone would succeed in trying to keep her from the battle.

Vancouver

"The information," Joe said softly. "I won't ask you again, Weiner. I want that tower area."

"I can't tell you." Weiner moistened his lips and glanced nervously at Stang. "Why did you bring him here? You know I can't talk to him. You know what Zander will do to me."

"Yes, but I thought it worthwhile," Stang said. "Tell him." He smiled. "And then get the hell out of here and hope Zander doesn't decide to make an example of you. He may not think chasing you down is worth his time."

"What about you?" Weiner said viciously. "Do you think he won't go after you?"

"No, because I'm not going anywhere." He grimaced. "I decided that it was time I stopped operating in a holding pattern where Zander was concerned." He glanced at Joe. "I'm not sure if Quinn is as lethal as Zander, but I know he's highly motivated, and that could make the difference. I'd advise you to give him the information before you make him angry."

"Step away from him, Stang," Joe said impatiently. "I don't have time for this. He has to talk now."

"Just trying to facilitate the matter." Stang took a step back. "I've never liked violence. It makes me—" He broke off as his cell phone rang. He gave a low whistle as he glanced down at the ID. "Zander. Remarkable." He turned and moved toward the door. "If you'll excuse me, I'll take this call. Feel free to carry on without me."

"The hell I will." He gave Weiner a cold glance. "Don't move from this room. You don't want to annoy me." He left the door open as he joined Stang outside. "I want to talk to Zander."

"No, he won't want to talk to you. He'll hang up. I'll compromise and put the call on speaker." He pressed the access. "Hello, Zander. This is unexpected. What can I do for you?"

"You're damn right it's unexpected. I'm sending you coordinates where I am right now. I want you to contact Dr. Eland and bring him here. Pronto."

"Someone is hurt?"

"Me. Compound wrist fracture. Nasty. I've been trying to set it myself, but I keep blacking out, dammit."

"Imagine that."

"You imagine. It's very clear and real to me after spending seven and a half hours climbing from that damn mine shaft."

"What?"

"Long story. You have to come in from the north, not the south. Get a helicopter and land on the opposite side of the mountain with the stream running through it. Then trek overland to these coordinates. No flyovers in that copter. And stay away from the south, or you'll blow everything."

"You keep saying you," Stang said. "You want me to come, too?"

Zander was silent. "Yes, I want you to come."

"Extraordinary."

"Just get Eland here within the next few hours. I have to get on the move. I don't know how much time I have."

"Eve Duncan?"

"I think she's alive. I couldn't find the body." He hung up.

"He **thinks** she's alive?" Joe said. "Call him back."

"Not if you want to find him at the coordinates he gave me." He pulled the door closed behind him. "Which you're now not going to have to pull out of Weiner. Convenient timing for him." He strode toward the car. "I'm sure he's extremely grateful."

He followed Stang. "Give me your phone. I want those coordinates."

"You'll get them when I give them to the pilot who takes us to Zander."

"I could take your phone from you."

"You could, but I'd fight. Since I've been wonderfully cooperative, I don't believe you'd want to hurt me unless there was no other way to save your Eve." He got into the driver's seat. "And there's a better way if Zander feels like cooperating. Evidently he's at least interacting with her if he knows she's not dead. He's ahead of you in all this, and that might make a difference. You go into that area without knowing what's happening, and you might start something rolling that proves fatal for Eve."

Joe was silent. Then he gave a low curse. "I don't want you to be right, dammit."

"Because you want to be totally in control, and now you may have to depend a little on Zander."

"A very little." He fell silent again, trying to see some other way that made sense. "He wanted you there in a couple hours. He must have thought it possible."

"Yes." He glanced at Joe as he pulled away from the curb. "And it's my job to make it possible. Three hours, and you may be near where Doane is keeping Eve. Think about that instead of having to work with Zander."

Three hours.

Joe felt a sudden rush of excitement as he thought about that short time span. He was close. In three hours, she would be near after all this agony he'd gone through. What the hell was he thinking? Who knows what she had gone through, what she was still going through?

"Let's move," he said crisply. "What about this Dr. Eland? Are you going to have any trouble rousting him out of his bed?"

"No." Stang reached for his phone. "Zander has an arrangement with him. He comes when called. I'll call him and tell him to meet us at the airport. Then I'll phone the pilot of Zander's jet and tell him the same thing."

"And does he come when called, too?"

"Of course, it would be dangerous for Zander to take a chance on someone who would fail him. He wouldn't tolerate it."

"You're failing him. You're taking me with you. What will Zander do to you?"

"I'm not failing him. I'm just entering into the picture instead of just staying on the sidelines."

"And you think that Zander will make that distinction?"

"I have no idea." He smiled. "But if he doesn't, I'll have you there to protect me."

"Don't count on it."

"But I do count on it," Stang said as he dialed the phone. "You're one of the good guys who should know better but don't. I knew it the minute I saw you in that library. That's why I took a chance on doing what I wanted to do without its interfering with—" He broke off and spoke into the phone, "Stang, Dr. Eland. Sorry to wake you, but we have a possible situation that Zander needs . . ."

Denver International Airport

"You'd better be prepared for a big payback, Trevor," Professor Hansen said sourly. "I can't believe you talked me into schlepping out to the airport at midnight to see this sketch."

"I'm prepared," Trevor said. "It's worth it if you can identify the area."

Hansen held out his hand and took the sketch. He studied it for a moment, then shook his head. "It's . . . familiar. But I can't identify the area for certain."

"You're sure?" Jane's hands clenched into fists. She had been hoping against hope. "Perhaps somewhere in Mineral County?"

Hansen frowned. "Maybe . . ." Then he shook his head again. "Wild country. It's my kind of country. I think I would have remembered it if I'd ever seen it before." His tone softened as he saw Jane's expression. "Sorry. Look, I'll go back to my lab and look through my photos in the computer. Maybe it will jog my memory." He turned and shook Trevor's hand. "I'll remember that you owe me. Expect a call." He turned and left.

"Zero," Caleb said. "You struck out, Trevor."

"And it could have been a home run," Trevor said coolly. "We have to try every avenue. What have you done lately except fly that airplane?" He looked at Jane. "I could go check out a few more sources in the forestry department at the university, but Hansen is the best man I know."

"That doesn't mean someone else might

not have been in that particular place at some time. It's a big country."

"It's your call."

She thought about it. She was tired of searching through books and making calls on the off chance a dream might have some basis in reality. "Yes, send e-mails and make phone calls, but we're not going to track anyone down for face-to-face interviews. I want to get out in those mountains and see for myself. Kendra actually sounded hopeful." She added wearily, "God, I need hope."

"I think a little of that is beginning to stir," Caleb's gaze was fixed on her face. "I feel it."

She tried to look away from him. Dammit, she could feel her body's response begin to heighten, heat, as it seemed to do whenever she was near him now. He had warned her, and it had come to pass.

Get over it. Once she became accustomed to the reaction, then it would surely lessen, and she could ignore it. "Well, I don't feel it."

"You will," he said softly. "It's buried deep, but it's coming to the surface. It might be

Kendra, or it might be instinct, or your Eve trying to reach you. Who knows? As I said, it's there, I feel it."

And looking at him, she realized she was beginning to feel it, too. The tiny flowering of hope and a deeper excitement mixed with determination. Of course, Caleb's effect on her always had hypnotic elements connected with it, but this was different. This came from within, and she welcomed it. She tore her gaze away from him and got to her feet. "Maybe you're right. At any rate, we're not going to get anywhere by sitting here."

Trevor nodded. "For once, I hope Caleb is right." He smiled. "It pains me to say that, but I hate the worry and the pain. I want you over it. It hurts me."

Glowing, golden, magnetism. Nothing dark or burning or hypnotic about Trevor. She drew a deep breath as she looked at him. It was like being held in velvet, protected, knowing that he would keep all pain and sadness from her path. Why had she turned away from him and walked away?

"I'll go get the car," Caleb said. "All this

sentiment is making me a little nauseous."

"I can see how it would," Jane said as she grabbed her bag. "Well, suck it up, Caleb. You'll get over it."

"Will I?" His brows rose. "We'll have to see."

"Not me. I could care less." She moved toward the terminal exit. She was suddenly brimming with strength, determination, and the beginnings of excitement. For the first time since she had learned of Eve's loss, Jane felt as if she was coming out of the darkness and heading toward her. Irrational? It didn't matter. She'd take it and run with it.

Caleb smiled faintly as he motioned toward the door. He said softly, "Told you so."

Pueblo, Colorado
Fourth Street

This section of the city was filthy, Blick thought in disgust. Bums lying in alleys.

Dealers peddling their dope on street corners.

Whores in short skirts and four-inch
heels strolling along, swinging their hips at
the men in cars cruising slowly by.

No class.

Blick knew this type of slum well. When
he'd joined the Army, before he had met
Kevin, he had often frequented the pot-
houses and whorehouses of whatever city
was near his base. It didn't matter whether
it was Detroit or Istanbul, they were all the
same.

But Kevin had changed all of that. He
had shown Blick new ways of pleasure,
new ways of power. He'd found himself
unable to go back to the old ways. He had
to follow the path Kevin had laid out for
him. Not often since he'd lost Kevin. He
had found himself too afraid to be as bold
as Kevin had been.

He could feel his eyes sting with tears. I
don't want to do this, Kevin. I know it's not
your way. But your father says it's the only
way that we can punish him.

He swallowed hard. He had been angry
with Doane since he'd received that phone
call. Doane had been ordering him around
and telling him that he was not doing anything right since it had begun. He was the

one who had been making mistakes, and Blick had been forced to risk his neck and change his plans and jump when Doane told him to do it.

It couldn't last much longer. Blick wouldn't let Doane give him orders. He only permitted Kevin to tell him what to do. Kevin was the master.

But he would do this last task for Doane because it might be the only way to get vengeance for Kevin. If Doane blundered and failed to make his fine plans work, then Blick would go his own way. He would find Zander and kill him himself.

After punishing Doane for failing Kevin.

His glance wandered over the street, with its filth that Kevin had found so unworthy.

Where to start . . .

The guy with pink-streaked hair and piercings in his nose and lip who was leaning against the wall and talking to a thin, young kid whose intensity was obvious. Drugs. He was trying to score, and the guy with the piercings was a dealer.

He pulled over to the curb and got out of the car. A dealer and an addict.

That's where Blick could start.

Ghost Town

This was truly a ghost town, Eve thought, as her gaze traveled over the barren streets and wood buildings, some of which were still standing and others that had fallen down. She could almost feel the lonely abandonment that was echoing through the town.

But the saloon was still standing. So maybe Zander had been telling the truth about being here and putting the extra weapon and phone under the bar in the saloon.

"You're very quiet," Doane said mockingly as he stopped the truck and turned off the ignition. "Don't you like your new home away from home? I was considering bringing you to this place first, but I decided the coin factory was safer, and it was easier to convert to my purpose."

"Yes, I imagine it would be difficult to install those gas vents in the ceiling of that saloon over there," she said dryly. "But it appears to be in one piece. Is that where you're taking me?"

"We may end up there, but I've decided that old barbershop down the street will better suit your purpose." He jumped out of the driver's seat and came around to the passenger seat. "Get out."

She jumped out of the truck onto the muddy street. The rain had stopped, but the cold mud was covering her shoes, and water was running rivulets down the dirt street. The rain had stopped, but the wind was still damp and chill as it touched her wet body. She was still soaked to the skin. When they'd stopped at the coin factory, Doane had not permitted her to change or even grab the few remaining garments that she'd left there when she'd escaped. The only things he'd taken from the factory were some of her tools and equipment, then he bundled her into the truck to bring her here. After handcuffing her to the steering wheel, he'd run back to the factory on some business of his own and not come back for a good twenty minutes. Then he'd driven down the mountain, slipping and sliding most of the way, even in this truck.

She stood there gazing at the ancient ruin of a town. People full of hope had once lived here and built their dreams. Now there was only desolation and loneliness.

A wolf howled in the foothills.

"I told you that the wolves would be after your Kevin," Eve said maliciously. "He can't get away from them. They're even following him down to this shambles of a town."

"Shut up about those wolves."

The idea of wolves devouring his beloved Kevin evidently bothered him. It was something to store and remember. "Barbershop?" Her gaze wandered down the street until she spotted a small wooden structure with a red, white, and blue barber pole that was hanging from a broken metal arm and looked slightly drunken. "It's very small."

"You don't need anything bigger." He grabbed the huge sack of equipment he'd taken from the coin factory. Then his hand was grasping her elbow and half pushing her down the street. "You're sculpting a skull, and you're no Michelangelo."

It wouldn't hurt to try to change his mind. "The saloon would probably still be better. It would free me to move around the reconstruction and I'd have more room to—"

"No." Doane said. "I'm not letting you more than a few feet away from me until you've finished that reconstruction. I don't want you to have room." He pushed the door of the barbershop open and shoved her inside.

Dust everywhere. Two ancient-looking barber chairs with cracked-leather seats. A broken mirror facing the chairs. "I can't work in conditions like this."

"You can and will." He opened the sack and pulled out the dais he'd taken off the worktable at the factory. He placed it on the seat of one of the barber chairs, then took off his backpack and pulled out the skull. He gently placed it on the dais. "Repair the damage you've done. Then finish him, Eve."

"I don't have enough light."

He pulled out a flashlight, and the dimness in the barbershop suddenly disappeared. He leveled his gun at her. "Finish him."

She hesitated, staring at him. She was cold, wet, exhausted, and discouraged. Why not refuse and let it end? Why was it worth going on with a battle she wasn't sure she wanted to win?

"I can see what you're thinking. I'm not going to let you do this to us, Eve. I've got to give Kevin what he needs, what he wants." His lips tightened. "And if you make me kill you, then I'll go after everyone you love. I warned you about that. You'll be responsible."

"I won't be responsible. I won't accept your sins, Doane."

But his words had reminded her that the battle was worth winning. If not for her, then for Joe and Jane.

And Bonnie.

Perhaps even for Zander, who could not be as evil as Kevin and Doane and might have furnished her with a path to freedom if she could get to that saloon.

So finish the damn reconstruction and try to get there as soon as possible.

"I'll finish him," she said curtly. "But I'm shaking, and my hands aren't steady. You were so eager to punish me that you didn't think about that when you jerked me down here without letting me dry off and change. Take off your jacket and give me your shirt."

"What?"

"My pants will still be wet, but the tails of your shirt will cover me almost to my knees." She kicked off her shoes. The floor was cool, but at least it wasn't as bad as feeling as if her feet were encased in ice from the mud. "Do it if you want me to be able to work."

He didn't move for a moment. Then he cursed as he shrugged out of his coat and began unbuttoning his shirt. "You deserved freezing your ass."

"We don't all get what we deserve, or you'd be in hell with your son." She took the flannel shirt he handed her, took off her own wet cotton shirt, and slipped on his shirt. It was warm from his body, but she received no comfort from it. She tried to block out the thought that he had been wearing it, the scent of him, the warmth that was coming from Doane and surrounding her.

It wasn't what she'd felt when Zander had put his vest around her, she thought suddenly. There had been no rejection with Zander. She still could not be certain whether or not he was an enemy. But she had accepted what he had given.

Given. That was the difference. He might be an enemy or a reluctant ally, but he had given to her.

And she was taking from Doane even though the thought made her ill.

But she had to survive. She **would** survive.

So take whatever she needed and get on with it.

She braced herself and turned to face the skull on the dais.

You've been waiting for me, haven't you, Kevin?

"Go on," Doane said impatiently. "Start it."

Kill you. Kill her.

Oh, yes, you've been waiting. But you won't kill me, and you won't destroy my Bonnie. I'll give you a little victory here, but you're going to stay in hell, and your father will be following you soon.

A huge wave of nausea hit her.

She fought it off.

Is that all you've got? I'm used to it now. Pretty soon, I won't notice it at all.

"Get to work." Doane was frowning. "Kevin is getting angry."

"As if I cared." Eve picked up a spatula and began to smooth the left side of Kevin's cheek. "He's dead, and he has no power any longer. He's getting weaker all the time."

"No!"

"And so are you, Doane."

"Am I?"

There was an odd note in his voice that caused her to stop. She turned to look at him.

Evil.

Strong, twisted, and full of fury.

And strangely alien.

Kevin. Not Doane. Kevin.

She inhaled sharply.

Then that impression faded, vanished.

And it was again Doane, vicious, also evil, but not alien. "You don't know what you're talking about," Doane said. "I have the gun. I have the power. I'm not weak, Eve."

Not when Kevin was that close, slipping over boundaries he shouldn't have been able to breach. That moment had frightened her. Doane was possibly changing, taking on Kevin's evil as well as his own.

"Evil isn't power." She turned back to the reconstruction. "You're both weak, Doane. You'll find that out soon. Now leave me alone so that I can finish this reconstruction. I want to be done with him."

"You'll never be done with him, Eve."

"Oh, but I will. I'll be done with both of you."

Work.

Hands smoothing, repairing, healing what should never be healed.

Give Doane what he wanted, then take what she wanted.

Find a way to get to that saloon.

Highway 145
Southern Colorado

"Did you find another town?" Margaret asked as she glanced at Kendra in the passenger seat. Kendra's fingers were flying over her phone's touch screen. "I admit I'm getting a little discouraged. We've already hit three gold-rush towns, and all we've come up with are souvenir mugs and guys trying to teach us how to mine gold."

"And you bought a mug at every place we stopped."

"I like souvenir mugs. They're usually funny or pretty and remind me of where I've been. Most memories are good, and during the bad times, you pull out one of those mugs and drink to the good times." She made a face. "But I may be stockpiling a few too many gold-rush mugs if we don't get more productive."

"Patience." Kendra studied the screen. "There are old gold-rush towns all over this area, and it looks like several of them had their own coinages."

Margaret's brows rose. "That popular? They could make real money?"

"Yes, according to what I'm reading here, anyone could set up their own coin factory. Private banks could do it. As long as the coins were made of real gold, it was legal tender. It was only after the early 1860s that currency had to be made in the official U.S. mints."

"So what's the plan? Are we going to visit every gold-rush town and antique dealer in Colorado?"

"I'm hoping that Venable and his resources at the CIA will be able to track down this specific model of coin press and narrow the field a bit. But there are a couple more old gold-rush towns nearby that are still standing and open to tourists. Since we have a pretty good idea that Doane was in this area recently, we might as well hit them, too."

"Okay, maybe they'll have different

mugs for my collection. How far is the nearest one?"

"About fifty yards."

"What?"

Kendra pointed ahead to a wooden sign on the right reading DRAKEBURY SPRINGS. "Turn here."

They followed a winding road that curved up to a parking lot packed with tour buses, SUVs, and RVs. It was a scene of bustling activity, contrasting with the almost desolate highway on which they had been traveling.

"It's like Disneyland up here," Kendra said, as they passed a fleet of parents pushing strollers. They parked and walked to a small kiosk, where they paid a donation and were given maps of the town, which was essentially a single street two blocks long.

They walked down a dirt road and passed two costumed actors pretending to be drunk prospectors. The men had attracted a crowd as each actor tried to outdo the other with their painful renditions of the song "In the Good Old Summertime."

"These buildings don't look very old,"

Margaret said, eyeing a general store where a woman in pioneer attire was selling cotton candy.

"They're not old. None of them are. I don't think any of these were built more than fifteen years ago."

"So what's the point?"

"The point? To make money, to draw tourists to hotels and restaurants nearby. The whole thing looks like a reconstruction. We may be wasting our time."

Margaret was studying the map. "The bank is up ahead and on the left."

A few minutes later, they were entering the one-story structure. There were two counters with balance scales. A chalkboard behind the counters listed the bank's current assets—circa 1857—and the buying price for gold.

Kendra shook her head. "Pretty sparse. Even if they once did make coins here, the equipment hasn't been here for a long time."

They moved down to the end of Main Street, where the town ended in a picnic area, several food vendors, and a tiny souvenir shop.

A white-bearded man in his late sixties

was working behind the counter of the souvenir shop. He looked up and smiled at Kendra and Margaret as they stepped inside. "Welcome. I'm Bill Johnson. Looking for T-shirts?"

Kendra shook her head.

"Shot glasses? Mugs? Bumper stickers? I just got some beer can cozies you might like."

"Nice color." Margaret took a yellow T-shirt from the table and slid it on over her own. She modeled the shirt, which read: STRIKE IT RICH AT DRAKEBURY SPRINGS. "I'll take this one."

The man smiled. "Looks good on you. That will be twenty dollars."

"Fifteen." Margaret smiled at him. "Or I'll pay twenty, and you can throw in that mug on the shelf over there."

He frowned. "That's nerve, little lady."

"You obviously have an overstock. I'm taking it off your hands."

He suddenly chuckled. "I do have an overstock. Twenty." He reached up and took down a mug and gave it to her. "No credit cards."

"Oh, I wouldn't use the credit card I have

for this." She reached into her pocket, pulled out a crumpled twenty-dollar bill.

Because it was Jane MacGuire's credit card, Kendra thought. She remembered Margaret had told her she wouldn't use it for anything that wasn't important.

He turned to Kendra. "What about you, young lady? You look like you could use a Drakebury Springs sun visor."

"Actually, we've just come here for information."

He glanced at Margaret and made a face. "And to steal from a poor tradesman who's only trying to earn a living."

"And had a big overstock," Margaret murmured.

He chuckled again.

It was clear Johnson liked Margaret and would have continued to banter with her. Kendra tried to get them back on track. "Information."

Johnson nodded. "You've come to the right person. My daughter wrote the book on this town. Literally." He motioned toward a paperback book displayed on the countertop. It was a thin book, obviously self-published, with the title **DRAKEBURY**

SPRINGS: HISTORY AND LEGEND. The author's name was Susan Johnson, with a young woman's picture rather immodestly placed on the front cover. "She was always crazy about gold mines and ghost towns from the time she was a kid. Always writing and drawing pictures. She's a great artist, but when she was in college, she wrote this book." He held it up and smiled proudly. "You can send it to her and have her sign it for you if you'd like."

"How much?"

"One for twenty, two for thirty."

Margaret opened her mouth to protest, and Johnson glared at her.

She changed her mind and gave him a sunny smile. "That's very inexpensive for a book that gives us a look at history. She must have worked very hard on it. By all means, let's buy it, Kendra."

"I was about to do that. I'll take one." Kendra paid him and picked up the book. "So are any of these buildings original?"

"Afraid not. The town is only a mock-up of a gold-rush town that went bust up in the mountains. Some of the stockholders of our company had ancestors who had businesses in that town and decided to capitalize on the Old West tourist craze. They built it as close to authentic to the family records as they could make it. But if you look at the photos in the book, you'll see it's a pretty good re-creation."

She glanced casually at the photos, then stopped. "What's this photo?"

"Oh, that's the original town. It's only a ghost town now. Pretty dismal, isn't it? And sad. It was in a valley surrounded by mountains that were supposed to be full of gold. The town was thriving, and everyone thought it would go on forever. But that area was mined out pretty quickly, so the town was abandoned. Too bad it all went bust because those mountain mines were in a beautiful spot. My daughter and some of her artist friends painted a mural showing the view from up there. You can see it on the side of this building, facing the picnic tables."

"Oh, we'll have to take a look at it on the way out. Would you know anything about old coin factories around here?"

"Well, there was a coinery somewhere up in the mountains near the original town, but by the time the miners moved on, they were taking their gold to Jeffreysboro."

"Jeffreysboro. Is the coin factory still there?"

He thought for a moment. "No, it was dismantled after the Civil War."

"Then where might we go to find an original coin press?"

"Well, I know there's one on display at the Denver Mint, but aside from that, I really can't say. Kind of out of my area of expertise, you know?"

Kendra nodded. "Sure. Have a good day."

"You come back now." He was looking at Margaret. "I can always use a little challenge to spark my day."

She grinned and waved her mug at him as she left the store with Kendra.

"Not much help there," Kendra said. "Waste of time. We'd better either look up some antique dealers who specialize in coin presses or move on to the next town."

"Yeah, kind of interesting though." Margaret looked down at her mug. "And not quite a waste, I got a nice mug out of it. Pretty scenery with the trees and those—" She broke off, her eyes widening. "Holy smoke."

Kendra's gaze flew to her face. "What?"

"My very pretty mug." She was staring at the mug with fascination. "It's only a little slice of a picture . . . but what does this look like to you?"

"I could tell you if you'd give it to me."

"Sorry. It just shocked me." She handed Kendra the mug. "Tell me I'm wrong."

Kendra was staring at the picture on the mug—mountains, trees . . . "Oh, my God."

"I'm not wrong?"

Kendra tried to tamp down the excitement and be objective about it. She didn't want to be objective. "Similar. But the picture on the mug is so small it's hard to . . ." Kendra was pulling her phone from her pocket. The next moment, she was accessing the sketch Jane had sent her. "It's damn close."

"I think we're there," Margaret said softly. "Bless Bill Johnson and his souvenir mugs." She took back the mug and compared it to Jane's sketch. "You're right, it's very small. We need bigger." She smiled. "And I'd bet we've got bigger. This mug must have been taken from some artist's rendering. What did Johnson say about that mural?" She was already half running toward the picnic area to get a better view of the mural on the side of the souvenir shop. She stopped short, gazing at the huge mural. "Oh, yes."

Kendra had caught up with her. "Incredible. It's the same, or so close it doesn't matter. The stream, the boulders, the mountainside, the cliff." She held up the phone to compare it to Jane's drawing. "Unreal."

"The angle is even the same." Margaret shook her head. "Are we sure Jane's never been there? Are we positive she didn't just subconsciously remember this?"

"I don't think so." Kendra took several photos of the mural, then punched in Jane's phone number and turned on the speaker. "How the hell do I know? But there's a way we can try to find out."

"Kendra. Anything happening?" Jane said when she answered. "Our interview with the forestry guru was a bust. We've left Denver, and we're heading your way. If I knew exactly where that was. You said you'd be moving around."

"And we have," Kendra said. "And right now we're in a tourist town called Drakebury Springs. We found something interesting." Hell, mind-blowing, but she was trying to keep her excitement on simmer. "I'm going to send you a photo. Okay?"

"Of course, but what—" Jane inhaled sharply. "Dear God, Kendra." She was silent a moment, and her voice was shaky when she spoke again. "There have been times in the last couple days when I thought trying to find this place was crazy. Maybe it is crazy, but it exists. It **exists.** It's everything that I—every detail." She cleared her throat. "It's obviously a painting. Can you track down the artist? Find out the exact location?"

"Are you sure this isn't a latent memory? That you haven't been there before? It's so close, Jane."

"If it's in Colorado, I've never been in the state before I landed in Denver. I know that I said I thought I might be a little crazy concerning my sketch, but I have to run with it. Now find me that artist."

"No problem. The artists painted this mural on the side of a souvenir shop, and I'll get in touch with them. I've already found the approximate location." She briefly filled Jane in on the history Bill Johnson had given them. "So that landscape is somewhere in the mountains in the vicinity of that ghost town. And there was a coin factory in that general area, too. Not in the town itself but somewhere up in the mountains close to the mines. Johnson was very vague about the exact location."

"We'll find out," Jane said. "You and Margaret have got us this far, we'll work on it from here. I'll call Venable and we'll—" She stopped, then said, "We have a chance. We can **find** her. I want to zoom up to those mountains and—" She drew a shaky breath. "But I know we can't do that. That's a good way to get Eve killed. We have to be careful. Doane can't know that we may be close to finding them."

"I'm glad you realize that," Kendra said gently. "We have to have an exact location and know what our best chance is to get her away from him before we move. No blundering around and showing our hand before we have a firm plan."

"Just listen to us," Jane said. "We haven't even found her yet. I'm hanging up and getting to work. You do the same." She paused. "Thank you, Kendra. Tell Margaret that there are no words to tell you both how much I appreciate what you've done."

"She hears you. You're on speaker.

There's no way I'd shut her out." She chuckled. "There's no way she'd let me shut her out. We'll get back to you." She hung up.

"She was happy," Margaret said. "That's good." She grinned. "And I'm glad you realize that I'm far too valuable not to be in the center of any important dealings and decisions that are taking place." Her smile suddenly vanished as she turned to look up at the mountains. "Is that where Eve is?"

"I think so. We won't know until we check maps."

"You were very serious when you were talking to Jane about moving too fast. It's happened before to you?"

She nodded. "An FBI kidnapping case. We tried to do everything right, but we still lost two children. You never know what a murderer will do when he's cornered. They panic and they kill."

"That can't happen to Eve. We can't let it." Her gaze never left the mountains. "It looks forbidding from here, doesn't it? The picture on my mug is so pretty but there's a kind of darkness . . ."

Kendra could see what she meant. Psychological? Perhaps. But she wouldn't deny the chill she was experiencing. "Then we need to get up there and chase all those shadows away." She turned back to the souvenir store. "And we can start by talking to your friend Bill Johnson and getting him to set up a meeting with his daughter and her artist friends."

CHAPTER

15

"Tears?" Trevor glanced at Jane from the driver's seat. "But, from what I caught of the conversation, not bad tears."

"I'm not crying." She touched her cheek. "Or maybe I am. But definitely not bad tears." She handed him her phone. "Kendra and Margaret struck it rich in the best possible way at that gold camp."

Trevor gazed at the photo and gave a low whistle. "If that mural weren't so crude, I'd think that you painted it from your sketch."

"May I?" Caleb reached over from the backseat and took the phone. He studied it for a moment, then returned the phone to Jane. "Okay, how do we follow up?"

"Kendra and Margaret are going to find out as much as possible about the area where the mural was painted. But they do know that a coin factory is located somewhere near the played-out mines in those mountains."

"Any recognizable point of reference?" Caleb asked.

"An abandoned ghost town. The original Drakebury Springs. It's in a valley that can be difficult to reach, and the coinery was some distance away in the mountains. But we may be able to locate it on the map and check roads going out of it into the mountains. The miners would have had a direct route from the mines and the coinery to the town."

Caleb opened his computer. "I'll start on that."

Jane nodded. "And I'll call Joe and Venable and tell them that we may be getting close to an answer." She closed her eyes for an instant. "God, that sounds wonderful. Now that we can give Venable a general direction, he's got to zero in on that coin factory."

"Anything I can do?" Trevor asked. "Or am I just a chauffeur? I admit I'm a little impatient with the role. I'm finding it less demanding than I'd like."

"It's a very important job. Just get us to Mineral County. Get us to those mountains."

Trevor glanced at her face, then slowly nodded. "Okay, I'll play any game you want me to play. It doesn't matter what I want to do. There's no way I'd let ego get in the way when there's a chance of getting this close to Eve." He added quietly, "Let me know if I can do anything else."

She smiled. "I will."

Caleb made a sound somewhere between a groan and a chuckle.

Trevor's brows rose. "You said something, Caleb?"

"No, just expressing my appreciation. You're really exceptional, Trevor."

"I wasn't trying to be. You just don't recognize sincerity."

"I recognize it. That's what's so difficult. Many times you do mean exactly what you say even when it sounds all noble and self-sacrificing."

Trevor grimaced. "Good God, I'm not noble. Are you being sarcastic?"

"I don't think I am. You irritate the hell out of me, but I'm beginning to understand you. That doesn't mean I won't try to undermine you if I get a chance. I don't have the same sterling qualities you seem to possess."

"And I understand you, Caleb. Much to my dismay," Jane said as she started dialing the phone. "Now, I'd appreciate it if you'd get to work."

"Yes, ma'am." He smiled as he bent over the keyboard. "No nobility, but I'll slave nonstop."

"Which might be termed nobility," Trevor murmured as he stepped on the accelerator. "If one wasn't picky about definitions."

Kendra stared down at the map spread out on the picnic table next to the gift shop, anchored by Margaret's coffee mug and Kendra's rolled-up jacket. Bill Johnson, the shop's proprietor, was on the phone with his artist daughter.

"Are you sure, hon? Your mural is showing us the valley just west of the old town, not east?" Johnson took the thick Sharpie pen from Kendra's hand and drew a large circle over a hilltop. He glanced at Kendra and nodded.

Kendra studied the map, trying to establish the location in relation to the town they now occupied. She turned to speak to Margaret, but the young woman had suddenly vanished. Where had she gone? she wondered impatiently.

Johnson finished the call and pocketed his phone. "That's the spot. It's several miles from the old town, up in the mountains. The ghost town sits in a sort of bowl surrounded by mountains." His finger traced a line on the ridge of the mountain slope. "Coming in from this direction, you can use this road above the old town to get to the area where she made the mural."

"Can we drive through the town itself?"

"Depends. The roads aren't the best up there, and with the storm we just had, some could be impassable right now. That's why we don't get a lot of tourists up that way. The town itself was always a muddy swamp after a heavy downpour." His finger traced a line on the map on the ridge of the mountain slope. "Coming in from here, you can use this road above the old town that bypasses the town and connects to the road that leads to that area my daughter painted."

"And where the coin factory is located?"

He shrugged. "Never been there myself, but I believe it's over this ridge." He pointed to a string of hills. "In any case, I wouldn't recommend going there right now." He checked his watch. "It'll be dark soon, and it can be dangerous trying to navigate those roads at night."

"Good advice." She grimaced. "Not welcome, but good. Thank you. You've been a huge help."

Johnson awkwardly gestured toward the map. "Uh, that'll be six dollars for the souvenir map."

"And worth every penny." Kendra paid him, and Johnson tipped his hat toward her and strolled back into his store. She immediately pulled out her phone and called Venable. "I've contacted the artist, and I believe we're on track." She filled him in on the new information Johnson had given her. "I don't like the idea of waiting until morning."

"It's the smart thing to do," Venable said quickly. "By that time, I should have an exact location for the coin factory and will be able to send up an attack team."

"No!" Kendra said. "What are you talking about? You show up with a show of force, and Eve is a dead woman. You know that Doane is crazy."

"Don't get upset," Venable said soothingly. "I know what I'm doing. I've dealt with Doane for years." He paused. "And it might be best if you let me handle the entire retrieval. You've done a fine job of gathering information, but it's time I took over. You could get in my way, Kendra."

"The hell I would," Kendra said. "You're scaring me, Venable. We're so close to being able to get Eve out of this. I won't let her die because you've gone trigger-happy."

Venable was silent. "You're right. Perhaps a more subtle, indirect, approach is best. I'll work on locating that coin factory and get back to you." He hung up.

Kendra stared blindly down at the map. She should have felt reassured by those last words. She did not feel reassured; she was uneasy. As she had told Venable, he had scared her. The CIA man was experienced and intelligent and should know better than to rush an operation like the one that might be facing them. Yet his first impulse was not intelligent at all.

She was tempted to call Joe Quinn, but evidently he wasn't presently available. Jane had called her back and told her that she'd not been able to reach Quinn by phone and had sent him an e-mail.

And what could he do anyway from Vancouver? Except maybe contact Venable and make sure he'd taken Kendra's protests seriously. It would probably be fine. It was just that she'd gone through a hideous experience in the past that had not gone fine but terribly wrong.

"You're frowning."

She looked up to see Margaret coming toward her from the picnic area. "Am I? I've got to stop that. I hear it causes wrinkles. Where did you go?" She watched Margaret drop onto the picnic bench beside her.

Margaret raised Kevin's journal. "I wanted to go someplace where I could concentrate on this. You seemed to have things under control here." She grinned. "Though I don't know how you could manage without my invaluable help."

"It was a terrible burden. But I now know where we're headed. We'll check into a hotel and set out first thing in the morning.

Jane will be here by then, and she can come with us."

"Good. In the meantime, maybe we can give this journal a closer look." Margaret snapped the cover band of the journal. "I just read something that makes me think we were right not to give it up too quickly."

Kendra's gaze flew to her face. "What?"

"Later. While we're getting something to eat. It may be nothing, but it made me uneasy."

"Uneasy?" It was strange that Kendra had been bombarded by that same emotion only moments before. At a time when hope should have been soaring, it wasn't good that both she and Margaret were experiencing doubt and apprehensiveness.

Margaret shrugged. "It will be okay. Don't worry. We'll work through it."

"Now that's one of your typically optimistic comments that has no basis on fact or reason." Yet Kendra felt a sudden surge of gladness that Margaret was here with her, and her words were giving her both warmth and comfort. She smiled. "But you know, I'm not only becoming accustomed to them, I've started to search for some inner wisdom in them. That's pretty frightening."

Margaret giggled. "It would be more frightening if you found it." She got to her feet. "Come on, let's find someplace to eat. I need something normal and megacalorie to balance all this high-powered brain drain."

CIA Field Office
Denver, Colorado

Venable leaned forward in his chair and stared at the photograph that the young researcher, Callie Burke, had just handed him. "What exactly am I looking at?"

"It's a coin press made by McGruber Mechanics and Associates between 1848 and sometime during the Civil War. Based on the photographs and measurements taken from Doane's car in Atlanta, this is what he had been transporting. And based on how little oxidation there is on the interior trunk marks, it was probably in the past couple of weeks."

Venable nodded. "Exactly what Kendra Michaels said."

"It's a different-model coin press than in the photo she sent. But it's similar. The team in Atlanta said they wouldn't have even thought of it if she hadn't tipped us off."

Venable placed the photo on his desk. Burke, the researcher, a slender woman in her mid-twenties, was obviously eager to impress. She had gone into high gear when he'd issued an order to speed up the research after he'd received that call from Kendra. Okay, impress me. "How many of these were made?"

She shook her head. "As far as we can tell, only about fifteen were ever in use in North America. It's hard to tell how many still exist. We're still combing ads and on-line auction listings to see how many have turned up in the collectors' market. But we did find something interesting: one of these was originally used in a coinery near Drakebury Springs, Colorado."

Yes. He tried to keep her from seeing the intense interest the last bit of info generated in him. "That's why I told you to look in that area. Doane's car may have been there."

"Yes, sir. And that old coinery is still standing. It was sold as a private residence about four years ago."

"Sold to whom?"

"A holding company. We're still running it down. It's not clear if the coin press was still there, but the real-estate listing did make a lot of the fact that it was a former gold-rush coin factory with many original features intact. We're still trying to contact the property's real-estate broker to ascertain if the coin press was there."

Venable nodded. "Good work. Let me know the minute you hear something."

The researcher hurried out of the room.

But Venable would bet that coin press was no longer in the factory. He felt a rush of fierce satisfaction.

I've got him, General. He's mine. I'm going to take him down.

He quickly got off an e-mail to Kendra Michaels with the information and leaned back in his chair. He thought for a long moment, staring at the photograph on his desk. Difficulties. Kendra Michaels, Joe Quinn, Jane MacGuire. He'd have to sweep those difficulties away.

So? He was good at eliminating difficulties.

He picked up his phone and dialed a number. "I need to pull a team together right away. See about borrowing one from the FBI. Tonight. We're heading for southern Colorado."

Drakebury Springs Ghost Town
Southern Colorado

"You have him almost repaired," Doane said as he studied the skull reconstruction. "Pretty soon, we'll be ready to put in his eyes."

"Déjà vu," Eve said, her gaze on the skull.

"Yes, we're back to square one." Doane got up from the barber's chair and came over to the makeshift dais. "All your agony and running didn't get you anywhere, did it?"

"It got me somewhere. I ran you ragged. I blasted your neat little plan to kingdom come. Or you wouldn't have abandoned the coin factory and brought me to this wreck of a town."

"Are you ready for the eyes now?"

"Not yet." She had the same reluctance she'd had before when they'd come to this point. She didn't want to see those blue eyes staring at her. It didn't matter whether or not they were glass. "I have to smooth the corner of the orbital cavity. One of the cavities is deeper than—"

"Hush!" Doane's head lifted. "A car! Do you hear it?"

She listened, and her heart leaped. Let it be help. "Yes." She moistened her lips. "Why don't you take the reconstruction and get out of here? You might be able to get away before—"

"Be quiet." He was peering out the broken window. Then he started to laugh. "No threat. It's our old friend, Blick. Right on time. Even a little early. I'm glad to see he was so eager."

She tried to hide her disappointment. "Time for what?"

"Wouldn't you like to know?" He took a pair of handcuffs out of his jacket pocket. "And I promise you will know very soon." He took one of her wrists and handcuffed it to the arm of the chair on which the dais was sitting. "I have to go greet him. I wouldn't want you to slip away on me."

"I can't work this way."

"I'll give you a little rest. Isn't that kind of me? This is more important."

"The car has stopped. I don't hear it any longer."

"Yes." Doane strolled to the window. "He's getting a little ahead of me. As I said, eager. I must join him and make sure that everything is as I want it." He headed for the door. "I'll be back soon. Now, you keep Kevin company."

The next moment, he had left the barbershop, and she heard his footsteps on the wooden sidewalk.

Why the hell was Blick here? And why was she even wondering, she thought wearily. Contending with Blick couldn't be worse than dealing with Doane. Blick was an unknown quantity, but she knew what a monster Doane could be.

For a moment, she had hoped that car might be salvation, or at least a passerby who might possibly change the equation. Deal with the disappointment.

And deal with the fact that she was handcuffed only scant inches from Kevin's skull.

Panic. There was no sense to it when she had been working this close to him all day. But she hadn't been chained and helpless before this. It made a difference.

Her heart was pounding, and she could feel the chill and nausea starting.

It was like being stretched on an altar to be sacrificed and not be able to escape.

Block him out. Doane would return soon.

Block Kevin out.

Blick was just coming out of the saloon when Doane strolled across the street from the barbershop. "You're very prompt, Blick. I trust you did exactly what I told you?"

"You say that as if you have the right to tell me what to do," Blick said sourly. "You had nothing to do with it. It was what Kevin would have wanted."

"You're right. We're both doing what my son would do if he were here." He looked beyond Blick at the door of the saloon. "Inside?"

"Yes," Blick said. "And it wasn't easy. Where's the Duncan woman?"

Doane jerked his head toward the barbershop. "She has a duty to do before I bring her here. But she's almost finished."

"You put me through a lot of trouble. It had better be worth it. How can you be sure that she wasn't safe up at the factory?"

"I'm not sure. But when she pulled a knife out of nowhere, I just had a hunch that things weren't as they should be."

"A hunch?"

"Kevin would know what I meant. And approve. Did you learn so little from him, Blick?" Doane could see that the barb struck home. He should really pull back, but he didn't give a damn. "But then you were more of an acquaintance, not kin. You couldn't understand Kevin."

"That's not true." Blick's face was flushed with anger. "He trusted me, he taught me."

"But I didn't need teaching," Doane said. "He was my son, one soul, Blick."

"No, he thought you were a fool. He used you."

Doane felt a bolt of pure rage and struggled to control it. "I'll forgive that poison from you, Blick. We mustn't have a break now, when we're so close to the goal."

"I don't need your forgiveness," Blick said roughly. "I've done my job, and now I'm going up to those trees in the foothills and set up. And you'd better be right, Doane."

"You're not going anywhere yet," Doane said. "Not until you show me how well you did your job. I've got to make sure you haven't made any slips." He strode toward the door to the saloon and threw it open. "After that, you can do whatever you want to do." He glared back at Blick over his shoulder. "Coming?"

Blick hesitated.

Doane waited. He'd said enough to play on Blick's pride. Don't say any more.

Come on, you son of a bitch.

Then Blick was moving toward him. "I didn't make any slips."

"Perhaps I wasn't being fair." Doane smiled as he stepped aside for Blick to enter the saloon ahead of him. "But I'm ready for show-and-tell, Blick."

Southern Colorado

"How are you doing?" Trevor glanced sideways at Jane in the passenger seat as she charted their course on her tablet computer. "You seem to be holding up pretty well. We've been on the road a long time since we left Atlanta."

"Good. Better than good, actually. Amazing."

She shot a glance in the rearview mirror at Caleb, who met her eyes and smiled. The smile was subtle and carefully not too self-satisfied but she knew exactly what he was thinking. She wanted to slap him. If only she didn't feel so wonderfully alive. Is this how it always felt to be him? Was Caleb's blood so different that even the little he had given her would serve to give her this exotic sense of excitement and exhilaration?

"I daresay she's never felt better, Trevor," Caleb said quietly. "I do good work."

"That remains to be seen," Trevor said. "If it's true, then I couldn't be more happy. I just don't trust quick fixes."

"Neither do I. But I'd rather fix the problem and go back and do it again if there's a breakdown. I'm far from perfect, but I can usually piece together a successful outcome." He tilted his head. "While you are probably close to perfect but not nearly as interesting." He thought about it. "Except to people who like the idea of safety and happily ever after. There are those rare souls who cling to that scenario and can't be pried away from it. Tell me, Jane, how do you feel about it?"

"I feel that we should be getting close to our destination," Jane said. "And that I'm in no mood to think about anything but getting to that hotel where we're supposed to meet Kendra and Margaret."

"Then let's think about them." Caleb leaned forward and rested his crossed arms on the front car seats. "You said we were close?"

"Yes." She checked the GPS app on her tablet. "The hotel is just ahead."

After another couple minutes, they rounded a bend in the highway to see the welcome sight of the Iron Peak Hotel. But as they pulled into the parking lot, Jane suddenly stiffened in shock.

"What's **he** doing here?"

Venable.

He was standing next to a dozen men attired in standard-issue, black, assault-team garb: flak jackets, baseball caps, and boots.

"What the hell? Stop the car!"

Trevor hit the brake, and Jane was out of the Jeep before it even stopped moving. She was standing before Venable with clenched fists seconds later. "What's going on?"

Venable's eyes widened at the sight of her. "Jane. It's good to see you looking so well. Your doctors told me that you were being released, but I had no idea that you were this far along."

"I'm fine," she said curtly. "Now what's happening here?"

"We have reason to believe Doane may be nearby with Eve."

"And you also believe that steamrolling in with a small army is your best bet? Doane is insane. Who should know that better than you? If he feels trapped, who knows what he'll do."

"Do you have a better alternative?"

"How about the alternative I've been suggesting." Kendra Michaels appeared from the other side of the black-paneled vans. "Leave the battalion behind and go in stealth with a smaller team."

Jane moved toward her. "Did you bring him into this?"

"No, there's no way we'd refuse help if it was a reasonable offer. I told him this wasn't the way to handle it, and I thought he was listening." She gestured to Venable.

"Margaret and I woke up to find them here using the lobby as a staging area. Kind of a nasty way to start a day."

"Only doing my duty," Venable said sarcastically. "Funny what passes for gratitude these days. Jane, I'm sure Quinn would agree that every means has to be used to get Eve back."

Jane stared at him in bewilderment. "Not every means. Not if it's this risky. I respect you, Venable. You're not stupid. Why are you doing this?"

"We have a different opinion. Mine is based on more experience than you'll ever have."

Jane gave up and turned to Kendra. "Is Margaret still with you?"

"She's bringing the car around. We were planning to meet you down the road."

"Why?" Venable asked. "You weren't planning on doing anything stupid?"

"No, you've got that covered," Kendra said.

"Problem?" Caleb climbed out of the Jeep.

"Maybe," Jane said.

Venable held up his hands. "Look, a stealth operation is easier said than done.

The road up the mountain to the coin factory goes along the ridge around that ghost town; it's narrow, and you can see it from miles away. You could be picked off with no problem. We need power and intimidation if we're going to make a deal."

Kendra glanced at the black-clad team. "Well, you've got enough for that."

"Enough to send Doane into a killing fit," Jane said. "If that's what you believe, why are you still here?"

"We have another unit coming in from Wyoming, right across the border. They should be here any minute."

Kendra nodded. "By all means, all you need is another dozen or so." She got into the rental car in which Margaret had just pulled up. "Good luck, Venable. I hope to hell you don't get Eve killed."

"That's not my intention." Venable's eyes were narrowed on Kendra. "And what do you intend to do?"

"Why should I tell you? You appear to like surprises. You sure gave us one this morning," Kendra said. "Maybe we're going to do a little sightseeing." Kendra motioned to Trevor, who was still behind the wheel. "Follow us."

Trevor nodded as Jane and Caleb climbed into the car.

Both cars turned wide to exit the parking lot.

As Jane looked back, it was to see Venable still standing there, and she could see his lips moving in what must be obscenities.

A mile and a half down the road, Margaret slowed to allow the Jeep to pull alongside.

"We're going to that coin factory?" Jane said.

"That's where I'm going. Your choice."

"There's no choice. Eve might be there." Jane's lips curved in the ghost of a smile. "And I have to see if that landscape really looks the way I drew it."

"From the mural, it appears that's already established," Margaret said. "You did well, Jane."

"And Eve could be held there," Kendra said. "I'd bet the coin press in Doane's car was from that coin factory. It's all coming together." She frowned. "And I'd wait for Quinn or Venable to make the first move, but I'm scared to death what Venable may do. I want to be there to see for myself.

Maybe I can stop him if he knows someone else is there but his team."

"I agree that this is a crazy idea of Venable's," Jane said, troubled. "But in spite of
your opinion of him, he's no fool."

Kendra was silent. "No, he's not. But
what if he's more interested in nailing
Doane than saving Eve? From that per-
spective, wouldn't his plan make perfect
sense?"

"That's a strong accusation, Kendra."

"It's a strong hunch, Jane."

And Jane believed in hunches. She also
couldn't stand the thought of waiting and
deferring to anyone else when she could
be on the spot, moving and using her own
judgment when it came to the person she
loved.

She hesitated, then glanced at Caleb
and Trevor. "I'm going to break a few rules
and probably get in trouble with the CIA.
Would you care to join me?"

Caleb smiled. "Venable has always
been suspicious of me anyway. It's only a
tiny step from suspicion to conviction in
the eyes of the CIA. I might as well push
him over the line. Trevor?"

"I've become accustomed to being your

chauffeur. What would you do without me?" Trevor said. "Point the way."

"Good God." Jane grimaced. "They actually agreed on something, Kendra. That may either be a celestial sign from above, or we may be in deep, deep shit."

"Okay," Kendra said. "You can handle it. I'll lead the way." She looked behind them. "But we'd better hurry. I want to be up at that coin factory when Venable gets there." She started the car. "And if we hang out here too long, I have a feeling Venable will try to stop us." She added sarcastically, "Purely for our own good and safety, of course."

Rio Grande Forest
Colorado

"It took over four hours, not three," Joe said as he pushed his way through the wet brush. "Zander was wrong."

"It might not have been four for him," Stang said as he checked to see if Dr. Eland was making good speed behind him as he followed Joe through the forest. "And we're getting close to the coordinates Zander gave us."

Joe nodded. "Jane sent me an e-mail while we were flying in here when she couldn't reach me by phone. This is the same region that Kendra Michaels told her was a high probability for where Eve might be held." He added impatiently, "We're closing in on Doane. But not fast enough, dammit." His pace increased. "And where is Zander? We should almost be where he told us to meet him."

"May I suggest you let me go first?" Stang said. "If he sees you, he may decide not to show. He doesn't like surprises."

"No, I don't," Zander said as he dropped down from the overhanging branch over the path ahead. He was cradling a rifle in his right arm. He added coldly, "Which begs the question, why the hell did you bring Quinn, Stang?"

"He wanted to come," Stang said simply. "And since I'd already done a good many things that would make you angry with me, I thought one more wouldn't do any harm."

"The hell it won't. He'll be in my way."

"Tough," Joe said. "I don't give a damn if I get in the way of your vendetta with Doane. I just have to make sure you don't catch Eve in the cross fire."

"She's not stupid, and she can take care of herself."

Joe stiffened. "You said that with confidence. You've seen her, talked to her?"

Zander didn't answer.

Joe was next to him in seconds. "Answer me. Or so help me, I'll break your neck."

"Quinn," Stang said warningly.

"It's okay, Stang," Zander said. "I won't hurt him."

Joe stared at him incredulously. "You're damn right you won't."

"Not because you don't deserve it," Zander said. "But I understand you can be lethal, and with this broken wrist, even if I put you down, you could probably do me more damage than I can afford right now." He stared him directly in the eye. "So I'll have to endure you until this is over. Providing you don't do anything that will keep me from taking out Doane."

"Have you seen or talked to Eve?" Joe repeated. "Do you still think she's alive?"

He nodded slowly. "The chase was pretty rough and the signs are that he caught her; but there was no body, so that probably means he didn't kill her. But he's got her again."

"Again? She was free?"

"She'd escaped and been on the run from him for the past few days."

Joe cursed. "Son of a bitch."

"Can we get to her?" Stang asked.

"Maybe. If I move fast enough," Zander said. "He may suspect, but he doesn't know for certain that Eve has help on the mountain. She'd be too smart to tell him." He was silent a moment. "Or perhaps too damn protective. He wants to finish the plans he made for her before he heads in my direction." He grimaced. "Which, hopefully, he thinks is Vancouver."

"Protective?" Stang asked. "Of you? Why should—"

"Zander, I'm going to charge you a small fortune for this idiocy." Dr. Daniel Eland had emerged from the shrubbery behind them. "Not only do you drag me out of bed and my own country, but you throw me into these woods and make me walk miles to get to you." Eland was glaring at Zander. He was a tall, spare man with gray-flecked black hair and a large nose and mouth. At the moment, that mouth was spewing curses and complaints that ended, "Now show me what you've done to yourself, so I can fix it and get out of this place."

Zander glanced at Joe, obviously not liking the idea of appearing vulnerable. Then he slowly lifted his left arm. "Set it and make it useable for the next twenty-four hours or so."

"Holy shit." Eland took one look at the bone protruding out of the skin of Zander's forearm. "You're lucky you didn't sever an artery." He pushed him to the side of the trail. "Sit down. This may take a while."

Zander dropped to the ground and leaned against a pine tree. "It can't take a while. We haven't got the time."

"Tell me where Eve is," Joe said.

"You're afraid I'll pass out or die, and you won't get the information you need?" Zander asked dryly. "I won't die. I don't promise I won't pass out for a while. And you don't go anywhere until I come around. I won't have you blundering in and causing Doane to scatter before I'm ready." He looked at Stang. "Keep him here."

"Who? Me?" Stang glanced at Joe. "Not my area of expertise."

"Do it anyway." He said to Eland, who was preparing a hypodermic, "Painkiller? I'll take that but nothing that will put me out for more than a few minutes."

"Be quiet," Eland said. "This is going to be excruciating, and if you hadn't given me such a bad trip, I'd almost feel sorry for you." He administered the shot. "It won't take effect fast enough to help much, but you're in a hurry." He reached in his backpack and started taking out his surgical equipment. He glanced at Joe. "You look fairly strong. Will you hold him down? I can't have him moving."

"I won't move," Zander grated through his teeth.

"My pleasure," Joe said as he dropped to his knees and grasped Zander's shoulders and upper arms and pinned him to the ground. "Now get this over, Eland. I want him back to his senses and able to talk."

Eland was wiping his hands on an antiseptic towel. "You do have such kind and sympathetic cohorts, Zander."

"Kind, no." Zander was looking up at Joe. "But somehow familiar. It's like looking in a mirror. Only something changed for you and made you—" He broke off and jerked his head toward Eland. "Do it!"

His back arched with agony as Eland set the bone. He didn't scream, but the blood ran from his lower lip as his teeth bit into it.

He passed out.

The first tentative pearl gray of dawn was lighting the sky, Zander noticed, as soon as he opened his eyes.

Not good, dammit.

"How long have I been out?" he whispered to Stang. "And where the hell is Quinn?"

"You've been out almost two hours."

"What!"

"Eland gave you another shot as soon as you passed out. He said that it was stupid to have you go through all that pain when he was going to have to work on you for a while," Stang said. "And he put you in a cast to keep the bone from shifting."

"Good. That arm wasn't doing me any good anyway." He added grimly, "But that doesn't mean I'm not going to have a word with Eland about disobeying orders."

"Eland said to tell you that you're going

to need extensive follow-up surgery if you don't want to do permanent damage. He didn't know how you managed not to go into shock with the amount of pain that break is causing you. He wants to check you into a hospital right away."

"No way." He glanced around the clearing. "Quinn?"

"He's just exploring the general area. He's not going to go after Eve until he has an idea where he's going." Stang smiled faintly. "He may be going through hell, but he's not going to risk Eve. He's even willing to put up with you if it has a chance of helping her."

"That held a hint of disrespect." Zander's eyes narrowed on Stang's face. "Something's different about you."

"Because something's different about you. I've never really been able to fathom Lee Zander, but I am beginning to get a tiny clue."

"Don't insult me. I refuse to be so transparent."

"Transparent you are not. Maybe just a little less opaque." He paused. "Why did you tell me to come along? Why me, Zander?"

"Maybe I thought I might need a business—" He shrugged. "You have a personal interest. You want Eve Duncan to live."

"Because you wanted me to have a personal interest. You wanted someone around you to spur you to save her." He tapped his chest. "I was the chosen one."

"Ridiculous."

"You're a very complicated man, and most of the time, I don't have a clue as to what makes you tick. But I think in this case somewhere there was a battle going on that even you didn't know about."

"Convoluted nonsense."

"Convoluted. Yes, that's an accurate description of you." He nodded. "And I think I have the answer to my question. You're going to go after Doane, and it goes against your grain not to do that with complete ruthlessness. But you wanted a safety net for Eve Duncan." He tapped his chest again. "The chosen one. You should be happy that I brought someone along who's better qualified. Of course, you can't control him. That will bother you. But you might be able to reason with him. He's very, very smart. He has only one goal.

He'll let you kill Doane if you'll protect Eve." He added softly, "Protect your daughter."

"I have no daughter. Ask Eve, and she'll tell you that." He paused. "Quinn told you?"

"Yes, not really a confidence. It just came out. I doubt if he'll confront you with it."

"Yet you're confronting me with it." He tilted his head. "You're not afraid of me any longer."

"Yes, I am. I'll probably always be afraid of you. But I'm so used to it that a little fear is exciting."

"That's sick."

"You don't really think that's true. That edge is the only thing that's kept you alive during these last years."

"I don't believe I like you psychoanalyzing me," he said with silken menace. "Particularly since I've never been sure if or when you might decide to kill me. Why don't we discuss that bizarre behavior on your part, Stang?"

Stang shook his head. "Someday, maybe. If I live that long."

"**If** you live that long," Zander repeated. "Now why don't you go find Quinn for me? I'm not sure I trust him not to go after Eve without me."

"I told you that he's smart and won't—"

"Tell me where that trail along the upper slope leads." Joe was striding toward them. "I was going to follow it myself, but I decided to give you another chance to fill me in on what I need to know." His gaze coolly raked Zander. "You don't look in such great shape. You should have Eland help you back across that mountain to the helicopter and let me handle Doane for you."

"Screw you." Zander struggled to sit up against the tree. "You'd go straight for Eve and Doane would skip out and I'd have to deal with him later."

"You're right, I'd make the right choice. Where does that trail lead?"

"I'll take you there." Zander got to his feet. "If you can exercise a little restraint."

"No promises. Not if Eve's at the end of that trail."

"She may be. I can't be sure. I tried to track them on the trail, but the heavy rain washed the signs away. I kept passing out, and I couldn't risk being helpless if Doane stumbled over me. He kept her at a house, an old coin factory, before she managed to escape. But I gave her my knife and, if Doane found it on her, alarm bells would ring."

"You gave her your knife?" Stang asked. "Why?"

"It seemed to be the thing to do at the time." He was picking up his backpack. He pointed toward a row of mountains to the left. "If you follow the trail over that ridge, you'll find yourself in a valley. It's shaped like a punch bowl. The only possible road spirals downward from its rim to an old ghost town at the bottom. But several miles back on this side of rim, we can hike to a cabin that I believe Doane occupied. It used to be a coinery. It was probably built up there so that the miners wouldn't have to go all the way to town to cash out."

"You might be proving valuable." He tilted his head. "I may be glad I stuck around."

"Let's get moving. With any luck, they'll still be at the factory. If they're not, I have a few other ideas."

"But now that I know where the trail leads, I don't need you," Joe said. "The last thing I want is to be saddled with someone who can't function. Go back to the helicopter with Eland."

Stang's eyes widened, and he gave a choked gasp.

"Saddled? Me?" Zander's voice was icy.

He turned and stared Joe directly in the eye. "I believe you should reconsider. Will I be able to function, Quinn?"

Joe's eyes narrowed as his gaze held Zander's for a long minute. Then he turned away and started back toward the trail. "Yes, you can function. Just keep up with me."

Zander watched him for an instant, then moved after him. His tone was low, almost conversational, as he said, "Do you know, you arrogant son of a bitch, I may take you out before we even get close to Doane."

CHAPTER

16

Ghost Town

"You're stalling," Doane said harshly. "You've done everything you had to do to repair what you did to my boy. Now complete him." He reached into the sack in which he'd stored all the equipment of hers that he'd taken from the coinery and pulled out the flat wooden box. "Give him sight."

"Don't be ridiculous. They're only glass eyeballs," Eve said. "He won't be able to see except in your imagination."

"And yours," Doane said softly. "That's what you're afraid of, isn't it? He's blind now, but you're afraid that he'll look at you and be able to see how to destroy you."

"I'm not afraid." Reluctant, not afraid, she tried to convince herself. This strange, overpowering, emotional involvement she'd developed with Kevin might be pure hallucination or something more malignantly mystical, but she must not let fear enter into it. "And he can't destroy me. Only I can do that."

"Then give my Kevin his eyes, and we'll see who is right."

She hesitated, then opened the box. "Blue eyes. The color of the sky. They should be pitch-black." She lifted the left eye out of the box. She took a deep breath and carefully placed the eye in the orbital socket.

Fast. Do it fast.

Get it over with.

She took the right eyeball and placed it into the socket.

"There it is. He's done." She stepped back, avoiding looking at the reconstruction. "Happy, Doane?"

"Oh, yes." His eyes were glittering with tears as he stared at the skull. "It's all there, all the beauty, all the power. How handsome he is. How could they kill anything that glorious?"

"How? With a great deal of skill and a strong stomach to combat the stench of him."

"Bitch!" His hand lashed out, backhanding her, bringing her to her knees. "Even at this perfect moment, you manage to spoil it for me." His fingers were buried in her hair, and he jerked her head back. "Look at him. He wants you to look at him."

She was looking at Kevin. She couldn't help it unless she closed her eyes, and she knew Doane would force her to open them.

Yes, Kevin was beautiful, as Lucifer must have been beautiful. She could even see the power that she had never meant to give those features. It had just come . . .

And, God help her, she could see the shining blue eyes staring, **seeing** her. It was not possible that adding those eyes had made his face come alive. She would not accept it. As long as she didn't accept that nightmare, it did not exist.

Mine. Have you. Have her.

The hell you do.

"So handsome," Doane whispered. "No one could ever resist him. You won't be able to do it either. He'll reach out for your

Bonnie, and you'll fall on your knees begging him to take you, too."

"Try me. It won't happen like that."

"Yes, he'll try you." He stroked her hair gently before releasing it. "Soon. Very soon, Eve." He stepped back. "Get up and get out of my way. I have to carefully package Kevin in his container, and I don't want you near him."

"Are you afraid I'll tear him up again?" She got to her feet and moved away to stand by the window in the front of the barbershop. "I might be tempted." But she stared out the window so she wouldn't have to look back at the skull. "I hear that wolf howling again. He sounds hungry. Kevin wouldn't stand a chance if he got hold of him."

"He won't get hold of him," Doane snarled. "I'm going to go out and shoot that wolf and shut him up. I'll bring back his head and throw it at your feet."

"Do you really have time to go hunting? Or maybe you've decided that all your plans to kill Zander should be tossed aside. They haven't been going so well, have they? Joe will find me, you know."

She glanced back over her shoulder. "When I got away from you, I gave him some extra time. He's probably closing in on you now. These mountains aren't safe for you any longer. Why don't you leave here and go on the run?"

"Why don't you be quiet?" He fastened the catches on the container in which he'd placed the skull. "I've considered the possibility that I might not be safe any longer. I'm taking care of it." He lifted his head and glared at her. "If I have to do without killing Zander, I will do it. Kevin would forgive me. He really wants you more now than he does Zander." His lips curled. "And he'll get you, Eve. If I die, I'll take you with me and give you to him to play with as he did the children. You'll be too busy protecting yourself to know what he does to your Bonnie."

"I believe both you and your son are full of hot air and bullshit," Eve said curtly. "If his spirit still exists, he has no power. He's just frantically scurrying around and trying to save those nightmare fantasies that don't exist any longer."

"You'll see. He'll enjoy—" Eve heard a

soft ping and watched Doane take out his cell phone and check it. He smiled and thrust the phone back in his pocket. "Perhaps sooner than you might think."

He strode across the shop, handcuffed her hands in front of her, and grasped her arm. "Come on. It's time to move to phase two of our visit to this wonderful town." He pushed her outside the door. "You were so interested in the saloon when we first arrived. Let's see if it still holds its fascination for you."

She stiffened. Had he found Zander's gun and phone? "The saloon? Why?"

He didn't answer, and a couple minutes later, she was across the street, and he was pushing open the door of the saloon.

Dimness.

Broken wood planks that served as a floor beneath her feet.

The smell of dust and mildew.

She could see the shape of a long bar across the large room with a broken mirror on the wall above it.

Yes.

But Doane wasn't pushing her in that direction. He was heading toward a cupboard against the opposite wall.

"What are we doing here, Doane?"

"It's sort of a holding cell for you. Don't you like it? I have to leave you for an hour or two, and the barbershop is too small and exposed to the street." He added maliciously, "What if those wolves came looking for Kevin and found you instead? Or perhaps Venable or Quinn might stumble on our little home away from home. I wouldn't want to make it that easy for them." They were next to the pine cupboard that must have been close to six feet high and four feet wide. "They used to store liquor in this cupboard during the wild days." He threw open the two doors of the cupboard, and Eve was suddenly assaulted with the overpowering odor of sour whiskey. "No one is going to take you away from me, Eve. If I'm going to lose you, it's going to be to Kevin." He thrust her into the cupboard. "Or maybe the roof rats I've seen running all over this saloon. You've got to hope there isn't one or two in that cupboard waiting to pounce."

"You've taught me how to deal with rodents, Doane." But the reference to Joe and Venable had made her nervous. She might have expected that Zander could have been sighted because she knew that was a possibility if Zander had managed to get up that ridge. But Joe? "Where are you going? Did Blick tell you that he saw any sign of Joe or Venable in the vicinity when he showed up earlier?"

"Do you think I'd tell you?"

"Or maybe it wasn't Blick who came. Maybe you lied to me."

He smiled. "Oh, it was most certainly Blick." He slammed the cupboard door shut, and she was in darkness. "As to where I'm going, you'll have to wonder. Did I catch sight of one of your brave heroes who want only to rescue you? Or am I only going after that wolf that you've been tormenting me with?" She heard the bolt of the lock slide in place. "I leave you to decide for yourself. Oh, and, if by some chance, the wolf or your lover do manage to kill me, then you may never be found in that cupboard. Not a pleasant death." She heard him chuckle, the sound of his footsteps crossing the saloon, then the door slam.

Darkness.

Sour whiskey.

Suffocating walls closing in around her.

A coffin, the cupboard was like a coffin. She took three deep breaths.

Okay, get control.

Doane had done his best to terrify her and make sure she knew how hopeless her situation was. Now she had to clear her head and look for a way out.

She had a few hours without Doane. The bar where Zander had told her he had placed the gun and phone were only yards away. If Zander hadn't lied to her. She had to believe he had not deceived her. She needed something to believe in right now. But how to get out of this damn cupboard . . .

It had been a bolt lock. The cupboard must be over a century old and been left to rot in this place. Pinewood was not strong like oak. She had managed to pry open the drawer of the desk at the coin factory by shattering the wood around the lock.

She looked down at her handcuffed wrists. She'd have to be Houdini to get out of them. She had no tool to pry anything.

She heard a scampering outside the cupboard. The roof rats with which Doane had been taunting her, she thought absently. She could almost see their sharp teeth gnawing at every piece of wood within sight. She and Joe had been plagued by those rats one summer at the cottage. They had been difficult to get rid of because they were voracious eating machines.

She stiffened. And those eating machines would not have left this pine cupboard alone without taking at least a few bites.

Perhaps weakening the wood around those hungry bites.

She began to carefully run the tips of her fingers over the surface of the wood. Nothing obvious. Doane would have noticed if there was anything that would herald a weakness in this coffin in which he had stuffed her. Nothing near the bolt itself.

She slid down to her knees and began to go over the wood wall close to floor level.

Nothing.

She moved to the corner of the cabinet.

Coolness.

Air!

Her heart leaped as she felt a tiny flow of air streaming into the cupboard from the bottom-left corner. She probed, explored the area. Two inches. The wood surrounding it was brittle, jagged and pointed like little knives. She pulled her fingers back and found one of them bloody.

Fine. She'd probably get blood poisoning.

Stupid. She was worrying about blood poisoning at a time like this?

She examined the rest of the cupboard but came up with no other openings. She'd have to go with the one she'd found in the bottom corner.

How much time had passed? Not long. It only seemed like decades had gone by since she'd been stuffed in this cupboard.

She pushed against the wood at the upper edge of the hole that could eventually lead toward the bolt. It moved. She pushed again.

It splintered!

She tried to be careful as she cleared the sharp splinters away and widened the hole. Three inches wide now.

She hit the area with the handcuffs binding her wrists, and the wood moved, then splintered.

Bruises instead of cuts. She'd take it.

She'd take anything that would get her far enough up in this cupboard to release that bolt. But she had an idea that she'd have to take a hell of a lot of more punishment before she got that far. But it was working. She had a chance if Doane stayed away long enough. She wanted to hurry, to rush it, but that would be a good way to do serious damage with those sharp splinters.

She started to carefully clear away the jagged splinters from the latest hole.

Stay away, Doane.

Your vicious little rat friends have betrayed you and given me a way out.

Just give me another hour . . .

Rio Grande Forest
Colorado

"The truck is gone." Zander stopped on the hill, gazing down at the coin factory. He muttered a curse. "I was hoping that they'd still be here."

"Maybe Eve's here." Joe started down the hill, his gaze raking the surrounding woods for possible ambush. "She could still be inside."

"Not likely. Doane wanted her to complete that reconstruction, and he'd be hounding her to do it." Zander followed Quinn toward the coinery. "The odds are that if he's gone, she's gone."

"You appear to have a handle on the situation between them," Stang said. "She must have confided a good deal to you."

"Confided?" Zander shrugged. "That's not the word I'd use. But I studied the dynamics between them, and I can make an educated guess about action and reaction." He called to Joe. "Check the windows and see if you spot any movement inside but don't bust into the house. Eve said that he'd rigged gas jets in the ceiling. It's almost certain to still be booby-trapped. Doane's son taught him a lot about military skullduggery."

"I wouldn't risk Eve by doing that," Quinn said coldly. "I was a SEAL. I know the advantages of a surgical strike versus an all-out assault. At least until we get her free." He'd reached the bottom of the hill and faded into the shrubbery that surrounded the house.

"He's very good," Zander murmured to Stang as his gaze followed Quinn. "Not even a rustle or hint of movement in those bushes."

"I'm sure he'd appreciate your approval," Stang said. "Not."

"He should appreciate it. It's not lightly given."

"You're not going after him?"

"Why? I don't think Doane's here." He grimaced. "And I have to conserve my strength. This damn arm is getting in my way."

"Since you should have fainted by the wayside by now, I wouldn't complain."

"But you're not me, are you? I'll complain if I like." His gaze was narrowed, circling the trees. "Interesting. This area looks amazingly similar to the photo that Jane MacGuire sent to Quinn." Joe Quinn had stopped on the trail about a mile from here and pulled up the photo and compared it to the landscape. "Coincidence, Stang?"

"I'm sure you think it is."

"But Eve Duncan would not, nor would

a certain priest I met in Tibet. So who is correct?"

"You tell me."

"Why, I am, Stang." He smiled. "I'm always correct."

"But you didn't tell me which way you were leaning."

"I didn't, did I?" He stiffened. "Quinn's coming around the other side. I hear him."

Seconds later, Quinn emerged from the shrubbery. "Lights blazing but no one inside." He frowned with frustration. "I'm tempted to go in anyway. There could be something that would give us a clue to where they went." He strode to the front door. "It's so damn—" He stopped. His gaze was on an object high up in the eaves. "What the hell? You told me there weren't any cameras here, Zander."

Zander went still. "There weren't any cameras when I was here before. Not in the trees. Not anywhere near the house." He was beside Quinn in seconds, looking up at the eaves. "And I checked there, too. No camera." He tilted his head. "It's not an entrance camera, it's pointed at the front grounds area and the trail." His gaze narrowed. "And it's running. It probably detected us on the trail and started operating."

"Who's receiving that picture? There's no one inside the house," Quinn said. "And if what you said is true, then the camera was probably put in right before Doane left. That means he wanted to keep tabs on anyone who might discover that this might be where he was keeping Eve."

"Why bother?" Stang asked. "If he was going to take her out of the area, what would it matter?"

"What, indeed?" Zander said. "Unless, he wanted Eve to finish the reconstruction and wasn't sure there was any danger. He'd want to set up a signal that would tell him if he should move out." He strode away from the door and around the corner of the house and gazed at the ridge that formed the rim of the punch-bowl valley. "Are you down there, Doane?" he murmured. "Wait for me, I'm coming."

"What the hell are you talking about?" Quinn was standing beside him. "What's down there? What's the story on the ghost town you were telling us about?"

"Just a ghost town called Drakebury Springs. I went there first when I was searching for Doane. When I was in the saloon, I found fresh boot tracks in the dust, and I thought it possible Doane had been there scouting out a place but decided against it. Then when I found the coin factory, I knew I'd struck gold." He shrugged. "But maybe Doane had second thoughts. Even with these foothills and ridges between that town and us, he might have had a clear enough signal so that he could feel safe down there even if we found this place."

"And any smartphone could be set up to signal him that the camera had turned on." He turned to Zander. "How certain are you that Doane could be down there?"

"Not certain at all. But it's a possibility." He started down the trail that led to the valley. "And it's also a distinct probability that if I'm right, Doane knows we're here and that the ghost town might be our next stop. I suggest we get down there before he takes off with Eve." He added over his shoulder, "My car is parked in the trees about a hundred yards from here. You and Stang are welcome to come along."

"Shit." Quinn was dialing his phone as he strode quickly after Zander. "Venable.

Jane said that he'd be heading in this direction as soon as he confirmed that coin factory. We need help."

"I don't want Venable."

"Screw you. I want everyone I can get." He spoke into the cell phone. "Venable, I need you to head for a ghost town, Drakebury Springs. It's near the coin factory you and Kendra were searching for. You can track my cell phone for the coordinates. We're heading there now."

"I have the coordinates for the coin factory. That's the target."

"We've been there. Doane has left. Zander believes he may be down in the ghost town. How fast can you get there?"

"Soon. Wait for me."

"Can't wait. Doane may know we're here. Get going!" He hung up and got in the car. Stang jumped into the backseat, and Zander took off.

Joe's phone rang. Kendra. "Quinn, I just heard from Venable. Wait for us. Don't go in alone. Margaret and I are on the ridge above the ghost town, heading toward you. We'll be there within five minutes."

Joe glanced at the ridge. He could see a dark gray sedan on the winding road around the mountain that would cross their path in the five minutes Kendra had designated . . . maybe.

"Stay back. Venable's coming."

"Yeah, I know. He's not too far behind us," Kendra said grimly. "And he's coming on a little too strong. I don't—There's a tree or something in the road ahead. I didn't need this, dammit. It looks like some kind of—"

The road in front of Kendra exploded into a fiery inferno.

"My God."

Kendra's car careened to the side of the road, and she was clearly struggling for control. The smoke was so thick that it was impossible to see if she'd actually plunged into the flames.

Then the smoke cleared, and they could see that she was hanging half-off the road, over the valley below.

"Get out!" Joe shouted.

"I doubt if she can hear you," Zander said. "She would have to have nerves of steel not to have dropped the phone." He glanced at the flaming plume in front of Kendra's car. "And I think the passenger door is opening. They may be okay."

The next moment, the two women emerged out of the passenger door onto the road.

"Run, dammit. Run, Kendra." Joe said through his teeth as he saw the flames licking backward from the blast to envelop the car.

They were already running.

The next minute, the gas tank of the car blew, knocking Kendra and Margaret to the ground.

"I'd say that Doane expected visitors," Zander said. "And decided to put out the DO NOT DISTURB sign." He glanced at Kendra and Margaret, who were getting to their knees. "I'm not stopping, Quinn. That blast might be Doane's first warning shot. I want to be there before he fires the second."

"I'm not asking you to stop." He glanced at the twin fiery plumes that were clawing at the sky. Then he looked back at the ghost town in the valley below. "He's down there. Eve's down there. Let's go get them."

The second explosion shook the floor of the saloon, causing Eve to lose her balance and fall to her knees.

What was happening? What was Doane doing?

She had just managed to slide her handcuffed hands through the broken wood and manipulate the bolt to free herself when the first explosion had gone off.

She had been on her way across the room toward the bar when the second explosion had happened.

Was it Doane? Or maybe Zander had shown up and set off both explosions. How the hell did she know? Her job was to take advantage of what might be a diversion and get out of here.

And find Zander's weapon and phone to protect herself before she did it.

She hurriedly crawled the additional few yards around the back of the bar. Zander had said he'd pushed it far back out of sight on a shelf beneath the bar . . .

She could see a shelf, but there was no weapon. Did you lie to me, Zander?

Don't give up. It could be at the other end of the bar.

She twisted around and quickly started crawling.

She suddenly stopped, frozen.

"Dear God," she whispered.

She could go no farther—the way was blocked.

By three kegs that were marked: DAN-GER. EXPLOSIVE. Several sticks of dynamite were fastened to each keg, neatly arranged in evenly spaced rows. On top was what appeared to be a triggering mechanism, with a red LED display glowing in the darkness.

"Bitch!" Doane was standing at the open end of the bar behind her. "How did you—" He was striding toward her. "Come out and join the party."

She had been so shocked that she had not heard his footsteps crossing the wood floor. She was cornered, huddled against the kegs of explosives. "What were you blowing up, Doane? I assume it was you."

"I'll take you to see for yourself." He grabbed the handcuffs on her wrists and jerked her to her feet. "And let them see you." His gaze raked her face and body. "Look at you, all bloody and scratched as if you'd been crawling through barbed wire. I couldn't be more pleased. You did me a favor by breaking out of that cupboard. You almost made it, didn't you?"

"I did make it. I would have been out of here in another few minutes."

"No, you wouldn't. I wouldn't have let you get away." He was jerking her toward the front door. "And now they'll see how determined I am to keep you."

"Who is 'they'? What was that explos—" She broke off as she saw the flaming wreckage on the ridge road. Through the smoke and flames she could barely make out the figures of two women moving some distance in the rear. Then a Jeep drew up beside the women, and another woman jumped out.

Eve would have known the identity of that woman no matter what the conditions.

"Jane."

"Yes, Jane MacGuire to the rescue," Doane said. "So clever. All the people who care about you were so smart about tracking you down. And you'll notice another car on the road coming down from our former home at the coinery."

"Who is it?" She moistened her lips. "Tell me."

"Why, Joe Quinn." He paused. "And he brought Zander with him. I didn't have to take you to Canada to see your dear father after all."

"How do you know?"

"The miracle of technology." He pushed her out into the street. "But now we have to make sure that everyone sees you . . . and me. Yes, you're in full view." He lifted his gun and fired one shot in the air. "That should do it. Jane MacGuire is coming to the edge of the road and looking down at us. I'm sure that Quinn and Zander can see us, too." He turned to face her. "Time for a demonstration."

He lifted his hand and struck her so hard that she fell to the ground.

She could taste the blood from her cut lip as she struggled to sit up. "Did you enjoy that, Doane?"

"Extremely. That hurt you, but I'd bet it hurt those people rushing to your rescue more. Get up."

She got to her feet. "It doesn't take courage to strike a woman who has her hands cuffed. Everyone will just think what a coward you are."

"No, everyone will see how you suf-
fered, and it will make them suffer to remember it." His head lifted, and his gaze
went to the ridge as a black van pulled up
behind Jane's Jeep, and uniformed men
poured out of it. "Ah, Venable. Very aggressive. That changes the speed with which I
have to work. Fortunately, I've planned for
every contingency. Have I mentioned before what a superb planner I am?" He lifted
his gun and fired one more shot. Then he
grabbed her arm and pulled her back into
the saloon. "Venable will read that last
shot as defiance. It may act as a trigger."

"You're cornered. Give up, Doane."

"You know I can't do that." He turned to
face her. His blue eyes were glowing with
excitement. "Cornered? I'm not the one in
a trap. You're the bait, and they're all taking it. Zander thought he'd come after you?
It only proves that you were wrong about
his not caring if you lived or died."

"No, it doesn't. It only proves he wants
to get rid of you once and for all."

"Well, he's here." He glanced at the bar.
"Let him come and get me."

He was talking about the explosives,

Eve realized, chilled. He had set off that explosion on the ridge, and it was clear he had enough left to take down a skyscraper. What kind of booby traps had he set up around this ghost town?

"Don't do this, Doane." She knew he wouldn't listen to her, but she had to try. "Leave this place."

"Oh, we'll leave it all right," he said softly. "I told you that the only way I'd give you up was to Kevin." His eyes were shining, his face illuminated by a light that held her, frightened her. "What better way to give you to him than have you burned on a glorious funeral pyre and let Zander watch it?" He reached out and touched her bloody lower lip. "And perhaps take him with us."

She couldn't take her eyes from him. Doane. Kevin. Who was standing before her? Evil. Pure evil.

Shots outside.

No! She couldn't just stand here. She had to warn them.

She whirled and broke for the door.

"That's not in the plan, Eve." He caught her, brought her down, his hands grasping her throat. "That will be your last escape."

His hands tightened. "Just a little pain, then Kevin will be there to take you."

Red haze. No breath. Bruising agony.

She was fighting desperately, her hands clawing at his fingers.

Red fading into darkness.

But beyond the darkness . . . light.

Joy.

Bonnie!

CHAPTER

17

"I'll **kill** him," Joe said between clenched teeth. "Get me there, Zander."

"Another few minutes," Zander said. "And in that few minutes, you'd better work out a way to get to the bastard to kill him. You're not thinking, Quinn."

Joe knew he wasn't thinking; he was only feeling. Seeing Eve stand there in the street, bloody, and looking like a holocaust refugee had torn him apart.

And then the son of a bitch had **hit** her.

"Easy to say," he said harshly. "You don't give a damn."

"Which is the best mind-set for removing obstacles like Doane." Zander was gazing straight ahead. "And the reason that you should stand back out of my way while I dispose of him."

Joe gazed at him in disbelief. "And let him kill Eve while you concentrate on killing him?"

Zander said quietly, "That won't happen, Quinn."

"Why not?"

"Are you expecting some maudlin emotional statement? You won't get it. If Doane kills Eve, it will be a victory for him. I'm not allowing any victories."

"Just get me there, and I'll go around back and see if I find a way to—" He broke off as the wood sidewalk in front of the saloon was spiked with rifle bullets from the ridge road. He glanced up and saw men swarming down the mountainside toward the town. "What the hell is Venable trying to do?" He dialed Venable. "Get your guys out of there. Are you trying to get her killed?"

"Intimidation," Venable said. "He's got to know that we're on top of him, and he can't—"

"Get out of there!"

But Venable had hung up.

Joe drew a deep breath, trying to smother the rage. "What do you know about that saloon, Zander? Can I get in from the rear?"

"I didn't do a thorough scan when I was here. I knew that Doane wasn't using the place to hold Eve, and I wanted to get on with the hunt. I remember a door and a staircase leading to the upper floor. The staircase was in lousy shape and missing four or five steps." He glanced at Joe. "You could swing up it, but it will take a bit of effort."

"Then take me around back." The gunfire had resumed, and Joe's hands clenched. "How long?"

"A minute, no more," Zander said quietly. "I'll drop you off, then dodge around front and draw Doane out and distract him." He turned to Stang. "When I jump out, you get in the driver's seat and get out of here. And stay out of the line of Venable's fire."

"I can handle that," Stang said. "But I should remind you that you're walking wounded."

"No, you should not remind me. I can't think of it right now." He glanced up the mountain. "Venable's men are nearly down to the foothills near the town. Once they get there, they'll head for the saloon, and there will be hell to pay."

"For Venable," Joe said grimly. "If he causes Doane to go crazier than he is right now, I'll take him down."

"Not Venable's usual pattern of behavior to go off like this . . ." Zander murmured. "He's usually cool, very cool." He swung the car wide as they entered the town and headed toward the rear of the saloon. "The ground is one giant mud hole. Get ready to jump out and run for it if I get stuck."

"Stop them!" Jane grabbed Venable's arm and whirled him to face her. "Are you nuts? You saw what he did to Eve a few minutes ago. He **wants** to hurt her. Now you're trying to panic him into killing her?"

"It's Doane who's nuts," Venable said grimly. He threw his arm toward the burning brush and the flaming wreckage of Kendra's car. "And that should prove it to you. We have to get him under control."

"Then let Joe do it. Give him backup, but don't try to take Doane out by yourself. Stop that shooting."

"I've given orders that my men not fire directly at the building itself but at the sidewalk and steps. Just enough to let Doane know he's pinned down and can't escape." His voice was soothing. "Trust me, Jane. It's the best psychological—"

"And what if a few of those bullets go astray?" Kendra had come up to stand beside them. "Those are hundred-clip assault weapons, not sniper rifles. Doane's not going to tolerate the front of that saloon being shot apart. If he feels threatened, Eve may be the one who suffers for it."

"You should approve of my taking action," Venable said. "You were within seconds of being blown up by that booby trap Doane set."

"It scared the hell out of Margaret and me," Kendra said. "But it didn't kill off any brain cells. The threat to us is over, and Eve is right in the crosshairs, where she's been all along. We don't need to make it any worse for her."

"I'm not making it worse. I'm trying to— Where the hell are they going?" His attention had switched to Trevor and Caleb, who were heading down the mountain toward the town. He started to curse. "They're not part of the operation. They have no business there. What are they doing?"

"Well, they won't be shooting up the town," Jane said. "They have too much sense. I'd guess they'll be trying to help Joe." She could see the car that must be Joe's enter the town and head for the rear of the saloon. "I don't want to guess. I want to be there." She went to the edge of the road and stood there, with hands clenched, her eyes straining to see any motion at the front door of the saloon. "I'm not as good at mountain climbing as Trevor and Caleb, so you find me a fast way to get down there, Venable. Or I'll be following them down this mountain. Either that, or you call off your attack dogs. Your choice. I'll give you three minutes."

"I'm not going to be—" His gaze was suddenly cool. "I've done what I thought best. You'll have to do the same."

"Right." Jane took off down the mountain. "And I'll be going straight to that street in front of the saloon, and any bullets from the gunfire you order will have to go through me."

"Come back, dammit. I'm warning you.

I'll be on the phone giving orders you're to be stopped before you get near that saloon, Jane."

"Go ahead." She heard him calling behind her, but she ignored it. The time was over for anything but action. She had to get down there.

"Let me go first." Margaret was suddenly beside her. "I grew up outdoors in the woods and hill country like this. I'm as steady as a mountain goat. Just step where I step."

"Okay." She tried to steady her voice. "If it will get me down there faster. Thanks, Margaret."

Margaret nodded. "I'll take you to her." She didn't speak for a moment as they made their way swiftly down the mountain. "She'll survive, Jane. I know you told me that she was strong, that she'd fight, but I never knew her, never saw her until a moment ago." Her voice was quiet. "And she stood there in the street, taking punishment and enduring, and I thought that maybe she was stronger than even you dreamed. Perhaps more than she knows. I watched her, and I wanted to hold her, help her. I came here for you, Jane. But now it's for her, for your Eve."

"That's all I ever asked. I'm so scared, Margaret," she whispered. "It's all going wrong."

"Maybe not. Joe Quinn is down there. All that love surrounding her has to mean something is right."

The gunfire had started again, and Jane felt rage and desperation choking her. She'd swear one of those bullets had struck the wooden bench beneath the saloon window. Too close. How near must a bullet come before Doane panicked? "Dammit, why don't they stop?"

Margaret says you'll survive, Eve. God, let her be right. Fight him. Fight all the stupidity that might destroy you. She's right, we all love you so much. We can't lose you. I can't lose you.

'We're in the foothills now," Margaret said. "Not long, Jane."

But where was Joe, and what was he doing? She hadn't seen him since he'd driven around to the rear of the saloon. He could even be inside the saloon by now. Stay safe, Joe. Don't let anything—

She saw the wall of flame first, reaching for the sky.

Then she heard the explosion, rocking the earth, rocking the mountain, rocking the world.

The saloon blew apart, shredding into pieces. One blast following the next, feeding on fire and smoke . . . and agony.

Jane screamed.

"Dear God," Margaret whispered. "No. No. No."

"Eve." Jane fell to her knees, her gaze on that inferno. No one could live through a blast of that magnitude. There was nothing left of walls or structure. The saloon was nothing but pure flame. The houses and shops around it were knocked flat, and the fire was licking, devouring the wood sidewalks. "Eve!"

Margaret was kneeling in front of her, wrapping her arms around her. "Hold on to me. You're not alone. I'm here."

But Eve wasn't here. Eve would never be here again.

It wasn't true. It couldn't be true.

She jumped to her feet. "I've got to go to her. I've got to help her."

"Jane . . ."

But she was running down toward the town, her gaze on that conflagration from hell.

She fell, jumped up again, and ran.

Joe. Where was Joe? Maybe he'd gotten Eve out before the explosion. That could happen, couldn't it?

Or perhaps Joe was lost in those flames, too.

Agony tore through her at the thought.

Nightmare. Loneliness. Pain.

There were people around her, Venable's team milling around in front of the saloon.

Caleb was coming toward her.

"Joe Quinn is alive," he said. "He was behind the saloon, and the blast blew him ten or fifteen feet away against a shop building. I think he'll be okay. Trevor is checking him out now."

"Thank God." She swallowed. "Now tell me Eve is okay."

Caleb didn't answer.

"**Tell** me. She has to be alive. She has to be okay."

Caleb's gaze went back to the fire. "Eve

went into that saloon and never came out. Dozens of witnesses, Jane, all focused in hopes that Eve would walk out of there. There must have been enough explosives in there to blow up a mountain. We'll see a hole big as a crater when we manage to get in there."

"Don't tell me that."

"I have to tell you exactly that," he said fiercely. "Do you think I want to do it? I **hate** it. I can't stand seeing you like this. I want to stop it. But I can't stop it. All I can do is cut you, and hurt you, and hope that you heal soon."

"She's not dead. She can't be dead."

"I hope you're right. But don't expect me to tell you that you are. I'll leave that to Trevor or Quinn. They'll comfort you and maybe even make you feel better." He stepped back. "Go on. Go to them. They're still behind the saloon." He turned away. "Or what used to be the saloon. I'm going to go talk to Venable and see if he has a way to find out . . . if there's a way of definitely ascertaining if there were any victims in that hellhole of a blast. I'll let you know."

Joe was struggling to get to his feet

when Jane reached him a few minutes later. His face was cut and bleeding, and his eyes were wild.

"No." His voice was hoarse. "No, Jane. It doesn't make sense. We can't lose her."

"I know." She went into his arms. Caleb had said there would be comfort, but that was not true. There was love but not comfort. The world was still barren. She had the horrible feeling it would always be barren. "I've always told people that I'd know if anything ever happened to Eve, that I'd feel it. But now I'm not sure. Maybe that's what I'm feeling now." The tears were running down her cheeks. "Is it, Joe?"

"No, because it's not true. I won't **let** it be true."

"Jane." Trevor was beside her. Warm, kind, loving. "There's a chance. Don't lose hope yet."

"That's what Caleb said you'd tell me. He said go to Trevor, and he'll comfort you." She said, "He's getting to know you very well, Trevor."

"Because I won't give up until we get an ID." He said gently, "And, give me the opportunity, and I'll wrap you in all the comfort that this world provides. It would be my privilege." He turned away. "I'll leave you two alone. You don't need anyone else right now. I just talked to a Howard Stang, who said he could get a doctor here right away. I think we need to get you looked at, Quinn. You may have some cracked ribs."

Joe wasn't listening, Jane realized. He was staring—stunned, numb—at the blazing firestorm that seemed to be growing in intensity by the moment, feeding on itself.

Devouring air, devouring life, devouring hope.

Eve went into that saloon and never came out. Dozens of witnesses. Jane, all focused in hopes that Eve would walk out of there.

Dozens of witnesses . . .

Give me a miracle, Eve. All my life with you you've made every day a miracle. I need a miracle now.

But the panic was starting, piercing the numbness, and desperation as she stared into the searing depths of that fire.

Oh, God, no miracle this time, Eve?

"I'm sorry, Jane."

She looked up to see Venable standing a few feet away.

He looked genuinely sorry, she thought dully. Too late. Everything was too late.

"That's nothing to how sorry you'll be if Joe finds out that it was one of your damn bullets that caused the saloon to blow." She gazed at Joe, sitting beneath the trees several yards away and being bandaged by the doctor that Stang had somehow managed to get down here. "He's in shock right now, but he'll go crazy once it hits home that Eve is dead." She moistened her lips. Joe wasn't the only one who would go insane. She was barely holding herself together now. "Caleb said he was going to go talk to you. Did you see him?"

"Yes."

She didn't want to ask the question. Her glance shifted to the flames. The fire had spread, jumping from house to house. Soon, the entire town would be ablaze. The final death of a ghost town, she thought.

As if in response, she heard the mournful wail of a wolf somewhere in the foothills. Mourning the end of a town. Mourning the end of Eve . . .

She braced herself, then looked back at Venable. "What did you tell Caleb?"

"That I wouldn't stage any attack without

attempting to determine the location of the people in the house. Standard operating procedure. We had infrared scopes trained on the building." He was standing very straight, looking her directly in the eye. "There were two people inside that saloon when it exploded."

She couldn't breathe. She felt as if she'd been punched in the stomach.

"Jane." He stepped forward with hand outstretched. "I can't tell—"

"Don't touch me." She jerked back from him. "I don't want anyone to touch me." No one but Eve. But Eve was somewhere in that hideous firestorm that was taking over the town.

Or maybe not. It could be that her Bonnie was beside her, taking away that horror. **I never believed that she came to you, Eve. I wish I could believe it now. God, I want to believe it.**

But Joe believed that Bonnie was always with Eve. Maybe if Jane went to him, touched him, stayed with him, he would make her feel it, too.

She got to her feet. "You've told me what you had to say. I don't want to talk to you any longer, Venable."

"I realize we had a disagreement about the way to free Eve, but it wasn't any of my men who set off that explosion. I want you to know that. It's going down in my report as a probable murder-suicide."

"Very tidy." She shook her head. "But I'm wondering how anything as chaotic as what went on here could be that tidy. Are you covering your ass, Venable?"

"I'm just doing my job. It's the truth and—"

"I don't want to hear any more," she interrupted. "Not now." She started across the distance to Joe. "I've got to tell Joe what you just told me, and I'm not looking forward to it."

Put one foot in front of the other. Look straight at Joe. He was staring at her. Did you see me talking to Venable? Are you hoping against hope?

There's no hope, Joe.

Except perhaps the hope that there's a little girl somewhere who will love and take care of our Eve when we cannot.

She reached Joe and sank down on the ground beside him. "Hi." Hold on. Don't cry. Then he'd feel as if he had to comfort her. She leaned against his shoulder, touching, trying to give warmth when there was no warmth. "I have something to tell you, Joe."

"You told her?"

Venable turned to see Zander standing in the shadows behind him. "Hello, Zander. Why are you lurking around here? Doane is dead. Your hunt is over."

"You told Jane MacGuire about the infrared?"

"Yes. How did you know about that?"

"I was up the mountain talking to your tech guy five minutes after the saloon blew. I had him show me the recording. I needed to know."

"Because you had to confirm the kill?"

He smiled faintly. "Of course, why else? You know what a stickler I am."

"But you're still here."

"Because I have a feeling things aren't quite right. You're not quite right, Venable." He glanced at Jane and Joe Quinn. "And I'm . . . disturbed. So I believe I'll stick around for a while." His glance shifted to the burning wreckage of the town. "She managed to create quite a stir, didn't she?"

"Eve?"

"Yes, who else is this about? She's the one who appears to reach out and touch everyone. Even you, Venable. Which is why I'm surprised that you'd risk her like that." He added softly, "Perhaps she even reached out and touched me the faintest bit because I find I'm angry that you'd do that to her."

Venable stiffened warily. "Is that a threat?"

"I don't threaten. You wouldn't even see it coming." Zander turned away. "But my curiosity is flaring as high as this bonfire of a town. You'll have to satisfy it, Venable. Or I'll do it myself."

The next moment he had faded once more into the shadows.

The wolf was howling again.

Margaret lifted her head and looked away from the blazing fire to the foothills.

At first, she had thought that the cry sounded mournful, but that was not the case. There was distress and anger and something else in that lonely howl.

And why was the wolf sticking so close to this hellish firestorm? she wondered curiously.

She glanced at Jane, sitting with Joe

and trying to hold away the horror that was already upon them. Jane did not need her right now. She probably wouldn't even know that Margaret was gone.

The wolf howled again.

I'm coming. I'm not the one you want, but I have to know . . .

She started to walk toward the trees.

By the time she reached the foothills, she realized the wolf was a male, and he was not alone.

Careful. Go slowly. A wolf pack was very dangerous. She could sometimes reason or soothe a single wolf if he proved intelligent. She had also even dealt effectively with packs. But the pack mentality often overcame everything else . . . and left only carnage.

Where are you? I won't hurt you. Let me come close, and I'll show you.

She stopped, listening, reaching out.

The grove of white birch.

She could feel the tiny hairs on the back of her neck tingle and lift as she approached. She could see flashes of gray and white weaving among the trees. How many were there?

She didn't want to know. Even three could bring you down and make a meal of you.

There were more than three.

She closed out all the wolves but the male who had been howling, calling. Kerak. Was that how he thought of himself? The impression was strong, but his mind was elusive . . . and very fierce.

But she was getting something else from him now.

Go away. He has to go away.

Not departure. Death. He was talking about death.

Not Margaret's death. Even though she was an intruder.

He? Who had to die? She formed a picture in her mind. **Doane?**

A fierce explosion of hate that was completely uninterpretable.

And it was coming not only from the male, Kerak, but from all the wolves skulking in those trees.

She shivered and stopped in her tracks. Should she turn around and go back? This could be fatally stupid. Why was it so important to her? It had started as curiosity,

but there was another element present
now. She had never joined with any animal that had displayed this complex an
emotional response.

And it had something to do with that explosion and fire in the valley.

She **had** to know what had triggered it.

She addressed Kerak directly.

**I can't be sure you're not angry with
me. Are you?**

No answer.

Just that wild flow of hatred.

**I'm coming into the grove, and I'm
going to sit down. I'll be very quiet, and
I'll let myself be open to you. Will you
let yourself be open to me?**

No answer.

She drew a deep breath and entered
the birch grove.

I'm here. I'm not going to hurt you.

She sat down on the ground and crossed
her legs.

She could hear a rustle in the shrubs,
and out of the corner of her eye saw the
soft flow of gray and white moving behind
her, on either side of her, in front of her.

Green eyes glowing in the dimness.

She could feel her heart pounding. She

could count at least six moving bodies en-
circling her in the trees.

Would they attack?

Too late to worry now. Open your mind.
Let the male wolf **see.**

She closed her eyes.

**You see who I am. Now let me see
who you are. Why were you watching
that ghost town?**

No answer.

Who has to die?

She heard a growl, and her eyes flew
open.

A huge gray-and-white wolf was standing not ten feet in front of her.

White teeth gleaming, half-crouched.

Who has to die? She gazed into those
wild, green-amber eyes. **Tell me.**

And she was suddenly bombarded, surrounded by a whirlwind of visions and impressions.

Rushing water.

Monsters.

Hunger.

**A little red-haired girl, eyes wide with
fear.**

Burned forests.

Darkness.

Silence.

Evil creeping on padded feet.

Death.

And in the midst of all that swirling chaos, the image of a red-haired little girl.

Margaret felt a surge of panic.

No, not the child! Don't kill the child.

She pulled back and started to jump to her feet.

Growling all around her.

The smell of sweat and animal.

She froze as she realized that she was completely surrounded. The rest of the pack had shown itself.

White pointed teeth, bared and ready . . .

Would the fire never go out? Jane wondered dully.

It had been hours since the blast, and the entire town was now engulfed in flames. She could see that Caleb and Trevor had joined Venable's team, who were digging a trench around the town to prevent the fire from spreading to the forests. The water source in town was limited to nearby streams, and help from the nearest towns had not reached here yet. She wanted to shut her eyes and close it all out, but she couldn't do it. It would be like closing Eve away from her since Eve was part of that fire. She supposed she should go look for Joe, but she would not be welcome. He had said he had to talk to Venable, to verify what she had told him. So she had stayed here, leaning against this tree, waiting for Joe, waiting for the fire to end.

Waiting.

"Jane." It was Kendra, coming toward where Jane was sitting in the trees outside the town's perimeter. "Good. You're not asleep. I was afraid that Dr. Eland had given you a shot."

"No, he tried to give one to Joe, but that wasn't going to happen. It may be killing him, but Joe won't run away from it."

"And neither will you." She fell to her knees beside her. "I won't pretend to know what you're feeling, but I want to tell you that I'm sorry that—"

"Everyone is sorry," Jane said. "I know that. I appreciate it. But I wish everyone would stop saying it. It won't bring her back. It won't stop the hurting." She wearily shook her head. "Now I'm the one who is sorry, Kendra. You're only being kind."

"And sincere. Don't forget sincere." Kendra hesitated. "And, right now, I sincerely wish I didn't have to disturb you. I told her that it wasn't the time, but she wouldn't leave me alone."

"What are you talking about?"

"Margaret. I just got a call from her. She told me that I had to go and get you and bring you to her."

"What?"

"I know. I know. You're grieving, and Margaret is being Margaret. I argued, but she wouldn't shut up about it. She said you had to come."

Jane shook her head.

Kendra sighed. "I knew you wouldn't do it. So did she. But she said to tell you that if you were grateful to her for saving your dog, Toby, that you had to come."

Jane gazed at her, puzzled. "This is hard for you. You didn't want to come and ask me. Yet you did it. Why?"

"Because it's Margaret, and sometimes she's Thelma to my Louise crashing into the Grand Canyon. And sometimes she's weird and kind of wonderful, like the good witch from Oz. I don't know which Margaret it is this time." She shrugged. "So I thought I'd take a chance on causing you more grief and go along with her. Will you come?"

"Where is she?" She looked around but didn't see her in the group fighting the fire. "The last time I saw her was when she came down the mountain with me. Why did she have to phone you?"

"You'll have to ask her. I told you, she said you had to come to her. She couldn't come to you." She jerked her head at the thick grove of trees to the north. "She's out there somewhere. Yes or no?"

Jane didn't want to go anywhere. She wanted to curl up in a ball and just ward off the loneliness and pain.

Toby. Margaret had saved Toby, and now she was asking one simple act in return.

Jane got slowly to her feet. "Take me to her."

Kendra nodded. "If I can find her." She turned and headed into the trees. "She gave me directions, but I'm not as woods savvy as Margaret. She'll hear from me if I get lost."

Jane quickly followed her. "How far is it?"

"Ten, fifteen minutes." She was climbing; they had gone through the trees and were now in the foothills.

Jane glanced back over her shoulder at the fire. It appeared even more intense from this distance. What was she doing wandering out here when everything that mattered was back in that town?

See Margaret.

Pay the debt.

Get it over.

"She should be up ahead," Kendra said ten minutes later. "In that grove of birch." Her pace quickened. "Margaret!" she called. "Answer me. I've stuck my neck out for you, and it had better be worth it."

"It's worth it," Margaret called back. "Of course, it will require a little work from you to help make it worthwhile. I can't do everything."

"Margaret, what the hell is going on?" Jane called wearily, as they entered the birch grove. "I really didn't want to come out here tonight."

"I know. But I couldn't come to you." The next minute she said, "I hear you. You're getting close to me. Slow down, and don't make any sudden movements."

"What?"

"I think we should do as she says," Kendra said, as they strode deeper through the trees. "I have a hunch she may be the good witch tonight."

Margaret giggled. "But I'm always good, well, almost always. And particularly tonight. I'm just around the next corner. Slowly . . ."

Jane moved around the corner.

She stopped, her eyes widening with shock.

Margaret was sitting on the ground only a short distance away. Lying half-on her lap was a magnificent gray-and-white wolf who lifted his head, his green-amber eyes shining warily as he saw Kendra and Jane.

"Shh," Margaret said softly to the wolf. "It's fine. You're safe." Then she smiled at Jane, a smile full of warmth and love that lit her face with joy. "It **is** fine. It's wonderful. We have a chance to make it right."

"Margaret?"

"She's not dead, Jane." Her voice was vibrating with the same joy that illuminated her entire being. "Do you hear me? Eve is **alive.**"